# BEFORE
# YOU
# BREAK

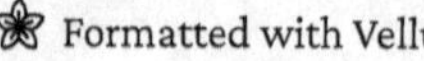 Formatted with Vellum

*To those whose battle lies within.*
*Your scars may not be visible,*
*But you are still a warrior.*
*Never give up.*

There was a star
riding through the clouds one night,
and I said to the star,
'Consume me.'
-Virginia Woolf

1

———

## LUX

My name means "light" in Latin. My mother gave me my name. Dad wanted something more traditional, like Laura or Taylor. But my mom got her way, as usual.

My mother loved the stars. She was obsessed with them, obsessed with the ebb and pull of the sun, the planets, the galaxies. She always said the placement of the stars and planets at the moment of our birth defined our destiny.

Sometimes I believed her. She could make you believe anything. She had that power. She could wrap you up in her warmth and send you spinning into a universe bright and sparkling.

She was the sun I orbited around. We all did, like moons reflecting her dazzling light. Sometimes, she seemed close enough to touch. But no matter how hard I tried, I could never quite reach her.

But she's dead now. Gone. An exploded star. A black hole. If you get too close to its edge, it sucks you in, its terrible gravity engulfing everything. Even light.

Mom deserted us. Then Lyra left. Now Dad's in the hospital. There's only me. Alone. Alone with my frantic, scrabbling thoughts. Alone with a darkness devoid of stars pressed against the backs of my eyelids.

We all have our secrets. Mom did. So does Dad. Probably even perfect, responsible Lyra. I know I do. Secrets so awful I can't speak them aloud, can't even think them.

I did a bad thing. A terrible thing.

Dad would say the truth will set you free. But he's wrong.

Some truths are dark and dangerous. And some sins can't ever be forgiven.

I would know.

2

—————

# LYRA

It's hard to breathe, like all the oxygen has suddenly been sucked out of the air. Things are tilting, swirling in and out of focus.

I stand in front of room 315, my suitcase pressing against my leg.

Everything seems far away—the hum of machines, the murmur of nurses' voices, the buzz of the florescent lighting, that sharp antiseptic smell.

The pain behind my ribs is a dark, pulsing wound. But I won't lose it. Not here. Not today. I can't. I've known this was coming for years, known it like how you can sense a storm by the electric charge singeing the air.

One breath in, one breath out. Stay. In. Control. Grief swells up inside me, and I shove it down. I have to.

Only a few hours ago, I was bent over trays of fixer and developer in the Art Institute of Florida's darkroom, working intently on a project for Advanced Portraiture II.

The nurse's voice on the phone had been tinny and distant, barely human. *I'm sorry to inform you . . .*

One frantic plane ride and a taxi later, I'm back in Michigan, facing the door to my father's hospital room, too terrified to enter.

3

My legs are stiff and heavy, my mind thick with fog. I stare down at the phone in my hand like it's an alien thing. I've messaged and called my younger sister Lux two dozen times today. She hasn't bothered to respond.

Where is she? She should be here. I shouldn't have to do this by myself.

But here I am. Alone.

My mouth is dry, my pulse a roar in my ears. I take a breath and enter the room before I can think about what I'm about to see, what I am or am not prepared for, what I'll feel.

What I feel is a sickening vertigo, my stomach wrenching up into my chest. "Oh, Dad."

My father lies in a too-small bed, the papery blue hospital blanket barely covering his immense body. Tubes run through his nose. An IV connects him to the humming machines crowding around the bed.

Everything is a glaring, alarming white: the shocking pallor of his skin, the walls, the floor, the papery curtain pulled between my father and the patient on the other side of the room.

He opens his eyes and attempts a smile. The structure of his face has crumbled before the onslaught of weight and the violence of the heart attack. The skin around his eyes is loose and puffy, folded inward half over his eyelids. His lips are a cracked grayish blue, and the right side of his mouth sags.

He tries to raise his head, but the strain is too much.

"Just rest," I murmur. I glance at a blue plastic chair in the corner, but I can't sit down. My spine is a rod of steel—if anything bends or gives way even slightly, my bones will shatter.

"Are you comfortable? Do you need medicine? More pillows? Are you cold?" I need a chore, a task, something to do, some way to help, to try and fix this, the unfixable.

"I'm fine." His baritone voice, normally rich and deep like an opera singer, is gruff, raw. "Just . . . tired. I'm glad you're home, Gingersnap."

My heart clenches at the familiar nickname. I clear my throat. "What did the doctors say?"

"Just another attack." Dad wheezes, grimacing. "This one a bit worse than the others."

I avert my gaze from the blinking machines, the zigzag pattern of his heart rate. Dad has suffered three heart attacks in the last six years. Each time, the doctors said he wouldn't survive the next one. Each time, he promised to do better. "I'm glad . . . I'm glad you're still here."

"Me too."

The silence stretches between us, nearly unbearable. "Dad, where's Lux?"

"She's around."

"Is she at home?"

"I—I don't know. I'm sure she's fine."

"She won't answer my calls."

Dad coughs and closes his eyes. He doesn't answer. This is his thing, ignoring everything he doesn't like, as if pretending something away could make it actually disappear.

Frustration flares in my chest. But this isn't the right time to talk. He's too exhausted, too sick. A wave of dizziness washes over me. I can't stay here a moment longer. "I'm going to find a nurse, okay?"

I flee the room as quickly as I can without running, acid rising in my throat.

There were no hospital visits eight years ago when my mother died. There was only the silent house. Then the funeral, the coffin and the gravestone, the soft weeping above the birds chirping, the breeze rustling the trees.

After the funeral came the visitors. Family and friends invaded the house, bringing their hunched shoulders and covered casseroles, their whispered apologies and awkward, pitying attempts at conversation.

I was only twelve, but I played the role of hostess perfectly, smiling and taking their dishes, tin-foiled turkey, meatballs in a Crock-pot, plates of muffins and croissants. I hung up jackets and sweaters, handed out tissues, made sure everyone had enough potato salad. All the while, the palpable grief in the house was so thick and heavy, I could barely walk through it, could hardly breathe.

I remember how Dad wept in great, gasping sobs. I'd never seen him cry before. Ten-year-old Lux sat in the hallway, knees pulled up beneath her chin, eyes glazed. I can see her so clearly, scrunched up in her pink silk dress with the tiny daisies all over it, the one Mom had loved.

Lux had stared at the wall as if transfixed. She didn't cry, speak, or respond to anyone. After a while, people just stepped over her in their suits and dark dresses on their way to the bathroom as if she weren't even there.

I clench my jaw and shake the memory out of my head. There's no use thinking about it now. I check my phone for the hundredth time. Still nothing from Lux.

I have to keep moving, stay busy. If I don't, I'll fall apart right here on the hospital floor, and I'll never be able to pick up the pieces. I can't fall apart. Instead, I find the nurse's station and wait until an older woman in a white lab coat introduces herself as Dr. Carter.

I meet the doctor's gaze. "Is my father dying?"

Dr. Carter smooths back her blond hair threaded with silver. "His previous two coronary artery bypasses were unsuccessful. The grafts have failed. He has severe systolic failure, with rapid onset symptoms of diastolic dysfunction as well. Your father has end stage congestive heart failure."

"What do we do next? Another surgery?"

"Due to repeated stents, significant scarring of the heart muscle is present. Another bypass would only fail. At this point, no further therapeutic options are available. I'm sorry."

There's a dull ringing in my ears. I barely hear her words, let alone comprehend them. "How long?"

The doctor touches my arm. "It is difficult to say for certain, but his time should be measured in weeks, Miss McKenna."

I close my eyes, a fresh wave of dizziness washing over me. No matter how prepared you think you are—you aren't. "What about a heart transplant?"

"I'm sorry, but your father is not a candidate for a heart transplant."

I focus on the doctor's face. Her skin is pale, almost translucent. I'd photograph her face in color, in a cool, natural light to capture the delicate netting of blue veins like scaffolding propping up her features, threading skin to bone.

The words are like stones in my throat. "What do you mean?"

"A donor organ would not sufficiently prolong his life. It isn't simply his heart. He has additional comorbidities, including morbid obesity, hypertension, and severe kidney damage. Nearly every organ in his body is failing."

I try to swallow, the hitch in my throat as large as a fist.

"Again, I am truly sorry. I've spoken with your father. He expressed a desire to go home. He's eligible for hospice care through Medicaid."

The shock rolls over me, unabsorbed. That will come later. Now there is planning, discussing, action. Something for me to do. "Is it something—I mean, could a family member take care of him?"

"If someone could be with him and take care of daily tasks. Certainly."

I try not to imagine the remaining weeks of spring semester slipping away. I can't miss the Central Florida Metropolitan Museum of Art photography competition. I've made it to the semi-finalist round. Winning could make my career, change my life. Photography is everything to me.

No, not quite everything. I can't bear the thought of strangers caring for my father on his deathbed. He's my dad. This is my responsibility. I close my eyes, pushing out thoughts of school, photography, the dream I've worked so hard to build. "I'll do it."

"I would like to discuss some things with you. You should know what to expect . . ." Dr. Carter continues talking, but I hear little of what she says.

My father is dying. My sister seems to have disappeared. And the painful, brutal memories of my dead mother swirl dangerously close to the surface.

But what I dread most at this moment is going back to that house. The home I haven't stepped foot inside in over two years, where the dust and darkness settle too quickly, where memories swirl and never really settle at all.

The house of my childhood, crouching silently, empty but breathing, rattled with tremors, the shivers of guilt, of loneliness, of secrets. Like a living thing.

3

———

# LUX

I've been lying here huddled beneath Autumn's blankets on the floor of her room for three days. It feels like three centuries.

My hair's knotted and tangled over my scalp, my mascara and eyeliner smudged over the hollows beneath my eyes. My mouth is thick and gunky, my throat scratchy from crying.

I clutch the phone, my fingers like claws. Like hands that don't even belong to me.

I've called the hospital so many times I've lost count. I need to make sure he's okay. I need to know what's going on. I punch in the number I know by heart. I ask the same questions. Finally, I'm transferred to a nurse who actually talks to me. *Your father's stable. He'll be discharged tomorrow morning. Your sister is with him.*

My sister. Lyra. Back home after all this time. The thought makes me want to scream. But still. Relief floods through me. Dad's okay. Lyra's taking care of him. Same old, same old. Nobody needs a screw-up like me around, just making things worse.

I hear the slamming of car doors, footsteps, then the key in the lock. Low voices in the hallway. Autumn is back, and she's brought someone with her. I cover my head with the blanket.

They walk into the room. Someone nudges my prone form. "Galapagos Tortoises sleep up to sixteen hours a day." Autumn's voice.

"Ugh." I groan. "Go away."

"Hello? I live here, remember?"

"Kill me now," a second, deeper voice says. Simone. "It stinks like the unwashed masses in here."

"The three-toed sloth sleeps twenty hours a day," Autumn says. "He moves so slowly algae grows on his back. You see any algae growth yet, Simone?"

"Nope. I do see some epically hairy legs, though."

Someone grabs the blanket and jerks it off me. I blink up at my best friends since fifth grade, Autumn Jián Yun and Simone Talebi.

Autumn tucks her straight black hair behind her ears and squints at me in concern. She's dressed in a gray sweater and loose khakis. She's full-bodied and curvy, like I am, but she's always hiding herself, hunching or slouching and wearing baggy, oversized hoodies. She's kind and loyal as hell, which is why I love her, forever and always.

"Seriously, you've got to get up," she says. "There's rice and Kimchi stew in the fridge. My mom made *jihnmandu* last night. Your favorite."

I just moan and close my eyes. "Someone turn the light off."

"Don't make us stage an intervention," Simone says. She's half-Iranian, half-Nigerian and full-on amazing. She's like six feet tall with these thick middle-eastern eyebrows and gorgeous brown skin. Her caramel-colored curls corkscrew around her head like the mane of a lion. She's fierce like a lion, too.

"Go away."

"I'm gonna bring Felix over here."

"Uh huh."

I feel her reach down and swipe my phone.

My eyes snap open. "Don't you dare."

Simone smirks and slides her black square-framed glasses up the bridge of her nose. They don't have prescription lenses. She just wears them for the heck of it. "Oh, Felix . . ." she mock-moans, pretending to text.

Felix Avery is my boyfriend of six months. I don't normally go for the smart, quiet, good-boy type. Usually after a few weeks or a month, I'm ready to move on. Lots of pearls in the ocean and all that. But Felix is different. He's got this sexy-nerd vibe going on, and coupled with his earnest sweetness, his puppy-dog desire to please—Felix Avery does me in.

Simone waggles my phone at me. "Smile for the camera!"

I'm a wreck. I can't let him see me like this. My makeup is a smeared mess. And I smell like a garbage can. "You wouldn't."

"Do you know me at all? I most certainly would."

She would.

"Taking an epic photo in three, two, one . . ."

"I'm up!" I drag myself to a sitting position and groan. Everything aches. Memories batter at my skull. I shove them away. Dad's fine. He's stable. Lyra's there, saving the day as always. Everything's fine. It's fine. Fine. Fine. I repeat the word in my head until it loses all meaning.

"Everybody at school is worried about you." Autumn sits down on her bed and pops a Tic Tac in her mouth. "Jayda says if you miss any more days, they'll have to kick you out."

"Jayda's an idiot."

"You need some sustenance," Autumn says. "When's the last time you ate?"

I gesture at my messenger bag leaning against her dresser. "There're some Twix bars in there."

Simone raises one thick, black eyebrow. "Is that how you've been surviving in here all week?"

"Nah, my mom's been bringing her egg rolls and *chap chae*. She doesn't even cook for me like that." As if on cue, Autumn's stomach growls loudly. She rattles her nearly empty Tic Tac container.

"Take some. I have five bars left." Lugging around a giant messenger bag isn't always convenient, I can keep a crapload of junk food in there: mini-boxes of Nerds, bags of Sour Patch Kids, Airheads, Jawbreakers, and handfuls of Starbursts, plus the occasional textbook and my folder of specialty paper.

"I can't." Autumn's shoulders slump. "I only have, like, four hundred calories left for today."

I shove my bangs out of my eyes and glare at her. "I did not just hear you say that. Simone?"

"I'm on it." Simone grabs my messenger bag, digs through it, and pulls out two king-sized Twix packages. She rips them open and doles them out. We've been doing this since seventh grade when Autumn's dad used to take us to the corner gas station on sleepover nights.

We always get a bucket load of candy—lemon drops, Skittles, peanut butter cups, jelly beans. And we each get a single Twix. The last one we always, always share, snapping it into thirds and splitting it between the three of us.

Autumn holds hers like it's something precious. And poisonous. She loves candy as much as we do, but she's been trying to lose the same twenty pounds for forever. Even though she doesn't need to. The zombie idiots at school make moronic comments about how Asian girls are supposed to be skinny, blah blah blah.

"Don't make me come over there and shove that thing in your mouth, Skittles," I say, using my favorite nickname for her.

She knows we will, too. "If you're forcing me, then I guess . . ."

"We're forcing you. You're beautiful, Autumn. Enough with the tasteless Tic Tacs already."

She takes a bite, closing her eyes in pleasure. "Mmm. This is so good."

I shove the whole Twix in my mouth, enjoying the crunchy butter cookie, gooey caramel, and creamy milk chocolate. The sugar injects itself directly into my veins. Almost instantly, I start to feel better.

"I'm seriously gonna call Felix." Simone shakes her phone at me. "You. Shower. Now. And for the love of all that's holy, please shave yourself."

"I'm going au natural. Armpit hair and all."

"Well, if you want friends, I advise you to rectify the situation. Pronto."

"That's how I roll. You don't like it, Jellybean, you can kiss my sweet ass."

"And . . . she's back!" Simone rubs chocolate off her upper lip and licks her fingers. "I'm still starving."

"Male penguins go without eating for up to two months." Autumn tosses the Tic Tac container into the trashcan next to her bed. "While they stand guard over their eggs, the females travel up to fifty miles one way to get fish."

Autumn does this all the time. It's not even weird anymore. Her mom is a veterinarian at Paws Plus in Dowagiac. Autumn wants to be a vet, too. She's crazy about animals, the weirder, the better. She's got posters of baby tigers and giraffes and fluffy sloths tacked all over her walls.

She's always spouting horrible facts you wish you'd never heard, like the fact that a blue whale's testicle weighs up to 150 pounds, or that female kangaroos have three vaginas. Three. I'm fairly sure I could've lived a happy, satisfied life without knowing that particular fact.

"I'm not a penguin," Simone snaps. "And neither are you. Lux, if you don't shower, I'm dragging you out as-is. Trust me, you do not want that. We're going to Chili's for chicken fingers and fries, so get your ass in gear."

I take a shower, comb the tangles out of my long, almost waist-length hair, and put on my makeup. Autumn turns up the latest *Beyoncé* hit, and we dance to the beat. The music pulses through me, pounding away the bad thoughts, blasting them to dust.

I grab my phone off Autumn's dresser and scroll through the messages. A couple from Felix. I tell him I'll see him tonight, same time, same place. I've got a ton from Lyra, the perfect sister I haven't seen in over two years. Who's so perfect, she hasn't even bothered to come home for two years.

Until now.

Ignore. Ignore. Ignore. I don't even read them. Who cares? Not me. Not one little bit.

We dig through Autumn's closet, pulling on thick knitted socks and draping ourselves in sparkly scarves. I fishtail-braid Autumn's hair and Simone swipes on her trademark crimson lipstick. I dot concealer over the pimples on my chin, adjust my nose ring, and circle my eyes with thick black liner.

I grin at Autumn in the mirror.

Now I'm ready.

I'm back.

4

LYRA

In my dream, everything is dark and shifting. My mother shimmers ahead of me, a barely discernible form in the shadows. I run toward her, tripping, scrambling, calling out for her. I can't see anything but my two pale arms stretched out in front of me.

My wrists are crisscrossed with red, pulsing wounds. Blood bubbles out of the cuts and spills down my arms, spreading across my nightgown. The blood is on my hands, my forehead, my cheeks, seeping between my lips into my mouth.

I'm choking on blood, my mother's blood as it fills my mouth and throat, great globs and clots of blood drowning my lungs and I can't breathe, can't breathe—

I wake up slick with sweat, thrashing at my blankets and gasping for air. I suck in huge breaths, my heart thudding wildly against my ribcage. My fingers clutch at my sheets.

I'm not dying. I can breathe. There's no blood anywhere—not on my face, my arms, or the oversized Ansel Adams landscape print T-shirt that serves as my nightgown.

A sudden pain grips me, my gut clenching against the grief striking me fresh and undiluted. I lay unmoving for several minutes, curled like a comma, eyes closed, willing the pain to drain away, willing the memories, jagged as glass, to fade and lose their sharpness.

They do, but slowly, gradually replaced by a jarring emptiness nearly as painful, like there's a hole in my chest where my heart should be. It was taken, stolen away that day eight years ago, just like everything else.

You get used to it, even learn to forget it for long moments, hours, even days. But it's devastating every time the knowledge comes crashing down again, when for just a moment, for just a dream, it wasn't there at all.

My eyes burn. I rub my face with the back of my arm and grab my phone off the nightstand. 8:33 a.m. Dad comes home today. He's coming home to die. How am I going to do this? How can I keep things together, take care of everything?

At school, it's simple. Everything is easier. The scholarships, the grades, the friends. I imagine all the things I'd normally be doing now, either breakfast in the cafeteria with my roommate Sarah or a meeting with the photo editor of the university newspaper. Then classes and more studio time in the darkroom unless Sarah dragged me out with her theater friends.

I sit up in bed. This is the new reality of my life. I'm not at school but home after a long absence, sleeping in my old bed that still smells faintly of the lilac shampoo and conditioner I used for years.

My room is the same as I left it: scarred wood floor, bare dresser, a bed heaped with blankets. Famous prints and posters are taped to every square inch of available wall space, from Lee Jeffries' blistering portraits of the homeless and Steve McCurry's work for *National Geographic* to the vintage celebrity photographs by Philippe Halsman and Angus McBean.

A minimalist, Dad always called me. A prison, is how my room seems now, like the entire house. A place you escape from and never come back to.

And yet, here I am.

A photo above my dresser snags my gaze. It's a close-up of me and Lux from three or four years ago. My forehead is too long, my nose too big, my skin veiled with freckles. My eyes are gazing off at some point in the distance, cerulean blue against the ginger of my hair. I look miserable.

Lux, on the other hand, hams at the camera, her grin lighting up her whole face. It's Lux who inherited the porcelain skin, lustrous ruby-red hair, and devastating beauty of our mother.

The only sound in the house is the dull thud of my heartbeat. The thought of Lux brings a sharp pain behind my eyes. Is she okay? Is she safe? Where is she? And how am I going to bring her back?

She's fine, I tell myself. She's fine. But fear still snakes around my heart.

"Where are you, Lux?" I say into the silence. "Where are you?"

But there's no answer. There's never any answer when it comes to Lux.

The last time I saw my little sister was Christmas of my freshman year. Lux broke two of Mom's china plates, hurling them against the wall. I don't even remember what the fight was about. It didn't even matter. We fought about everything.

Dad begged me to come home every break, but I couldn't. I couldn't bear it. Since then, I've spent Christmas in the dorm and filled up my summers working as an aide for my advisor, Dr. Wells.

My advisor. I need to tell him. I check my phone again for a message from Lux—still nothing—and call him.

"Dr. Wells," he answers gruffly. I imagine him sitting ram-rod straight in his office chair, his skin the color of walnuts, his lean, brooding face as he squints behind the sheen of his glasses.

I explain what happened, why I'm here and not there. The words sound alien, like they're coming from someone else.

"I'm sorry for your loss," Dr. Wells says with uncharacteristic kindness. He's not one for social niceties. But over the last few years, we've become something like friends.

"I'll be back soon," I force out, like saying it aloud will make it true. "I'll do whatever I have to in order to make up the work. I'll—"

"You need to focus on your family, now."

My throat tightens. "I know, but—the competition." The photography competition for the Central Florida Metropolitan Museum of Art is huge. The finalists' prints will be displayed next to the likes of Annie Liebowitz and Steve McCurry. The winner receives a $10,000 grant and an internship and stipend with *Photography* magazine. With Dr. Wells' guidance, I've made it to the semi-finalist round.

This is my big chance, my dream. Until yesterday, it meant everything.

"The committee needs to see your submission by March twenty-eighth," Dr. Wells says. "That's two and a half months away. If you make it to the finalist round, the gallery is . . . April eighth. The rules state you must be present to win. Lyra—"

Surely, I'll be back long before then. "I'll be there."

"Do you have prints ready?"

My gut clenches. I've been working on this project for months, but nothing is good enough. "I will."

"I'm truly sorry about your father," he says roughly. "Keep in touch."

His kindness is going to undo me. I grit my teeth, shoving back the emotions hovering at the edges of everything, the grief creeping up my throat. "Thank you."

I end the call and stand up, the shock of the cold floor knifing my bare feet. I stumble from my room to the downstairs bathroom, turn on the tap, and splash water on my face.

The bathroom is a makeshift darkroom. A sheet of black felt covers the window over the bathtub. The table Dad built out of two-by-fours stands across from the toilet. The solutions, the timer, and trays are placed neatly on one side of the table with the enlarger on the other.

I spent much of my childhood down here. I pick up a pair of tongs. Maybe I could set everything up again. Maybe I could still find time to prepare for the competition, even while I care for Dad. I place the tongs gently on the counter and head up the basement stairs.

On the main level, the morning light oozes between the curtains. In the cramped kitchen, dishes pile in the sink and overflow onto counters tattooed with juice stains.

The living room is heavy with shadows. Books and papers are strewn across the floor, crumpled pop cans and a crusting cereal bowl left on the glass-topped coffee table. My stomach clenches in dread. What happened here?

The lamp next to the couch is on the floor, the shade bent, the glass bulb shattered. Is this where Dad had his heart attack? Where he fell, hurting and terrified? What happened? And where was Lux?

Where is she now? Why isn't she here? *What did she do?*

Tears sting my eyes. I fight them back, swallowing my grief. If I start to cry, I won't know how to stop.

5

LUX

Thirty minutes after Autumn goes to bed, I push the covers off and climb carefully to my feet. I'm dressed and ready to go. I grab my purse and Autumn's house key from her dresser.

"Where are you going?" Autumn asks groggily.

"Shhh," I whisper. "I'll be back soon."

"But it's a school night." Autumn's great at English and writing and

history. And science, pretty much everything but math. I used to love science, but school sucked all the joy out of it.

"So?" I hate school so much. I've had senioritis since freshman year, but now as an actual senior, it's for real. I haven't been to classes in four days. The thought of all the work I've missed is overwhelming, so I push it right out of my head. "I'm not going tomorrow. Sweet dreams."

She groans and rolls over. Tomorrow she'll give me a big fat lecture, but it's not tomorrow yet. I blow her a kiss and slip quietly out of the house.

Twenty minutes later, I'm at the park, driving the old single-lane gravel road to the massive clearing Mom always took us to on her

20

midnight picnics. It's the best stargazing spot for miles, far enough from the small towns to keep the light pollution minimal.

Stark, leafless trees hunch like black shadows around the perimeter of the clearing. It's so quiet out here. There's the occasional rustle of tiny feet in the snow, the crack of something breaking and falling, a twig, a frozen acorn.

I'm grabbing my stash of blankets from the backseat when Felix Avery pulls up in his battered Ford F-150. We pile our blankets and pillows in the bed of the truck and climb in.

"Hey, hot stuff." I pat the space beside me.

Felix grins, his large hazel eyes bright in the moonlight. "I can't stay too long. I've gotta study for that Physics exam." He hands me one of the cappuccinos he picked up at the gas station and runs his fingers through his mop of muddy brown curls. I'd rather have some peach schnapps, but really, it's too cold for that and Felix doesn't drink.

He's a nerd through and through. His current life goal is to be valedictorian. But it's like he thinks he's going to earn it by sheer will and sweat alone. And unicorn tears, because that honor is going straight to Jayda Washington-Clark, who can recite the periodic table in her sleep.

He's always worried about tests and essay deadlines, even though he already got into Notre Dame on early admission. Felix never drinks, and he always leaves parties by eleven to get his beauty sleep. Until me, that is.

Since we first got together six months ago, we've explored a dizzying array of make-out session locations: on his bed, on my floor, in the front seat of my car, on the bean bag in his friend Raj's basement, and here, out in the big wide open beneath a sky full of stars. I've kept him up way, way past his bedtime.

"You okay?" he asks me, concern lining his voice. "You haven't been at school. I've been texting and calling all week."

I lean in and kiss him. I don't want to talk about that anymore. It's over and done. There's only now, only the sharp air and the brilliant blue-black sky sprinkled with stars like crushed ice.

I sink down, and he hovers over me, kissing me harder, deeper. Stars and planets and whole galaxies explode in my stomach. Even after all this time together, it feels amazing. Like swallowing lightning.

After several long, spectacular minutes, we break apart. We lay back, and I snuggle into his chest for warmth. I listen to the steady beat of his heart. The thing about Felix is, we do way more than just make out.

The other guys—they always pushed for more. I like a hot make-out session as much as any girl, but I'm not ready. Not yet. Felix gets that. He never pressures me. We're so much more, go so much deeper. We cuddle. And laugh. And talk about everything, anything.

The white puffs of his breath mingle with my own. We gaze up at the stars. "Show me," he says.

I trace the shapes in the velvet sky. "Canis Major, the one that looks like a dog. Taurus the bull is there, to the right of Orion. See his horns? And above and to the east, there's Auriga."

"I see them. This is seriously off the hook, Lux."

"I know, right? Look high in the sky, over that tall pine tree. That's Gemini. It's two figures, holding hands. See, legs, torso, arms outstretched? That bright star that's the head of the figure on the left? That's Pollox."

"What's their story?"

It's so cold, my ears burn, my throat seared with every breath. A memory flashes through me. Me and Lyra, lying next to Mom, staring up at the same dazzling sky. Mom gripping my hand, whispering the myths in her husky voice. She said astrology was the language of the heavens. She said, "If you listen closely, the sky speaks to you."

"They were brothers, born to Leda, queen of Sparta," I say to Felix. "The twin Castor's father was the king of Sparta. Pollux's father was Zeus, so Pollux was born immortal, while Castor was fully human. The twins grew up handsome and strong. They loved each other deeply and did everything together, fighting in the Trojan war, chasing the golden fleece with Jason and the Argonauts.

"One day, Castor was killed. Pollux was overcome with grief, distraught without his brother. He begged his father Zeus for help. He was willing to do anything to be reunited with his brother. Rather than killing Pollux so he could be with Castor in death, Zeus decided to make Castor immortal. He placed them both in the sky, so they could be together for the rest of time."

Felix finds my hand beneath the blankets and squeezes it. "Anybody ever tell you that you tell the best stories?"

"All the time." I used to love telling stories, spinning magical tales the way my mother could, back when it was me and Lyra, Lyra and me. Back during those long days and endless hours and minutes alone in the house, just the two of us. Back when our fears were too large to see, just hulking shadows at the edges of our vision. Now the only stories I can tell are the ones already in the sky.

"Superhero of the day. Go," I say to distract him. It's a game we play. Felix loves comic books. He's watched pretty much every superhero movie and TV show ever created.

He thinks for a second. "Squirrel Girl."

"Huh?"

"Squirrel Girl, from the Marvel Universe. She's got an awesome tail and has like, every squirrel in Central Park under her control. She's tough, fun, and creative. She single-handedly defeated Iron Man's nemesis, Doctor Doom. She's always underestimated because: squirrels. I mean, what's better than an army of adorable, furry little critters that'll swarm and kill you?"

"The attack of the kamikaze squirrels."

"You wanna know a secret? She might be my favorite of all of them."

"Is she hot or something?"

"She's totally hot. But not as hot as you."

I mime gagging. "You're such a nerd. You're lucky *you're* hot." "I know." He kisses my forehead.

The winter night is still. Nothing moves. Nothing breathes. The meadow is bathed in moonlight. Next to me, Felix's eyes gleam like dark stars. Above our heads, the constellations wheel in the frozen bowl of the sky.

Right now, right this second, everything is perfect. Beyond perfect.

My heart is a galaxy of shooting stars.

6

LYRA

Dad arrived home two days ago. Each morning, I remember all over again that he's trapped in bed, waiting to die.

It's my job to prop him up, to feed him, turn on the fan when he gets hot, help him change positions so he doesn't get bed sores. It's my job to help him to the bathroom, to change his bedpan when he can't make it, to go to him when I hear his voice rumbling down the hallway, to prepare his pills and medicines, and comfort him on his journey toward death.

My sister is still gone. The night before last, she finally replied to the dozens of texts, emails, and phone messages I sent her. *Leave. Me. Alone.* One text, then nothing. So, she's alive and well. And exactly the same.

Dad doesn't seem concerned. She's at her friend Autumn's house. She's safe, she's alive. She'll come home in her own sweet time.

I shove thoughts of Lux out of my head. It's time to prepare the first cocktail of pills: two small yellow capsules, a round red one, one huge and white that looks like chalk. I place the pills in little paper cups and balance them on a tray with a large glass of water.

After only two days, we've already fallen into a reassuring sort of schedule: first batch of pills before nine, breakfast at ten, bathroom check after breakfast, lunch at one, second batch of pills after lunch, bathroom break, snack at four, third batch of pills at five, supper at seven, television until ten.

Even though Dad rejected regular hospice care, he's been assigned a hospice nurse to check up on him once a week. Her name is Ellie Delmonte. She's in her mid-40s, a large, pillowy woman with a booming laugh. She's all movement, noise, and sparkle. Her burgundy hair is a glossy helmet, her long fingernails painted peacock blue.

When she first arrived, she had bustled around the bedroom, setting things up, sorting, arranging, and humming to herself, her brightly patterned satin shirt billowing around her. "Don't hesitate to contact me if you need anything, dear. We have volunteers who can assist with daily activities, spend time with your father, whatever your family needs."

I shook my head. "I'll ask him, but I think we're fine."

"Let me know if you change your mind, darling," she said, her broad face crinkling, dimples forming in her peach-colored cheeks. "I'll be here every Friday at 3:30 p.m. I'll always stay for a couple of hours so you can take a break. Have coffee with friends, see a movie, or my personal favorite, shopping. Shopping is a great distraction when you need one."

I just stood in the middle of my father's room, nodding, my hands hanging helplessly at my sides. I couldn't even imagine such inane things as shopping, movies, coffee with friends.

She paused, smiling kindly, her eyes full of empathy. Or pity. I couldn't tell which. "I know this is a difficult time, but I'm here to help you, honey."

She was trying to make me feel better, but I just felt more alone.

Even with Dad here, what I feel more than anything is a dark, oppressive loneliness. But I can't think of that now.

"Good morning," I say brightly, standing in the doorway with my tray of Dad's pills.

The bedroom is almost the same as it was a decade ago. There's the faded rose curtains, the white wallpaper dotted with tiny cornflowers, the outrageous salmon pink comforter Mom loved.

Mom's oak dresser stands next to a large floor-length mirror.

Perfume bottles, a fake pearl necklace, and her fancy silver-handled brushes are all exactly where she last placed them. The ceramic, heart-shaped box she used to keep her earrings in is gone. An origami star sits in its place.

"Lyra." Dad blinks up at me. The light from the bedroom window slants directly into his eyes.

"Here, I'll get that." I set the tray down on the nightstand and move to the window.

The yard is brown and patchy with dirty mounds of snow. The sun's already bright above the bare maple tree, but a mass of clouds gathers on the eastern horizon, fat and foreboding. A storm is brewing.

"How are you feeling?"

"Oh, you know, the same old." A forced laugh gurgles in his throat, then dies.

Across the street, the cornfield still lays fallow, a flat expanse of taupe that bleeds into the darkening sky. The world is silent and lonely outside the window.

I close the curtains. "You hungry?"

"Negatory."

"10-4," I say, because I know he wants me to.

"Remember how much you used to love that?" Dad asks wistfully.

When Lux and I were little, we thought Dad's CB radio, or squawk box as he called it, was the coolest thing ever. He used to let us climb into the cab of his big rig 18-wheeler and tune into Channel 19. Dad had been a long-haul trucker ever since I could remember. He was gone for five, seven, ten days at a time.

I remember a thousand bedtimes when he'd call to tell us good night. I always asked him where he was. "I'm on the big road, headed eastbound for Bean Town," he'd say. Another night, I asked, "You made it to Cincinnati yet?" And he'd say, "Already in my back pocket, Gingersnap."

He always said stuff like, "I gotta stop for some go-go juice, some motion lotion," when the big rig needed diesel, or, "I got myself another driving award" when he got a ticket. Mom wore a T-shirt he bought her that said, "My heart belongs to a trucker." But after a while, she stopped wearing it.

After Mom's death, Dad switched from long haul to short haul so he could be home on weeknights. Sometimes I could see the long stretch of highway reflected in his eyes. I never asked if he missed the independence and loneliness of the road. I didn't want to know.

I turn away from the window. My stomach rumbles. I haven't left the house yet to go to the grocery store. I haven't wanted to leave him. That and Lux took Dad's car on her great escape. "We're pretty much out of food."

"Why don't you run to the store?"

I don't want to leave him alone, but the food will run out before the hospice nurse, Ellie Delmonte, returns. And I need to shop for a low-sodium diet per the doctor's instructions.

"I'm *fine*, Gingersnap. Look at me. I'm not gonna fall apart if you're gone for an hour."

I sigh. "How am I supposed to get there? Lux took your car."

He blinks a few times. "You could take the bulldog."

Mom's minivan, aka the bulldog. We loved Dad's slang for the other vehicles on the road—school busses were cheese wagons, motorcycles were crotch rockets, tow trucks were dragon wagons, septic trucks were toilets on wheels.

The Honda Odyssey has sat in the garage for most of the last eight years. Like everything else of Mom's, Dad refused to get rid of it. And I refused to drive it. Until now.

"Yeah. I suppose I could," I say slowly.

"My credit card is on top of my dresser, next to my wallet and keys."

I watch him take his pills. The hitch in his throat as he swallows is barely visible through his rolls of fat. The thought of leaving, even for an hour, brings both guilt and relief. I should be here when it happens. I must be here. It's my reason for being home in the first place.

It's my role, my duty to make things easier, to help him with the dying. Still, it terrifies me, the thought of entering the room one morning and finding him cold and rigid, his face locked in agony, the smell of death already infused in his pores.

Canned laughter floats from the TV, old reruns of M*A*S*H. He sighs, closing his eyes as he sets the half empty glass of water back on the nightstand.

I gather the little plastic cups, crinkling them on the tray. "Is there anything else you'd like to do, Dad?" I don't know my father well enough to know what he likes. He loved photography once upon a time, but I haven't seen a camera in his hands in years, maybe since he bought me my first SLR Nikon 35mm camera on my eighth birthday.

Since Mom's death, he's either eating or watching TV or gone on a truck run. We're like strangers, but intimate strangers who've survived a crash together.

"You know, the hospice nurse said they have these volunteers who come in and spend time with you. They can talk, read, sing, even play the guitar. Would you like that?"

"Can't you do all those things?"

I snort. "Not the guitar. You already know you don't want me singing, unless you want your ears to start bleeding."

He grins at me, a flash of his old self. "We don't need anybody but us."

"I thought you might say that. How about a book then?"

"Reading is hard on my eyes."

"Oh."

"I've been wanting to read this more." He picks up a large book from the nightstand. A Bible.

My throat tightens. Mom used to read us the Bible around Christmas and Easter, and for a while when Gran died. It hadn't done her any good. "What for?"

"There's a lot of good stuff in here I didn't know. It's—comforting. I've been going to church, the one on the corner of Culver Street."

My eyebrows shoot up. "For how long?"

"At least a year. There's some real nice people over there. And I've been trying to read a few chapters every day. You think you could read it to me?"

I sigh. What I wouldn't give to be back at school, surrounded by all the things that make up my safe, predictable life, the routine of classes, hours in the dark room, dinners with Sarah or some of the other art majors. "I don't know, Dad. Maybe later, after I go to the store."

"I wish Lux was here."

"Well, me too, Dad," I say, clipping the rise of anger at my sister's name. I could use someone to help, to clean the filthy house, to keep me from feeling so totally and completely *alone*. "I hope she's okay."

"She's okay." He turns his head away from me. The TV blabbers in the background.

"Why is she at the Yuns?" I ask carefully, watching my father's face, the muscles ticking beneath the folds of skin. "Why isn't she here with us?"

"Does it matter?"

"It matters to me. She should be here. This is important."

"She needs some time. She'll be back when she's ready."

"Was she there—when you had the heart attack?" I chew on my lower lip, worrying a flag of loose skin. "Was she fighting with you?"

"It doesn't matter." With his face in profile, I can't see his eyes clearly.

I see only the flare of his nostrils, the tightening around his mouth.

"Who called 911?"

He sighs. "Lux did."

"So she was there. Then why wasn't she with you at the hospital?"

"Lyra—"

"Did she do something? Is that why she's gone?"

"It's done. It's over."

"What did she do?"

"She didn't do anything."

"She screwed up again, didn't she?"

"Lyra, just leave it."

But I can't leave it. I can't help myself. "How could she leave you?

When you needed her most? What kind of person calls 911 and flees the scene?"

"That's enough!"

I clench my jaw. "You could have died. You—"

"But I didn't," he says in a weary voice. "Now, please. I was thinking I'd like to look through some of those old photography books. Remember the ones I used to read to you?"

I take a breath, willing myself to calm down. Riling Dad up will only weaken him further. I speak as slowly and calmly as I can manage. "I think they're still in the laundry room. I'll get them."

I walk downstairs to the laundry room. Something happened. I'm not sure what, exactly, but anything involving Lux tends to become an epic disaster. She did or said something terrible, I know it. Anger flares through my veins, sparking at the tips of my fingers.

I sink to my knees on the gray cement next to the cardboard boxes stacked in the opposite corner of the washing machine and furnace. The boxes are labeled in my mother's elegant script: *Summer clothes—3T-5T, Dad's tools, Lux's Breyer horses.*

My fingers tremble as I unstack the boxes, shove them aside. I've got to stay calm, compartmentalize my emotions. There'll be plenty of time for anger later.

I dig through the boxes until I found the one labeled *Dad & Lyra's photo books.* I yank the lid off and almost smile at the worn spines of books I haven't seen in years: *World's Best Photography, Landscape Photography of Michigan,* and *Faces and Places.*

My gaze snags on another box: *Lyra's photos/negatives—2003 to 2009.* I run my thumb along the black marker scrawl of my twelve-year-old hand.

My lungs burn for air. There are so many memories locked away in these boxes. Beautiful photos of our beautiful, broken family.

We had no idea, back then, how it would all burn to the ground. I rub the wetness from my eyes and head back upstairs. How quickly we lose everything that matters.

## 7

## LUX

Snow spirals down, swift and furious, slapping the windshield of my car. I've got Lorde cranked up loud on the radio. The heater is dialed as high as it will go. It's Friday night, and me, Autumn, and Simone are on our way to Jayda Washington-Clark's party.

Autumn sits up front with me, squeezing her Faygo diet orange pop between her legs while she fiddles with her phone. Simone's in the back seat. She texts with one hand, balancing the French vanilla cappuccino we picked up at the gas station in the other.

I squint into the gloom, the gray sky turning a murky blue over the tops of the trees lining either side of the two-lane road. Our headlights glow like halos in the darkening night.

I grip the steering wheel with Autumn's pink fingerless gloves. The silvery tank top and black mini are hers too, since I'm still crashing at her house.

I left my own house with nothing but the clothes on my back. Luckily, I was wearing my jean jacket and the three-inch wedge heels that make me feel like I can pulverize whatever gets in my way. Which is how I feel right frickin' now.

"What's the agenda for tonight?" Simone asks, leaning forward between the front seats.

"What else?" I say, thumping the steering wheel. "A whole night of dancing our asses off with hot guys! Or in my case, one very specific hot guy."

Autumn giggles.

"Ugh. Spare me the details, please." Simone pretty much hates the male species. Scratch that. She's got a ton of guy friends, but she's not interested in taking it to the next level. I've seen boatloads of guys hit on her. She's never returned the favor. She always keeps a pink can of Mace in her purse next to her inhaler, and she's not afraid to use it.

Autumn, on the other hand, is nearly as guy-crazy as I am. While I'm currently attached, Autumn is free to play the wide-open field. But she's too embarrassed to even talk to most of them.

"You think Dominic will be there?" Autumn asks.

"You know he will be." Dominic Harris is the high school quarterback for our lousy football team, the Wildcats. He's your typical jock through and through. Autumn's been half in love with him since freshman year.

"You actually going to talk to him this time, Skittles?" Autumn shrugs. Of course she won't.

"Rumor has it he just broke up with Jayda," Simone says, snapping her gum. "He's a free agent."

"This is your chance. Talk to him."

Autumn blushes. "Well, maybe. He's just so ... hot." "I've seen better," Simone says.

"Seriously?" I say. "And who would that be?"

"His chin looks kind of like a butt. Which: *meh*."

My phone rattles in the console's plastic cup holder. A text.

"Want me to get that?" Autumn asks, already reaching.

"No!" I know exactly who it is. I have zero desire to get reamed out by Lyra right now. Or ever. I take a hard curve in the road. The wheels of the Honda Accord drift across the icy road.

"Lux, can you slow down please?" Autumn grips the side door handle.

"You're going twenty over the speed limit."

"So?" Jayda lives ten miles outside of Brokewater on a long-ass country road surrounded by deep forest and the occasional farmhouse. There are no streetlights, no stoplights. There are no other cars even on the road.

"But it's *snowing*."

I grin at Simone through the rearview mirror. Autumn's always so serious about everything. She needs to lighten up. Just a bit. This is southwest Michigan. Every year, we get pummeled with lake effect storms curtesy of Lake Michigan. We know how to deal with a little snow.

I jerk the wheel and veer the car into the oncoming lane, then turn the wheel again and swerve back.

"Stop it!" Autumn shrieks.

I step on the gas pedal and do it again.

A car appears over the curve of the hill ahead of us. I slide into his lane. The car honks and flashes his lights.

"Lux!" Autumn pounds on my arm.

My pulse hammers against my neck. Adrenaline flushes through me and I'm alive, so alive. A hundred times better than last week, when I could barely drag myself off the floor for four damn days. But that's over. Done and gone.

Tonight, I'm free. Free to party. Free to chill the hell out. Free to be wholly, 150% *alive*. And what better way to feel alive than a good old-fashioned game of chicken?

The other car—a boring, beige Toyota—lays on the horn. He heads into the right lane, trying to avoid me.

"Kiss my sweet ass!" I yell, sliding back over to match him.

He swings to the left. Only thirty yards away now.

"That's enough!" Simone says in her throaty voice, leaning so far forward she must not be in her seatbelt.

But I'm in complete control. I have perfect depth perception. I can tick off the seconds until impact, grid the distance between the two cars, measure the space like a straight crease on an unfolded piece of paper.

"Wuss!" I crow, cranking the wheel to block him again.

Simone grabs the wheel from me, jerking the car back into our lane. Only she overcorrects, and the Honda skids.

A roaring fills my ears. Autumn screams. My heart jackhammers against my ribs.

We slide across the icy road, almost weightless. I slam on the brakes, but it's too late.

The wheels can't catch enough traction to stop. The backend of our car swivels, our headlights flashing across the oncoming car, the looming trees.

We slip slide across the ice, plowing straight into a snowbank.

My body snaps forward, jerking against the seat belt. A burning pain slashes across my neck. Simone lets out an "oomph" sound as her body bangs into the back of my seat. Autumn's opened pop bottle splashes liquid all over her thighs.

The other car roars past us in a blare of horn and a spray of sleety snow.

For a second, we all just sit there, breathing hard.

"What the heck?" Autumn yelps.

"Not cool, Lux." Simone rubs her shoulder.

I whip around and glare at her. "We were *winning*. I was *fine*. Then you had to go and twist the wheel on me. *That* was not cool!" "You could have killed us." Autumn's face crumples.

"Sorry about your pants. But that was Simone. Not me."

"You're too much sometimes, Lux," Simone says. Her eyes are watery, her breath wheezing in her chest.

"You guys are the wettest blankets I've ever seen. The epitome of party poopers. It's called *fun*."

"If you call being stuck all night in a snowdrift while we miss an epic party *fun*." Autumn reaches into the glovebox for a handful of old Taco Bell napkins and dabs at her wet jeans.

"We are not stuck. In fact, we can—"

Simone starts coughing, one hand fluttering at her throat, the other shoved in her purse, searching.

"You okay, Jellybean?" I ask, twisting around in my seat.

She nods breathlessly, grabs the inhaler and brings it to her mouth. We watch her suck in her asthma medication. After a minute, her breathing sounds normal again. Simone's allergic to practically everything. She carries her inhaler around like an accessory.

"Code red averted," she says, rolling her eyes. "Can we please get out of here?"

I turn back to the front and check out the snowdrift our front wheels are currently buried in. The snow is mounded three feet high. Just beyond it, a line of thick, bristling pine trees. "We might have to do a bit of digging first."

"Are you freakin' kidding me?"

"It won't take long, I've got the shovel in the back and—what's that?"

Something dark moves just to the right of the snowbank. Just outside the glow of the headlights, stark trees stoop, huddled against the onslaught. I shove open the car door, a blast of frigid air striking my bare skin.

Thick clouds block the light of every star, the snow swarming down like confetti. Even the moon is only a dim shadow of itself. It feels like being cut off from the whole world, the entire universe.

"It's just a trash bag," Simone says. "Get in here and shut the door."

She's right. The trash bag is half buried in the gray, slushy snow at the edge of the road, black plastic flapping in the wind. But there's something else.

I clomp through the snow in my three-inch heels, sucking in my breath as I sink ankle-deep. Snowflakes flutter against my face, landing on my eyelashes, my cheeks, my nose.

"Lux!" Autumn yells.

"I saw something move."

"Whoop-de-freaking-do," Simone says. "I'm freezing my ass off!"

"Hold on a sec." It's twilight now, making it hard to see the details of the bag. I bend down, balancing precariously, and reach inside.

I feel something small, furry, and stiff. I pull it out. My stomach drops. "What is that?" Autumn's voice goes high, hysterical. "Is that what I think it is?"

I hold the little body in my hands. The yellow glow of the head-lights reveals the spiky black and white fur, crusty with ice. Its eyes are closed. A kitten. Dead.

Tears collect at the corners of my eyes, hardening into crystals in my eyelashes. Who could do this? Who could stuff a litter of tiny, innocent creatures into a bag and leave them by the side of the road to freeze to death, like nothing, like trash?

I imagine them alone, abandoned, waiting for their mother to come back to them, waiting for the rescue that will never come.

I can see them, confused and hungry, making sad little mewling sounds. Crawling together for warmth as the freezing temperature sucks the life out of them. Each one going slowly cold and stiff without warmth, without life.

Suddenly I'm weeping, sobbing, gasping for breath. It hurts. It hurts so much, holding this tiny lifeless kitten in my hands.

Simone climbs out of the car. "This sucks, Lux. I get it. But we've got to go. Your lips are blue. Literally."

"No. We can't just—we can't leave them. We have to bury them."

Simone throws up her hands. "Where? How? The ground is frozen, in case you haven't noticed."

I slip the dead kitten carefully back into the trash bag. I wipe my cheeks with the sleeve of my jacket. "Pop the trunk of the car."

"What? We can't—"

"Pop the trunk! We'll put them there for now and figure some-thing out later."

Simone's thick eyebrows lower into a straight line. "You've got to be kidding me."

"Do I look like I'm kidding?" I nearly scream at her. "Autumn, open the damn trunk."

"This is a terrible idea. You cannot put dead, decaying corpses in your car! That's disgusting!"

Autumn looks back and forth between me and Simone. I glare at her. "It's my car. I decide."

Autumn shrugs, leans over, and pushes the button beneath the steering wheel. "Sorry, Simone."

"Don't apologize to her!" I say, my teeth chattering. I lift the trash bag gingerly and hold it in my arms, trying not to think about how many dead kittens are in here. Six? Eight? More? Acid rises in my throat as I carry the bag to the trunk. Simone follows me and takes out a flashlight and the shovel we'll need to get out of the snow drift.

I'm lowering the bag when I feel it. The slightest push against my forearm.

I drop the bag with a thud. "What in the—!"

"What's your deal?" Simone asks, glowering at me.

I wish I had better gloves than these flimsy fingerless things, but I don't. I steel myself with a deep breath and plunge both hands in the bag.

More stiff bodies, more frozen, ragged fur. And then something moving. "Turn on the flashlight."

Simone points the flashlight at my hands. I pull out a tiny, smoke-gray kitten. It's alive.

The little thing wraps its tiny paws around my wrist. I hold the kitten easily in one hand and unwind my fuchsia knit scarf with the other. Carefully, I wrap it up in the scarf.

I knock on Autumn's passenger window. "Here. Warm her up."

She caps her diet pop, rolls down the window, and takes the kitten. "Poor baby!"

"How old is she?"

Autumn cradles the tiny creature in her lap. "Her tail isn't curled around her body, and her eyes are open and bright. Maybe seven, eight weeks?"

I pat her shoulder. "Beautiful *and* brilliant."

"It might not be a girl."

"It's a girl."

"Girls have a dot and slit under the tail and males have two dots. You want me to check?"

I've already decided she's a girl, and I don't want to be told differently.

"No! No checking. It's a girl, okay? No further discussion needed."

Autumn wrinkles her nose. "Did you know oysters can change their gender multiple times over the course of their lifetime?"

"Whoop-de-freaking-do!" Simone hollers. "Come on! Help me dig out of this mess."

Simone and I duck our heads against the onslaught of snow. We shovel ourselves out of the snow bank and jump back in the car.

"What's the plan here?" Simone asks, shivering and blowing into her hands.

I back the car up and turn around. "The pharmacy's only a few minutes back. We need milk and a syringe." "What about the party?" Simone asks.

"We'll be late. So what?"

"Look, Lux," Simone says. "I know you want to save that thing, but it's practically frozen. You're getting your hopes up. It's just gonna be that much worse when it dies."

"Don't you dare say that."

Simone rolls her eyes, but I don't care. Autumn's crooning softly to the kitten, stroking her head.

"Me, Skittles, and the kitten disagree," I say. "You're outvoted and you know it."

We head to the pharmacy, snow swirling in the twin circles of our headlights, crunching beneath the tires.

Whatever happens tonight, I'm going to save that kitten. It's a fighter.

Like me.

8

---

## LUX

The party whirls and churns around me. The music thrums in my chest, in my bones. People swirl in and out of the massive kitchen, where all the beer and wine and chips, brownies, and bowls of M&Ms are stacked nice and neat on the marble island. There's a massive pool table and big screen TV in the basement.

Out in the living room, the couches, chaises, and coffee and end tables are all pushed back against the walls, making a dance floor for dozens of gyrating couples. The sliding glass doors to the deck keep opening and closing. Girls strip down to their bikinis and climb into the steaming, ten-person Jacuzzi.

Usually, I'm one of the first ones to jump in. Usually I'm dancing and grinding and drinking and laughing the whole night away, spinning and whirling, bright and dazzling as a sparkler on the Fourth of July.

But not tonight. Tonight, I'm all business. I'm saving a life.

I sit at the farmhouse-style kitchen table, hunched over the tiny kitten.

She's nested inside one of Jayda's sage green towels I warmed in her dryer.

I hold the kitten carefully in one hand, trying to get her to drink heated milk from a syringe. Her whole body is trembling. She laps tiredly as I give her the milk, one drop at a time.

"To what nefarious purposes are we up to tonight?" A shadow looms over me as Felix gives me a hug from behind. The chair next to me scrapes against the floor as he flops into it.

He's wearing a vintage T-shirt that says, "My Weekend is All Booked Up," with a printed stack of books beneath the words. His nerdy clothes are always slightly rumpled, like he's too busy solving quadratic equations to spend time on personal hygiene. "You look— amazing. Like Black Widow in the original comics."

I try not to blush, but with my porcelain skin, I pretty much blush at anything. I love how effusive Felix is with his compliments, how he always compares me to some epically gorgeous comic book character. He's so adorably geeky. "Hey, hot stuff. What's up?"

"Sweet mother of—is that a cat?"

"Great deductive skills you have there, Sherlock." I tell him everything that happened on the way here. Well, not everything. I leave out the insane game of chicken with the Toyota. He's like Autumn. He doesn't appreciate certain versions of fun.

He pets the kitten's ear. "He's handsome."

"It's a 'she.'"

"How do you know?"

"Isn't it obvious?"

"Should we check?"

"What is with you people and your obsession with gender identity? She is who she is. What she really needs is a name. And not Fluffy or Cuddles or anything lame."

Felix gives me his wide, dopey grin. "That white streak between her eyes looks like a lightning bolt. How about Harry Potter?"

"Just, no. She's much too refined for that. Plus, hello? She's a girl."

"That's undetermined."

I glare at him. "Whatever. Are you gonna help me or not? Her fur is the color of ash."

"Well, that's a depressing comparison. How about something more conventional? And, you know, not about death. Like Stormy."

I roll my eyes. "Too cliché."

"How about Jean Gray?"

"That's an X-men character, right? What's her other name?"

"You mean Phoenix?"

"That's it! She died and then she was reborn out of the ashes. It's perfect!" I lean in and kiss him on his perfect lips. "I love it."

Felix scrapes his hand through his scruffy curls. "Happy to be of service." He rubs the kitten's tiny head. "You need a break? I can take over if you wanna dance or chill for awhile."

My heart melts. "I'm good for now."

"Cool. You want a Mountain Dew?"

"How about some schnapps?"

Felix brings me a sweating bottle of schnapps and a bag of Doritos. He kisses me on top of my head. My stomach does little cartwheels. He's too perfect for words.

"Thanks, babe."

He smiles at me, but the smile doesn't reach all the way to his eyes.

I don't want him to be sad. I want him to be as happy—no, euphoric—as I am. "What's wrong?"

Just as he opens his mouth, Jayda Washington-Clarke saunters up. She's wearing a silky maroon strap dress that flatters her light brown skin and the mahogany stripes streaking her shoulder-length hair. She points at us. "No food outside this kitchen, *comprende*?"

Jayda's a cheerleader, wildly popular and super smart, and the host of the best parties. Her parents are *never* home. But she's tough as nails when she wants to be. If you so much as drop a Dorito on her parents' white carpet, you're out. And if you don't want to go, one of her linebacker boyfriends will firmly escort you.

"We got it," I say.

She glares at the kitten.

"Is that thing going to pee in my house?"

"No way. She's potty-trained. She can even use the toilet."

"Mmmkay ..." She twists up her face, as if deciding. Then she smiles her trademark brilliant white smile and turns to Felix. "How 'bout that

Physics test? It was totally brutal."

"Yeah," he says, but he sounds distant, like he's thinking about something else.

Jayda wrinkles her nose. "Wait. Is that weed I smell? Is some scum-sucking idiot actually stupid enough to smoke in my house? I'm gonna kill them!" She barrels out of the kitchen.

"Someone's about to be booted out on their ass," I say. Felix doesn't even crack a smile. "Okay, now you really have to tell me what's going on."

He tugs his hair behind his ear in that adorable way of his. "That Physics test? It *was* brutal. I got a C minus."

"That blows." I know it sucks for him, but I haven't given a flying fart about my grades since I was nine.

"I have to get an A in Physics."

Phoenix gives a little mewl. She's lapping the milk harder, getting stronger. Her suckling makes a soft sucking sound. Her little belly is round and full, her fur drying into a silky blue-gray. "Getting a B is not the end of the world, you know."

He gives a short, hard shake of his head. "I need a scholarship to pay for Notre Dame's astronomical tuition. I'm gonna have to study more."

"Okay, I guess?"

Just then, Autumn and Simone wander in to refresh their drinks. Simone leans against me, wheezing. She loves to dance, and usually it doesn't affect her asthma as long as she takes her medicine beforehand.

"You need your inhaler?"

"Nope. I'm good."

"I'm so gonna ask Dominic to dance," Autumn says, her cheeks two pink circles. "I totally am. Hey, Felix." "Hey," Felix says back.

Raj Patel walks up and slaps Felix on the back. He's Felix's best friend and fellow geek. They both love Star Wars, comic books, and arguing about Marvel versus DC worlds, which Avenger kicks the most butt, and other nonsense.

"Nightwing versus Daredevil," Raj says, not even saying hi to the rest of us. He and Felix have this superhero battle thing going on.

"That's easy." Felix sits up straighter, preparing his argument. "It's a good fight, but Matt has 360-degree perception. He hears human heartbeats. He times bullets. Daredevil knocks Nightwing out flat. End of the sixth round, tops."

Simone stares at them, her eyes bugging out.

"Nightwing can throw his batarang so hard he cuts through metal chains," Raj says. He's super-skinny, with ears that stick out, these huge dark eyes, and a serious mouth that makes him look like he's always frowning. "He tears open punching bags with his fists."

"The humanity!" Simone mock-clutches her chest. "How can you bear it, Lux?"

Autumn giggles.

"Haven't you heard?" I deadpan. "Pocket protectors are the new sexy."

"I don't wear pocket protectors." Raj pats his button-down shirt pocket anyway, like he's checking just to make sure. He glances at me for the first time. "Is that a cat?"

"No, it's a skunk bomb," Simone says, shoving her black-framed glasses up the bridge of her nose. "For nerds, you're both dumb as a pile of rocks."

"I resent that statement." Raj frowns. In spite of—or maybe because of—his almost perfect SAT scores, he completely lacks any sense of humor.

"Please," Felix says with a grin. "Nerd is so passé. I prefer the term 'intellectual badass.'"

I rub his bicep with my free hand. "See? Sexy as hell."

Simone groans. "I can't even."

"As I was saying," Raj continues. "Nightwing would use one of his sonic grenades to hobble Daredevil's senses."

"Not a chance. Heck, Daredevil can swat bullets with his cane. He'd be on Nightwing faster than he could react for sure."

I sigh and slant my eyes at Felix. "We're boring our friends to tears over here."

Felix is smart enough to take the not-so-subtle hint. "Hey Raj, I heard they've got World of Warcraft set up on that massive TV downstairs. Wanna check it out?"

Raj nods curtly and leaves the kitchen.

"Thank goodness that torture's over," Simone says. "I came over in the first place to tell you that guy's here again. The one with the greasy hair."

"Um, hair gel much?" Autumn snorts.

The last party we went to, this older guy named Reese crashed the party. He had to be in his early twenties, and he stared at all the girls like we were his prey. We figured out later he's the guy all the stoners get their dope, E, and Molly from, so someone must be inviting him. But still. Gross. I make a gagging mime with my free hand.

Simone sneezes, takes her glasses off, and wipes at her eyes. "Sorry, Lux. I think I've had enough of that thing and its allergy-laden fur."

"It's a 'her.' And her name is Phoenix, thank you very much. Go tear up the dance floor."

"Hells yes!" Simone shakes her hips. She loves to dance. Last year she was into a heavy jazz phase, the year before that it was hip-hop. This year it's swing. It doesn't matter whether she's just walking across the room, she moves with the grace of a ballerina, like she's skimming the surface of the world. "Come on!"

"Five minutes, I promise." The kitten's movements slow. She curls into a little ball, tucking her nose beneath her paws. The tiniest hint of a purr vibrates against my palm.

Simone grabs Autumn's arm and they head back out to the party.

Felix clears his throat. "Anyway, back to our conversation. What I'm trying to say is, I need to spend more time studying. And less time, you know, hanging out."

My body tenses. "What's that supposed to mean?"

"It means ... we can't spend so much time together. We need a break."

It takes a second for the words to sink in. A break. *Breaking up*. I leap out of my seat, adrenaline flushing through me. "You're breaking up with me? At a frickin' party? While I'm trying to *save* this kitten's life?!!"

He shakes his head, eyes widening. "No! It's just a break. Just—"

There's a roaring in my ears so loud I can barely hear his words. "A break? A frickin' *break*? Are you for real right now?"

"No! I mean, yes. Sorta. You're not listening—"

Pain explodes inside me. This is not how tonight is supposed to go. A dark thing wakes up inside my chest, rears its ugly head. "Then what is it? You think you're better than me?"

"No!"

"You think I'm too stupid for you. That's it."

"That's not what I said!" His voice is rough, pleading. "Please, can we just back up for a minute here?"

"I heard exactly what you said. And how you said it." I shove the chair against the table with my hip. My mind blazes with indignation, with humiliation. I can't believe it. All this time. He's just wanted to use me, like the rest of them. "Screw you, Felix Avery. I wasn't that into you, anyway. You're just a social pariah posing as someone who's cool, someone who matters. News flash: you don't. You don't matter at all."

I storm out of the kitchen, leaving him sitting at the table with his mouth hanging open. Serves him right. No one screws me over. No one.

The music surges through my blood, lighting up my synapses. The volume is turned way up, blaring through me. I shove past the couches full of people chatting and drinking and clatter upstairs in my heels.

I open doors until I find Jayda's room. A few rooms are already occupied. Curses follow me down the hallway. No one's in here. No one would dare.

It's dark, but I've visited enough times to feel my way to her massive walk-in closet. She keeps the boxes for every pair of shoes she's ever purchased. I fumble for the top box, open it, make a little bed with my scarf, and tuck the sleeping kitten inside. No one will mess with her in here.

My phone vibrates in the pocket of my jean jacket. It's Lyra. Again. Screw that. I don't want to think about any of it right now. Or ever. I can't. I won't. I dump the phone inside the shoe box without looking at it.

Phoenix is safe. Now I can focus on what the heck just happened. How my tongue tastes coppery. How my head is buzzing like a thousand wasps are trapped inside, batting around against my skull. How my whole body's trembling with outrage. *How. Dare. He.*

Something bad is about to happen. I can feel it.

And I'm the one who's going to do it.

9

LYRA

It's almost 6:30 p.m. and dark by the time I make it out to the garage. I spent the afternoon scrubbing and organizing the house until it gleamed.

Now I stand, my hands limp at my sides, staring at the minivan my mother drove for four years, until she didn't have a need for driving anymore.

She used to say, "Ready to rumble?" mimicking Dad's deep voice. It always made Lux laugh and laugh.

I make myself press the key fob. There's no reason to freak out. It's just a car. Dad and Lux have driven it plenty of times since Mom's funeral. It's not like her essence still lingers inside it, drifting like blue smoke, like a ghost.

I shake the thoughts out of my head and climb into the van. A pine air freshener hangs from the rearview mirror. There are a dozen gum wrappers stuffed inside the two plastic cup holders, a bunch of *Us Weekly* and *Cosmo* magazines scattered on the passenger's seat. Lux.

The van coughs and sputters as I back out. I head for the grocery store, the vehicle groaning in protest. It bumps and jolts down the road as I make a mental note to ask Dad if it always sounds like this.

The headlights are two cones of light in the winter darkness, the

48

world beyond drenched in inky shadows. Street lights are few and far between in a small country town like Brokewater.

Brokewater has only one grocery store, Browne Meat and Grocery. Main Street boasts two gas stations, a McDonald's, Taco Bell, Delia's Ice Cream Shoppe, and a Chili's. Bill's Bar and Grill is ten minutes out of town, and if you want Walmart or Meijer's, you have to drive twenty-five minutes into St. Joe.

There's a huge dairy farm just out of town. At certain times of day, if the wind is blowing a certain way, you catch a whiff of something foul, the faint stench of manure.

By the time I park, the van is making raspy, clunky noises. I can't worry about that now. I tighten my coat and duck inside.

I don't want to see anyone I know, don't want to answer questions or endure the pitying looks and muffled whispers the town has bestowed upon my family for years. For months after the funeral, everywhere we went, people whispered behind their hands, "Those are the girls of that woman." Like we couldn't hear, like we didn't already know.

I grab a bag of shredded cheese and toss it in the cart.

"Freckles? Is that you?"

I freeze, instantly recognizing the smooth, rich voice behind me.

Ethan Kusuma walks up to me, a carton of eggs in one hand and a dazzling grin plastered on his face. Ethan Kusuma, star wide receiver of the Wildcat's varsity team and one of the most popular guys in my graduating class. Ethan Kusuma, still as appallingly handsome as ever.

Junior and senior year, I was the yearbook photographer in charge of covering athletics. I attended every single Wildcats game, roaming the sidelines, camera up and ready, taking pictures of every play. None of the jocks ever noticed me.

During our senior year, the Wildcats actually made it to the state playoffs. That first game, we were down by three with the seconds ticking on the clock. Ethan ran a simple button hook play, but the quarterback was in trouble, just trying to elude the defenders swarming him. Ethan went long.

I was already near the end zone, so I followed him in my viewfinder, snapping shots as the quarterback launched the ball his way. Ethan had two defenders flanking him, but he leaped high, stretching for the ball. I managed to grab the perfect frame: Ethan's hands grasping the ball with his fingertips, his body arcing in mid-flight, both defenders pulling at him but unable to bring him down. His Hail Mary touchdown catch won the game.

The photo made the local paper. Then the Cass County Gazette picked it up and ran it on the front page. He noticed me after that, enough to nickname me Freckles and flash me that devastating grin every time he saw me on the field or in the hallways. But his smile always had a hard edge to it, like there was some joke only he was getting, and it was at my expense.

My heart clenches at the memory. "Um, hey."

"I thought I recognized that hair. It's nice to see someone my own age around here. Aren't you supposed to be at some artsy-fartsy college in Florida?"

I wince. "I'm taking a furlough. Weren't you going to Michigan State on some scholarship?"

His grin widens. "I guess you could say I'm taking a furlough, too." His scruffy black hair falls to the top of his plaid shirt collar. I've always hated long hair on guys, but on him ... It works. Everything about him works. His eyes are the color of amber, seeming to capture all the light in the room. His Asian features are perfectly aligned, his olive-toned skin sculpted over his cheekbones and jawline.

I try not to imagine how I would photograph him in deep shadow, how the light would highlight the fine lines of his face, the brightness of his eyes. I clear my throat. "It's nice to see you again. I've got some refrigerated stuff in my cart, so I should probably hurry up and finish."

He puts his hand on my cart, tapping his fingers against the metal. "Wanna catch up? Chat about old times?"

I highly doubt we had a single similar high school experience. He was the most popular guy in school, the jock with all the girls. I was a dork, the frizzy-haired nerd who stuck to the sidelines, capturing other people living their lives behind the safety of my camera.

I wish I had it now. My face burns. Once upon a time, I would've chatted politely until he was the one who got bored and left. But things are different now. "Those 'old times' were only three years ago, and we weren't exactly friends."

His cocky smile almost falters. Almost. He's still so arrogant, like he expects the whole world to capitulate to his every whim and desire. It probably does.

Seeing him brings back a torrent of memories I'd rather not relive. Like every other girl at Brokewater High, I fell victim to his charms. But not now. I'm smarter now. Older. Stronger. But still, my mouth is dry. My heart thuds in my chest.

"Come on, now. You're not really gonna leave me hanging, are you?"

"Actually, I'm really sorry, but I am." I jerk the cart out of his grasp and walk purposefully down the dairy aisle. A toddler giggles nearby. To my left, an old guy with a puff of white hair picks out a tub of sour cream.

"I still have that photo on my wall," he says behind me.

For a second, my legs won't move. The same photo is framed and hanging above my bed in my room. It's the one thing that connects us.

"That's cool," I say woodenly. "See you around, I guess."

This isn't like me. Even with people I despise, I'm polite, demure, meek. But today, that veneer's been stripped away. My father is dying. My sister is gone. I have zero emotional reserves to deal with anything else. I just need to end this conversation.

I walk around the corner to the frozen foods aisle, grab a box of waffles, a bag of frozen peas. But he doesn't take the hint. He never did. He pushes his cart up beside me.

I glare at him, about to tell him off, when I notice the little girl sitting in the front seat of his cart. The one who was giggling a minute ago. She's almost a mini-me of Ethan, but her skin is darker, her curls kinkier. Her huge eyes shine like topaz.

"Lyra, I'd like you to meet Hadley. Hadley, this is Lyra. Hadley is my daughter."

The little girl is bundled in a knit sweater, her round cheeks dimpling as she grins. She grips a small red polka-dotted purse in her chubby hands and shakes it. "Yook!"

My face must register my shock, because Ethan laughs. "You might remember I was with Nyah the last half of senior year. She was five months pregnant at graduation."

I'd left in June for a summer photography study tour in Washington D.C., so I never heard the news. I glance at his left hand. No ring.

"We never married," he says in a low voice, his brows knitting together. "She took off three months after Hadley was born. She needed to live her life. Now I live in my mom's basement and spend my weekends with a two-year-old, changing diapers and scraping spaghetti off the ceiling. Not quite what you imagined, huh?"

"I didn't know," I mumble, unsure what to say.

He shakes his head, a scrap of hair falling into his eyes. "It's not so bad. We have fun don't we, Chipmunk?" He makes a goofy face, and she bursts into a fit of giggles. The sound is pure and bright as church bells on Christmas morning.

"I'm happy for you."

He steps closer. "How about some coffee at Delia's later? Or a walk by the river. Hadley likes to play at the park."

Instinctively, I take a step back, banging into my cart. My head is a thicket of confusion. I can't square this new version of Ethan with the suave, arrogant ladies' man I knew before. Besides, I'm not here to fraternize with a member of the opposite sex, no matter how hot he is. I'm here for one reason only. "I'm sorry, I really can't. My dad is—he's sick. I'm sorry. I have to go."

I leave him in the frozen foods aisle and finish my shopping, quickly tossing items into the cart. He isn't my type, like at all. So why is my mind replaying that cocky grin over and over? I close my eyes, take a breath, and force Ethan Kusuma out of my head.

I make it to the checkout without seeing anyone else I know. The

Hispanic girl behind the register is tall and extremely thin, nearly gaunt. Her black hair is pulled back in a low bun, a single side lock dyed Windexblue. "You look the same as I remember," she says as I put a box of Golden Grahams on the conveyer belt.

I look at her again. Narrow, pinched face and a tilt to the corners of her mouth, like she's about to slip into a scowl or sneer at any second. She does seem familiar.

"Isabel? Hello?" she says in a bored tone.

Now I remember. Isabel Gutierrez was also in my graduating class. Her mother, Maria Gutierrez, used to babysit me and Lux occasionally when Dad was on a long-haul run and Mom had the presence of mind not to leave us alone by ourselves.

"Hey, Isabel. What's up?" I stack the rest of the groceries on the conveyer belt.

"Oh, the same old stuff, obviously," Isabel says airily. The scanner bleeps as she scans cans of low-sodium tuna and tubs of non-fat yogurt.

Another worker starts bagging the food. "Sorry to hear about your father. Your poor family." Her voice has that same insincere edge to it that I remember from high school.

The hairs on my neck prickle. I'd hoped no one here would know, but who was I kidding? Isabel's mom is a nurse at St. Joseph Medical Center. She was probably the first to hear. "Yeah. It sucks."

"And your sister, how is she?" Isabel smirks. "Still partying like it's 1999?"

The smugness in her voice tells me she knows exactly how far Lux has slipped down the rabbit hole, and she's happy about it. "Lux is fine.

Thanks for your concern."

She shrugs. "Just making conversation."

I remember now how much I dislike Isabel. "Why are you still stuck in this town?"

Isabel glances down at the jar of peanut butter in her hands. Her mouth is puckered, her small dark eyes glinting. "Just taking a break from school. Saving up money. Most people don't get fancy scholarships. They actually have to work to pay for things."

I narrow my gaze but say nothing. She's bored and baiting me, just like she did when we were kids, when I was forced to play with her even though I knew she hated me. She'd always ask which doll or stuffed animal or coloring book I wanted, then choose it herself, a sly, triumphant smile playing across her face.

Isabel makes a clicking sound with her tongue as she passes a tub of margarine over the scanner. "While I'm stuck here, I'm taking a couple of classes on natural remedies. Margarine is one of the worst foods for your body, you know. It's made of chemicals and partially hydrogenated soybean oil, which just goes straight to the arteries. You should so try the raw food diet. When you cook foods above 116 degrees, they lose all their essential nutrients and enzymes, their vital life force. You should try sprouted millet and barley bread. I bet if your dad went on this raw food diet I've been on, he would totally get better. It's cured all kinds of cancers and stuff. Since I've been on it, my skin like, completely cleared up."

I jerk Dad's credit card out of my purse. "I don't think zits and congestive heart failure are on quite the same level, Isabel."

"Hello? I know that. But seriously. You can special order these totally great pressed juices? Kale, ginger, and beet juice. They're like, uber healthy." She's got this virtuous look on her face, like she's the only one with some magical elixir with the power to purify the sins of the world.

"I'll keep that in mind."

Isabel tosses a disdainful glance at the eggs, boxes of Kraft mac and cheese, and dark chocolate bars. "These foods are all toxic, you know. We put so many poisons into our body, it's no wonder we're dying left and right."

Death might be a blessing at this particular moment. "Yes, well. I hope your diet works out for you."

Isabel rings me up. "I have all these books I could recommend. They're a real eye-opener."

"I'm sure they are. How's your mother?" I always liked Maria

Gutierrez, in spite of her daughter. She was kind and warm and soft-spoken, everything I'd always thought a real mother would be like. How she managed to produce a pretentious, self-absorbed daughter like Isabel is one of life's many mysteries.

Isabel hands me the receipt. "She's still single and alone. Probably always will be. She never tries, you know? She's just a dowdy, miserable old woman."

"I'm sorry to hear that."

Isabel stares at me impassively. "Thanks for visiting Browne Meat and Grocery. Come again. Have a most excellent day."

I sling the bags into my arms and brace for the blast of cold as I hurry out to the parking lot. I duck my head against the hard little bits of snow flung down from the night sky. The asphalt is a slushy, icy mess, and I nearly slip twice. I kick my boots against the tires before climbing into the van.

My breath puffs out white and steaming, my fingers already stiff from the cold. When I turn the key, the van makes a growling, grinding sound, then putters into silence. I try again. Nada. Nothing. Zilch. I slam my fists against the steering wheel. "Come on!"

Something knocks against the passenger side window. It's him.

Ethan Kusuma grins at me beneath the beanie pressed down over his ears, straggles of black hair poking out in all directions. Beneath the parking lot lights, his eyes are dark gold. "You need some help?"

I clear my throat, trying to ignore him. I start the engine again. It groans to life, only it sounds like a mangled robot screeching in its death throes. I roll down the window. "I don't need a man's help, but thanks so much for asking."

"Not even a man who's a mechanic?"

I glare at him. "You're kidding me."

"This face wouldn't lie to you. I've worked full-time at Ross's Engine Repair for the last two years." He tugs off a glove and wriggles his fingers at me. His fingernails are rimmed with black. "See? Engine grease."

"You're telling me you know what's wrong with this thing?"

"Yep. You smell that slightly sweet, burning odor? That puddle of transmission fluid that's dripping underneath your van right now? I'd say it could just be worn gaskets or a damaged bell housing, but not coupled with that whining, grating sound. It's your transmission."

I know enough about cars to know transmission issues are expensive. "That's just fantastic."

"I can fix it."

"You sure about that?"

He levels me with his most charming smile. "I can do anything with these hands, darling. Catch a game winning ball. Fix up a car good as new. Change a badass diaper. The ladies are especially impressed with my skills. I can even—"

I clear my throat, trying not to blush. I know exactly what he was about to say. "Got it, thanks. Look, the damn thing's working for now, so I'm just going to go home."

The flirtatious grin slips from his face. He frowns, his thick eyebrows crinkling. "You shouldn't be driving like this. Follow me to the shop. It's closed, but I've got a set of keys. You can drop the van off and I'll get you set up with a loaner. I can't look at it tonight 'cause I've got Hadley in the car with me. But I'll check it out first thing tomorrow."

I sigh. Just when I thought things couldn't get any worse, here's another problem pressing down on me like a hundred bricks, strangling the air right out of my chest. "I really just want to go home."

He frowns. "I'm serious. It could die any second. And if you're in the middle of an intersection, that's gonna be bad news for you."

"Do I have a choice?"

"Not if you want to avoid more expensive repairs, or an accident that leaves you a braindead vegetable." He smacks the van door. "Follow me. I'm in the junky pea-green SUV with the 'Baby on Board' sticker on the back window, compliments of my mother. Afterward, we can grab that coffee. Or ice cream. Or whatever. Think you can handle that, Freckles?"

Irritation flares through me. He's getting under my skin. "Could you please not call me that? Coffee's not really a good idea right now. I'm pretty busy."

He just laughs and strides back to his SUV, brushing off the snowflakes collecting on his shoulders.

Even in the dark, I can see the thick, iron-bellied clouds hanging low over the trees. Another snowstorm is coming.

I follow Ethan to the mechanic's shop, my heart filling with a mixture of dread and anticipation.

# 10

# LUX

I leave Jayda's room and make my way down the first few steps. From this vantage point, I can see Felix across the living room stuffed full of dancing, writhing bodies.

He's slumped on the white leather couch, his head in his hands. Jayda Washington-Clarke sits next to him, her manicured fingers caressing his back. Of course. I should've known. She just broke up with Dominic. So she and Felix can be together. That disgusting, two-timing jerk.

My thoughts dart around the edges of my skull, my brain on fire. I'm not a cheap toy he can just trash when he gets bored. I will not be cast aside and ignored. I'm not that girl. No way.

I go downstairs and grab a cup right out of the hand of one of the freshman bimbos. I chug it down, ignoring her half-hearted protest. It's time to dance. But not with Simone, who's swaying in the corner with her hands outstretched, the object of a dozen guys' slack-jawed awe.

I scan the crowd. I know exactly who will hurt him the most.

I stride up to Dominic Harris. He's chatting with a couple of foot-ballers, but he turns toward me when he sees his friends eyeing me. "What's up?"

An image of Felix flashes through my mind. I can almost feel his warm hands, his fingers laced through mine. For one fleeting second, I hesitate.

I glance across the room and see Felix. He's turned toward Jayda. She actually wipes a frickin' tear from his eyes.

Flames of rage erupt inside my skull. My hands ball into fists. Felix Avery can kiss my sweet ass.

I turn to Dominic and cock my hip. "Wanna dance?"

"Do you even need to ask?" He runs a hand across his close-cropped fade, a slow smile spreading across his face. He's got gorgeous earth-brown skin, a chiseled jaw, and those piercing dark eyes romance novels always blabber about. And his body is to die for, even though it's currently hidden beneath his American Eagle hoodie. Simone's right, though. He does have a butt-cleft chin.

A few of his friends wolf-whistle as I grab his arm and drag him out to the center of the dance floor. We dance hard and furious, careening into and against each other, until I'm glistening and breathless. I press my body against his, and he wraps his strong arms around my waist.

The stuffy air makes me dizzy. My head pounds, my heart thumping faster than the music, jerking frantically against my ribcage and I don't care, I don't care, I don't care.

I catch a glimpse of Felix and Jayda. Jayda's glaring at me, her face fixed in a nasty scowl. Her hand is on Felix's knee.

The world is shrinking into something small and ugly.

I dance harder, faster, until the room is whirling, pulsing, radiating sparkling light. Bright liquid colors spin in fantastic eddies and swirls around me.

Dominic leads me back into the kitchen, sweaty and stumbling, where a bunch of guys are throwing potato chips at each other, trying to catch one in their mouths.

"Hey, Lux," Jamal Randolph says. "You're looking fine tonight. Fat in the best possible way." He gestures at my cleavage.

I slant my eyes at him, flash that smile all the guys love.

"Is that your natural hair?" Owen Wittenburg asks, adjusting his Lions baseball cap.

"No. I soak it every night in the blood of my enemies." "That's sick, brah!" Owen grins.

Jamal guffaws. "No, but it is, isn't it? Your sister's a ginger, too."

I grab a fresh beer and guzzle it down. "I'm all natural, baby. Unfortunately for you, you'll never know for sure."

"Oh, burn!" Dominic laughs.

Someone shrieks out in the hot tub. Dark energy sparks at the tips of my fingers. An insistent buzzing, like bees beneath my skin. Like an itch I'm desperate to scratch. I need to do something. Anything. Everything.

I turn to Dominic. "I dare you to go outside and run a lap around the house. In the snow. In your tighty-whities." The guys howl.

Dominic's slow, smug smile slides across his face. He takes a step toward me. I can smell his Axe body spray, and underneath it, the odor of sweat. "I'll take that dare. But you gotta do it, too."

Adrenaline flushes through me. The colors in the room are amplified, saturated, spinning and pulsing around me. There's a small voice in my head—Autumn's voice—warning me not to do it. But I have to. I've got to bury my thoughts in an avalanche of cold, shocking adrenaline.

I stare at Dominic, not breaking eye contact. I slip off my jean jacket, then my tank top. The cool air from the opened sliding glass door hits my stomach, my chest.

"Well played, dude!" Owen yells. "Well played!"

Dominic strips off his hoodie, then his shirt, revealing chiseled abs and a broad, defined chest. My breath catches in my throat. Before I can chicken out, I slide out of my mini skirt, dropping it on the floor.

He unbuckles his belt and nearly trips taking off his jeans. He's wearing red plaid boxers, left over from Christmas. My bra and panties are black lace, but they cover just as much as the bikinied girls in the hot tub.

Dimly, I hear guys hooting and whistling. Something about underwear seems to drive people out of their minds.

"Hot damn," Owen says.

"Lose twenty pounds, girl, and you'd be a dime," Jamal says.

"Nah," Owen argues. "More to grab, bro."

For one furious second, I get why Simone despises guys. Then my smile stretches across my face, taut as a rubber band. "Screw you, Jamal."

"Lux—" someone says unhappily. Autumn, somewhere behind me. I ignore her.

I raise my eyebrows at Dominic. "We doing this or not? Let's blow this joint."

"Go!" Dominic shouts. He scoops me up, carrying me like a damsel in distress, and dashes out through the sliding glass door. He slip-slides on the deck, nearly dropping me. A bunch of people crowd out after us.

He wants me to sling my arms around his neck. But I'm no damsel. I elbow his chest and scramble out of his arms, shrieking. I gallop ahead of him.

The frigid air bites at my exposed, tender flesh, needling my belly, chest, and thighs. My feet sink deep in the snow, a shock of icy pain spiking up my heels. I barely feel it.

Things are careening around inside me, things I can't think, can't feel. *He doesn't want you*, a voice whispers in the back of my head. *No one wants you. He left you, just like everyone else.* Humiliation quivers through me, helpless fury billowing at the corners of my vision. *Make him pay.*

I run through the dark, rounding the corners of the house. Dominic's laughing, trying to grab me. My skin is numb, slick. I slide away from his fingers.

I make it back inside before he does, breathing hard and dripping melting snow all over the kitchen floor. Jamal and Owen high five me. "That was lit!"

Jayda stands at the front of the crowd, her full lips pressed into a pout. "Overkill much?"

"Shock and awe, baby. Shock and awe," I say, shaking out my hair. My bangs are plastered to my forehead. Icy water drips down my neck.

"That's just how I roll."

She thrusts a towel at me. "Clean yourself up. You look like a ho."

"Don't be jealous," I snap.

"Me? Jealous of you?" Jayda's gaze travels up and down my body.

"Bless your delusional heart."

When Dominic stumbles in, she turns without a word and stalks away.

"You wanna chill sometime?" Dominic asks, wiping his glistening pecs with his T-shirt. He gives me his hoodie to put on. Since I'm so short, it falls to the middle of my thighs.

"Come on, bro! Why'd you have to do that?" Owen groans. "I was enjoying the view."

"Sure. Sometime." I scan the kitchen crowd, urgently searching for Felix. I need him to feel as horrible as I do. I need him to feel worse. I don't see him. He must've limped home already, tail between his legs.

I'm picking up my clothes and shoes when Simone grabs my arm. "What the hell do you think you're doing?"

"What's it look like? I'm having *fun*. Ever heard of it?"

She points to the kitchen table, where Autumn slumps, shoulders hunched and trembling, head in her hands. "Any particular reason you picked Autumn's long-time crush as your boy toy of the evening?"

My heart lurches in my chest. That thought hadn't even entered my fevered brain. The adrenaline leaks out of me, in its place a bone-deep chill.

I wanted to hurt Felix. I didn't think about Autumn and her crush. I should have, but I didn't. She's my best friend and I didn't think about her at all.

I've done it again. Hurt the ones I love the most.

I move toward her. "Skittles, I'm—"

Simone jerks me back. "Don't. She doesn't want to see you. Especially not in that." She gestures at Dominic's hoodie.

Autumn looks up then, her eyes red and raw. She sees us. Hurt flashes in her gaze. Hurt I caused.

"I didn't mean it," I stammer, frantic, full of anguish. This is my M.O.

I do things. Stupid things. Selfish things. Then I can't undo them. I can't ever make it right. "Autumn, you gotta believe me!"

Dominic and Owen stride up to us, half-baked grins plastered across their faces.

"Girl, you must be made of coffee, 'cause you grind so fine." Dominic slings his arm across my shoulder.

I wriggle out of his embrace, heat flushing my face. "Get off me."

"Is your name homework?" Owen says, leering at Simone. "'Cause I'm not doin' you, and I should be."

Simone whirls on him. "You kiss your mother with that mouth? Get out of here. And by here, I mean the whole state of Michigan."

"You on your period or something?" Dominic asks with a hard laugh.

"Yep. What's your lame excuse?"

Owen pulls down the bill of his hat. "Gross."

Simone glowers at him. "You asked. Now leave."

"You're utterly mental, sometimes, you know that?" Owen says.

For a second, Dominic looks like he might be pissed, too. Then his face loosens into a grin, and he claps Owen on the back. "Come on. There's far too much estrogen in here." He winks at me. "Check you later, girl."

They wander back out to the deck, laughing.

Simone rolls her eyes and turns her fury back on me. "Just what is your issue?"

"What's yours, *Jellybean*?" I snap, my voice rising.

"You're seriously being a total asshat right now."

"So are you! It was an accident, okay? I didn't mean it."

Whoop-de-freaking-do." She folds her arms over her chest, her eyes dark and cold, accusatory. "You are incredible. And not in a good way."

"I said I was sorry. What more do you want?"

I don't wait for her answer. There's nothing she can say that I haven't heard a hundred times before. I turn and stumble out of the kitchen, into the living room, into the whir and pulse of bodies, pushing through the tangle of sweaty arms and legs, the thrum of music hammering my skull.

"Lux." It's Felix, slouching with his hands stuffed into his pockets, looking miserable. "Can I talk to you?"

I shake my head, tears clogging my throat. "No. Stay away from me. I'm no good for you. Just—stay away."

"Lux—"

But I'm gone, pushing through the crowd. I almost trip over someone's foot. A hand grabs me. "Woah, there. Watch your step."

I look up at Reese Havestar. He's long and lean, with stringy brown hair slicked to the side with too much hair gel, a thin, hawkish nose and red slash of a mouth. He leans against the wall next to a girl I recognize.

Darcy Ackelsen graduated last year, but she still hangs around town, working at the auto shop her parents own. Her wheat-blond hair is shaved on both sides and long on top, tucked into a braid that falls to the middle of her back. She's got a stud in her nose and two rings in her upper lip.

Her pupils are huge in her ice-blue eyes. "Hey, Lux," she drawls.

"Hey."

Reese's hand still encircles my wrist. "You're missing some clothes."

"So are you." He's thin, dressed in a T-shirt and baggy shorts, even though we're only three weeks into January, the coldest month of the year.

I rub my arm over my face, scrape away the moisture. Flip the switch that pastes that glittering smile on my face. The one that says 'I'm flying' when really, I'm falling.

Reese drops my wrist and shoves his hands into his pockets, leans back against the wall. "You like to party? You look like a girl who likes to party."

Yes. I want to. Whatever he has, I want it. The alcohol is a sour pit in my stomach. I need more. Everything's hot and sharp inside me. Dangerous and ugly. "In case you haven't noticed, I'm pretty much up for anything."

Darcy raises one eyebrow. "Trust me. He's noticed."

My tongue is thick and gunky, my mouth dry. The way his gaze drifts over my body sends spiders crawling underneath my skin. I tilt my head at the clothes I'm holding. "I've got to change."

"You need any help?"

"Not this time."

His lip curls. "Next time, then."

"Ignore him," Darcy says, grinning like there's some sort of joke going on that I'm not a part of.

"I guess I'll see you," I say, backing away.

"See you," he echoes back at me, still staring.

I escape back up the stairs to Jayda's room. I stumble in the dark, hands out-stretched, feeling for her dresser. I find it and fumble urgently until my fingers close on the little Ballerina lamp I teased her about during one of her sleepovers sophomore year.

I switch on the lamp, let my eyes adjust, then yank on my clothes. I spread Dominic's sweatshirt on top of Jayda's bed. That'll serve her right.

I go back to her dresser, searching for what I need. I pick up her plum purple nail polish and put it in the pocket of my jean jacket. I examine the photos tacked to a display board above the dresser, a bunch of selfies and mall photo booth strips of Jayda and Dominic, Jayda and a bunch of her pouty friends.

There's a receipt from Delia's Ice Cream Shoppe next to a photo of her and Dominic. Someone wrote "You + Me = 4 Ever" in blue pen on the bottom, next to the tip line. This will do.

I unpin the receipt and start to fold. It's not the best paper, not like the thick, parchment-like Wyndstone Marble Paper Dad buys me, but it'll work. I've memorized the folds. My fingers are trembling, but they still know what to do. I pull the point between the outer layers of paper, creating the inside-reverse fold.

Origami is like a beautiful puzzle. You have to tease out the shapes with your hands, from corners to edges to petal folds to crease lines. I make a bend, decreasing the radius of the curve. I check the positions of the edges with my fingers, then flatten the bend and adjust the roll of the flap, until the crease intersects the corner of the paper.

For just a moment, while I focus intently on my task, the world fades. The throbbing inside my head ceases, the thunder of my heartbeat recedes, the loathsome thing slinking through my veins like black sludge slows to a crawl. The receipt gradually transforms from a simple rectangle of paper into the elegant shape of a swan.

I do this because it calms me. I do it because I want to. I do it because you can turn anything—even trash—into something beautiful. I place it carefully on Jayda's dresser, right where she left her purple nail polish.

I sink down next to the kitten's shoebox, leaning against the wall. I stroke Phoenix's soft fur. My phone buzzes inside the shoebox, but I just stare at it, willing it to go away. It buzzes again, calling to me, pulling at me.

Finally, I pick it up. I snort as I scroll through the messages, all from Lyra. Six missed calls. Eleven missed texts. Perfect grammar, perfect spelling, perfect punctuation. That's so Lyra—perfect.

*Where are you?* Monday, 3:31 p.m.

*We need to talk.* Monday, 5:56 p.m.

*Are you okay?* Tuesday, 9:24 a.m.

*I'm at the hospital. Where are you?* Tuesday, 6:47 p.m.

*Stop ignoring my calls.* Wednesday, 2:51 p.m.

*Just tell me you're okay. Okay?* Wednesday, 4:48 pm.

*What's wrong with you? Pick up.* Yesterday, 10:10 a.m.

*Please come home.* Yesterday, 11:42 p.m.

*I have to talk to you.* Today, 1:12 p.m.

*Are you even listening to your messages? Call me back.* Today, 2:45 p.m.

*Why are you doing this?* Today, 10:54 p.m.

*Dad is dying. For real. Please come home.* Today, 11:11 p.m.

It's like an ice pick plunged into my gut. I thought Dad was discharged because he was okay, like last time. And the time before that. But I was wrong. So, so wrong.

Shame is a smoldering coal in the center of my chest. I slam my head back against the wall, hard enough to make my ears ring. Then slam it again. Pain spikes up and down the back of my neck. No. No, no, no. I bang out my frenzied thoughts.

The scream is coming, rising up from the depths deep down inside me. Lights spark behind my eyes and I need to move, do something, anything. Everything.

I leap to my feet, grab the shoebox and hurtle down the stairs, through the dancing throngs, until I'm facing Reese. People are watching, their gazes like fire licking my skin.

Reese stares back at me, unmoving, waiting for whatever I'm going to do. What am I going to do? What do I want to do? Need to do. Have to.

There's nothing like taking that step. Crossing the line. No more boring. No more normal. No more unoriginal world where nothing ever happens. You take that step, leap into the wild, perilous unknown. It's an ice-cold rush. A thrill like flying, like falling.

It's crossing into the bad. It's shameful and treacherous and dangerous. It's exhilarating, my heart pumping pure adrenaline all the way down.

I grab his shirt and pull him to me. I kiss him on the lips, hard. His mouth is dry and tastes like cigarettes and something else, something smoky and sickly sweet. "Whatever you have. I want it."

"You got it, Princess. Come with me."

"I'm out, bitches!" I yell, twisting around, seeking out Felix, Simone, Autumn in the crowd behind me. Seeing no one. No friendly faces, no eyes lighting up in recognition. Screw them.

"Have fun, you two," Darcy calls after us, smirking.

Reese takes me out to his car, a beat-up Thunderbird. I arch my neck, gazing up at the heavens. The clouds are thin and straggly now, like strips of faded rags. I find Orion's glowing belt, then follow the constellations up the ladder of the inky sky.

"Canis Major, Canis Minor, Gemini," I say under my breath.

"You coming or what?" Reese says, throwing open the passenger door.

The trees are looming shadowy shapes turned bleached bone in the beam of the headlights. I climb inside and nestle the box with the sleeping kitten safely between my feet.

"What's that?" he asks.

"Do you really care?"

He shrugs. He pulls a thumb bag with two white pills out of his jacket pocket.

"What're those?" I smoke plenty of dope and I've done my share of Molly and E. These pills look like Oxy, but I'm not sure.

"Do *you* really care?" He raises his eyebrows. "Relax, it's not like it's

Crank."

My stomach tightens in warning. I ignore it.

I need this. I need my thoughts ripped right out of my skull. I don't care how it happens, as long as it does. Thoughts of responsible, faultless Lyra, back from her shiny, perfect life. Thoughts of my father, weak and dying and my fault. My fault. Thoughts of my mother, red hair swirling in red water. My fault. "Will it make everything go away?"

He cups the back of my head with one hand and gently presses one of the pills between my lips. "I promise."

I crunch down on my back molars and chew the gunky, bitter-tasting pill. Reese hands me a can of Budweiser and I chug it down, almost gagging.

Then he's kissing me and I let him because this is who I am. This is what I do. Everything is bad and I'm bad and I just need it all to go away.

What does it matter? What the hell does any of it matter?

11

## LYRA

I spend the afternoon organizing the basement, laundry room, and sorting the disaster that is Lux's bedroom. I straighten the origami animals cluttered on her dresser, pain like a razor slicing through me.

Why won't she come home? Why won't she answer my texts and calls? What's going on?

I rub my palms against my sweatpants. I can't think about that now. Other thoughts dart in my head, almost as dangerous. Ethan Kusuma. I shouldn't let myself think about him, his dimpled smile or his adorable little girl or how intelligent and competent he acted yesterday at the auto shop.

I'm supposed to go back in later today. The thought starts an anxious fluttering in my stomach. I managed to avoid agreeing to a coffee date, but only by repeatedly reminding myself that Ethan Kusuma is a knuckle-headed jock, a cocky, presumptuous jerk.

Ethan's just a distraction, one I don't need and can't afford. Not now. I push thoughts of him out of my head and check in with Dr. Wells, who reminds me again of the looming competition deadline. I assure him I'll have a portfolio ready, even as worry gnaws at the back of my mind.

I finally make myself call the university, ignoring the knot of resentment tangling in my gut as I withdraw from classes. School is my life, my haven, my escape from the haunting memories of my past. The thought of not returning for another five months fills my veins with lead.

I need to do something, distract myself. I need to work. So I clean. The act of taking chaos and putting it in order soothes something inside me. It's putting something right in the world, however small.

I dust the coffee table with the ceramic vase with the daisies Mom adored—until she threw it on the ground during one of her screaming matches with Dad. I spent most of a night trying to glue the shards together. It's mangled and ugly, but Mom kept it.

My mother is everywhere in this house, in the dent in the wall in the kitchen where she hurled a frying pan, scrambled eggs and all, in the general direction of my father. The permanent divot in the green plaid couch where I used to lay for hours, curled up with a photography book while my mother stretched her own canvases or set up her easel next to the window.

"Lyra," Dad calls.

I shove down the memories and head to his room. "I'm here."

He's switched off the TV and propped himself into a sitting position, *The Black and White Handbook: The Ultimate Guide to Monochrome Techniques* opened in his lap.

I take the plate and glass from the nightstand. "What do you need?"

"Do you remember these?" He spreads his thick, swollen fingers over an image of a forest landscape. "We spent so many hours going through them, pointing out the ones we liked, then trying to replicate them ourselves."

I remember a few of those times, when we'd sprawl on the living room floor and study my black and white photographs and discuss focal plane and length, tonal ranges, image composition.

But mostly I poured over the books myself and showed Dad my efforts when he returned from a long haul. He always seemed interested, but he was also distracted and restless, murmuring, "Top notch, Gingersnap," though I knew he wasn't really seeing it, not really even seeing me.

"I remember, Dad." I force a smile, my fingers tightening around the plate.

"Those were some good times."

"Yes, they were."

"We still have all your pictures. I kept them."

I swallow a thickness in my throat. "I saw a box of them in the laundry room the other day."

Dad smiles, deep lines appearing in his face. "I'd like to see them again. Remember how you used to creep around, snapping pictures of everybody when they weren't looking?"

"Yeah. I thought I could capture their 'true selves'. The part they didn't let anyone else see."

Dad says, "Remember, you don't take a photograph—"

"—You make it," I say, finishing his favorite quote by Ansel Adams.

Dad's smile slips from his face, like it's taking too much effort. "You should bring them up."

Dad saved every picture I ever took, the negatives too. I haven't opened that box in years. The thought sends a shiver of nervous energy up and down my spine. Pictures bring ghosts to life.

I've been trying to bury my ghosts for eight years. I don't want to go down there. I don't want to take the lid off of memories so painful, they threaten to unravel me.

I take a step backward, toward the door. "I will. I've got errands to run first. I'm gonna check on the bulldog. Will you be okay?"

"I'll be fine. I love you to the moon."

"I love you all the way back," I say, my throat closing around the words we used to say every bedtime when Dad was home, and on the phone when he wasn't. How many more times will I get to hear him say it?

"Watch out for all the yahoos on the road."

"10-4, Dad." The air in the room is stuffy. It's starting to smell like sickness, like dying. I need to get out of here. I need to breathe.

I bundle up in my coat, scarf, and gloves and drive the loaner car —a burgundy Nissan Altima—the five minutes back into town, to Ross's Garage.

The place is a low red brick building with several open single stall garage doors, the bays within servicing a half-dozen cars, some up on hydraulic lifts. I walk in through a side glass door with a little Welcome sign.

The office area is clean, with a row of brown chairs, a water and coffee station against the far wall, and plastic end tables scattered with *Automobile, Popular Mechanics*, and *Motor Trends* magazines. It smells like coffee and those pine air-fresheners.

I ding the bell on the counter. After a moment, an older Indian lady comes out of the back. She adjusts her glasses and smiles at me. "Ethan's girl, yes?"

I stiffen. "Um, no, sorry. I'm not his—You must be confusing me with someone else."

Her smile widens. A fine net of wrinkles expands across her light brown skin, crinkling around her eyes. She would photograph beautifully. "I apologize, of course. He's in the shop, working on your Honda Odyssey right now."

"Can I see him? He promised me an update." I realize I should've just given him my number. He could have called with the information. Or even texted. He wanted me to come in. He wants to see me. Heat creeps up my neck.

The woman just nods and gestures for me to come around the counter.

The shop is heady with the scent of gasoline, motor oil, and grease, the air bursting with the sounds of electric drills, idling engines, banging and clanking, and shouted conversations between the mechanics. Tools, spare parts, and stacks of tires clutter the workbenches against the walls.

I step over several oil stains and make my way past two vehicles on lifts to get to the minivan.

I recognize Ethan's dark locks under his dirty baseball cap as he bends beneath the Honda's hood. Another mechanic balances on a rolling creeper, his upper half hidden beneath the car.

Ethan's wearing a loose, faded blue jumpsuit. He moves gracefully, his hands sure and fluid, like he's conducting heart surgery, not plowing around inside greasy engine parts. My pulse jumps.

"Hey, Freckles." Ethan straightens when he sees me. He drops his wrench on a rolling tool cart next to him and wipes his hands on a rag sticking out of his pocket. "Meet Darcy Ackelsen."

The second mechanic rolls out from underneath the van and stands up. And it's not a guy like I'd assumed, but a girl. She's stunning, with light, ice blue eyes and golden hair shaved on the sides. The top chunk is tied back in a French braid that swings down her back. Her cheekbones are sharp in her wide, square face, her skin perfect, nearly poreless.

I want to photograph her so badly, my fingers twitch.

"Hey," she says, stretching out her hand.

"Nice to meet you, Darcy."

"Darcy's worked here longer than I have. Her father, Fredrik, owns the shop. She also takes weekend shifts at Bill's Bar and Grill and takes online classes in accounting in her spare time. I'm lazy in comparison."

She rolls her eyes. "I doubt that. Nice to officially meet you, Lyra. I've heard so much about you."

"I doubt that," I say, my cheeks reddening.

"I just graduated last year. I see Lux around sometimes."

I try not to flinch at the sound of my sister's name. "Have you seen her lately, by chance? I'm actually looking for her."

Darcy shrugs, her gaze flickering to somewhere over my shoulder. "Sorry, not in the last few weeks."

I swallow my disappointment. "Well, let me know if you do. So, what's wrong with my car?"

Darcy swings the wrench she's holding, points it at the engine. "You need a new transmission. The front axle needs immediate replacement, and the oil's practically dry. When's the last time this old girl got an 80point inspection, or even just a basic oil change?"

I shrug helplessly. "It hasn't been driven much in the last eight years. Or at least, not by responsible drivers. It was my mom's car."

I watch for their eyes to shutter in pity, but it doesn't happen. Ethan opens a metal drawer in his rolling toolbox and picks up a piece of paper. "Front office worked up this estimate, but Darcy and I can get it done for less. I've got a rebuilt transmission we can use."

I try not to stare at the staggering size of the numbers. It's probably more than the van is even worth. But I can't imagine getting rid of the bulldog, no matter how much I hate driving it. It was Mom's. Her skin cells are still in there, invisible to the naked eye. "Okay," I stammer.

Ethan walks me to the front desk. "I get off work in two hours. You wanna grab dinner with me and Hadley at Bill's? Remember his mushroom burgers? They're still fantastic."

I shake my head. "I don't think that's a good idea." But a different thought is niggling around in the back of my brain.

He leans closer. I can smell the sweat and grease on him, some kind of musky aftershave. "Why not? A two-year-old isn't an appropriate enough chaperone for you? Afraid you'll lose control and jump me right there in the restaurant, in front of truckers sipping coffee and 70-year-old retirees?"

I blush furiously, untucking my hair from behind my ear so it falls across my face as I fill out the paperwork. The words keep blurring in front of me. "Of course not. That's—that's not what I meant."

He cocks his head at me, the cool light from the windows slanting across his features. He would make a great subject. So would Hadley, with those chubby cheeks and amber eyes.

I need prints for the gallery. I have to have them. And Ethan seems ... if not innocuous, then at least slightly less of an arrogant asshole, softened at the edges. "I was going to ask you if Hadley would sit for me. I have this art gallery thing coming up, and—"

"We'd love to. But I have to warn you, Hadley won't be doing much sitting." He leans against the counter, crossing his legs and cocking his head, preening. "But you can always use me to win your little competition."

"It's not a little competition. It's very prestigious, actually."

"I'm sure it is," he says, suddenly serious. "Tell me when and where. I get off early on Fridays."

The hospice nurse comes Friday afternoons. And the light will still be good. "Like around four? River Run park?"

"Perfect." We exchange numbers. He grins, amusement flickering in his gaze. "Just text me the date and time. And then afterward, dinner."

I wipe my damp palms on my jeans. My pulse thuds against my throat. "Thanks for the offer, really, but I just don't think that's a good idea. No offense."

"I'm wearing you down, Freckles," he calls over his shoulder as he heads back into the shop. "I can feel it!"

# LUX

I don't think and feel like normal people. I get that. When I'm flying, the world sparkles. Everything is sunshine and bright sparks of color and crazy, spinning laughter.

It's not like being high or manic, it's just that everything is painted in vivid, saturated LIFE. Joy and happiness just bubble up inside me. I'm energized, exhilarated, intoxicated with it. People laugh at my jokes. They want me at their lunch table, at their party. Guys look at me and want me.

I'm the queen of my own universe, flying through the world on a carpet of rainbows. Absolutely nothing can stop me.

When I'm falling, well, that's a whole other story.

It's been four days since the party. I didn't come back to Autumn's house that night until after 3 a.m. I tossed pebbles at her window until she came to the front door and let me in, hissing for me to be quiet. But I was stumbling around in the dark, drunk and high on whatever Reese gave me. I woke up her parents.

"I'm so sorry," I said, hiccupping. "Thank me for my hospitality. I mean, yours. Thank you so, so much."

I don't really remember their faces or what they said, but Mrs. Yun has looked like she's sucking on a lemon ever since. Autumn's mortified. She never gets into trouble. Usually, I can charm my way out of any situation.

Parents love me, nose ring and all. Luckily, Mrs. Yun likes me. She makes me kimchi stew whenever I come over. She knows me, gets my moods.

Autumn told her parents about my dad, so they're cool with me here. They think they understand why I'm so upset. But they don't. They don't have a clue.

I'm off my A game. I'm spinning off into darkness. I can't stop, can't slow my fall. I can't get my footing.

When I crash, I go down hard. When I'm like this, every day I don't stab someone with a pen or have a stark raving meltdown right in the middle of Physics class is a victory. Then there are the days when even school seems like an insurmountable mountain, one I'm unable to even think about climbing. Like now.

I've spent the last few days in a pile of blankets on Autumn's floor, my phone clenched in my hands, staring at the text from my sister. *Dad's dying. Dad's dying. Dad's dying.*

I haven't showered. Haven't gone to school. Every morning, Autumn shoulders her backpack and stands in the doorway, staring at me with a concerned, perplexed look on her face. Every afternoon, she comes home and does her homework and practices guitar and eats dinner with her perfect family and does all the things that Autumn Yun does. She's barely talked to me.

I cluck my tongue and call Phoenix's name. "Here kitty, kitty, kitty." The kitten is playing in the corner with one of Autumn's stray socks. When I move toward her, she leaps into the air and scrabbles across the wooden floor. She stumbles and slip-slides like an adorable dust bunny.

She's a feral little creature. Wild-eyed and sharp-clawed. Terrified of everything. I haven't been able to hold her since the night of the party, when I nursed her back to life.

"I saved you, little one." I pick up the sock and flutter it in front of her face. She stares at it. Her enormous eyes follow every movement, her body a tightly wound spring. I move my hand toward her. She spits and hisses, hackles raised. "I'm gonna make you love me. You're already doomed. You just don't know it yet."

I have to get up. I can't stand the stench of my own body. My head throbs, my stomach a shriveled, aching pit. I force myself to take a shower, scrubbing off the filth and grime from the party. From that night with Reese in his car.

I yank on a pair of Autumn's gray sweatpants and her blue Detroit Lions hoodie and scrape my hair back into a ponytail. I get my eyeliner, lipstick, and extra concealer out of my messenger bag. I shove my bangs out of the way and line my eyes with thick, black liner.

Autumn's mirror reflects my image back at me like an accusation. My face seems disjointed, fragmented. I only see parts of myself: watery, red-rimmed eyes, silver hoop nose ring, too-white, ghostly skin, the cluster of pimples on my chin. Dad always says I look like Mom. Her face in my memory is only a faded blur. I avert my eyes.

I walk around Autumn's room, restless and edgy. On one wall, there's a huge framed print of her at nine or ten. She's riding a speckled pony, holding a third-place trophy. The tops of her bookcases are clustered with her glass-blown hummingbird collection. Some of the glossy little figurines hang from a jade jewelry tree on her dresser.

Above her desk, she's decorated a bulletin board with all of her A+ English tests. I lean in to inspect a 100% essay, something about the South Korean immigrant experience in the 1960s and 1970s. I run my finger along the shelf full of sports and music awards and ribbons. Not even an iota of dust.

My stomach growls. Autumn's house always smells faintly of garlic and cabbage. Like home-cooked meals and love. Like what a house with a real family should smell like.

A thorn of jealousy pricks me. Everything comes so easy for her. I take a blue Cass County Regional Debate Team third place ribbon and slip it into my pocket. She won't miss it. She's not even on the team anymore.

Still, she's been good to me, letting me stay here for almost three weeks, even though she's so furious she can barely speak to me. That's something.

I find my messenger bag in a heap next to Autumn's bed and pull out my folder of paper. I pick a blue 6-inch square sheet and sit down at her desk.

My hands move instinctively over the paper, forming the base creases, the valley folds from corner to corner, pulling out the center layers to inside-reverse-fold a flared section for the tail feathers, then a few mountain-folds to create the head and pinch down the long, slender bill. I pleat the wings with alternating mountain and valley-folds, until it looks like the little bird is in midflight.

I tuck the hummingbird on her shelf, in between two second place soccer trophies.

Autumn has volleyball practice after school on Tuesdays, so it's 4:30 by the time I hear her key in the lock. She pauses in the bedroom doorway when she sees me, like she's shocked I'm actually off the floor and dressed.

"We need to talk," we both say at the same time.

She doesn't laugh. She sits down on the bed, dropping her heavy backpack to the floor. She clutches a half-empty bottle of Faygo diet orange pop in both hands.

I pick at my plum nail polish. I know she's angry. She probably hates me. I would hate me, too. I do hate me. But I can't stand this wall of silence between us. I've tried to explain, over and over, but the excuses fall flat, even in my own ears.

Simone barely responds to my texts. She's disgusted with me, too. Autumn is the one we both protect. I'm not supposed to be the one who hurts her. I've messed everything up. Again. I always screw up. I'm losing my best friends.

With everything else imploding right now, I just can't deal. I've got to win her back. "I'm so sorry, Skittles," I say. "I'm a terrible, horrible person. You must hate me."

She tugs a strand of black hair out of her French braid and chews on it. Her eyes are hooded, wary. "I don't hate you, Lux."

"How can you not? I was basically all over the only guy who should've been off limits."

"Yeah. I know. I was there."

Phoenix tears in crazed circles around the room, jumps into the litter box and leaps out again, granules of kitty litter sprinkling across the floor. The day after I brought Phoenix here, Autumn brought home cat food and made up a cardboard box filled with kitty litter. My heart hurts at how good she is. I don't deserve her.

"I don't know what happened. I was crazy in my head, how I get sometimes. It's like I didn't know what I was doing."

I wait for her to finally yell at me, but she doesn't. She sucks in a breath. "I mean, it's not like he's my boyfriend. It's not like he's a Gray Wolf or Sandhill Crane. I know that."

"Wait—what?"

"Animals that mate for life." Her shoulders slump. She rips off the pop bottle label in strips and watches them drift to the floor. "Like seahorses. Seahorses are monogamous. They mate for life."

"Yeah, you've told me. The male gets pregnant and gives birth. Which makes it Simone's most favorite animal ever."

Autumn rubs the sleeve of her sweatshirt over her face. "Look, I know a guy like Dominic will never want a girl like me. I'm not stupid."

Guilt spears me. She's so sweet, so good. "That's not true. And anyway, he's kind of a tool. *You're* the one who's too good for him."

She just shakes her head. Tears tremble in her lashes. "It just—it still hurts."

"It wasn't really me who did it, okay? It was like I was someone else, outside my own body. I didn't mean to. I didn't want to. I would never— " But of course, I did. I would never, but I did. I do. My own tears scratch the back of my throat. "I screw everything up, every good thing. I'm so sorry."

"It's okay."

"I'm a terrible friend."

She sighs. "No, you aren't."

We make eye contact. I want her face to be open and happy again, same old Autumn. But it's not. She's stripped off the whole label, and now she just holds the bottle in her hands. Empty. "There's something else. My parents said, last night they said that they've been happy to have you here these last few weeks, but—"

I don't even hear the rest of her words. A great black void yawns open in front of me. A black hole. It only takes a second to tumble in. "You're kicking me out."

"No, no. I don't want you to leave. But, Lux, you've been here a long time. It's like, almost the end of January already. What are you hiding from? Why don't you want to go home?"

Indignation sweeps over me, anger bubbling up inside me like water boiling over the sides of a pot. "What's it to you? I thought friends were there when we needed each other."

"I am! I have been! But you can't—I mean, you know you can't just like, live here, right?"

"Of course not!" I leap to my feet, suddenly frantic. "I can't go home, okay? I thought you understood that. I thought you understood how it is there, how horrible it is for me."

Autumn just blinks at me. "I'm so sorry, Lux. But my parents—"

"This is because of the party, because of Dominic. You're getting back at me."

"No! I already said—"

"Just stop it!" My heart plummets. Howling despair sucks me down. Everyone leaves. Everyone abandons me. Even Autumn. I'm never enough to make anyone stay. "Do you even care about me? Don't pretend you care about me and then go and do something like this."

"Of course I do!"

"Never mind," I growl. "I don't need you."

She sniffles, wiping her nose with her sleeve. "Lux, please. That's not true. You're my best friend!"

I need to escape. I've got to get out. Now. I grab my clothes and shoes and the bag of cat food and hastily stuff them in my messenger bag. "*Simone's* your best friend. You always did like her best."

"No. You don't understand. I'm not trying to—"

"I won't bother you or interrupt your precious life anymore. You can be sure of that!"

Phoenix turns away from me, her little butt in the air as she stalks one of Autumn's hair ties. I grab her, her wiry body twisting and writhing to escape me. She hisses and yowls. Her claws scrape across my hand, but I don't let go. I stuff her inside the front pouch of my hoodie. "Don't worry. I'll get your ratty clothes back to you. Have a nice life."

"Lux, stop!"

"Dominic Harris doesn't even know you're alive, okay? You have no right to lay a claim on him!" I storm out of Autumn's house, hot tears blurring my eyes.

Behind me, I can hear Autumn crying. She always cries to get her way, to get people to forgive her when she's just stabbed them in the back. She pretends everything's okay, all the while plotting her revenge for whatever slight she thinks you've committed against her. I mean, give me a frickin' break.

I jump into Dad's old Accord and peel out of her driveway, leaving black skid marks on the perfect white concrete just because I can.

13

———

LYRA

It's dark by the time I make it to the basement. I'm running out of errands, running out of things to scrub and scour. I'm afraid of what thoughts will come unbidden if I allow myself to be listless in this house. Inaction is dangerous. Inaction lets the demons in.

The gray cement walls of the laundry room rise over my head, cold and pitiless. The air is heavy, thick with the dust of secrets. The lone light bulb in the middle of the ceiling sheds a circle of yellow light.

I sit cross-legged on the concrete floor, searching through boxes overflowing with bundles of photos and dozens of envelopes stuffed with negatives and scrawled with dates.

I flip through the snapshots in my hand, all of them monochrome. I've formed two small piles, filtering out pictures of my mother unless Dad specifically asks for them. I doubt he will.

He seldom talked about her, after. When he did, it was as if he lived a different life than we did, remembered an entirely different person. When he was forced to mention her death, he called it her 'passing,' like she was a ship sailing out the mouth of a harbor.

My father is so fragile, his heart sloshing within the shell of his skin like an egg. He must have suffered, finding her like that. He'd driven through the night to be home early, to surprise her with flowers, with daisies, her favorite. I remember seeing them later, wilted

83

and crushed against the carpet in front of the bathroom door, white petals bruised beneath the shoes of the EMTs.

I picture Dad in my mind, much younger and slimmer, his face lit with boyish excitement. I imagine him noticing the light, the steam sifting beneath the bathroom door. What did he think? That she was taking a bubble bath?

I see him opening the door handle with one hand, daisies twisted behind his back with the other. Then his face, frozen in horror, his eyes locked on the scene before him, hideous and unreal and red, so much red.

This is as far as my mind travels in my waking hours. It's at night, racked in the clutches of my nightmares, that the red water comes, the blood-soaked tub, the thin arms slashed to pale bone, the dead white eyes.

It was weeks after the funeral before I realized this scene was meant for me. I was the one who came home right after school on Thursdays. Lux had flute practice. Dad was supposed to be gone for another day.

Maybe I could've protected him somehow, lifted some of the weight of his guilt if he'd been spared from finding her, from that ruthless judgment that he'd failed at the only thing that mattered to him—keeping his wife alive.

I will those thoughts from my mind. I've already played this 'what if' game a thousand times. It always ends the same way, with more questions than I'll ever have answers.

I finish the first batch and take out another. Most of the pictures are of my mother: Mom sleeping with her hands beneath her head like a prayer, Mom cross-legged on the floor with a stapler in one hand and a canvas frame in the other, Mom sitting at the table, bent over her daily horoscopes, Mom dancing with Lux in the living room, her head thrown back in laughter.

I was obsessed with capturing her then, of trying to understand her by freezing her image on paper. Mom always seemed like this unpredictable stranger, a wild creature of the forest, of the moon or maybe the stars, of places I couldn't go or understand.

She was volatile, her moods erratic and shifting like oil in water, so much rage and joy and sorrow shut up in one woman's body that she was never the same person on any given day.

I toss another picture into the pile, one of Mom slumped on the couch watching TV, face blank and glassy. The next photo stops my breath.

I hold it up, examining it in the halo of light. I've forgotten this picture almost entirely. Now everything comes flooding back. Maybe … but no, the face is too small, the features too indistinct to make anything out.

The negative. I drop the picture and grope through the jumbled box for the envelopes, searching for the right date. I find it and withdraw the sleeve of negatives.

Do I still have photo paper? Enough developer? I leap to my feet. The air hums against my skin, raises goose bumps on my arms. Am I ready for this? It doesn't matter. I have to do it. Maybe I'll find something … an answer, a reason … something. At this point, I'll take anything.

My fingers tremble as I hold the negative. This is the last photograph of my mother ever taken, the last image of her, warm and breathing and alive.

I don't know why she decided to leave us, why we could never manage to make her happy. I did everything I could think of to earn her love. I tried to be perfect. I never whined or complained or threw temper tantrums. I did all my chores without being asked. I earned good grades. I watched after Lux.

But it was never enough. We were never enough. I was never enough.

After all these years, I still don't know why.

14

# LUX

I'm alone. Always alone. Trapped inside my own skin, with nothing to do. Nowhere to go. Last night, I used the last of the cash I stole from Dad's top drawer on the Village Inn Motel a few miles outside of Brokewater. I spent a sleepless night tossing and turning on a thin, lumpy mattress.

Today I've been driving around town for what seems like an eternity. The gas needle drifts lower and lower. Dread builds up inside me like a brick wall.

There's nowhere to go. Nowhere to go but home.

I don't want to go home. Lyra is there, with her perfect little life. Always taking care of everything and doing everything right. Always reminding me of all the ways I fail. All the ways I'll never measure up.

She'll take one look at me and she'll know. She'll see the guilt scrawled all over my face. She'll know what I did to Dad.

Dad. *Dad is dying.* Acid fills my throat. I can hardly breathe as I choke it down. Dad is dying for real this time. It's my fault. I caused it and then I ran, just like a frickin' coward.

I shove those thoughts out of my head. I can't think about that. The black hole will swallow me if I let myself think like that. But I still don't have anywhere to go. It's too effing cold outside. I have to go home. I have no choice.

When I get there, everything is different. Because of Lyra. She's scrubbed every inch of the house until it's gleaming. There's no dust, no messy clothes strewn across the couch, no dirty dishes overflowing the sink and piling the counters, no mess anywhere. Instead of the gratitude I'm supposed to feel, resentment jolts through me.

The house is silent but for the creak of my footsteps. I walk down the dark hallway on legs like jelly. Phoenix is tucked inside my hoodie. She yowls angrily and kneads at my stomach, her tiny claws puncturing my sweatshirt.

I stand in front of Dad's closed door, my heart throbbing in my chest, my eyes burning. I have to see him. I have to tell him how sorry I am, beg his forgiveness. I'm sorry. I'm sorry. I'm sorry.

I reach for the door knob.

"He's sleeping."

I whirl around. Lyra stands at the end of the hallway, her hands balled into fists on her hips. One of the old boxes from the laundry room sits at her feet. I didn't even hear her come upstairs over the thundering of my own heartbeat.

"Where have you been?" Her voice is sharp.

That familiar bitterness ripples through me, all the old wounds rising to the surface. "Around."

"Around where?"

I lift one shoulder, let it drop. "With friends."

"Friends? What friends? You've been gone for almost three weeks!"

"So? You're my keeper all of a sudden?" "Can't you even—wait. What is that noise?" Phoenix lets out another yowl.

"My new cat."

"Your new—?" Her face contorts, her nostrils flaring. "You disappear for three weeks and come back with a *cat*?"

"So what?"

"And just who's going to take care of it?"

I bristle at the insinuation in her voice. "I am. Obviously. What's your deal?"

"What's my deal? Do you have any idea how worried we've been?"

"I was fine."

"I sent you texts. Called you a dozen times. Aren't you worried about Dad?"

"He's fine."

"He's not fine." Her jaw clenches. "Dad is—he's dying."

I taste acid in the back of my throat. "They've said that before."

"No. It's for real this time. He has a hospice nurse. He's going to die."

Her words strike me like hammer blows. I can't bear to hear her say it out loud. I can't stand here even one more second. I turn away from Dad's door and open my own door, grasping the handle with shaking fingers. I shove my way inside and lock it.

Lyra rattles the doorknob. "Lux!"

"Leave me alone!" I yell. "Just stop it!"

Phoenix hisses and scratches. I pull her out of my hoodie pocket and drop her to the floor. Three stinging red welts appear on my wrist. I stand there, staring at my room, my eyes throbbing.

The paper star mobile hanging over my bed, its dozens of colorful, three-dimensional stars attached to fishing line. The paper star chains draped over my curtain rod, twined around my bedposts. My origami creatures on my dresser next to my mom's old perfume bottles I never use. The clothes usually strewn across my floor are now folded neatly on my bed.

It feels like a stranger's room. Like I haven't been here in months, maybe years. Everything is the same. Everything is different.

Lyra pounds on my door again.

I hear Dad's voice. "Lyra," he says, his voice muffled. It sounds different, weaker.

Lyra's footsteps walk away. "I'm coming, Dad," she says.

I clamp my hands over my mouth, stifling the low moan rising up in the back of my throat. My father is dying.

What have I done?

15

LYRA

In the darkroom fashioned from the downstairs bathroom, in the silence and the warm red glow of the safelight, I work. I scrub a stray strand of unruly hair off my cheek with my forearm and remove the glossy eight by ten from the enlarger using a pair of chemical-resistant plastic tongs.

I drop it emulsion side down into the tray of developer chemicals set on the makeshift wooden counter and start the timer. Wetness seeps over the surface of the photo paper, coils around the edges, drags it down and under.

It's been two days since I found the photograph, two days for the question to spread like mold, festering through my brain, obsessing every thought, every waking moment. I'm both drawn and repelled, entranced and terrified.

I pick up the edge of the photo paper with the tongs, flip it over, and gently rock the tray. The paper moves in its chemical bath, swells and falls in tiny waves. I check the timer.

Dark smudges form over the whiteness, lines and shapes and patterns. A rope of dark hair, the curve of an ear. The first marks are a light gray, the color of fog. They darken and expand like a stain, the gray of clouds swollen with rain, the gray of shadows, of silver hair, of dusk, of ashes.

The shades of gray deepen to charcoal, then to pitch. Crisp ebony lines strike out, developing from a white void into the ladder of a spine, the gentle arc of a shoulder, a bowed head and silvery eyes like two beads in a string of Catholic prayers.

I lift the paper with the tongs. The excess liquid runs in clear streams off the developed photo. I dip it into the stop bath and then the fixer solution, completing the steps from habit, everything in a precise order, for the precise time, at the precise temperature. I put the photograph on a rack next to the others to dry.

After I wash my hands, I tug the next negative from its protective sheath, touching only the square edges. I've been experimenting with the last four prints, readying myself. Nervous energy thrums through me. Memories ride close beneath the mantle of my skin.

I'm sick of this purgatory. My father's way doesn't work. Ignoring doesn't work. Pretending doesn't work.

Nothing works. I need to see, to know, to discover what I never thought I'd find: a reason. And if not that, at least a way to understand.

I place the negative in the enlarger's carrier, emulsion side down, slide the carrier into place, and flip the knob, throwing an image onto the easel. I adjust the aperture to full open, fiddle with the grain focuser until every shape and line tapers to a fine razor point.

My heart pulses in my throat, blocking my air.

The picture is of my face—solemn, mouth tight, eyes downcast—in the full-length mirror in my parents' bedroom. The angle is wrong, the flash glancing off the glass. I'm fuzzy and unfocused. But reflected in the mirror, above and to the right of my face and the white starburst of the flash, a figure sits on the bed. She is crystal clear, as if the camera knew something the twelve-year-old photographer did not.

Her narrow shoulders hunch inward like broken wings, hair like a molten river flowing down her back, fingers woven tightly together, hands clasped like a prayer. There's no color in the negative, but I know every hue and shade in that room: the tiny blue cornflowers in the white, white wallpaper, her faded mustard-yellow nightgown, the gaudy salmon-pink bedspread.

Her eyes gaze at something off-camera. I squint, examining the purse of her lips, the slight flare of the nostrils, the tilt to the corners of her eyelids.

What did her eyes reveal when she believed no one was looking? What secrets did they release? I can't tell from the projected negative. I need more. There's too much gray, too much ambiguity.

I crank the enlarger's body up, cropping out my face, the bed, her hands and torso. I want only the face, the eyes. I place a sheet of photo paper under the easel's arms, activate the timer, and make the first print exposure.

For the next two hours, I work tirelessly, using up and abandoning dozens of prints, constantly adjusting aperture size and exposure time, trying different filters, varying the lengths of processing time in the developer solution.

Each print is capable of perfection. And each print fails miserably.

My mind drifts back, trying to remember that day, everything that happened. Mom was in the middle of one of her frenetic art phases. She always worked in the corner of the living room, parallel to the large picture window for the best natural light.

She primed a canvas and set it on the easel. She set out her tubes of paint, sap green, cadmium red, brown madder, alizarin crimson, and burnt sienna, squeezing the tiniest bit onto the wooden palette.

She used long-handled camel hair brushes. I once asked her if the camels hurt when the artists took out their hair. She laughed and laughed, until she could breathe enough to explain the hairs were actually from squirrels, horses and goats, not camels. She was sure no animals were hurt in the process.

"Always paint back to front," she told me, like she forgot I used a camera, not a brush. "It's easier to paint over something than to try to paint around it."

I was curled up on the couch with a book, watching her more than reading. Dad was on a truck run. Lux was in her room, building a diorama out of her origami animals for a school project.

It was Tuesday afternoon, two days before she killed herself.

"You want to create the value contrast to catch the eye of the viewer." She laid in all the shadows to establish form, darkening the background. She dipped the tip of the two-inch brush in the blue and used feather-light strokes to blend in the sky. She stippled in grass and bright yellow flowers.

Slowly, the shape of a girl appeared, rimmed in shadows, her back to the viewer as she fled, her hair flying behind her, her head half-turned. "Add something dark to frame your center of interest. It draws the eye. Don't be pedestrian or boring. There's nothing worse than boring."

"There's nothing worse than boring," I echoed. The sharp smell of turpentine stung my nostrils.

"Exactly." She stared at the canvas and sighed. "It's not right. Something's not right."

She picked up a rag and wiped excess paint from the brush before dipping it into a cleaning jar. She scrubbed her hands and punched out a text on her phone. "I need your father. Where is he?"

She slammed the phone down on the end table and returned to the painting, a frown etching a line between her eyebrows. "What's it missing?"

"It's perfect, Mom."

But she didn't hear me. She dashed into the bathroom and returned with a toothbrush.

"That's your toothbrush!" I said, like she didn't know, like she just needed reminding.

She waved it at me. "Always be prepared to sacrifice everything for your art, Lyra. Everything."

She riffled the bristles of the white paint-laden toothbrush, snapping her wrist and flicking paint from the brush, spattering the canvas like snow.

"There can't be flowers and snow," I pointed out.

"Of course there can," she huffed. "It's *art*. Art is magic. Art is dual. It can be more than one thing at once."

"Okay," I said, not really understanding.

She checked her phone with her clean hand, her face darkening.

"What's your father doing? Why isn't he answering my calls? Am I not important to him anymore?"

She returned to the painting, glaring at it in disgust. "There's no soul." "I like it," I said in a small voice.

"It's trash. Any true artist can see that."

She picked up the brush again, her mouth taut. She painted wildly, frantically, slapping on strokes of alizarin crimson, burnt umber, and olive green, filling the canvas with shadows pulsing with dark, brooding color.

I just sat there, my fingers tightening around the book. I watched the picture turn from bright and beautiful into something dark, confusing, and unsettling.

"How come your pictures aren't nice?"

She looked up, her eyes burning like embers. "Art isn't *nice*, Lyra," she said fervently. "It isn't pretty. Art is powerful and provocative and painful and ugly. Art is brave. Art makes you *feel*."

"What am I supposed to feel?"

"You'll know when it happens." Her voice came out hard and fast. She punctuated each word with a stab of her brush at her painting. "Don't be afraid to put your whole soul into it, Lyra. Put your whole self in, even when it's not polished or lovely or what you think people want to see. Your art is not for them. Your soul is not for them. You understand?"

My throat was closing up on itself. There wasn't enough air in the room. "Yes," I managed, but I wasn't fast enough, convincing enough.

She turned on me. "Am I wasting my time with you? Do you get it, yes or no? You can't be like them!" She flailed her arms. "Do you see it? Do you see my soul in my art? Is it there or not?"

I didn't know the right answer. It sounded like she wanted me to say yes, but just a moment earlier, she'd called the painting trash. I didn't know, but I was desperate to get it right, to make her happy again. "Yes!" I gulped. "Yes, I see it."

"No!" She leaned over me, shaking the paint brush inches from my face. "You don't! It's crap. It's worthless. And so am I. I'm a lousy, worthless piece of—" She slumped down into a sitting position, the brush dropping to the carpet. She cradled her head in her hands. "I can't. I can't do it anymore. Where's Jacob? Where is he? He's barely returned my calls. He's ignoring me. He's found someone else. He's found a better family than us, I know it. He hates me. He hates us."

I shrank back against the couch, tears springing into my eyes. "Dad hates us?"

Before she could respond, her phone rang. She snatched it. "Jacob? Where are you? What are you doing? I've called you twenty times!"

She accidentally hit the speaker button. "... area with bad reception.

I'm so sorry. Is everything okay?"

"No! No, everything is not okay, thanks to you! How am I supposed to do this? I'm so stressed out, I can't even work. Do you understand how critical my art is to me? All I want is to talk to my FRICKIN' HUSBAND and you won't even do that. Are you planning to leave us, is that it? Is that why you won't return my calls?"

"What? No! That's crazy."

She leapt up like the carpet was on fire. "What did you just say? You think I'm crazy?"

"No!" he said loudly, then again, more softly. "No, of course not. Look, Eve, I have three more days, then I'll be home."

Mom's back was to me. Her narrow shoulders shook. I could see the knobs of her spine through her flimsy nightgown. "Work is always more important than me," she said, her voice trembling. "Is that how it is now, Jacob?"

"Eve, I love you. You know that. This isn't the best time. I've got a black eye to take care of." I knew that meant a broken headlight. "Let's talk tonight."

"When did you stop loving me?"

Dad let out a long, slow sigh. "I can't just leave. I'm half a day from delivery. Then I can head back."

Mom clutched the phone with whitened fingers. "I need you here."

"I can't lose another job," he said in a tired, defeated voice. "You know that."

A single tear tracked down my mother's face. "You don't love me. You never loved me. Just admit it. Tell the truth for once in your pathetic life."

There was a long hiss of silence. Finally, Dad said, "I'll be home soon.

Please, just hold on."

But he wasn't home soon. Not soon enough. Not until it was too late.

At the time, she hadn't seemed any worse than usual. I was used to her wildly vacillating fluctuations in mood. I thought I was.

That night, I took her picture in the mirror. The next day, she retreated to her bedroom and refused to come out. That was the last conversation we ever had. It was the last time I saw her alive.

My focus returns to the image in front of me. Slowly, slowly I blend the grays, sharpen the lines, blacken the blacks and whiten the whites, patiently bringing out clarity and purity.

Still, her eyes are obscured, shielding whatever truth is there, must be there. Her eyes had to reveal something in those last desperate moments before she took her own life. Didn't they?

She must have known. She was already plotting it out, her escape from her family. So where was the sign? What had I missed?

There has to be something. I don't know what it is, what form it took, or how I'm supposed to recognize it. I don't even know what I want to see. Fear? Regret? Love for her daughters, her husband? Or even just an awareness, the truth of what was about to happen.

My stomach twists as I start the final print with the last piece of photo paper. This one will reveal everything. I'm so close. Anticipation and dread thrum through my veins as I expose the photo paper in the enlarger.

The bathroom door crashes open.

The Velcro tears, and the felt curtain ripples to the floor. Light explodes against my eyes.

# 16

# LYRA

"Hey!" I throw my arm across my face. The glare of daylight strikes my retinas like blazing arrows.

"Oh," Lux says. "I didn't realize you were in here."

I step back, blinking rapidly. The print is ruined. Anger balloons inside me so hot and fast, I can barely speak. "You knew! You always do this—"

"I said I didn't know!" Lux crosses her arms over her chest. "Did I mess you up?"

"Yes. As a matter of fact, you did." I stare at her, fighting the anger down.

She's even more beautiful than when I last saw her over two years ago. And older. Her features are delicate, a fine spray of freckles across her porcelain skin, a thin silver ring in her nose. Her red hair falls in layers almost to her waist, thick bangs cut just above her green, kohl-rimmed eyes.

She's wearing a loose pine-green sweater over faded jeggings, a chunky-knit fuchsia scarf draped around her neck. She's several inches shorter than I am, and heavier, her body full and sensuous. She's one of those girls aware of every motion, of every eye following the curve and sway of her body. She's confident and self-possessed in a way I never was and will never be.

"Sorry. Like I said, I didn't know you'd set up the darkroom again."

I turn away, banging my trays together. I dump them in the bathtub and run the water. I rinse the trays and tongs, feeling my sister's presence like a bur in my back.

"What are these?"

"Pictures. Nothing."

"They're all of Mom."

"Yep."

"I have to use the bathroom."

"Go upstairs."

"I don't use that bathroom."

"Not my problem."

There's a protracted silence. "I seriously didn't know you were in here."

"Sure you didn't." I bend over the tub, scrubbing the developer tray vigorously.

Lux doesn't respond. After a moment, I glance up. She's gone. A headache gathers like storm clouds behind my skull. I stack the trays next to the enlarger, wipe my hands on my sweatpants. I need more paper.

I glance at my phone on the counter. It's almost three. Time for more pills and a bathroom trip, then maybe I can head to the closest photography store, which is two towns over and a forty-minute drive.

I take several deep breaths. I will stay in control. I just need more paper, then I can keep trying.

I pick up the Cass County Gazette from the front steps on the way upstairs. For the last several days, I've been reading it to Dad. He still wants me to read him the Bible. But I can't do that. Not now, when I've lost so much.

Where was God when my mother killed herself? Where was God through the dark and lonely shadows of my childhood?

I pause in the hallway outside Lux's door. "I'm going to the store. Will it be too much trouble to stay here until I get back?" Silence. I slap my palm against the door.

"Whatever," Lux mumbles.

"Lux—!" I smack the door again, my hand stinging. "Don't you dare leave. You hear me?"

She doesn't bother to answer.

"Lyra," Dad calls from his bedroom.

My jaw aches from clenching so hard. I go in his room, twisting the newspaper in my hands. "What do you need?"

"It's that time again," he says, embarrassment flashing in his eyes. "Time to pay the water bill."

It's his old trucker slang for using the bathroom. He slings his arm around my shoulder and I help lift his bulk. He can mostly make it on his own, he just needs me to steady him.

When we're done, he sits up in bed and I sink into the frayed, navy blue La-Z-Boy I hauled in from the living room a few days ago, the one I puked on the day I turned six and stuffed my face with too much cake.

The fan is switched off. The air is stale, thick with the stench of sickness.

"Why are you fighting with Lux?"

"She always starts it."

"She's your sister," Dad says, coughing. It's a ragged, phlegmy sound.

I look down at the newspaper in my lap without really seeing it. "Then maybe she should act like it."

"She's going through a rough time."

"Seriously? And you aren't? We aren't?"

A sharp breath whistles through his teeth. "Please, Gingersnap. Can't you forgive?"

The muscles in my jaw bulge and contract. The headache hits full force, striking the tender space just behind my eyes. All the trouble she's caused, the messes she's made. "Has she even come in to see you?"

"She deals with life in her own way. Like her mother."

"That's bullsh—"

"She feels bad."

I grip the front page of the newspaper and rip the paper into tiny squares. The shredded pieces slide off the newspaper and flutter to the floor. "Leaving you like that—you could've died!"

"She's sorry."

"How do you know?"

Dad touches my arm. "The eye should learn to listen before it looks." He's quoting one of his favorite photographers, Robert Frank.

"What does that even mean, Dad?"

"Don't judge her too quickly. I've already forgiven her. Can't you do the same?"

"What am I even supposedly forgiving her for? You won't tell me what that happened."

He sighs, a long shudder of breath that trembles his whole body. I know he wants to escape me, to just walk away or leave the way he used to, whenever Lux or I asked any questions, whenever we dared dip below the surface of things, question the why of what happened to us, the implosion of our family.

Even when Mom was still alive, he would flee during the bad times, take every job he could find. He ignored the things he didn't want to see. But now he can't. He's trapped in this bed. He must hate it.

"I want to talk about Mom."

"Comeback?" he says, more of his trucker slang.

"I said I want to talk about Mom."

He closes his eyes, gray smudges staining his skin. "The past is in the past, Lyra. Let it rest."

"I found some old pictures. I found one from two days before she — before her suicide."

"Your mother passed. There's nothing we can do about it now."

"Passed? She passed? Is that what you call slicing her wrists open to the bone?"

Dad flinches. "Lyra, please."

I rub my temples, my jaw tightening. I can't release this rage building up inside me. I have to stay in control. "I remember other times. I remember her being gone, visiting her in the hospital. All the doctor and psychiatrist appointments."

"We don't need to dwell on the negative things."

"I dream about her. She tried before, didn't she? More than once."

"There's no reason to discuss this. Not now."

"Yes. There is." We never talked about it. Not after, and not before. My father didn't tell us there was something wrong, that a vast black pit had opened in the center of our living room. That we were all balanced precariously at the very lip of it. That only one misstep by any of us and we would all tumble in. He never said, "Be careful." He never said, "Watch your step."

"Your mother was sad. Is that what you need to hear?"

"She was more than sad, Dad. You know that." What we don't talk about, what we've never talked about: the times her anguish filled her up to overflowing, until her heart couldn't contain it all and it turned, transforming into something harsh and ugly. The three tiny half-moon scars on my upper arm, remnants of her fury, her grip so hard her nails pierced my skin.

"Yes," he says so softly I almost don't hear him. There's something in his voice, a sharpness like a razor blade.

"She hurt herself. Sometimes she hurt us."

"Why must you talk about this? Please, just stop."

"Because I need to know, Dad. It's my history, too. I need to know why. There are things only you can tell me." The words I don't say hang heavy over us anyway: soon, it'll be too late. "The doctors—did they tell you what was wrong with her?"

"Your mother was just who she was, no more, no less. Labels never helped anything."

"They gave her medication," I say, remembering. "Sometimes she didn't take it."

"She tried her best. Can't we just leave it at that?"

I think of that last photo of her, of the mysteries captured in her dark, impenetrable eyes. I've tried it his way, just ignoring everything, pretending it never happened. It doesn't work. I'm still as burdened with grief and shadows as the day the ambulance and the EMTs came to our front door. "No. I can't."

He stares up at the ceiling, refusing to meet my gaze. "I'm the one who failed her. She tried her best. If you want anyone to blame, blame me."

"That's not what I mean."

"Guilt and blame destroy everything they touch, Lyra. I know that better than anyone. I want something different for you. Just remember the good times. You had a roof over your head, didn't you? Food and clothes. Isn't that enough? Forget the rest."

In the months after Mom's death, after that night of the funeral, I never saw him cry. His eyes were always bloodshot and watery, red-rimmed and empty. He took on this stooped, hunch-shouldered look, like he was perpetually slogging against a high, harsh wind. Like he wasn't equipped, wasn't built for a life steeped in so much responsibility, so much raw, devastating emotion.

The headache throbs against my skull. "I can't do that."

"Please, I need to rest." His voice is weak, defeated. He turns his face to the wall.

I stand up, the remains of the newspaper cascading to the carpet. Everything I don't know but should is swirling inside me. It feels like trying to grab a fish underwater, sleek and frantic, always slipping just out of reach.

I may never find the answers I'm searching for. Not from him.

I grab my coat from the closet and the car keys from the kitchen counter. I stumble down the hall and out the front door.

———

It's in the photo supply store, in the middle of aisle three, my hands reaching out to lift the white box of resin fiber paper off the top shelf, the harsh glare of the overhead florescent lights stinging my eyes.

I recall one of Dad's favorite sayings. He always quoted the photographer Diana Arbus, saying, "A photograph is a secret about a secret. The more it tells you, the less you know."

The truth comes, sudden and sharp. The print will never be

perfect. None of them are. It's not in the pictures, not in my memories, not in my dreams.

I won't find what I've been chasing after, what I've both yearned for and buried deep within myself, unwilling to face it, to search it out and name it—it's simply not there.

I can wipe out every speck, every iota of gray. In the final purity of flawless black and pure, unadulterated white, my mother's eyes will be what they have always been to me.

Empty.

17

## LUX

I try not to listen to their voices, my father's choked and rasping, Lyra's sharp and shrill. I want to hook my earbuds in my ears and blast everything into oblivion with roaring, head-splitting sound. But I can't.

I sit frozen on my bed, smoke from the cigarette clutched in my fingers wafting out the open window. It's the first week of February, and the sharp air pebbles my bare arms with goose bumps. I hear every word.

After awhile, my sister leaves, her feet stomping down the hall, out the door. I sit perfectly still. The house descends into silence heavy as a tomb.

I snuff the cigarette against the window ledge, drop it into the snow-clumped bushes below. The house is too quiet. I should be in school, but I just can't seem to make myself go.

Inertia clamps down on me, cementing my limbs, pressing against my chest like an ice block. I could die here, this very moment, and no one would even know.

I have to escape. I have to get out of here. Screw what Lyra said. It's not like Dad's going to die *today*. He's lucid, talking and eating just fine.

I force my sluggish body to move. The origami elephant I've been working on all afternoon slips off my lap and falls to the floor. I was wet-folding it, but Lyra's argument with Dad distracted me.

Now the paper's hardened, the elephant only half-formed. I toss it in the trash, then tug on my jean jacket and wind a scarf around my neck.

Phoenix's little gray paws slip out from beneath my dresser and bat at my toes. She spent twenty-four hours under there my first day back home. Now, I can get her out sometimes, if she has something worthy to attack. She tackles my feet, spitting and growling, as I pull on my striped knee socks and leather boots.

"Hey, girl. Here, girl." I lean down slowly, clucking my tongue and holding out my finger. She barely sniffs at me before skittering back beneath the dresser.

I kneel and try to reach beneath it. She hisses at me. She's still feral, refusing to be tamed.

I pause at Dad's door. I listen to the slow, unsteady rhythm of his breathing, the uneven cadence of his snores. I need to see him. I have to. I know that. I push the door open, catch a glimpse of his dark slumbering form.

I freeze. Nothing moves. The room is the same as it has always been: bed, dresser, closet, the new full-length mirror leaning against the wall. I still think of it as new, even after all these years.

Memories of Mom sweep over me, a savage ache clenching my chest. I must have been six or seven the day we broke the mirror.

I was chasing Lyra around the house, playing my favorite spirit animals game. Lyra careened into the doorway of our parents' bedroom, lost her footing in her socks on the wood floor, and crashed into the full-length mirror.

I skidded in right after her, barely missing the worst of the shattered pieces scattered across the floor. Lyra crouched in the center of it, completely still, her face frozen in shock and fear. Several red spots bloomed on her hands and feet.

We thought Mom would be furious, but she wasn't. She rushed in, stepped right over the jagged shards, and scooped Lyra into her arms.

"What happened? Are you okay? Why are you shaking?" "Aren't you mad at me?" Lyra whispered, aghast.

"Why in heaven's name would I be mad at you?"

Mom set her on the closed toilet lid and slowly peeled off her socks. "Oh, baby," she said, making a pained sound in her throat. She stroked Lyra's feet as she pressed antiseptic cotton balls against her cuts and checked for slivers of mirror inside her skin.

I watched them, a sharp jealousy pricking me. After Mom bandaged Lyra up, she went back to the bedroom to survey the damage.

"Are we gonna throw the mirror in the trash?" I asked.

She chewed on her lower lip, her hands on her hips. "Breaking a mirror is seven years of bad luck. I'm afraid the entire course of your future has just been irrevocably altered." Lyra's eyes widened.

"But I won't let that happen. Not to my Lyra. There's one thing we can do to avert this disaster. We have to bury the mirror beneath the moon. You know what this means?" We both stared at her.

"Midnight picnic!"

"What about school?" Lyra asked, but her voice sparked with anticipation. She wanted to go as much as I did.

"Bah!" Mom scoffed. "I can teach you plenty."

While Mom gingerly picked up the shards of broken mirror and stuffed them into a couple of canvas shopping bags, Lyra and I packed the picnic basket with peanut butter and honey sandwiches, fruit snacks, apples, and string cheese.

That night, we went to bed like usual. I couldn't sleep. My body thrummed with impatience and excitement. Finally, sleep took over anyway. Mom woke us up a little before midnight.

Still in our pajamas, we all snuck out to the car and drove several miles to a clearing next to a playground and picnic tables. We could've just buried the mirror in our backyard. That wasn't Mom's style.

The August air was hot and cloying, even at midnight. Once our eyes adjusted, we could see the dim shapes of the trees huddled at the edge of the clearing.

Mom spread out the red and white checkered blanket on the grass.

Lyra and I drifted back to sleep beneath the stars. Mom grabbed her shovel, dug a hole, and buried our bad-luck mirror. When she finished, she lay down on the blanket next to us, smelling like dirt and her jasmine-scented shampoo.

"There," she said, nudging us back awake. "See that hazy band stretching across the sky? That's the Milky Way. Look south, there's creeping Scorpio with his long, deadly tail and brave Sagittarius with his bow."

Her words were like a song in my ears: Delphinus, Aquila, Cygnus, Corona Borealis. "I can see it," I said, squinting, searching for the figures Mom seemed to find so easily. An ant crawled along my arm.

Lyra shook her head. "I can't."

"Look for a teacup shape. Follow the handle of the big dipper to that blue-white star, Spica, right above that tall pine tree. Can you see the winged maiden clutching her sheaf of wheat? That's Virgo, your sign, Lyra, the largest constellation of the Zodiac. It means you're loyal, practical, methodical, a heart-helper. You're always trying to help others, but you never ask for help yourself."

"Cool," Lyra mumbled. She sounded like she was falling back asleep.

I wanted to be a winged maiden. Instead, my sign was just an ugly, nasty scorpion.

"Your element is earth, and your ruling planet is Mercury. Virgos appreciate the arts, just like Cancer, my sign."

"What about me?" I asked, suddenly furious.

"Scorpio," Mom said, tracing the shape in the sky. "Emotional, passionate, exciting. A force to be reckoned with. But also, obstinate, resentful, full of secrets." She reached out and tapped my chest with a single finger. "A jealous heart."

I felt my heart beating in the exact place my mother had touched me. How could it be jealous? Of what? I felt like I was shrinking and expanding at the same time, a thunder of anger building in my ears. "I do not."

Before I could say anything else, Lyra pointed at the brightest star in the sky. "Is that the North Star, Mom?"

Mom shook her head. "Polaris isn't the brightest star. It's the forty-eighth. That one you're looking at is Sirius, the dog star. It's the closest star to us, but it's still eight light years away. That light you're seeing right now? It's eight years old."

"Older than me," I said. I stared up at the black velvet sky with blurry, gritty eyes. The stars were so bright, so very close. I stretched my arms, grasping to touch one.

"Then why's the North star so famous?"

"The axis of the earth is pointed directly at it," Mom said. "Polaris does not rise or set. It remains in nearly the same position in the sky, while the whole fleet of stars wheels around it. If you're lost, you can use

Polaris to find your way home."

"Awesome," Lyra breathed.

"The stars can chart your future, if you let them," she told us. "The sky is a map to your destiny. Never forget that."

She was always reading our horoscopes, plotting our personalities, our fates. She told us extravagant fortunes like, *Your strength will conquer the world* and for Lyra, *You will bring your dreams to life.*

Lyra was different. Lyra had Mom's beloved constellations etched on her skin. Lyra was the artist, just like Mom. Lyra was the perfect one. I didn't have a single special thing about me.

I was right there with them, but I wasn't. I looked up at that sky and wished on every star I could count. I tried not to blink, so I wouldn't miss a single one. I stared until my eyes burned in their sockets. I wished my mother would love me.

She was like the stars themselves, magnificent and sparkling, blazing so bright. She seemed so close, but no matter how hard I tried, I could never quite reach her.

I blink rapidly. She's gone for good. And Dad will be, too. I could never reach either of them, these planetary bodies that made up the universe of my family. We rotated around each other, never quite touching.

I can't think these thoughts. I don't want to remember. Even the good memories are dark and frayed around the edges.

I back out of Dad's bedroom. I flee, slamming the front door against the scrabbling, whispery silences of that house.

# LUX

I text Reese with trembling fingers. It's still so damn cold. My breath puffs white in front of me while I wait for the heat to kick on. Outside, everything is still. The snow is a sloppy gray mess, the trees stark against the washed-out sky.

He texts back. *Come over.*

Thirty minutes later, I'm in Reese's cramped apartment. Everything is old and shabby, but it's clean. The table is clear, the counters scrubbed, the video games and controllers heaped in orderly stacks on the shelf below the TV. Posters of old rock bands like AC/DC, Pink Floyd, and Nirvana hang on the walls in plastic frames. Instead of couches, he has giant bean bags.

I scrunch down in a lemon-yellow bean bag, a bottle of Jack Daniel's between my knees. He gave me a pill as soon as I walked in the door. It's already starting to kick in.

In the kitchen behind me, the refrigerator drones. The ceiling fan over the kitchen table sputters, recycling stale air.

Reese sprawls on the bean bag next to me in shorts and a pumpkin-orange T-shirt, smoking a joint. A musky, burnt-popcorn smell fills the room. "You want some?"

"Yeah."

Reese hands me his joint and leans over, jerking the bottle from between my legs. He takes a long swallow. The bottle is already a third empty. "Just going to town, aren't you?"

"I need it."

"You aren't cranked enough already?" His voice is smooth as satin, his eyebrows scrunched in false concern. He puts the bottle on top of a neat stack of *Maxim* magazines on the coffee table.

I suck down the sweet, thick smoke. I need to get numb, to forget, to be obliterated. The apartment spins and buzzes around my head. Objects in the room swim in and out of focus, shrinking and enlarging like shadows on a wall.

I gesture at the weight machine in the corner behind him and the pull-up bar attached to the doorway in the hall. "Nice décor you have there."

He flexes one skinny arm. "We all have our dreams, Princess. Mine is to be a MMA fighter someday. What about yours?"

"Not everyone has dreams."

"Seriously?" I shrug.

He squints at me, like he's seeing me for the first time. "Aren't you supposed to be in school?"

I blink at him groggily. His image keeps slipping around in my head. "What do you care?"

"Just wondering."

"I'm dropping out." Dropping out of school was as easy as slipping into the freezing water of Lake Michigan. It seemed impossible at first, the harsh shock of it sucking your breath from your lungs. It only took a few days before school seemed like a whole lifetime ago. Something that happened to someone else.

"You sure about that?" He takes the joint from me. "Isn't it your senior year?"

"School's stupid. Who needs it? I'll just get my GED or something." My voice sounds slow and strange in my own ears.

"You shouldn't drop out. You're too smart."

I just shrug.

Reese stares at his joint, turns it between his fingers, and hands it back to me without smoking it. "You hungry? I've got cold pizza and beer."

The thought of food trembles the liquid swirling in my stomach, makes me want to vomit. I shake my head and sink further into the bean bag.

He swaggers into the kitchen. I gaze around the room, my vision swimming. I move the liquor bottle, pick up one of his magazines, and flip through it.

There's a beautiful redhead, her hips cocked, her lips curled in a seductive smile. I want to keep her. I rip out the page, fold it up, and tuck it into the pocket of my jeans.

That strange, urgent need wriggles through me. I check my folder in my messenger bag and pull out a stiff and heavy black paper. I crease it and rip on the diagonal, forming a triangle.

I work silently, my hands moving too slow, too sluggishly. My fingers keep stumbling over each other, messing up. I manage to close and flatten the awkward diamond shape, then twist the ears and open the mouth with the tip of my fingernail.

I open the wings and shape scalloped curves on the outer edges of the wings with my fingers. By the end, I'm focusing so hard my head feels like it's about to split open.

"Hey, is that a bird?"

"No, Sherlock. It's a bat."

"Aren't bats all nasty and diseased and stuff?"

"Bats are good. They eat mosquitos. In China, they're considered very lucky. So here, I've brought you some luck."

"No one's ever made something like this for me before." Reese slides down in the bean bag next to me. He takes the bat and cradles it in his hands. Something changes in his face. "This is totally jacked, Princess. Can I give this to my sister?"

"You have a sister?"

"She's eight. She'd love the crap out of this." He's grinning, and for once his eyes look almost awake, alive. Softened, somehow.

He puts it down carefully on the carpet next to him, then takes another drag. A thin curtain of smoke hangs over us. He leans in and kisses me, his mouth tasting like ash and pepperoni.

He doesn't kiss like Felix. Reese's kisses are bigger, sloppier. They don't turn my stomach inside out. They don't send my heart shooting into the stratosphere.

But right now, his eyes are soft. Right now, his hands are on me. His attention is on me. He wants me. He wants me and Felix doesn't, so screw him. I don't care about the rest.

A sweet, syrupy half-dream pulls at me. Everything warm and smoky and far away. My internal organs start to glow. I can feel them. See them in my mind's eye, drifting apart. Glowing like jellyfish, like flashlights blinking beneath my skin. Thoughts becoming more and more slippery, slowly disconnecting from everything.

Still, darkness remains, shifting just beneath me, a shining oily black sucking at the edges of my consciousness. That bleak, desperate knowledge that tomorrow I'll remember it all again.

But right now, tomorrow is so very far away.

19

---

## LUX

Hours later, the high wears off. It's after ten and completely dark by the time I get home. I would've spent the night at Reese's place, but he already had plans. Plans that clearly didn't involve me.

I've got nowhere else to go. My phone is radio silent. No texts or calls from Autumn or Simone. Fine. Let them be that way. They obviously don't value our friendship the way I do. They're punishing me.

They're probably together right now, sprawled on Autumn's bed, painting their nails and gossiping about me. I bet they're sharing a damn Twix bar and laughing their asses off. I know it.

My empty stomach clenches in pain. And hunger. I didn't eat that pizza at Reese's, even after the munchies set in. I stop in the kitchen and grab a can of Campbell's Chicken Noodle Soup out of the cupboard. Soup was Mom's favorite remedy for any sickness, from colds to fevers to the flu.

Because my timing is always exquisite, Lyra picks the exact same moment to make her own meal. She's here all day, and she chooses now? Anger slithers through me. I slam the cabinet closed with a loud bang.

"Hung over?" Lyra asks in a sweetly nonchalant voice. She opens the fridge and pretends to examine its contents.

"Like you care." I jerk a bowl from the cupboard next to the fridge, standing as far away from Lyra as possible.

"I do. I'd really like to know why you look so tired, seeing as you don't appear to be attending school, don't have a job, and don't lift a finger around here. You've been home for two weeks. You don't even do your own cat's litter, Lux! Guess who makes sure she has food when you disappear?"

Lyra's the one who looks tired. Gray smudges rim her eyes. But that's not my problem. She chose to come back after all this time, waltzing in like she's gonna save the day. That's on her. I shove my bangs out of my eyes and glare at her.

"Dad's gotten a bunch of letters from the school. The vice-principal keeps calling and leaving messages. They're going to expel you."

I tense, square my shoulders. Ready for a fight. "They can't. I'm dropping out."

"That's ridiculous. It's your senior year! What about college? You can't do that."

"Try and stop me. Can you move? I need the microwave."

The microwave is on the counter directly across from the fridge. The small kitchen is too cramped for both appliances to be used at once.

"I'm getting sandwich stuff." Lyra grabs the bread and rummages behind the jug of orange juice for the peanut butter.

"I was here first."

"What, are we little kids now?"

I sigh loudly. Lyra grabs her food and moves out of the way. She sets out the bread for two sandwiches on the counter next to a knife and a jar of honey.

I pop the lid off the soup, dump it into the bowl, and shove it into the microwave. Every cell in my body bristles with resentment. She acts all high and mighty all the time, but she's the one who left. She left me all alone and she didn't come back, not until now. When it's too late. When the damage has already been done.

"I was wondering what you did," she says.

"What do you mean?"

"What you were fighting over, with Dad. What you said to him."

"That's none of your damn business."

"He's my father, too. You causing his heart attack with your stupid recklessness counts as my business, don't you think?" She spreads a dollop of peanut butter on each piece of bread.

"I have nothing to say to you." I swallow hard, my voice rising against my will, cracking on the ends of my words.

"I just hope it was worth it, whatever you were fighting about. Worth breaking our father's heart. Literally."

I flinch, blood rushing to my head. "Why do you always have to be such a bitch about everything?" There's no way I'm telling her a damn thing. Still, her words bring the memory to sharp relief in the center of my brain.

We *were* fighting. Dad and I fought about everything. Without Lyra there to play peacekeeper, things fell apart. Like an abandoned city returning to the jungle state from which it came, disintegrating into ruin.

The two of us were like strangers trapped in the same house. We either ignored each other or we fought. Dad didn't want me to go out on school nights. I did anyway. I got letters from school about my grades, detentions. He thought my clothes were "inappropriate." He caught me smoking.

I don't even remember what started it that night. I'd been drinking, half a bottle into the peach schnapps Simone and I convinced her older brother to get for us.

Dad had gotten all religious all of a sudden, always quoting the Bible at me. I couldn't stand it. He was the last person in the world to be getting all high and mighty and righteous.

I was livid, my body shaking with fury. I screamed things, spat out every hateful, hurtful thing I could think of.

"What'd you fight about?" Lyra squeezes honey on the bread slices.

"Something about curfew? Your skirt too short?"

I don't respond. I'm dizzy, my ears ringing. Emotions churn and tumble in my gut.

"You get knocked up?" she asks in this vaguely condescending way that makes me want to punch her in the throat.

The microwave timer dings. I cover my hands with a dishtowel and cradle the steaming bowl close to my chest. My fingers are quivering, my pulse a roar in my ears.

"Screw you, Lyra. Where do you get off? Like you have the perfect life. Oh, wait. You ran off and abandoned us, leaving all the crap you didn't want to mess with behind. So I guess you probably do."

"What's that supposed to mean?"

"Why don't you go back to your perfect life? No one even wants you here."

Her eyes narrow, the muscles in her jaw clenching. "Are you on drugs?"

I want to rake my nails across her haughty face. "Just shut up!"

"I just think it's fair, you know, that you tell me. What you killed our father over."

"Why can't you ever shut up?" My fingers shake so badly, steaming broth sloshes over the lip of the bowl. I barely feel the burn. Blood surges to my brain, my thoughts tumbling, spinning and pinballing off each other.

I remember the blazing indignation I felt that night, the rage overtaking me. I was yelling, shouting, barely coherent. I remember what I said. I wish I didn't but I do. I remember every ugly, despicable word.

"I know what you did!" I screamed at him. "You think you got away with it, but I know!"

"Lux, stop," he begged. He grabbed at his arm, his bloated face leached of color.

I didn't listen. I didn't hear, I didn't care. I'd kept the buried secret so long inside me, it almost felt good to vomit it out. "You're the reason Mom is dead!" I hissed, my lips pulled back over my teeth, ferocious.

"She killed herself because of you!"

I didn't even notice what happened at first. I just kept yelling.

He slipped down against the wall. I thought he was just sitting down, but he looked funny. He was floppy and saggy, like a lopsided stuffed animal tossed aside by a tantrummy toddler.

He gripped his arm and made a hitching, gasping sound in his throat, like he couldn't talk, like he was in too much pain to talk. His head slumped over. His eyes were still open, but they weren't looking at anything.

I froze. A cold, dull dread crept over me. "Dad? What's wrong? Dad!"

But I already knew. I fumbled my phone out of my jacket pocket and dialed 911 with urgent, trembling fingers. I told the guy on the other end our address, barely remembering the numbers, the street name of the house I'd grown up in. I ended the call even though the 911 guy was still talking.

I stared at Dad with growing horror. He wasn't moving. He was dead. I knew it. A fissure opened up inside me, a crack for all the bad things to fall into.

A dark moaning sound filled the room, sucking all the oxygen out of the air. Finally, I realized that terrible gutted sound was coming from me. I bent over, clutching at my stomach, unable to breathe.

I couldn't stay there, not one more second. I fled. I ran away from my own father when he needed me most.

"Lux," Lyra says, pulling me back into the moment.

I stare at her, my eyes raw and burning.

"Just tell me the truth. Please." Her face crumples, the hostility leaking out of her. "Can't you give me that, at least?"

"You don't know anything. You left, Lyra. You don't get to judge me. You weren't even here!" I bolt from the kitchen, slamming my bedroom door so hard the whole house shudders.

I bang the bowl of soup down on my dresser, more hot liquid sloshing over the sides, and throw myself on my bed. I cover my mouth with my hands. Bite the skin of my palms to keep the scream inside.

Phoenix claws up the bedspread and races along the length of the bed, mewling frantically. Everything I can't think skitters around in my head, crashing into the walls of my skull. My eyes throb in their sockets. Suffocating shame chokes my throat.

It's my fault. I know that. The shadowy truth I can't escape from, no matter what I do.

We both have our secrets, Dad and I. I have mine. Secrets so terrible I can't speak them aloud, can't even think them.

It's Dad's fault that Mom is dead.

But also, it's mine.

# LYRA

I bring Dad his afternoon pills, watch him swallow them down, then make him a tuna sandwich with an apple for lunch. I rinse the dishes and scrub down the counters, even though they're already clean. The thought of how scuzzy and crusted they used to be makes me cringe in revulsion. When I cleaned out the fridge last month, I found more than one container of left-over Spaghettios sprouting a nasty green-white mold.

If the kitchen does not glimmer and gleam, it is at least very, very clean. There's comfort in these daily chores, action a refreshing release from having to think.

I'm meticulously picking lint from each plaid couch cushion when Lux prances into the kitchen around three. She hums and sways to the music piping through her earbuds. She digs through the fridge, grabs a green apple, a jar of peanut butter, and a knife from the drawer, rattling the silverware as she bangs it shut with her hip.

Lux looks haggard, like she hasn't slept in days. Her skin is blotchy and gray. A blade of guilt slides between my ribs whenever I think about the fight we had two days ago. I went too far. I got upset and I said things …

I rub my eyes with the sleeve of my sweater. Lux has the uncanny ability to bring out the absolute worst in me. When she's around, I say terrible things, even when I don't want to. I always hate myself afterward.

"Hey," I say. "Are you okay?"

She just stares at me, hostile, belligerent, not even bothering to take out her earbuds.

"Look, I'm sorry. I overreacted before."

She rolls her eyes and heads back to her room without saying a word.

I can't wrap my mind around the concept of my sister. Lux is a stranger to me, completely foreign, incomprehensible. Where is the little girl who loved stories, make believe and pretend? Who loved dancing and clomping around in Mom's high heels and games of hide and seek? Where is the girl who'd grab my hand beneath the table when the yelling started, squeezing so hard my fingers went numb?

A memory takes hold of me. How she used to sneak in my room at night, how I'd be tucked in my bed under a pile of blankets when I'd feel her breath grazing my cheek. Half-asleep, I'd groan and lift my arm so she could scoot against me, a curled-up puppy, small and warm.

Some nights she came in long before midnight, when the house was too quiet. Even then, it wasn't the creaking floors, the ping of the furnace, or even the shouting that got to us. It was when everything fell silent, as if we both knew the silence was the most dangerous of all.

Those nights when anxiety pricked us awake, Lux would ask me to draw the constellations on her back. I'd trace the shapes of Aquila the eagle and Capricornus the sea goat, the flying horse of Pegasus and the great bear of Ursa Major. She always knew the right answer, could always tell before I'd even halfway finished.

Where is that sweet, creative little sister? She's gone. In her place, there's a girl oozing defiance, cynicism, disdain. I can't imagine screaming matches with my father, the drinking and the parties, taking off for days at a time, the insolence that seems stamped across Lux's whole being. Are there no boundaries? No lines Lux is unwilling to cross?

My own world is black and white. There's right and wrong, acceptable and unacceptable. There are no grays.

I sigh and glance at the clock. 3:30 p.m. The hospice nurse, Ellie Delmonte, will be here soon. I promised Ethan I'd meet him at the park at 4:00. I've been putting it off for a few weeks now, but it's already the second week of February. I can't wait any more.

Restless energy thrums through me. It's been so long since I've held my camera in my hands. I need this, I need it like breathing.

The thought of Ethan sends a nervous flutter through my stomach. Ethan gets under my skin in ways I don't want to think about. He's so cocky, so sure everyone loves him. I hate how often he's right, how easy it is to let myself get carried along, taken in.

But I need to do this, for my art, for the competition. Ethan and Hadley will both make gorgeous subjects. It's just one afternoon. An hour of taking pictures, making small talk, then I'm done.

The promise of the photography competition is the only thing connecting me to my old life, to the normal, regular world I've worked so hard to build.

I can't give it up completely. Photography is the only thing anchoring me to sanity. Focusing on my art helps me forget, filters out everything else.

The hospice nurse arrives promptly at 3:30 p.m. She sweeps into the living room, the fruity scent of orange blossoms wafting after her. She's wearing dangling emerald tear-drop earrings, her fingers stuffed with vintage sterling rings, their stones as big as my knuckle.

She hugs me to her enormous bosom. "How are you doing, my dear?"

"Fine," I say, barely able to breathe.

She asks me a few questions about how Dad's doing, his sleeping and eating patterns and how he's managing the pain. She notices my camera and asks about my art.

"My niece is an artist. Drawing mostly, but painting now, too. Everyone should have a hobby, preferably one less expensive than shopping," she says, eyeing her rings ruefully.

I don't tell her the truth—art isn't my hobby, it's my life. "Do you think it's okay if I leave for awhile?"

"Of course! That's one of the reasons I'm here. Go, have a wonderful time."

When I hesitate, she shoos me away with her hand, the bangles jangling on her wrists.

———

I arrive at the park first and scout out a flat spot next to the river's edge. The last three days have been sunny. The snow is mostly melted, the rocky ground still firm and relatively dry, not yet soggy with the warmth of spring.

Brokewater Creek is more like a river, wide and strong, snaking all the way to Lake Michigan thirty miles west. But here, by the park, the river is mostly shallow, muddy brown water rippling over sandbars and clusters of smooth stones.

I load a cassette of panchromatic 400 ISO film, attach my zoom lens, polarizer, and UV haze filter. The portrait lens is better, but Hadley will probably run around like a hooligan. I need flexibility.

I snap a few shots of the water, the way the sun strikes a spray of droplets into diamonds, a clot of brown and red leaves slick with snow, the glistening belly of an overturned rock. I already know I won't use these.

I photograph faces, the geography of emotions, the hills and valleys of physical features, the ravine of the mouth, the caverns of the eyes, the well of an ear, the knoll of an eyebrow. The terrain of a face reveals layers of meaning and depth that a simple tree or bird or slope of earth never could.

"There you are."

I look up to see Ethan trotting toward me, little Hadley bobbing along beside him, holding his hand. Hadley wears fur-lined boots, white tights, and an orange sweater dress. She's holding the same red polka dot purse from the grocery store.

Ethan's dressed in loose stonewashed jeans and a gray waffle-knit shirt beneath his leather jacket. I try not to notice his broad shoulders, the curl of his hair over his collar, the way his dark clothes bring out the topaz of his eyes.

"Hi, guys. Thanks for coming."

I glance at the sky. The daylight is just beginning to take on that glow around the edges that photographers covet, soft and golden.

"How's the van?" Ethan asks.

Last week, I picked up the Honda and switched out the loaner, but Ethan was at lunch and I didn't see him. True to his word, the final cost was almost a third less than the quote.

"Purrs like a kitten," I say. "Thank you."

"No problem."

"I wanna swing!" Hadley chirps, gesturing her pudgy fingers back toward the playground. Her curls bounce in their pigtails.

"After pictures. That's the deal," Ethan says, squatting down in front of his daughter. He takes the purse from her. "You want to smile and be in the pictures for Miss Lyra, right?" She nods solemnly.

"Remember that cookie we talked about," he says with a wink and turns to me. "She's a ham for the camera. Since she was six months old."

I kneel on the cold ground and squint into the viewfinder. "Hadley, do you want to go to the edge of the water and pick up a stone for me?"

Hadley obeys. I turn the front ring on the lens barrel until she comes into focus, the trees behind her blurring. I zoom in on her face, adjust the f-stop, and compose the image within the viewfinder.

Over the next thirty minutes, I take a few rolls of film, snapping wide shots of Hadley skipping toward the river, bending down, the rock in her hand, then closer shots as she examines stones glistening with jeweled water, her exuberant expression as she holds it up toward Ethan to show off her prize.

I'm too aware of Ethan ambling along behind me. It's hard to focus for reasons that irritate the crap out of me. "Thanks for agreeing to this."

"No worries. Hadley needed to get out of the house."

The sun skims the tops of the trees, the light just about perfect now, though it's getting colder. "Hadley, will you come sit by me for a minute?"

I photograph close-ups of Hadley, sharpening her face, blurring out the river in the background. The sun glitters in her saucer eyes, her thick lashes shadowing her round cheeks.

She sits patiently for about four minutes. Then she's scooting back and forth on her bottom, begging Ethan to let her swing.

"Can you wait just one minute more?" he asks.

"No!" she shouts.

"Hadley, that's not okay. No yelling."

"No!" she screams again, leaping to her feet.

"Five-minute time out," Ethan says. "Sit right there."

"No! No! No!" Hadley tries to dash away, but Ethan grabs her and sits her down. Her face scrunches up and she bursts into tears.

"Stop it," Ethan says, frustration lacing his voice. A few moms standing over by the slide glance our way. Ethan's shoulders hunch almost imperceptibly. "Please, Hadley. No screaming."

Hadley tries to jump up, and Ethan firmly, gently pushes her down again. She throws herself on the ground, flailing her arms, wailing as loud as she can.

The other moms purse their lips, shoot us judgmental glances.

"That's it." Ethan pulls his phone out of his pocket and starts scrolling, his expression grim.

"What are you doing?"

"I downloaded this book, *Happiest Toddler in the Neighborhood: How to Raise Cooperative and Respectful Kids*. I'm still waiting on the cooperation.

And the respect. And the sanity."

Hadley shrieks an ear-piercing scream. "No! No! I don't wanna!"

"It's okay," I say. "I think I've got enough good shots. We can be done now."

He chews on his lower lip, scanning his phone. "That's great, but I can't let her out of the time-out early. The author says that would just reinforce her bad behavior. Right?"

"No, Daddy!" Hadley wails. "Please! Me wanna swing!"

He looks at me. "Don't ask me. I don't know what your book says."

"*Daddy!*"

"I mean," I say over her shrieks. "Really, it's our fault for asking too much of her."

"Okay, great. I was thinking the same thing. Go ahead, Chipmunk."

Her face instantly breaks into a dazzling smile. She scrambles to her feet and scampers off toward the playground.

"I'm supposed to ignore it and stay calm," he says wryly, running his hands through his dark hair. "It's a little difficult when the perfect mommies over there are taking in the whole show, probably thanking their lucky stars their own husbands aren't stuck with all the parenting duties. I'm screwing up, scarring her for life as we speak."

"Just start her therapy savings account now and you'll be good."

He laughs. His features are so open when he laughs, there's none of the false charm and bravado from earlier. My stomach tightens. Something inside me wants to keep that soft, easy expression on his face, wants to see it directed at me.

"Seriously though," I say. "Forget those supermoms. They're just the queen bees from high school, version 2.0. They get off on feeling superior to everybody else."

"Yeah, you're probably right."

We follow Hadley up the hill. "I am right. Trust me, I know these things."

"Thanks for that," Ethan says, nudging my shoulder with his.

My cheeks flame. He's too close. I raise my camera, hiding my face. "Your turn."

I snap a few shots of Ethan leaning against an old maple tree, the rough bark a sharp contrast against his olive skin and gold-flecked eyes. He stares straight at me, eyebrows cocked, a cheeky grin spread across his face.

I try to focus on the composition, the shapes, lines, textures, and shadows of the image in my viewfinder, but it's not working. My pulse quickens, palms sweating.

Dad always said, "Don't shoot what it looks like. Shoot what it feels like." He sounded like Mom when he talked like that—like art had a soul, like its purpose wasn't just to be, to exist, but to bring something out of you. Right now, I'm not sure I can handle what it feels like.

The wind picks up, whipping a few strands of hair into my face. I smooth them back, tucking them behind my ears. "Okay, I've got enough," I say, my voice cracking.

His smile only widens. "You sure about that?"

"Yep. Used up a whole roll."

He pushes himself off the tree trunk and ambles toward me. "I didn't know film still existed. That camera looks ancient."

"It was my dad's," I say, gripping it tighter. Dad never used a digital camera, and he didn't want me to either, although I do occasionally for school projects. "Dad thinks Photoshop is cheating. Art is made when it's just the camera, the photographer, and the subject. That's what he likes to say, anyway."

Ethan nods. "I get that. Technology doesn't always change things for the better."

"It's not about better or worse, really. Digital is fine. I just like the darkroom. I like physically developing the film and making the prints. It's peaceful. Everything goes calm and still." "Daddy!" Hadley yells.

"Unlike now, right?" Ethan winks at me. He jogs over to the playground and puts Hadley on the swing, curling her fingers around the chains. "Hold on tight."

I take a few photos of them from different angles. "Hadley is about the prettiest little girl I've ever seen."

"Thanks. It's hard to pick out which features came from where. Nyah's from the Dominican Republic and I'm half-Indonesian, half-Argentinean. I think my great-grandmother was Armenian or something."

"She has your eyes, and your smile."

"Thanks, Freckles," he says, that same magnetic smile playing across his features. "How sweet of you."

I blush. Again. I stare at the ground and kick at the mulch. Ethan pushes Hadley higher and higher. She shrieks and thrusts her legs at the sky.

"I heard about your dad," Ethan says after a few minutes. "I'm sorry."

I stiffen. It's still hard to talk about. "Yeah. Well, we've been waiting for it for awhile now."

"That doesn't make it any easier. I know it's not the same, but Petulu, my grandfather, died in a motorcycle accident when I was thirteen. He lived with us. It was awful. I'm not sure what's worse, dying suddenly without a chance to say goodbye or having to deal with a slow, painful death."

I look at him, but he's focused on pushing Hadley. "I'm sorry, Ethan. I've had both. It's hell either way. It's like asking if you would rather die by fire or freezing to death. You still die. The outcome's the same."

"By fire. Freezing is slower. It can take days. Parts of your body die and turn black while the rest of you is still alive. All you can do is wait and watch it happen, and you know what's coming next."

"Sounds like you've thought about this a lot."

He smirks. "You have plenty of time to think when you're wandering the house at three a.m. trying to soothe a colicky baby."

"High, high," Hadley squeals. Ethan pushes her a little harder. She sticks her feet in the air, giggling hysterically.

It's getting too dark for pictures. The sky is slate. Sharp stars poke through the drifting canopy of clouds. The air is colder.

I take my gloves out of my coat pocket and tug them on. I pack my camera in its leather bag, place it next to Hadley's little red purse, and settle into the swing next to Hadley. "That's a fancy purse your dad's got there."

Hadley giggles. "Mine!" she shrieks.

"She's a collector of rocks, sticks, leaves, whatever she can find. It all goes in that purse and then ends up all over the house. It's fantastic."

I laugh. "I'm so disappointed it's not yours."

Ethan rolls his eyes. "How's college? It must be exciting, getting to follow your dream. I always thought you were so cool carrying your camera around all the time."

I snort. "Are you sure you're remembering correctly? I was never cool."

"Sure you were. You don't have to hang out with the popular kids or go to all the parties to be cool. You had a passion, a focus. You knew what you wanted. I always admired that. I felt the same way about football. Football was everything." He doesn't say the words we both hear: until it wasn't.

I glance at him. The lines around his mouth are taut. I've got no clue what to say. "I'm sorry."

"Yeah, that part of it sucked."

"I'm sorry," I mutter again. I'm an idiot. "You never regret it?"

"Sometimes I wonder what things would have been like, if I was still at school, still playing ball. But I can't have both, you know?"

I understand that pull all too well, the battle in your head and heart between your dreams and your responsibilities, your future and your family. "I know."

His face smooths out. "If it's football or Hadley, Hadley wins. Just don't ask me that question in the middle of an epic tantrum. But still, I'd make the same decision again."

"High, Daddy! High!"

"Okay, Chipmunk. Just a little higher."

I watch the white puffs of my breath in the gray light. "Do you like your job? You seem good at it."

"You know what? I actually do. I still want to go back to school, maybe study engineering and design cars instead of fix them. But for now? Like I said, I'm good with my hands. I like taking something broken and putting it back together. One of the assistant managers is leaving in a month, and I'm in line for the promotion. A fatter paycheck means we actually get to move out of my mom's basement. Score one for self-sufficiency."

"That's cool." I clear my throat and kick at the mulch with the toe of my boot.

"How's your sister? She back home yet?"

"How'd you know about that?"

He shrugs. "It's a small town. Honestly, I get most of my news from

Darcy. She still hangs with the high school crowd sometimes."

Darcy's name in his mouth makes my stomach drop. My heart constricts treacherously, like I actually care. I try not to look at him. "So, um, is Darcy, like—" Ugh. I sound like a clueless fourteen-year-old.

"My girlfriend? Freckles, why do you ask?" Amusement sparks in his eyes.

My face flushes with heat. I'm sure I'm bright red from my chest to the tips of my ears. "No reason. Just making conversation."

"Well, since we're *making conversation,* no, she's not. She's a great friend. She's funny and smart and knows more about car engines than most guys I know. But to be honest with you, she parties a little too hard. She's not really the type to settle down or get serious."

My capricious heart loosens in my chest. "Oh. Okay."

"Why? You jealous, Freckles?"

"Nope," I say, forcing my voice to sound normal. "Whatever gave you that idea? You just think everyone's into you, don't you?"

He smirks. "They aren't?"

"Not those uber-moms, that's for sure."

He laughs. "Touché, my lady. Touché."

"All done, Daddy!" Hadley announces.

Ethan stops the swing and helps Hadley get down. He presses the back of his hand against her red, chapped cheeks. "It's getting pretty cold, huh? Put your hoodie on, baby. Five minutes and it's time to go."

Hadley nods, her eyes wide and white in the growing twilight. She grabs his leg in a fierce hug, then races off toward the slide as we follow behind her.

"Darcy said she knows my sister."

"Yeah. Darcy parties with Lux sometimes. Lux is quite the wild child,

I hear."

My jaw clenches. "You could say that."

"What's she like?"

I give him a sideways glance. He seems genuinely interested, like he really wants to know. "I think she's on drugs. She took off for almost three weeks. Our father is lying in his bed, dying—and she disappeared. She's out of control."

"That's tough," Ethan says.

"I can't talk to her at all. She's this stranger living in my house. All we do is fight. She doesn't care about anybody but herself."

He stuffs his hands into his pockets and leans against the slide. "Sometimes you have to let the ones you love go their own way and make their own mistakes. Maybe all we can do is love them and pray for them until they find their way back. That's what my mom did for me. It worked."

"Are you a Christian, then? That's totally not how I remember you."

"My mom's devout. Like, church every weekend and Bible study every Wednesday night. I lapsed and now I'm ... I don't actually know. In between? I take Hadley to the church's children's program every week. It's cute. What about you?"

"No offense, but prayer and church never did anything for my family."

"Maybe you just can't see it yet. God doesn't just come in and fix all of our problems. It's not like that. It's not about that."

"Then what's it about?"

"Having faith in something bigger than yourself. Knowing you're not alone."

"Well, that sounds great and all, but I don't think—"

"Just a sec." Ethan pushes himself off the slide. "Where's Hadley? I don't see her."

It's nearly dark. Stars wink and glimmer in the dusky sky. The trees are black looming shapes along the outer rim of the playground. There's no one else here. The hairs on the back of my neck prickle.

"Hadley!" Ethan calls.

Then I see her. By the river. Near the bridge, where the water's the deepest. A small, pale shape. Teetering at the water's edge.

I suck in my breath. "Hadley!"

2 1

---

## LUX

Some people think origami isn't art. After all, it's just paper, right? But in some ways, folding is the most difficult art form of all. Carving in stone or wood or ice is subtractive—the artist removes material to reveal the final shape. Building sculptures from clay, metal, and glass is additive—the artist adds and brings together materials to create something.

But folding is different. You start with a piece of paper. You end with a piece of paper. The form is still itself, and yet it's transformed. Its beauty is in its expression, proportion, and detail.

I sit cross-legged on my bed, Imagine Dragons piping in through my earbuds. I glance at the opened pages in my *Advanced Origami Techniques* book, sight reading the diagrams.

I've been working on a squirrel for over two weeks. I've discarded a dozen rough drafts made with the cheap Kraft paper I use for my practice pieces. When I'm ready for the final draft, I use the hand-made Japanese Washi Paper Dad gets me, a soft, fibrous paper perfect for my needs.

I shape the squirrel beneath my fingers, focusing on creating smooth surfaces and flowing lines. I form each fold carefully, burnishing the creases with the back of my thumbnail. I trace an arch with my thumb and index finger in the paper, drawing the shape I need. I make the base folds and creases and inside-reverse-fold the large section of the tail, then crimp the belly.

I'm thinking of Lyra. I'm thinking of my father dying in his room. My mother dead and rotting beneath the earth. No longer my mother. No longer anything but shriveled flesh and white bone.

I remember my childhood in fits and snatches, a handful of dream sequences. A sound here, an image there. My father's sandpaper voice. My mother's glossy smile. Mom so happy, so gloriously bright.

When she turned her brightness on you, it was like staring straight into the sun. I remember Lyra basking in that sunlight. I remember cowering in shadows.

I remember Mom drifting out of her bedroom after hours, maybe days locked inside. She wandered the house in her nightgown, a confused look on her face. She didn't even see me unless I was right in front of her. Once, she stumbled over me, then stared at me in bewilderment, as if I had sprung up overnight. As if she didn't even remember I was there.

For the finishing touches, I mountain and valley-fold to form the nose and crimp the triangle face to suggest eyes and cheeks. The little squirrel stands on its own on my bedspread, balanced by the large tail arcing over his head.

Phoenix instantly starts stalking it, her little butt in the air, the fur along her spine sticking straight up. I reach out to her. She hisses at me and backs away.

"I'll get you to love me," I whisper. "Just you wait."

There was never enough sun. There was never enough love. It felt like starving, reaching and scrabbling for something only to have it knocked out of the way, handed to someone else. Lyra was bigger, stronger. She had the gifts. I didn't.

She was my best friend. And she was my mortal enemy. She stole my mother's affection, my father's attention. I survived on the scraps. Sloppy seconds. I had to claw and fight for what I got. I didn't play fair. I couldn't.

A memory tugs at my mind. I must have been only seven, Lyra ten. Dad was gone. It was just the three of us. Outside, the rain washed the whole world in sheets of gray. It pounded against the roof, slashed at the windows. The trees slumped against the onslaught, their leaves torn off and slapped to the ground.

Mom and Lyra were in the living room. Mom sitting cross-legged on the carpet, building one of her canvases out of wood and a loose canvas sheet. Lyra on the couch, hunched over her photography books. They were talking about art stuff, the rule of thirds and composition and shadow versus light.

I was supposed to practice piano, but instead I curled into a ball on the floor. Mom didn't even realize I wasn't playing. The carpet was rough and nubby against my cheek. I listened to the groaning of the wind, the hiss of the rain, the soft lilting voices of my family.

They created their own little world, the two of them. It was Mom and Lyra. Or it was Dad and Lyra. Always Lyra.

I didn't want to hear them anymore. I got up and stalked down the hallway. They didn't even notice. I went into Lyra's room. Before I could let myself think about it, I pocketed one of her pearl earrings she'd gotten for Christmas. I felt a twinge of guilt, but the thrill that thrummed through me was stronger, more powerful. Intoxicating.

I wandered into my parents' room. Mom kept the jewelry she never wore in a glazed ceramic box. I opened the lid, let her necklaces spill through my fingers. There were several prescription pill bottles on the dresser next to the box.

I picked one up and rattled it. The lid popped off, all on its own. I pocketed a handful of round yellow pills. They were colorful. I wanted them. I wanted to take something away from her.

I wanted to hurt both of them. So I did. I remember this so clearly, remember that first exhilarating thrill of stealing, taking, hurting.

I felt a presence behind me. Mom, hovering in the doorway. "What are you doing?"

"Nothing." I turned around fast, shoving the pills and the pearl earring deep into my back pocket.

She looked at me, her head slightly cocked. "I have an idea. Let's go dancing!"

Lyra came up behind her. "But it's raining."

"Don't be a party pooper," Mom said, winking at me. "My element is water. Getting wet never hurt anybody, besides the Wicked Witch of the West, anyway." She tugged on my hand.

I followed her down the hall to the front door. "What about my rain coat?"

She made a dismissive sound in the back of her throat. "You have to feel it, every drop. That's the whole point." She threw open the door and ran outside. I ran after her.

The rain was cold and sharp on my skin. I stopped on the gravel sidewalk, watched Mom twirling in the grass. She spread her arms and tilted her head back toward the sky. Her avocado-colored dress clung to her hips, her stomach, her breasts. Tendrils of red hair stuck to her neck and cheeks. She opened her mouth and drank the rain.

"Come on!" she called to us.

Lyra stood in the opened doorway, her arms crossed over her chest.

She slanted her eyes at me. "There's lightning. You're crazy."

But I followed my mother. I would've followed her anywhere. The thrill of hurting her faded into the thrill of being with her, the sole spotlight of her attention, swept up in her giddy joy. Instantly, I forgot everything but my overwhelming, aching love for her.

She took hold of my wrists and spun me. Our skin was slick. It was hard to hold on. Rain splattered my face and drenched my clothes and hair. Above us, a crash of thunder shook the sky.

She gazed at me, into me, her eyes so bright, her whole face laughing. We whirled and whirled around the front yard, our bare feet slipping and sliding in the wet grass.

When we finally stumbled back inside, Mom told Lyra to get us towels. She wrapped me up and hugged me so tight, I didn't dare breathe.

Lyra watched us, glowering, her blue eyes a darkening storm.

I felt victorious, like I'd won something precious. And Lyra hadn't.

It's one of the few things I remember clearly, like a shiny stone I can rub and rub until I can see my own glimmering reflection. But so much else is still fuzzy. There is so much missing, so many gaping holes.

Sometimes, my own past feels like a half-formed thing. Some spots are blank or vague—like a work of origami completely unfolded. When you fold a piece of paper, you change its memory. I can still see the creases, can feel the places where life imprinted itself on the paper —but I can't make out the form of it. I try to hold it in my hands, examine the dim shape from every angle. But mostly it remains as it is, a ghost of itself.

I need to get out of here. I can't think these thoughts. I can't.

I pick up the origami squirrel, feel the soft folds between my fingers. I crush it into a ball and hurl it into the trash.

# 22

## LYRA

I see the small shape of Hadley right at the water's edge, leaning over a rocky drop-off beneath the bridge.

"Over there!" I reach for Ethan's arm, but he's already gone.

He sprints toward her. "Hadley! No!"

I run after him. Hadley looks like she's turning, stepping back. She slips on a rock. In one swift movement, she goes down, her little body pitching into the black water.

My heart leaps into my throat. My legs are too slow and heavy, like I'm barely moving even though I'm running full-tilt.

Ethan reaches the bank first. He plunges into the icy river and dives under the water. For a long, torturous moment, I can't see either of them.

The water closes over their heads with barely a ripple, as if they never existed.

In the sudden silence, I hear only the rapid thud of my own heart over the breeze soughing through the leafless trees. How many seconds since Hadley went in? Thirty seconds? Forty-five? Come on.

*Come on.*

Ethan surfaces, gasping, chest heaving.

He climbs up the bank, cradling Hadley in his arms.

I grip his arm, jerking the sleeve of his jacket, helping him stay upright when his foot snags on a tree root. It's so dark, for a second I can't see whether she's moving.

"Is she okay?"

"Hadley!" Ethan yells into her face.

She chokes and sputters. "Daddy!"

I put my hand on her leg. She's soaked to the bone. And freezing cold.

"What do we do?" Water drips down Ethan's face. His hair is matted against his scalp. His eyes are wide, frantic. "Do we take her to the hospital?"

I shake my head. "The hospital's fifteen miles away. She needs to get out of those clothes and get warm. My house is less than a mile from here. Come on."

He follows me without a word. We take my car, Ethan in the back seat, cradling Hadley, me driving. For once, I'm grateful for country roads. I speed home in less than three minutes.

We carry her inside and bring her to the living room. Her whole body's shivering uncontrollably.

"Take off all her clothes," I tell Ethan. I run to the upstairs bathroom and fill up the tub with lukewarm water.

For half a second, I freeze. I hardly use this bathroom. And I've never used the tub, not in eight years. Blood-soaked images flash behind my eyes. I push them away. This is not the time.

I go back to the living room and help Ethan peel off Hadley's drenched clothes. We carry her into the bathroom and lower her into the tub. I kneel next to the tub, holding her head up.

"It's okay, it's okay, honey. You're okay. You can relax now."

She's still and quiet, staring at me with her enormous golden eyes.

Ethan paces behind me, wringing his hands. "Is she going to be okay? You sure we shouldn't just go to the hospital?"

"She'll be fine." I can already feel the warmth seeping back into her limbs. "She was in the water for less than a minute. You saved her." "No. I let it happen," he says savagely.

"It was an accident."

"I wasn't paying attention."

"There's no point in blaming yourself."

He looks on the verge of panic. "It was my fault."

"She's okay. Do you hear me? She's okay."

"Are you sure?"

"I'm sure. Here, take over for a minute."

Panic creeps into his voice again. "What do I do?"

"Just keep her as submerged as possible. Warm up her face and head with this washcloth. I'll be right back."

I stick my head in Dad's room. He's slept through the whole thing. Lux's door is still closed, so she's either not paying attention or she took off again. Either way, I can't worry about it now.

I grab a bunch of towels from the linen closet, then head downstairs to my room to pick out the smallest clothes I can find. When I come back up, we rub Hadley down with towels, then dress her in one of my hoodies that falls to her shins, pajama shorts that I cinch at the waist with a ribbon, and a pair of my winter socks that go past her knees.

"There. You look adorable."

"T'ank you," she says solemnly.

"How about some hot chocolate?"

Her little face breaks into a smile, her eyes glimmering. "Yummy!"

Ethan paces the living room like a caged tiger. He jiggles his car keys in his hand. "You sure we shouldn't—"

"Look at her, Ethan. She's acting normal. She's warm. She's happy."

"Okay." He takes a deep breath. "Okay."

"But you're freezing. And you're shaking like crazy. Go take a warm shower. Make sure it's not hot. I'll try to find some clothes." Ethan looks at Hadley, hesitating.

"I'll put the clothes outside the bathroom door. We'll be in the kitchen, making hot chocolate. Now go!" Finally, reluctantly, he goes.

"Hadley, do you want to help me find clothes for your daddy?"

She grins and takes my hand. Dad's clothes will be way too big, plus I don't want to disturb him, so I end up finding an oversized pair of apricot-colored unicorn pajama pants in Lux's bottom drawer. She's gone, of course.

I grit my teeth. No time to get pissed off now. I grab the oversized Detroit Lions hoodie hanging up in her closet and hold it up to my chest. It should fit him. I'm about to shut the closet door when I notice something else.

Mom's heart-shaped ceramic box, the one from her dresser. It's sitting on the top shelf of Lux's closet. I take it down and carefully lift off the ceramic lid. It's full of junk. Trash. Gum wrappers, Canadian quarters, a rusty lighter, a couple of lipstick tubes, nail polish, receipts, a tiny glass figurine, paper clips, several earrings, an origami swan.

I recognize my single pearl earring Mom bought me for that last Christmas before she died. It's been missing for years.

Hadley tugs on my jeans. "All done?"

"Yeah, sweetie. Let's go." I tuck the earring in my pocket and put the ceramic box back on the top shelf. What the heck is going on with Lux? Yet another question to add to the growing list. I push my anger down and turn to Hadley. "Your daddy's gonna look awesome. Almost as fantastic as you."

By the time Ethan comes out of the bathroom, I've got two bowls of steaming chicken soup ready and waiting. The hot chocolate is brewing on the stove, and Hadley's sitting at the kitchen table, scarfing up marshmallows.

I laugh when I see him. I can't help it. The unicorn pajamas fit him at the waist but are much too short, riding up to the middle of his shins.

"Hey, at least the sweatshirt is manly, right?" he says with a grin. He preens and takes a bow.

He pokes Hadley's belly and she bursts into giggles.

Then he kneels down and wraps his arms around her. It's a hug so fierce and intimate, I feel like I should turn away. "I love you," he whispers into her hair.

My heart clenches. I don't know why I'm surprised, but I am. He's a good dad. A great dad. I have the sudden, inexplicable urge to hug him too, to know what it's like to be wrapped up in those strong, safe arms.

He comes over to the stove. His damp hair curls over his ears. He smells like soap, and beneath that, the deep, musky scent that is distinctly male. "What smells so great over here?"

"Homemade hot chocolate," I say, stirring the chocolate a final time. I pick up the pan, pour the liquid chocolate into three mugs, and sprinkle in the mini marshmallows. "You boil whole milk and add in a bar of melted dark chocolate. It's really quite easy. My dad always made it for us after— " I pause, my mind snagging on a memory. Shouting, broken glass, tears. I shove it down. "When we were sad."

"I've never had anything but the powdered kind."

"You're missing out on an essential life experience. Here." I hand him his mug and start to give one to Hadley.

"Maybe put it in the fridge for a few minutes, so it isn't so hot? Do you have a plastic cup? Ceramic will break if she drops it."

"Sure. Your parenting books teach you that?"

He grimaces. "Real-world experience, unfortunately."

A few minutes later, Hadley's all settled, her chubby hands wrapped around a plastic cup of cooled hot chocolate. "Urse! Urse!"

"Huh?"

"Her purse. And your camera. We left them at the park. I'll go back and get them."

In the chaos, I'd forgotten about the camera. I feel a sudden sense of impending loss, but no. It's dark and cold. No one's at the park. My camera is safe, for now. "Drink your hot chocolate first. It's never gonna be as good as it is right now. That's what my dad always says."

Ethan takes a long sip. "This is delicious. Like, mind-alteringly good."

I shrug, my face reddening. "My pleasure."

"Thank you for what you did today."

"For what? You're the one that jumped in the water."

He shakes his head, his brow furrowing. "I totally freaked. I always thought I'd be smart in an emergency, but I wasn't. All I could think about was losing her. You were the clear-headed one, calm under pressure. You took care of her." He tugs at the unicorn pajamas and grins sheepishly. "Guess I'm losing manly points left and right, huh?"

I take another gulp of hot chocolate. It scalds on the way down. I try not to notice the chocolaty mustache skimming his upper lip. "I don't think so," I whisper.

"What?"

I take a step back, untucking my hair so it falls across my face. "I said you're welcome."

His grin widens. "No, you didn't."

"I'm sure I did."

"We'll just have to agree to disagree, Freckles—I mean, Lyra."

The way he says my name sends shivers up and down my spine that no amount of hot chocolate could help.

## 23

## LYRA

The third week of February passes, gray and bitterly cold. I spend as much time in the darkroom as I can. No matter how often my thoughts stray to Ethan and that day at the park last week, my responsibility is here. I need to be here.

My father is getting worse. His skin is sallow, splotchy with the effort of breathing. The doctor warned me of this: his heart can't pump enough blood to keep up with his body's demands. His legs and feet are swollen. I can't stand this agonizing, creeping death.

The darkroom is my relief. I've always found comfort in the quick movement of my hands, the safelight making everything dark and red like a womb, the slowly emerging images floating in their trays, images I created and can make better, always better.

The competition is a constant reminder niggling in a corner of my brain. I've worked with several prints of Hadley, a few of Ethan, but somehow I can't make myself leave the snapshots of my childhood.

Everything rushes back so clearly. They aren't memories so much as mirrors, reflecting back in an instant the years I'd thought I'd forgotten, had tried to forget, both the bad and the good.

The photo I'm resetting in the enlarger brings a slow sharp ache to the pit of my stomach. A pile of daisies tossed in the trash, the flowers half-escaped from their paper bouquet wrapping, their stems bent, the petals ripped and torn.

My parents fought almost constantly in the last year Mom was alive. Sometimes I crept into the hallway and listened to them. I both wanted to hear and dreaded it simultaneously.

Less than a month before her suicide, Dad came home from a week-long run. They were in the kitchen, supposedly making supper.

"How could you forget?" Mom's voice, loud and high-pitched.

Dad's voice, quiet and placating. "I'm so sorry, Eve. I've been on the road six days. I was just focused on coming home. I wanted to see the girls."

"You always remember to bring them their fancy paper and film. You used to bring me flowers every time. Every. Single. Time. The most beautiful daisies. Do you remember? Do you even care anymore?"

"Of course I do, but I—"

"You know the last time you remembered to bring me flowers? Do you?"

A pause. "No."

"Eight months, Jacob! No one forgets things that are important to them. You show your true feelings loud and clear. You don't love me. Admit it. Tell me the truth."

"I love you."

"Those are just words. They don't mean anything. Anybody can say that. I just can't do this anymore, I can't be here while you're off doing who-knows-what-with some whore—"

"I'm working! I'm on the road, that's all."

"Liar!" Something slammed against the table. I heard a sharp slapping sound.

"Eve, stop!"

I clapped my hands over my ears, but it didn't matter. I could still hear every single thing.

The slapping sound came again. She started to cry. "Do you see what you do to me? Do you see how much pain I'm in?"

"Don't do that, baby. Please."

"What do you expect me to do? What am I supposed to do when you cause so much pain?" Another slap. "Do you see? Do you see now how much you hurt me?"

A chair scraped back. "Please. Eve, I love you. I'm so sorry. I'll do anything. Tell me what you want me to do. Just—just stop."

"Why don't you love me? Do you want me to climb onto the roof and jump off? Do you want me to tie a cord around my neck and hang myself from the ceiling fan? Would that make you happy? You'd be free then."

"No! Please don't talk like that, baby. I'll do better, okay? I promise."

"I'm all alone. You just leave me, every time ..." Her voice dissolved into sobs.

My father's voice, exhausted, defeated: "I have to leave for work. That doesn't mean I don't love you. Okay? Eve?" She didn't respond.

"I'm so sorry about the flowers. I'm sorry I forgot."

There was only the sound of her gasping, hiccupping sobs.

"Why don't you relax? Don't worry about supper," Dad said, his voice artificially cheerful. "I'm gonna go out and grab some pizza and bring it back for the girls, okay? I'll be right back."

I crept from the hallway as he grabbed his jacket out of the coat closet. "Hey, Gingersnap," he said softly. "Keep your mom company for me, will you?"

Obediently, I went and sat next to her. She was slumped at the table, her head in her hands, her shoulders trembling. "Mom?"

She raised her head, tears streaking her mascara down her face in two black lines. One side of her face was bright red. "Your father doesn't love me."

"I love you," I whispered, pain and loyalty squeezing my heart.

"Do you really?"

"I love you, Mom. More than anything. More than the whole world."

She shook her head. "No one understands. How it is to be trapped here, in this house all alone. What it's like for me."

"I understand," I said, but the only thing I really understood was how unhappy she was to be stuck here with us, with me. I was desperate for her to gather me up in her arms and tell me everything would be okay, that *she* loved *me.*

But she didn't.

She scrubbed her arm over her eyes. "You're just a child. You can't possibly understand."

"But I love you. I love you to the moon." My mistake was repeating the line Dad always said to us at bedtime.

Instead of finishing the last line, she flinched. "Don't tell me you're on *his* side."

"No!" I cried.

But it was too late. She looked at me like I'd committed some terrible crime against her. She got up, went into her bedroom and shut the door.

Lux crept out of her room and sank down in the chair beside me. Her small hand slipped into mine. "Is it over?"

"Yes," I said. "It's over."

When Dad came home, Lux and I sat with him and ate greasy pizza slices and butter-soaked breadsticks on paper plates. The bouquet of daisies he'd picked up at the gas station stayed on the table. Mom didn't leave her room.

"Tell me about school," Dad said brightly. He said nothing about Mom's absence.

"I made this with the art papers you got me," Lux said, showing him a roughly shaped origami creature. "What is that? An elephant?" "No!" Lux giggled.

"A rhinoceros?"

"No! It's a llama!"

"That was my next guess, I swear."

"Look, Dad, it's road pizza," Lux said, opening her mouth full of food. Road pizza was Dad's trucker slang for roadkill. Lux thought it was hilarious.

"Ha. Good one." He ruffled Lux's hair. "Who wants homemade hot chocolate?"

"I do! I do!" Lux cried, leaping out of her seat. "Can I help you? I know how to stir super good."

Dad and Lux chattered on like nothing was wrong, like there wasn't a bottomless chasm gaping in the center of our lives. But I couldn't. I sat there numbly, eating cheese and sauce and crust I barely tasted.

The next morning, I found the bouquet in the trash, the delicate daisies crushed and broken.

What happened to us? Who would we have been if Eve hadn't been our mother? How fundamentally have we been changed, altered off our potential course?

And Lux—where was the little girl who used to follow Dad around and hide in his closet, waiting patiently for the moment he would notice her? She would creep around the house, borrowing things that belonged to him—his cologne, the remote control, the latest *Photography* magazine. How had she gotten so lost?

I turn away from the photograph. It seems pointless to think about now. We're both damaged. We're both lost.

I set aside the photographs in neat piles and clean up. I should talk to Dad again. I need to talk to him. If there's some truth that can help me understand my mother's life, her death, all of it, then I want to know it. Dad can tell me.

He's still here, still alive. For now.

# 24

## LYRA

When I enter the bedroom, at first I think he's sleeping. His eyes are closed. The National Geographic's *Greatest Landscapes* book is lying open on his chest. It rises and falls with each labored breath.

When I turn to leave, he calls my name in a strained voice. "Lyra."

"Do you need to rest?"

His face is sallow, the whites of his eyes beginning to yellow. His lips are tinged blue. "Negatory. Come sit. Talk to me."

I obey, settling into the armchair by the bed. I swallow hard. He's getting worse. This is my father, and he is dying. "Are you in much pain?"

"Nothing I can't handle. Don't worry about me, Gingersnap."

"That's impossible."

"I've been worried about you."

"Don't be silly. What for?"

He lifts his hand and passes it across his face. "You haven't been talking much. Are you upset with me?"

"It's—" I want to say, "All right," but I can't. Not anymore. It isn't all right, and never will be. "I just—I want some answers, Dad. I'm tired of all the secrets. I want to talk about our family, our past. Everything. The good and the bad."

He blinks slowly. "It won't do any good. It's over. What does it matter?"

"It matters to me! This is my life, too."

"It's all darkness, Lyra. It's mistakes and bad choices and guilt. Why relive it? God has forgiven me. I have peace."

"Do you? Because I don't. And that's not fair."

He raises his eyebrows. He's not used to push back from me, the good daughter, the obedient one. "Why are you making such a big deal out of this now?"

The silence stretches between us. There's so much I can't bring myself to say. This thing—this prison Mom condemned her own family to—it demands explanation.

We were the ones closest to her. We're the survivors. We deserve an explanation, a reason, an understanding. We deserve to know. I need to know.

"I'm glad you found religion and all that, Dad," I say finally. "I really am. I know you hate talking about it, but—I still need to know. Don't you think I've earned it?"

He stares up at the ceiling. The room fills with the sound of his ragged breathing. "What do you want to hear?"

Conflicting emotions tangle like snakes in my belly. "Tell me about Mom."

"I loved her more than life itself. I tried to make her happy." He pauses, the lines around his mouth taut. "She had a hard time being happy. Things were difficult for her. But I tried. I was on the road so much. I always felt bad about that, but you were so responsible. You took care of things."

I run my fingertips along the ridged cords of the armrest. "I was just a kid."

He coughs. "You were always so strong."

"I shouldn't have had to be." He doesn't say anything.

"How many times did she try to kill herself?"

"I don't remember."

"How can you not know?"

"Three or four, maybe. Sometimes she just took too many pills. She wanted to sleep. She felt overwhelmed."

"She hurt herself," I say.

There's a silence punctuated only by the creak of the bedsprings as he adjusts his bulk.

"She hit herself."

"Yes. I couldn't stop it."

"Why? Why would she do that?"

"I don't know. To try and show me how much pain she was in, I guess."

"Did you love her?"

"Of course. I loved Eve. But it was hard sometimes. She wanted love—she craved it—but she couldn't receive it. Couldn't believe she really had it, even when she did."

My fingers curl into fists in my lap. "I remember fights. I remember her screaming at you, accusing you of not loving her anymore."

"She could never believe she was loved. It didn't matter what I did. It was never enough."

"Did you ever worry about us? Home all alone with her? Did you worry about her hurting us? Because I remember—"

"Yes! Is that what you want to hear? Yes. I worried about her all the time. I know she loved you girls with all her heart. But yes, I worried about you there, with her. Constantly."

Anger sprouts in my gut. "Why didn't you do anything? I don't remember you ever doing anything. You'd come home after being gone for days, and we'd be in the same clothes you left us in. All the food in the fridge was spoiled. One time, we survived on Cheerios and peanut butter because Mom never left her bedroom."

The memories seep into my mind, dark and painful. Once in a while Mom would call to me—never Lux—to bring her water or a plate of crackers. Entering the bedroom felt like an invasion. The drapes drawn tightly over the windows cut off most of the light. The stench of sweat and body odor permeated the stale air. The dark, cloistered room was a mausoleum.

We survived by making it a game. It was Lux who made it seem real. She was vibrant and animated, throwing herself into the role she'd chosen. She made our fantasies come alive through sheer force of will.

Wooden spoons became swords or wands, our father's oversized dress shirts ball gowns or wedding dresses, a scrap of cloth tied around our heads a crown or American Indian headdress, a bowl of stale Cheerios a feast fit for a king.

We lugged our mattresses into the living room and made castles, dungeons, and labyrinths with the couch cushions. We scavenged the cupboards for food, camping out beneath the kitchen table like it was a cave.

Lux made things seem almost normal. She called Mom's depressions 'vacations': "I'm sorry, my Mom can't come to the phone right now. She's on vacation." In reality, Dad was gone and Mom was too sick to brush her own hair, let alone make us breakfast or help us get ready for school.

There was only us. "Why didn't you do anything?"

"I tried," Dad says. "I asked her—I begged her—to get better. She went to three different therapists. Each one prescribed medications that didn't work, or she wouldn't take them. I didn't know what to do. I didn't know how to stop her from being so sad."

My heart thuds against my ribcage. I rub at the slim half-moon scars on my upper arm. "She wasn't just sad."

He shakes his head wearily. "No. She wasn't just sad."

I turn my head so Dad won't see the wetness gathering at the corners of my eyes. "Sometimes she was so angry. Like when she screamed at us, or grabbed our arms. Once, I forgot to hug her when I got home from school. She shredded my homework. She'd get so upset, no matter what we did. And you were either gone or you just watched it happen."

"What do you want from me, Lyra?" His expression hardens. "You want me to admit I was a terrible father? That I escaped through work but left you and your sister to fend for yourselves? That I couldn't love your mother enough to make a difference? That I wasn't a good enough husband to make her want to stay alive?"

My mouth opens, closes. My bones are filled with lead, my limbs too heavy to move. "I didn't mean that."

A shudder ripples through him, his breath coming in ragged gasps. "You're right. I wasn't the father you needed. Or the husband she needed."

His admission only weighs me down more. Maybe he's right. Maybe dredging it all up just causes more pain. "Dad—"

"It's the truth. I betrayed her. Is that what you want to hear?"

"No. I—"

"It was my fault, why she died—why she chose to leave us. What I did ..."

My stomach churns. "What are you talking about?"

But he only shakes his head, panting. His face is an unhealthy, papery white. "It's hard—to breathe."

Instantly, I'm on my feet. "How can I help? Should I call the nurse?"

"Water. Please."

I race to the kitchen and hold a glass beneath the tap with trembling fingers. I see now how his health crumbled beneath the immense load of his guilt, the mass of his body like a weight of shame and remorse crushing him into the grave.

He blames himself. He's suffered every moment since Mom's death. His guilt has destroyed him almost completely.

When I return, I hand him the water and watch him drink, watch the hitch of his Adam's apple in his throat. "Should I call Ellie Delmonte? Are you in pain? She said she can give you something stronger."

He shakes his head and takes another swallow.

I take the glass and put it on the nightstand. Tears tremble in my eyelashes. "She was sick. She would have done it anyway."

He turns his face to the wall. "Maybe."

But the word is empty, and we both know it.

## 25

## LUX

I close the front door to Reese's apartment and hug myself as I step out into the blustery snowstorm. It's been snowing heavily since mid-afternoon.

Everything—the lawn, the driveway, the top of the car, the trees—is carpeted in a thick layer of white. The wind swirls up the loose snow on the ground. Wet flakes pelt down from the rapidly darkening sky.

I follow Reese to his Thunderbird, shivering while he unlocks the doors. It's less than thirty degrees, but Reese is dressed in khaki shorts and a long-sleeved skateboarding shirt.

I slip inside the car and cup my hands over my mouth, breathing hot air on my freezing fingers. "There's only like one day left in February. You'd think it'd be frickin' spring already."

"Remember where we live?"

"Southwest Michigan," I deadpan. "Where we shovel snow to make room for more snow."

"It could be like this for the next two months. Or it could be sunny and seventy next week." Reese flicks on his headlights as he pulls out of the driveway.

"I vote for seventy and sunny."

"You'd be warmer if you wore more than that stupid jean jacket all winter."

I glance at him, his hawk-nosed profile silhouetted against the light from the street lamps flaring through the car windows. "What do you care?"

He just shrugs. We pass a cop car, and Reese swears softly, tapping the brake pedal. The cop keeps going. Our headlights are dim circles of yellow in the gauze of swirling snow.

I kick at the backpack crumpled at my feet. "What's this for?"

"Nothing to worry your pretty head about."

The car is warm now. I fan my fingers in front of one of the heating vents. I'd rather be back at the apartment getting wasted. I haven't had anything all day. The familiar urge, that scrabbling, itching need, that *wanting* starts its dark rustling beneath my skin. "Who is this guy again?"

"I told you before. He's like my uncle."

"*Like* your uncle or your uncle?"

"Anybody ever tell you that you talk too damn much? Chill out, Princess."

He's wound up tight tonight. I settle back in the cracked leather seat and leave him alone. Get through this and then we'll head back to Reese's, where he'll give me what I want, what I need.

I pull my phone out of my jacket pocket. I scroll through my messages. Or lack of them. I still haven't heard from Simone. I click on Felix's name. A single text. *R U Okay?*

My eyes go hot and gritty. I stare at the screen, my fingers hovering over the keys. I hit delete. I can't talk to him. I won't.

At least Autumn is finally texting me.

*Room stinks like cat food. How's Phoenix?*

*Bitchiest. Cat. Ever.*

*Hahaha. Forgive me?*

I don't hesitate. *Always.*

*Where U @?*

I text: *With Reese.*

She responds a second later. *He's sketch, girl.*

*Whatever. Plans?*

*@Simone's*

I click off my phone. Autumn is loyal to a fault. No matter what happens, she always comes back around. Simone, on the other hand, is fierce and territorial. Once she picks a side, it takes forever for the smoke to clear. But it's the three of us. It's always been the three of us.

I imagine what the two of them are doing right now without me. At Simone's, we always watch marathon reruns of Fresh Prince of Bel Air on BET, then work our way through her collection of movie musicals for the thirtieth time. *Moulin Rouge!* is her favorite. Autumn and I always lobby for *Les Miserables*. Or she'll break out an impromptu class and try to teach us swing dancing, lecturing us on the differences between Modern Jive and the Lindy Hop.

Last time we had a sleepover, Simone had a whole stack of books by Naomi Wolf, Gloria Steinem, and Virginia Woolf for her Feminists of the 20th Century research project. She picked up a Kate Chopin book called *The Awakening* and handed it to Autumn. "You'll really like this one," she said with a wink and a pop of her gum. "It's all about sex."

"What—what's that supposed to mean?" Autumn sputtered, almost spitting out her mouthful of Nerds.

"Come on, Skittles. You haven't noticed that almost all your bizarre animal facts are about doing the deed?" I said, giggling so hard I could barely get the words out. Autumn seized the opened bag of peanut M&M's and flicked one at me.

"Candy war!" I cried, chucking a handful of Sour Patch Kids at Simone.

The food fight was truly epic. We laughed so hard my stomach muscles were sore for a week.

My gut twists. I miss them like a phantom limb.

Reese jerks the wheel, and we turn into a long driveway. He parks the Thunderbird next to a red truck covered in snow. "Don't forget the backpack."

I sling the empty pack over my shoulder and climb out of the car. I bow my head against the slanting snow and step inside Reese's boot prints.

The house is an adorable two-story with a wide front porch and crisp yellow siding. There are two white rocking chairs and window boxes that'll hold flowers if this frickin' snow ever stops.

Reese knocks twice. We wait a moment before the door swings open.

"Well, hello and come in," a middle-aged, balding man says, beckoning us into the living room. We step inside, stamping our feet against the threshold.

He closes the door and thrusts out his hand. "My name's Floyd. You're a mighty pretty girl."

I shake my bangs out of my eyes and smile at him, the way I know Reese wants me to. "I'm Lux."

His hand is warm and a little oily, like he's just lotioned it. He looks like a kindly neighbor or someone's favorite uncle. His face is broad and ruddy, his eyes friendly beneath the pale dome of his forehead.

"Nice to meet you, Lux." He steps back and makes a wide gesture with his arms. "Please, make yourself at home. I've got hot chocolate, tea, and cookies in the kitchen, if you'd like some."

"No, thank you." The living room walls are paneled with a rich, dark wood, the carpet a plush, creamy white, and the furniture is all gleaming black leather. A huge entertainment center takes up an entire wall, including a seventy-inch, curved-screen TV. "Nice place."

"You sure about that hot chocolate?" Reese says, slanting his eyes at me.

I remember Dad's version, homemade and the best, richest hot chocolate I've ever tasted. "I guess so. I don't want to cause any extra work." I duck my chin and flash Floyd a shy smile.

"No problem, sweetheart. I already set out a mug and a couple of cocoa packets. The kitchen's right through that archway there. You can leave your bag here, by the door."

I'm being dismissed. "Okay. Thanks." I scrub my feet on the mat, drop the backpack, and head into the kitchen.

The kitchen is so shiny with steel and glass, I have to blink a few times to adjust my eyes. It smells like something burnt, toast or maybe popcorn. Wooden blinds are drawn over all the windows, so I can't see outside.

"Have a seat," I hear Floyd say to Reese. Their voices become hushed. I heat up a mug of water in the microwave, stir in the powdered chocolate, and sit at a round glass table. Smudges and fingerprints smear the underside of the glass, like whoever cleans it only bothers with the top.

I glance at my hands wrapped around the mug. Three long scratches scrape my skin from my knuckles to my wrists. Phoenix. She's doubled in size, at least. She spends her time streaking around my room in snarling, hissing outrage.

She attacks anything that moves, my feet in particular. She won't let me pick her up or even pet her, and she's bitten me more than once with her tiny, needle-sharp teeth. Still, sometimes she'll claw up my bedspread and curl into a ball at the foot of my bed at night. I'll wake up to her warm little body pressed against my ankle or the arch of my foot. It's progress.

I sip my watery drink, the gritty granules sticking to my tongue. It's nothing like Dad's. Thoughts of Dad always seem to slip into my mind unbidden. I don't want to think about him. *He's dying.*

So what? The doctors have said that for years. *This time it's true. This time, it's my fault.*

I jerk myself from my seat, nearly spilling the hot chocolate. I can't sit here like this, allowing my mind to wander. This is when the darkness boils up, when the demons start creeping into the hidden corners of my thoughts. I need to do something, anything.

I head down the hallway, looking for the bathroom. Which door is it? They're all closed.

I push on the second door to the left. The latch gives way with a muted click, and the door swings open. I fumble for the switch, flooding light into a room that's most certainly not the bathroom.

It's a small room lined wall to wall with glass cabinets, every shelf crowded with weird objects. I glance quickly down the hallway, listening as Reese cracks a joke and Floyd laughs. I step into the room.

The first two cabinets contain a display of feathered tomahawks, bent and rusted knives, and ancient guns probably used in the Civil War. The next cabinet is filled with Nazi paraphernalia: a folded flag, a couple of faded red armbands, a beige uniform, stacks of yellowed pamphlets marked with swastikas, and a framed black and white photograph of Hitler. In the picture, Hitler looks benign and almost friendly.

The hairs on the back of my neck prickle.

The next cabinet's shelves are lined with skulls. Some of the skulls are bleached white, others are yellowed. Most are of small animals, probably squirrels, rabbits, and coyotes. One looks like a cat. A few others might be dogs. I shudder.

Three large skulls gape out from the center of the middle shelf. They're unmistakably human. These are not the bleach-whitened bones from the skeletons in science class. These are ochre-stained, almost brown.

My heart plummets, all the blood draining from my head. I take an involuntary step backward. Where would someone get something like this? You couldn't just buy them, could you? I mean, eBay sells some crazy crap, but certainly not this level of disturbia.

Where do you get a human skull? And what kind of twisted, messed up person wants one? Suddenly I can imagine Floyd as one of those serial killers you hear about who used to coach little league and host neighborhood barbecues. The neighbors never had a clue. The whole time, a psychopath lurked behind that bland, innocuous face.

I should leave. I don't belong here. My mouth is dry, my throat thick. Thoughts buzz like bees in my head, nervous and agitated. I wipe my sweaty palms on my jeans. The skulls stare at me accusingly with their blank, empty eye sockets.

Yet, that familiar urge is there, niggling at the back of my brain. I have a bad habit of doing the opposite of what I should. It'll only take a second.

I wiggle the tiny metal key and open one of the glass cabinet doors. I look for something small, something innocuous, something not imbued with evil or death.

The sound of voices drifts from the living room. I reach in, careful not to touch any of the dusty artifacts, pick up a flint arrowhead, and slip it into my pocket.

I flip off the light and hurry out of the room, quietly shutting the door. I pause for a moment in the hallway to calm my thudding heart. The voices in the living room grow louder. Reese and Floyd must have moved from the couch toward the front door.

I dash down the hallway into the kitchen and slide back into my seat at the glass table by the time the two men enter through the archway.

"How was it?" Floyd says, smiling. He looks different, somehow. I imagine the shape of his skull beneath his sloping brow and shiny, pink skin.

I tighten my fingers around the mug to keep my hands from shaking. "Huh?"

His eyes are too big. They stare at me, unblinking. "Your cocoa. Did it hit the spot?"

"Um, yeah, thanks. It was great," I mumble.

He comes closer until he's hovering over me. I sense the heat of his body, smell something stale and slightly sour. "You're a real pretty girl, you know that?"

The arrowhead in my pocket is a burning coal. "Thank you."

"You've got the body of a woman. Reese treating you like a woman?"

My heart jams in my throat. He's not actually saying what I think he's saying. He's old enough to be my dad. Ten minutes ago he seemed bland as milk. Not anymore.

I slide out of my seat and catch Reese's gaze. *Let's go.* "Thank you, sir, for your hospitality."

"Anytime," Floyd says, smiling hard.

I cross the kitchen, aware of Floyd's eyes on me the whole time. I slip my arm around Reese's waist. "It's getting late. My family will be worried. Can you take me home?"

"Yeah, we gotta split." Reese shakes Floyd's hand. "See you next week."

"I'm looking forward to seeing you again, Lux," Floyd says, and there's both desire and threat in his voice.

I stare at my hands as we pull out of the driveway. They're trembling. The headlights reveal the black bodies of trees lining both sides of the road, their gnarled roots draped in snow.

"What's wrong?" Reese asks.

I thrust my hands between my knees. My whole body is freezing. I don't want to tell him.

It's Felix I want to tell. I want to slip my cold fingers between his large, warm hands. I want to press my cheek against his chest and let his calm, steady heartbeat merge with mine. It's his voice I want murmuring in my ear, promising me everything will be okay. But Felix isn't here.

We drive in silence for several minutes. Reese lights up a cigarette at a stop sign and hands it to me. "This will calm your nerves."

I take a drag, roll down the window, and blow the smoke outside. The chilly air pimples my skin. "That guy has skulls in his house. Human skulls."

"You saw those, huh?"

"What the hell? Who does that?"

Reese just shrugs. "They're collector's items, I guess. Like Civil War relics or something? Floyd said you can buy them on the black market."

A shiver runs through me. "Who is he, anyway?"

"He owns that pawn shop in St. Joe, next to the strip mall."

"But that's not all he does."

"What's it to you?" Reese's voice goes hard.

I look out the window at the shadowy darkness. My heart sticks to my ribs like a magnet. "You bought drugs from him. To sell."

Reese blows out a mouthful of smoke. "Get off your high horse, Princess. Don't pretend you care about anything but getting high. Where do you think that comes from?"

"That's not true." But to Reese, it is. That's all he knows about me.

It's all he wants to know. I think of Felix again. Felix with that dopey smile and mop of curls.

Felix was a good thing. I ruined us, like I ruin everything in my life. Hot tears sting the back of my eyelids. I cannot, will not cry. Not for him. And certainly not for me.

We pull into Reese's driveway. I duck my head against the snowflakes twirling down and dash into the apartment. What the hell am I doing? I need to get away from this guy. I need to stop. Pull myself back from the edge.

But first, I need to forget.

I need to drown everything away in a warm liquid haze.

# 26

# LYRA

The doorbell rings. It's early on Wednesday afternoon, and I've just fed Dad his lunch. He can't feed himself properly anymore. Most of his meals now consist of applesauce, yogurt, eggs, and other easily digestible foods.

The days pass slowly and then all at once. It's already mid-March, and I can see the signs now, markers on his slow descent toward the end.

The doorbell rings again. I dump the dirty dishes into the sink and hurry down the hall to the front door.

For a moment, I don't recognize the girl shivering on my front porch. The faux-fur lined hood of her coat is pulled low over her face. She scrubs at her forehead with a gloved hand, revealing a chunk of inky hair.

"Hey, Isabel."

"Hey." Isabel Gutierrez shifts her weight, adjusting the aluminum foil-covered casserole dish tucked under her right arm. Her face is small and sharp. She looks uncomfortable. "My mom wanted me to bring this over."

"Oh. Thanks." The cold air pimples my skin. I'm only wearing loose jeans and a long-sleeved baseball tee. The cold weather hasn't broken. It's still as frigid as January. "Um, do you want to come in or something?"

Isabel glances back toward her car parked in the driveway, which is still running. "No thanks. I've got work in like, fifteen minutes. It's *carne asada* tacos with cilantro pesto. The food, I mean."

It snowed last night. Harsh sunlight reflects off the unbroken plane of white, dazzling my eyes and blurring Isabel's features. "Sounds good."

"I wanted to make an organic seaweed, kale and artichoke dish, but my mom wouldn't let me. Sea greens are actually chockful of nutrients, but she thinks organic food is a ploy by the big companies to charge more money for the same food."

I smile. "When your mom used to babysit for us, she'd always make baked enchiladas smothered with cheese. Remember those warm, gooey churros dusted with cinnamon and sugar?"

Isabel tucks a few strands of hair back beneath her hood. "Horrible for the arteries."

"Yes, well, we didn't worry about that back then." I rub my arms to keep from shivering.

"How's your dad, by the way? I'm supposed to ask."

"Not so good. I think it'll be pretty soon."

"That sucks. But it's for the best, right? I'm sure you don't want him suffering."

"I don't want him to suffer. I don't want him to die, either." I reach for the casserole dish but Isabel doesn't let go. Her arms are almost skeletal, but stronger than I expected.

"I hear you've been hanging out with Ethan Kusuma."

I glance down at my feet. "Yeah. Some."

"Shy nerd-girl and the star football player?"

"He's more than a football player and I'm not a nerd."

Her eyebrows shoot up. "So the rumors are true. How the hell did that happen?"

"We're just friends," I say, suddenly protective of our non-relationship.

Her full lips pinch into a frown. "I guess he's truly fallen off his pedestal big time, hasn't he? Getting Nyah knocked up senior year, giving up his hoity-toity scholarship, and now he's the one saddled with the brat. He's a walking advertisement for birth control."

I clench my teeth so hard my jaw hurts. "You know what I think?"

"What?" she says, the corners of her mouth curling.

She wants this. She wants to piss me off. I jerk the casserole out of her hands. "Thanks for bringing this by. I always did like your mother."

Isabel's face flattens, her features going hard. "I know you're all enamored over him right now, but watch yourself. He's not right for you."

"What's that supposed to mean?"

She shrugs. "Just saying."

"Do you have a problem with me?"

Her smile is like Teflon. "I don't have a problem. Do you?"

I remember how she used to kick me under the table when her mother wasn't looking. How she always took the prettiest Barbie to play with, leaving me with the one with the missing arm or chopped off hair. How I hated going over there, only relishing the moments at the kitchen table with her mother, Maria. I won't let her see that she's getting to me. "Tell your mom thank you."

I shut the door in her face, all the scathing words I want to say burning my tongue. I take several deep breaths, willing my anger down. I don't know her, I don't even like her. I don't care what she thinks. I used to, though. The wild-haired dork desperate for everyone to like her, even the perfect, popular girls. But I was invisible to them.

I shake my head. It doesn't matter now.

I head into the kitchen and put the casserole dish in the fridge. Part of me wants to chuck it in the trash. Dad probably won't be able to eat it, but it'll feed me for several meals, and Lux if she wants some. If she's ever at home.

I check on Dad. "Who was that?" he asks.

"Isabel Gutierrez. You remember that lady who used to baby-sit me and Lux? That's Isabel's mom."

Dad's gaze darts to my face, then skips away. "Maria Gutierrez?"

"Yeah."

"Maria's daughter was at our house?"

"Yep. And she hasn't changed much at all. Hey, are you okay?"

"I—yes, I will be." He takes a deep, shuddering breath. "Just memories."

I lean against the doorway. "You could have her over, if you want. To say goodbye."

He shakes his head vehemently. "No visitors. I don't want anyone seeing me—not like this."

"Your friends won't care what you look like."

He coughs, wheezes hard. "No."

"Fine. If that's what you want. Did you know her well?"

"She was friends with your mother."

I hazily recall Mom picking us up. She and Maria would spend a few minutes chatting. It always took awhile to gather our book bags, coats, shoes, and toys.

Maybe they went out for coffee a few times? I don't remember. I don't remember Mom having many friends. Not at the end, anyway.

Dad has another coughing fit. He struggles to breathe.

I move to the bed. "Here, we need to elevate your chest." I prop some extra pillows against the headboard and help Dad raise himself into a reclining position.

His breathing eases. "Thank you."

"How often is it hard to breathe like this?"

"Mostly at night, but more and more now." He smooths the comforter with his hands. His fingers are swollen sausages. The swelling, the difficulty breathing, the blue-tinged lips, they're all signs the end is near.

"Dad, Ellie said there are things we can do ... to make things easier.

Drugs. Opioids, I think she said. Morphine. It can take some of the pain away."

"No. I don't want any drugs. No relief."

The way he says it, 'no relief.' He's already been in a lot of pain, more than he's let on. And he wants it that way. My throat tightens. "But Dad—"

"That hospice nurse already tried to convince me a dozen times. I don't want anything."

"You're not making any sense."

"It's my choice."

"Mom wouldn't want this."

"I've made up my mind, Lyra."

It's useless to argue with him. This is another of his punishments, his penance.

Desperation builds up inside me. I can't bear the thought of the suffering he's enduring for no reason. "I thought you said God forgave you."

"He has."

"Then why this?" I gesture wildly. "Why are you insisting on feeling all this pain when you don't need to?"

"This is part of it. Please, I need to do this."

"But why? I don't understand."

"Let it go, Lyra." His voice is gravelly, thick with the effort of speaking.

"Dad—"

"Maybe it's time to talk about certain things, while I still can."

I sink heavily into the blue armchair. "What do you mean?"

"I have a life insurance policy."

"No, Dad—"

"Listen! I need to rest soon. Let me say this. Got your ears on?" he says, using his old CB slang.

I nod mutely.

"I have a life insurance policy for five hundred thousand dollars. It cost an arm and a leg with my health, but it's worth it. In my will, the money is split between you and your sister. I want Lux to finish school, go to college. I'm entrusting the money to you. Help her out of this rut she's stuck in. I'm hoping I can talk some sense into her, but in case that never happens, it's up to you.

"Some of that money will go toward my medical expenses and the funeral. Use the remainder of your share to cover the rest of your college education. Promise me you'll go back to school next semester."

I nod again. I can't do anything else. I'm numb. I want to scream, to howl with grief, but nothing comes out. My father's about to die. He's talking about his own funeral like he's going grocery shopping.

The reality of his death strangles me like a creeping vine, roping me to the chair, to the harsh, terrible here and now I don't want to think about, let alone experience.

"Promise me, Lyra."

"I promise," I manage to say.

"You can sell the house or keep it, it doesn't matter to me. Don't spend a lot on the funeral. Don't even have one, if you don't want. I'd like to be buried next to Eve. I've already purchased the lot. Just call the RoseHill Funeral Home, they'll help you with the process and the papers and whatever else needs doing."

"Okay, Dad."

"You've done such a good job. I'm sorry this had to be asked of you." My eyes burn. I rub them with the heels of my hands.

"Will you read a little something to me? Then I'll try to rest. First Corinthians thirteen."

"The love chapter."

Dad raises his eyebrows.

"I went to church, Dad. Remember?"

"Yes, we did, didn't we?" He leans back and rests his head against the pillows. His skin is gray. He looks tired. Bone-tired.

I reach for the Bible on the nightstand. I find the spot and begin to read: "'Love suffers long and is kind; love does not envy; love does not parade itself, it is not puffed up; does not behave rudely, does not seek its own, is not provoked, thinks no evil; does not rejoice in iniquity, but rejoices in the truth; bears all things, believes all things, hopes all things, endures all things. Love never fails. And now abide faith, hope, love, these three; but the greatest of these is love.'"

"Those are the most beautiful words ever written."

I close the book and hold it in my lap, stroking the nubby surface with my fingertips.

The fabric of my skin is too thin, insubstantial, like I could slip into the nothingness that hums around the edges of things. "You wanted me to hear it."

"I hope it'll carry some meaning for you, like it does for me."

I rub my temples. How much can love really suffer? How long can it endure before it cracks, before it's beaten and trampled beneath the brutality of life? Mom loved us—in spite of everything, I still believe this—but love wasn't enough to tether her to this world.

My love for Dad won't bind him to life. And my love for my sister? Do I still even love Lux? Or has my anger obliterated it? Love seems so tenuous, so weak, so easily crushed. "If only love like that really existed."

"It does. It's the way God loves us."

"It sounds nice."

He coughs several times into his fist. "It's more than nice. It's true."

I place the Bible back on the nightstand. My hands ball into fists in my lap. It's all I can do to stay seated. Every fiber of my being screams at me to flee, to get away from the awful sound of his breathing, the stale, heavy air pressing down on me.

"God calls us to love others in the same way." He sucks in a breath.

"No matter what they do. Love endures all."

"You need to rest."

"There's still time for you and your sister. I ran out of chances. Don't waste yours."

"Dad—"

"Please." He's almost gasping. "Make things right with Lux."

I shoot to my feet. Beneath the pain and the grief for my father, there's something else. A deep ache, an empty space lodged behind my heart. I can't. I don't know how.

"I've got to work on my pictures. I need to send them on Monday to get them to the committee on time."

"I'm praying for you."

Prayers won't do any good. They never have.

I hurry from the room before he can see the sudden tears trembling against my eyelids.

# LUX

I try to ignore the knocking on the door, but Lyra doesn't answer it. Then I remember she's out, getting groceries or gas or something. The hospice nurse is here, with Dad in his room. She's not going to get the door.

The knocking doesn't stop. It's insistent, like a little dog that won't stop yapping. Finally, I yank out my earbuds and drag myself to the front door.

It's Felix. "Hey," he says, grinning nervously. "How's Phoenix?"

"If you get too close to her, she'll claw your face off."

"Oh. Um. Good?"

"What are you doing here, Felix? Shouldn't you be in school?" I tighten my sweatshirt around myself.

The day is gray, cold, and miserable. Heavy iron-bellied clouds slink low over the horizon. The snow is slowly melting, the first patches of brown grass starting to show through. I haven't seen the sun in weeks.

"First, it's like 3:30 in the afternoon. And anyway, it's spring break." Felix kicks at a stray pebble on the cement porch. "Look, don't get mad. Autumn asked me to come."

"What? Why?"

He scrapes his hand through his hair. "You dropped out of school,

Lux. No one sees you anymore. Word is you're hanging out with a drug dealer. What's going on?"

"What do you care?"

His smile dissolves. "I do care."

"You sure have a funny way of showing it."

"I messaged you."

I shrug. "I've been busy."

"I'm worried about you. Autumn and Simone are worried about you. We're concerned."

A gust of wind bites into my exposed neck and face. I shiver and thrust my hands beneath my armpits. "Thanks for coming all the way out here to show your *concern*. But I'm *fine*."

"I get that you're mad at me. I'm not so happy with you myself. But still—I care about you, Lux. I want you to be okay."

My throat constricts. I throw him a lethal glare. "Maybe you should've thought about that before you broke up with me."

"I didn't—"

"Save your excuses for someone who cares. Jayda, maybe?"

He looks at me, aghast. "Please don't do this."

"Do what? Call you on your B.S.?"

"No. That's not what I meant. It's not what I'm trying to say." His hands clench and unclench at his sides.

Where's he been all this time? Nowhere. He left me, abandoned me just like everybody else. "I don't really care what you have to say."

"Why are you acting like this? What's wrong?"

"Nothing," I spit out. I've had enough of this conversation. I've had enough of his puppy dog eyes and his sad, confused face. "Please, do us both a favor and go away."

"We really cared about each other. I believe that. We had—"

"I don't know what delusions of grandeur you're under," I interrupt, "but you seem to be exaggerating your importance in my life. Frankly, you were boring. You're the human equivalent of a sweater vest."

His eyes go dim. He steps back. "You don't mean that."

"Yes, I 100% do." The words are like a blade twisting in my belly.

"Okay," he says, almost to himself, like he's deciding something. "Okay."

The look on his face deflates me. Hot energy drains out of my veins and suddenly all I can think about is how much I've missed him. How it felt when he touched me. The prickling heat of it. The fire.

What it was like, the first time we went to the park that muggy July night. It was our eighth date, and I was falling hard, harder than I ever thought I would. We spread a blanket on the bed of his truck and looked up at the sky unfolded like a scroll. He asked me to show him the stars.

He held my hand and I listened to him breathe. I told him the myths my mother had taught me during all those midnight picnics staring up into the dark. I didn't know yet how much he would share my love of astronomy, of galaxies and stars and planets all spinning above us in space.

I hadn't retold the stories to anyone but Lyra, and that was years ago. I loved Simone and Autumn with all my heart, but they didn't understand. They didn't see the magic. I wanted him to see, to feel it in his bones like I did.

"Tell me a story," Felix whispered. He traced circles on my bare arm.

I took a deep breath and gazed up at Leo the great and terrible lion, whose coat could not be pierced by sword or arrow. And Orion, the mighty hunter, whose boasting caused the gods to punish him for his vanity, sending the small Scorpius to sting him to death.

"My favorite is Andromeda," I said, trying to ignore the fireworks exploding inside my skin. "She was a princess, the beautiful daughter of King Cepheus and Queen Cassiopeia. The queen boasted throughout all the land that her daughter Andromeda was more beautiful even than the Nereids, the lovely companions of Poseidon, god of the sea. Infuriated by Cassiopeia's hubris, Poseidon sent a sea monster to ravage their kingdom.

The only thing that could stop the beast was to sacrifice Androm-eda. Heartbroken, the king and queen did as they must, chaining their daughter to a rock in the middle of the sea.

"Luckily, the hero Perseus was nearby and heard Andromeda's cries. When the monster emerged from the sea, Perseus slew the beast and saved the princess. They were married and had many children. After her death, the goddess Athena placed her in the sky as a testament to love."

"I get why you like that one." Felix told me the origin story of all his favorite comic characters, from Daredevil and Wolverine to Jessica Jones and Squirrel Girl. I tried to focus, but all I could concentrate on was how my skin was turning to liquid fire.

Finally, finally, he bent and kissed me, his lips soft and warm. It was sweet and slow and dazzling. Insects buzzed in the grass. The trees rustled softly in the breeze. The stars above us flickered and winked like candles.

My heart was a jar full of fireflies.

But that was before.

I watch him trudge back to his car, shoulders hunched against the wind. He's abandoning me all over again.

The dull gray light drains all the color out of the world.

2 8

---

# LYRA

I spend hours every day in the darkroom while Dad rests. I've made several good prints from the negatives of Ethan and Hadley. My favorite is one of Hadley cupping a wet stone in her outstretched hands, her face alight with the thrill of discovery.

But it's still not right. Technically, the print is perfect. The composition, the exposure, the clarity—everything is good. But I'm not satisfied. The picture is missing something, something I'm not giving it.

I groan and lean back against the sink. My legs and back ache from hours spent standing and bending. The wooden table is scattered with dozens of technically perfect prints, but I've rejected all of them.

The photographs for the competition must be better than perfect. They must be art. Anyone with a bit of skill could create these pictures. There's nothing in them that speaks to me.

Mom always said art was supposed to speak. Sometimes it was beautiful or ugly or painful, but it always said something. It always had a soul.

There's no soul in these pictures.

It's the candid snapshots of my family I keep turning back to. My father, my mother, my sister. The negatives aren't great. Most are over or underexposed or unfocused, the composition lopsided or cramped. And yet, they're beautiful in their imperfection. They make my heart ache with a pain so savage I can barely breathe. They make my veins bleed, my bones splinter.

It's a risk, using these photographs instead of the safe landscapes, portraits, or even the abstract art other students will submit. The final prints I've managed to cobble together create a portrait of a fractured family, a cluster of damaged, wounded people lost in the orbits of their individual pain and heartbreak.

It's a dangerous thing to display loss so openly, without regard. It's the only way I know how.

I push aside the images of Ethan and his daughter, the photographs of the river, the house, the ones I convinced Darcy to let me take at the mechanic's shop. Instead, I spread out the photographs that make up my past.

Beads of sweat gather at my hairline. I rub the moisture away with my forearm. I feel lighter than I have in days. Down here, in the quiet warmth and the red haze, I'm free to relive my memories, to relish some and discard others, to create my family anew, as we used to be, as we could have been.

Who might my mother have been, without her illness? An artist, a mother, a wife. Who might we all have been, without that blot in her brain?

I sift a picture out of the pile in front of me. In it, Mom looks happy. She's seated at her easel in the living room, newspapers spread below her to catch any stray blobs of paint. Her gaze is directed at the painting, her delicate eyebrows scrunched together and her lower lip pinched between her small white teeth. Her long braid loops over the wing of her shoulder, and she grips a loaded brush in her right hand.

Behind her, slightly unfocused, Dad sits on the edge of the couch. He's much younger, and thinner. Grief hasn't yet etched itself upon every cell of his body. He's watching his wife, a smile tugging at the corners of his lips. His face fairly glows with devotion. He really loved her. We all did.

I pick up another picture, one Dad or Lux must have taken for me.

I'm in my pajamas, sitting next to Mom and gazing up at her with what can only be described as adoration. My face is blotchy with hundreds of freckles. Freckles down my arms, across my collarbone, my chest.

A memory surges through me. My mother, curled next to me in bed, nested in a pile of blankets. I was in fifth grade. It was nearly Christmas, and Mom and I had strung white fairy lights across my window.

Mom was telling me a bedtime story about the myth of Chiron the half-man, half-horse centaur. "He offered to take the place of Prometheus, who was doomed to an eternity chained to a rock while an eagle pecked out his liver," she said. "Gross, right?"

I usually loved Mom's stories, but that night I couldn't concentrate on the lilt of her voice. I lay stiffly, my arms at my sides, my eyes stinging with tears until the fairy lights above me blurred into pointy stars.

"As his reward, the Greek god Jupiter placed Chiron in the sky as the constellation Sagittarius." I didn't say anything.

"Tell me what's wrong," Mom said, stroking my arm.

Bile roiled in my gut. "Jamal Harris said my freckles are ugly," I choked out. "He said I have some kind of skin disease."

Beside me, Mom's body went still. Her nostrils flared. "That is completely unacceptable. What did your teacher say?"

"I don't know."

"You didn't tell her? Lyra, you must report bullying. I'll call a meeting with the principal tomorrow."

"No!" Acid burned the back of my throat. I knew what would happen. The kids would get even meaner. I didn't tell her it wasn't just Jamal. Sammy Amlaner told me I had "gingervitis" in a voice dripping with disgust, and before that, LouAnn DeNido announced to the whole class that my freckles looked like bloody pimples. My freckles were ugly. I was ugly. "Please don't, Mom."

"Why in the world not?"

I rubbed my fists against my burning eyes. "It will just make it worse."

She stared at me, that blue vein in her forehead throbbing. "Lyra—"

"Please, Mom." I tensed, waiting for her rage.

"I just can't believe a child could be so cruel! How could—?"

"Mom!"

She took several deep breaths and closed her eyes. She pressed her hands over her chest, like she was physically forcing down her anger. "All right. If you're sure."

"I'm sure, Mom. Please. Don't make it a big deal." She traced her finger along my jawline, my nose.

I flinched, turning my head toward the wall.

"Oh, Lyra," she breathed. "Do you know how lucky you are?"

"I'm not lucky."

"You have the stars etched on your skin. Here's the bull's horns of Taurus on your arm and Sagittarius with his bow and arrow beneath your collar bone. And look, there's Leo, his lion's head and body right here above your elbow. You don't have to look to the sky to chart your future. It's mapped right here, on your own body. This is a gift, Lyra. People like us, we determine our own destiny."

I breathed in the scent of her jasmine shampoo. Her green eyes were so big, so bright, so close. I wanted so badly to believe her. Anything she said, she believed in that moment with her whole self, and she could inject that belief right into the center of your beating heart. "Really, truly?"

"Really, truly," she said, stroking my hair. "You are so, so special."

The door banged open. Lux stood in the doorway, little fists on her hips, eyes blazing. "I wanna be special, too!"

Mom sat up quickly. She sucked in her cheeks, her half-smile frozen on her face. "You are, Shortcake. Of course you are. Just in a different way."

Lux didn't buy it. Her lower lip jutted out, tears springing into her eyes. Her skin deepened to a mottled shade of crimson. "You love her more!"

"That's not true." Mom's voice hardened. "Stop it."

"I hate you!" Lux shrieked. She whirled and ran down the hall.

Mom's mouth contorted, dark emotions flitting across her face. She leaped off the bed and ran after Lux. "What did you just say to me?"

I shoved back the covers and followed her into the hallway, dread curdling my stomach.

Mom caught Lux by the arms. "Take it back! You know how hard I try for you? How much I've sacrificed for you? Take it back right now!"

But Lux's face was frozen in shock, her mouth hanging open, her eyes wide and terrified.

Mom shook her. "You don't love me? That's what you're telling me?"

I shrank against the wall. Lux's terrified gaze flickered toward me. I tried to say something, but no sounds came out. My mind was spinning. Everything changed so fast, I couldn't think straight.

I felt like I'd been dumped from the warm safety of a lifeboat straight into a cold, surging sea. I was flailing, swimming down into darkness instead of up, into the light.

"Tell me you love me, you ungrateful little brat!" "You're hurting me!" Lux wailed.

"Say it to my face! Say it!"

"I love you!" I yelled it as loud as I could. "I do! I love you!"

She didn't hear me, or she didn't care. She shook Lux hard, digging her nails into her upper arms.

Dad's footsteps pounded down the stairs. "Hey guys," he said in a bright, forced voice. "Who wants my special homemade hot chocolate?" "Daddy!" Lux cried.

"Take it back," Mom said, grimacing. She was shaking. Her eyes were huge, rimmed with red. "Just take it back."

Dad put his hand on her shoulder. "Eve, how about you help me in the kitchen?"

"Please!" Her voice changed, taking on an edge of panic, despair. "Tell me you love me."

"Eve."

She stood up, slowly releasing her grip on Lux's arms.

Lux sagged to the floor, sobbing. Even from several feet away, I could see the dark red divots in her skin, the red blooming in the cracks.

"She hates me, Jacob. My daughter hates me."

"No one hates you," Dad said. "We all love you, Eve. Don't we girls?"

I nodded fiercely. "I love you, Mom. I love you."

Mom stared down at her hands. She opened and closed her fingers, like she was supposed to be holding something, but had forgotten how. "I try so hard, Jacob. I'm trying."

Dad put his arm around her. "I know. We know. Why don't you head upstairs? We'll get that hot chocolate started right away."

He gently pushed her until she moved on her own. She shuffled up the stairs, leaning heavily on the railing.

"Dad," I said.

He crouched down in front of Lux. He touched her arm and gazed at the red on his finger like he'd never seen blood before. His jaw clenched, his face hardening into an emotion I didn't recognize. It looked a lot like fear. "You're all right, Shortcake."

But she didn't respond. She rocked back and forth, her arms crossed over her chest.

"Hey, hey." He patted her shoulders gently.

Still nothing.

"It's okay, Lux," I said.

"Come on, Shortcake," Dad said, a hint of alarm entering his voice. "I love you to the moon."

She took a ragged breath, finally looking up at us. Her lower lip trembled.

"You can say it, sweetie. Come on. Do it for me."

"I love you all the way back."

"That's my girl. Good girl. Let's go get a treat, okay?"

She nodded through the tears leaking down her cheeks. Dad hefted her into his arms, and we went upstairs.

Mom sat at the kitchen table, pale and shaking. Her hands were clenched in her lap, the vein throbbing in her neck. "I don't know what happened. I didn't mean to. I just—I'm a terrible mother. I'm so, so sorry."

I ran to her immediately and threw my arms around her.

Dad put Lux down. She stood there for a moment, hesitant.

"I'm so, so sorry, baby. I don't know what came over me." "I'm sure it was an accident," Dad said.

"It was an accident," I echoed, squeezing my mother's bony shoulders.

"Come here, baby."

Lux went to her, the tide-pull of our mother too much for her to resist. Mom hugged her fiercely. "Please forgive me," she whispered into her hair. "I didn't mean it. I'm so sorry."

We forgave her instantly, every one of us.

That's what it was like, all the time. Good bled into the bad. Things could change on a dime, one second happy and content, the next a black storm of misery or rage.

I rub my eyes and blow out a mouthful of air. The memories are like tacks hammered into the tender flesh of my brain. I force myself to keep working.

I take a pair of scissors and cut the photos at different angles, until each picture is separated into four or five triangular shapes. I carefully glue each photo onto black mounting board with spray adhesive, recreating the photo like a puzzle with slight spaces between the pieces.

The result is a slightly disjointed image—you know what it is, but you also see the fracture. I stand back and look. My breath snags in my throat.

I see now what I couldn't see before.

There is so much pain here.

But there is a kind of beauty, stark and brave amidst the ugliness.

Sometimes, it's the ugly things that make us feel the most.

This is it.

This is what I need.

———

There's a sudden banging sound at the front door. I leave the darkroom and head for the stairs.

Lux stands in the foyer, balancing a khaki messenger bag on her hip as she tries to finagle her key into the deadbolt to unlock the front door. It's one of those double-key deadbolts, the same one we've had ever since I can remember. You need to unlock the door from the inside.

I rest one foot on the bottom stair. "What are you doing?"

Lux's shoulders flinch and hunch inward. She half-turns to look down at me. Her skin is blotchy, her eyes jittery, her gaze flitting from me to the door to the floor. "Nothing."

"Look, this isn't a good time to leave. Dad needs us here."

Lux jiggles her keys in her fist. Her pupils are pinpricks in her watery green eyes. "You're not my keeper. I can go wherever I want."

"Are you even listening to yourself?" I pause, staring up at her. "Are you high?"

Her gaze flies to me and flaps away. She shifts her weight and again tries to jam her key into the lock. The key clicks against the metal, nowhere near the hole.

I stomp up the stairs and stand in the foyer, only a few feet from Lux.

My jaw clenches. "Dad keeps asking for you."

Lux stiffens. She says nothing for a long moment. "I don't have to explain myself to you."

"Look, I'm telling you. There's not much time. Whatever it is you're doing—it can wait."

"You don't know anything. You think you do, but you don't."

I put up both hands. "Okay, fine."

"Besides, he's got you, doesn't he?" Lux says in a gritty, strangled voice. This time she hooks the key in the lock and swings open the door. "That's all he really wanted, anyway."

I blink against the daylight flooding the foyer. "Are you in some kind of trouble?"

"Always trying to fix everything, Little Miss Perfect. Sorry to burst your precious bubble, but I'm beyond fixing."

I think of the memories the photographs dredged up. I think of Lux as a little girl, who used to make up all those games and stories. The one who used to crawl into my bed and wrap her scrawny arms around me late at night.

Where is that Lux now? Somewhere along the line, she cut herself off entirely from me and Dad, encasing her heart in barbed wire that ripped your flesh if you got too close, if you tried to touch her.

When did that happen? When Mom died? Did the process of ossifying her heart begin then? Did we betray Lux by not being there for her when she needed us? Entangled in our own grief, did we inadvertently do something Lux saw as unforgivable?

I reach out and touch her arm. "That's not true."

She snatches her hand back like she's been burned. "It's not like you care anyway. You hate me."

"I've never hated you."

Something closes over Lux's face. "You always were a horrible liar." And then she's gone.

After a moment, the car roars out of the driveway. The front door's still open, letting in drafts of freezing air.

I just stand there, paralyzed on the top step.

Alone.

## 29

## LYRA

Ethan texts me Friday afternoon. *Is the nurse there? H wants 2 go sledding. U in?*

There are a few softly rolling hills in southwest Michigan. The biggest one is at Brewster's Farm. The owners charge five dollars for a giant black tube and hot chocolate in Styrofoam cups. I haven't been there since senior year, when Edward Thorpe tried to stack two tubes, fell off like an idiot, and sprained his ankle. Besides, it's the third week of March and there's hardly any snow.

*No snow,* I text back.

*Hello? Snow Machines. Closed for season this week. Last chance. H misses U.*

My stomach somersaults. Just Hadley? My fingers hover over the screen. But no, this isn't me. I can't type that. I'm not a flirt. I'm the quiet one, the wallflower. I don't know how to do this stuff. But still, I want to go. Badly.

*When?*

*4. See U There.*

It's already 3:45 p.m. I throw on some insulated leggings and track pants, a sweater, and my puffy black coat. I peek my head in Dad's room. Ellie is sitting in the navy La-Z-Boy, a book in her hands. She's reading *The Wizard of Oz* aloud, one of Mom's favorite books. She must have pulled it from the bookshelf, or maybe Dad asked her to read it. Dad's eyes are closed, his breath ragged in his chest.

Ellie looks up, her giant hoop earrings swinging. Ropes of rose-colored pearls encircle her neck. The light winks off her rings, the amber stones the size of nickels. "How are you, my dear?"

"Is he sleeping? I heard you reading."

"I like to think we can still hear each other, even in the deepest sleep. I'm hoping it gives him good dreams."

"Is he—is it almost time?"

"I'm afraid so, honey. He'll be at peace soon."

"Okay," I mumble, because what else is there to say?

Ellie gestures at my clothes. "You going somewhere? Please tell me it involves a boy."

The bright red creeping up my neck tells her all she needs to know.

She smiles wide, her raspberry lipstick bleeding a little into the fine lines around her mouth. "Well, you look lovely. Look how you want to feel, that's what I always say. Have fun, darling. You deserve it."

On my way to Brewster's, I stop at the post office to overnight my package of prints for the committee's March 28th deadline. If they approve me, my spot in the gallery is ensured—my shot at the prize money, the internship, my chance at a whole new life.

I say a quick prayer over the box, not knowing to whom exactly, maybe to the universe.

If I deserve anything, I want so badly to deserve this.

———

I shield my eyes from the sun. It's such a relief from the dark foreboding of the house, the walls closing in. Death crouching in the corners, waiting to pounce.

I need a distraction.

Who am I kidding? Ethan Kusuma is more than a distraction. My stomach somersaults again when I see them waiting for me at the bottom of the hill.

Hadley's bundled in a fuzzy pink coat and a hat with yellow pompoms. She squeals and hugs me like we're best friends. It doesn't take much to earn the complete loyalty and adoration of a two-year-old.

Ethan's dressed in dark jeans and a black leather coat, a gray knit cap squashing down his hair. The corner of his mouth twitches. "Hey, Lyra. You prepared for an adventure of epic proportions?"

The sound of my name on his lips sends an uncomfortable zap of electricity sparking through me. I clear my throat. "Let's do this thing."

We pay the fee, grab our tubes, and trudge up the hill. There are a dozen families with little kids yelling, laughing, and slip-sliding down the hill. No one our age. Because they're all away at college or working, I think with a twinge.

Ethan settles in a tube at the top of the hill. I help Hadley climb on Ethan's lap and sit down next to them on a second tube. "I must warn you," Ethan says. "Hadley and I play to win. Are we gonna demolish her, Chipmunk?" "Yeah! Me win!" Hadley yells.

"That's my girl."

"Then let's race!" I push off with my hands and whoosh down the hill. The cold air nips my cheeks. My hair lifts off my neck and flies behind me.

Ethan and Hadley's tube punches into mine at the bottom of the hill.

"Me win?" Hadley asks hopefully.

"You sure did," I say, trying to climb out of the tube without falling on my face like an idiot. "Just you, though. Not your daddy. He definitely lost."

Hadley giggles. "Again!"

We go again. And again. After an hour, I can't feel my fingers anymore. We stop at the little station at the top of the hill to grab steaming hot chocolate in Styrofoam cups. Hadley plops down on her butt and plays happily with clumps of snow. I sip the watery hot chocolate through a straw, warmth filling my stomach.

Ethan stands next to me, his presence like a wall of static electricity. "How's your dad?"

"It's almost time."

"I'm sorry. That sucks."

I kick at a clod of snow with my boot. I realize I want to tell him everything. It hurts too much, keeping it all inside. "He keeps telling me he's found peace, but he seems upset, and he won't talk to me about it. Like he feels guilty about something."

"We all do things we regret in life. Maybe when your life flashes in front of your eyes, all you see is everything you did wrong."

My throat tightens around my words. "He refuses to take pain medication to make the end easier. That's the real reason he wanted to come home to die. He wants to suffer."

"That must be really rough for you," Ethan says gently. His eyes are warm and kind.

I blink rapidly, look away. "I hate seeing him in so much pain."

He touches my arm. "I know."

"Daddy!" Hadley holds up two handfuls of snow.

"You rock, Chipmunk."

Her face lights up when he looks at her. My heart twists in my chest.

"Ball! Ball!" She mashes the snow between her fingers.

I squat down in front of her. I don't want to think about death now, here, when I'm surrounded by so much life. "Watch my cup, okay?" She takes the Styrofoam cup and holds it carefully.

I mash up a chunk of snow and roll it between my gloved hands until it's mostly round. She trades me the hot chocolate and I hand her the snowball. "Ball. Right?"

She grins so hard little dimples pop out on both sides of her cheeks. "Ball!"

"What do you say, Hadley?" Ethan says.

"T'ank you," she says in the most serious, adorable voice I've ever heard.

I stand up, brushing snow off the knees of my pants. When I glance at Ethan, he's staring straight at me. The corner of his mouth tugs into one of his cocky smirks. My pulse jumps in my throat, my palms suddenly damp even though I'm freezing. "What?"

"You," is all he says. It's a line, probably one he's used a dozen times before on a dozen different girls. He's looking at me like he knows my heart is palpating and my thoughts won't organize themselves properly. He knows, and he likes it.

Heat flushes my neck and travels up into my face. He might like it, but I don't. I'm exposed and vulnerable in all the ways I hate. A sharp, spiky resentment pricks me. "Can you stop please?"

Ethan rolls his shoulders and clasps his hands behind his back. His smug grin only broadens. "Stop what?"

"Nothing. I just—I don't know."

"Don't leave me hanging. Spit it out."

I lick my dry, chapped lips. "Just—everything was fine a few minutes ago. But now you're acting like you used to, back in high school."

"What does that mean?"

"Arrogant. Entitled."

His eyebrows knit together. "Big words, college girl. You think I'm arrogant?"

I shrug uncomfortably. I need to shut up. I'm making things worse, but the words keep tumbling out of my mouth. "Honestly? You're a jock.

In high school, you strutted around like a male queen bee. No offense."

His smile fades. "No offense?"

"I mean, why wouldn't you, right? You had everything—popularity, good looks, sports, all the girls."

"And you think that makes me what? Shallow? Stupid? An asshat?"

My face flames. "No. I mean, I don't know. Maybe."

He takes a step back, folds his arms over his chest. "Wow."

I hate the way he's looking at me, like he's disappointed. "I'm not trying to judge you or anything."

"It sure sounds that way." His voice has an edge to it. "You know, I'm not an awful guy now, and I wasn't then either. I never bullied anybody or treated girls badly. Do you have evidence to the contrary?"

"No."

"You know what else? I kind of resent the implication. Yeah, I loved to play football. I went to some parties, drank some beer, had fun. I loved my girlfriends and was good to my mom. My life was pretty good. I'm not going to apologize for that."

"I never said—"

"You did." Ethan keeps his gaze on me, his face inscrutable.

For a long moment, neither of us says anything. The cold seeps in through my track pants. Hadley draws designs in the snow, giggling to herself. I've upset him, and the suckiest thing is I don't even know what makes me do crap like this.

This is what I do, what I always do. This is why I've never had a real relationship. I go into retreat mode. I can't let anybody in. Because why? Because I need control. I need things ordered and neat, in nice predictable boxes. Because I know this doesn't mean anything to him.

This is all just a game, a distraction, a conquest. And what is it to me? More than that, whether I want it to be or not. It is. My heart is pulling me in directions I'm afraid to go. Standing here, it's becoming increasingly clear that I'm not in control of anything.

Abruptly, he lets out a hard laugh.

"What?"

"You're so dead set on pigeonholing me a jock, and yet I've spent most of my life fighting against the nerdy Asian stereotype. You should have seen them at MSU. My roommate, all the guys in the dorm—they were shocked my scholarship was for *athletics*. Like we can't jump, hold onto a damn ball." There's something else in his voice now, a sliver of resentment.

"And that's funny?"

"Yeah, yeah it is." He shakes his head, a dark lock of hair falling into his eyes. "Maybe you're right. Maybe I played a jock too well."

"No," I say firmly. "I was out of line."

He goes silent again. We both watch Hadley scooping up piles of snow. The wind picks up, scraping through the trees at the bottom of the hill. "I need to tell you something."

"You don't have to tell me anything."

"No, I want to. When Nyah got pregnant, I was as scared out of my mind as anybody. But my dad ran out on us when I was seven. I still remember it. It was the worst day of my life. He went back to Indonesia and got himself a brand-new family. No need for the old one anymore.

"There was no way in hell I was turning into him. It wasn't really even a decision. I knew I was gonna be there for this kid. You know what else? I didn't fully get what that would mean, that it would be me giving up my dreams. I was the guy, so of course I'd still get to go to college, still get to play ball. Sounds selfish, doesn't it? You pegged me as just that kind of guy."

Shame forms a stone in my throat. It's hard to swallow. "I'm sorry if—"

But he just keeps going. "Nyah's parents kicked her out. They were hardcore born-again Christians, and not the forgiving kind. We took her in. She moved in with my mom when she was six months pregnant. I went off to college, and then Hadley was born. Instead of partying on weekends, I came back here. I changed diapers and fed her bottles while Nyah tried to sleep. But it wasn't enough. Nyah was exhausted, depressed, and when Mom called me, I knew from the tone of her voice. Nyah was gone. I spent a week wrestling with my own conscience. And then I came home."

I hear the pain in his voice, the sacrifice that a decision like that cost him. He had big dreams, just like I do. He had the talent and the scholarships to go with it. He's only twenty-one, still at the beginning of his life, yet he gave up that big shiny future in exchange for diapers, exhausted nights, and long hours stuck in a small-town job.

And all this time, I've still thought of him as who he was—or who

I thought he was. I didn't have a clue. "Ethan, I didn't mean what I said."

"I think you did."

"I was wrong."

He just looks at me.

This time I don't look away from his gaze, even though my mouth goes dry and my stomach drops down to my toes. "I'm sorry." I want to say more. I want to put my hand on his arm, his chest, feel the beat of his heart. But I can't. I don't.

"Apology accepted," he says finally.

"Thank you."

"Forget it. It's not like you're the only one who's ever stereotyped a baller."

I sip the last of my hot chocolate. Behind us, kids squeal and shriek in delight as they sled down the hill. "Are you angry at Nyah?"

"For awhile, yeah. I resented the hell out of her. But you know what? It takes two to tango." He scoops up Hadley and brushes snow off her fuzzy pink coat. "And now I have this."

"She's wonderful."

A shadow crosses his face. "I still miss football. I miss my friends. I miss college. It's right, what I'm doing. I know that. But that doesn't make it easy."

"It's hard trying to figure out how to be loyal to your family *and* have your dreams." I think about my mother and her painting, my father and his photography. I think about Lux, drifting so far away I can barely see her anymore.

I got away. I escaped. I left Dad and Lux all alone in that cramped, shadowed house. I got to chase my dreams. Where did that leave her? I blink the thoughts away. "Maybe it's impossible."

"Exactly. Most people don't get both."

Hadley whispers something in Ethan's ear. He grins. "The Chipmunk wants to know if you'd like to go get ice cream."

I raise my eyebrows. "You aren't frozen enough?"

"Not yet. I can still kinda sorta feel my toes. So? You in?"

"Wanna icy?" Hadley says to me, making a goofy face.

"Ice cream in winter is one of our things, just so you know."

"Seriously?"

"Yep. Superman ice cream is our absolute, all-time favorite dessert. We love to make our lips blue, don't we, Chipmunk?" He tickles her ribs and Hadley squeals with delight.

"Now you're just weirding me out." But I can't help it. In spite of everything, I'm smiling.

This feels right. It feels good. I don't want to fight this warm, happy feeling infusing my very pores. I don't want to retreat, to shut down, to run away.

I want to be right here, right now. Nothing more and nothing less. "How can I say no?"

# 30

# LUX

It's been three days since the last fight with Lyra. I can't bear it in that house. Every day, I pause outside his door, determined to go in this time.

The harsh sounds of his breathing keep me up at night. I can hear it rattling deep in his lungs. It sounds like someone is pressing Saran wrap over his face. Each ragged breath is a battle for survival. A battle he's losing.

Sometimes, the breathing noises stop. My heart clenches in my chest as I wait, ticking off the seconds, my mind screaming, *Breathe, breathe!* Just as abruptly, it jerks to a start again. Each time, fear lodges in my heart like a splinter. Each time, I back slowly away from the door, my heartbeat thundering in my ears, my stomach churning.

Tonight, I stand in front of his door like every other night, staring at the grains in the fake wood. My body weighed down, my legs cemented with dread. The thought of facing him, of meeting his sad, defeated eyes and knowing the truth—that I caused this, that I caused it all—It makes me want to sink through the floor and disappear. Forever.

He doesn't really want to see me. Why would he? Why dredge up sleeping monsters? Why remind him of the complete and utter failures of his youngest daughter? He must hate me. If I were him, or even Lyra, I would hate me too. I do.

Still, I have to do this. He's my father. My legs are jelly, my heart sloshing like water in the cavity of my chest. I push open the door, listen to it creak on its hinges. I take a step into the room, then another. I stand there and stare at him.

The light is on, but he's sleeping. Dad's eyelids are stained eggplant purple, his lips blue. His sagging jowls are yellowed with fatigue and sickness.

He looks nothing like how I remember him. When I was little, I used to shadow him like a spy. I sat for hours behind his blue La-Z-Boy when he crashed in front of the television, creating my little menagerie of origami creatures and waiting for him to wake up.

I followed him to the kitchen or laundry room, creeping at his heels. I hid in his closet, crouched among his shoes, the bottoms of his dress shirts curtaining my head. Sometimes I hid under his bed, lying flat on my belly, my cheek pressed into the carpet, trying not to sneeze as I breathed in the dust.

Occasionally, he would notice me. "Hey, Shortcake, you scared me," he'd say, placing his hand over his heart. "Don't get lost in there." He would pat my shoulder or ruffle my hair.

Sometimes I went through his things, dumping out the hamper when no one was around, smoothing the wrinkled clothing, or picking through his drawer in the bathroom.

I explored his pockets, fingering the quarters and dimes, a rubber band, bits of lint, crumpled receipts from meals and hotels on the road. Certain things I tucked away in the top drawer of my dresser: a chewed pen cap, a paper clip, a stale, unused stick of gum.

If someone asked me back then, I couldn't have explained why I did those things. It was a game, a mystery, the only way I had of knowing my father. It made me feel close to him, like we shared a secret. He belonged to Lyra, the same way my mother belonged to her. She stole their love and attention with her talent, her art. All I could do was make useless shapes out of stupid paper.

I stare at my father. He could be dead but for the labored rise and fall of his chest, the hoarse sounds as air grates from his lungs. He's my father. The only parent I have left. And he's about to die.

The black hole opens in front of me. Dark, dense gravity pulling me in. I'm teetering on the edge. Then toppling, falling, spinning down, down, down.

I back out of the room and flee the house.

31

# LYRA

Death is near.

I've spent most of the last three days sitting by my father's bed, holding his hand or reading to him. I sleep curled in the navy armchair, my nightmares punctured by the constant rattle of Dad's breathing.

His hands and feet are frigid, mottled a sickly whitish-blue. Half the time, he's no longer aware of my presence. He slips in and out of consciousness, sometimes waking up confused or frightened. Several times he's called me Eve.

I contacted the hospice doctor. He told me this was normal, a common part of the process. *How is death normal?* I wanted to scream. But of course, it is. It's the most normal thing in the world.

When I called Ellie, she offered to come straight over. I declined. Only family should be here. It is what Dad wanted. I can do this, I can bear witness to his pain.

It's Lux who should be here. She's a ghost, coming home to sleep or grab food or change her clothes. I'm the one taking care of her cat, making sure it has food and water, cleaning out the litter. I've texted and called her dozens of times, but she won't respond. I don't know how to reach her.

I'm so emotionally exhausted, I can barely spare a thought for anything other than Dad, other than this slow, horrific process of dying.

It's six thirty in the evening on Tuesday night. March 28th. Four hours ago, I received the email I was waiting for.

The committee loved my work.

I'm a finalist.

I should be happy. I will be. I know I will be, but now? It registers in my mind and slips away like everything else that suddenly seems meaningless.

I grip my father's cold hand, staring out the window at the rectangle of gun-metal gray sky. I wait. My eyes are hot and grainy. My eyelids keep sliding like a cool black curtain over my vision. I doze for a few moments and jerk awake.

I examine Dad's face, reassured by his irregular grunts and wheezes that he's still among the living. For now. I haven't prayed in years, since I realized God wasn't going to come down and bring my mother back to life.

But now I do. I plead with God to make it easy for him, to make it quick, to give him that peace he craves. He's suffered enough. We've all suffered enough.

I lean my head against the back of the chair, rubbing my eyes with the forearm of my free hand. My eyes drift closed.

"Lyra." Dad's voice is weak, barely a whisper.

I squeeze his hand. "I'm here. I'm right here."

His breathing is labored, his lips purple. "It's time."

"Don't say that."

"Tell your sister ... I'm sorry."

"Tell her yourself. Just hold on a little longer. I'll—I'll try to find her. She'll come. She has to."

He squeezes my fingers, so weakly I might have imagined it. "I wish I could undo ... so many things."

My heart is splitting in two. "There's nothing to be sorry for anymore, Dad."

He chokes, then manages to clear his throat, making a gurgling sound like something thick and wet in his lungs. "I need to tell your mother ..."

"She knows."

He closes his eyes. "Tell her I'm . . . sorry."

I feel loosened, my bones and ligaments coming unglued. My head is wobbly on the stalk of my neck. I thought I'd be ready, but I'm not. I'm not ready at all.

"Your sister ... Please—forgive her."

There's a roaring in my ears, loud and pulsing and ugly.

"Take care of her ... Promise me ..."

"I promise."

"I love you ... to the moon ..."

"I love you all the way back," I whisper.

I hold his hand, utterly helpless to do anything else.

An hour later, he's dead.

## 32

## LUX

"How's your cat?" Jayda asks, glaring at me with her fists on her hips. She's wearing white skinny jeans and a thin, tight jacket that shows off her slim waist.

She stands in front of the dilapidated front door of the old abandoned warehouse out on Highway 9. They used to make pencils or erasers or something back in the 80s. Now it's a place to escape, to party, hook up, get high, and do pretty much anything you want.

I raise my voice over the pulse of the music blaring from inside. "She's bitchy and spiteful. Seriously reminds me of someone I know."

Jayda purses her lips. "Whatever. You ever planning to return to school?"

I shrug, hunching against the wind. Above me, the sky is black, the stars obscured by low, ominous clouds. The weather is warming up during the day, but the nights are still frickin' freezing. "Haven't you heard? The man uses structured education to turn us all into zombies. You want to turn out like your parents? Like your parents' parents? I don't. I'm so over it."

"What are you even talking about?"

"Going to school is terrible. Just think about it. You sit on your butt all day, listening to people drone on for hours about dates and wars and formulas that are useless to everyday life—any rational, logical person would detest it."

"You're seriously dropping out your senior year," she says, incredulous.

"Label it however you want. I'm experimenting with the vagabond lifestyle. You can enjoy your three hours of homework a night slaving away for a piece of paper. I pass."

Jayda throws up her hands. "Sometimes you sound really mental, you know that? Like off-the-wall bonkers."

The wind howls around the corners of the warehouse. I jam my hands under my armpits, stomping my feet. "You gonna let me in or what? It's freezing out here."

Jayda steps back. She tucks her purple-streaked hair behind her ears and chews on her lower lip like she's got something to say.

"What?"

"You should stay away from Felix. He doesn't want to see you."

I flinch at the sound of his name. "You aren't the queen of the world, Jayda. You aren't his girlfriend either, last time I checked. Unless you've already moved in on my sloppy seconds?"

I don't wait for her reaction. I don't need to. I push past her into the fray. The warehouse has been empty so long, moss and weeds and even flowers burrow their way up through the crumbling concrete floor in spring and summer. The first tendrils of green peek between several cracks. Moonlight glimmers through several gaping holes in the roof.

It's still frickin' cold even though it's almost April, but the walls keep out the wind chill. That's a big deal in Southwest Michigan.

I'm dressed to impress and when I walk into the party, I feel the approval of everyone's eyes on me, guys and girls. The top I'm wearing is all silvery and falls in glittery folds around my cleavage. I'm moonlight on water, I'm turned all the way on.

Jamal Harris always brings a portable generator, so we have music. String lights are draped along the concrete block walls. I shout, "Hey" to a bunch of people, including Dominic and Owen, and the girl with the shaved blonde hair, Darcy something or other. Then Autumn is at my side.

"I've been looking everywhere for you," she shouts.

I grab her arm, squeezing tight. I missed her more than words can say. "You drunk, Skittles?"

She holds up a red Solo cup and leans against me. "I'm mostly sober. Cross my heart. You wanna dance?"

People are already dancing in the center of the room. More are clustered around the keg table in the back or sitting in the rusted metal chairs lining the walls.

My phone buzzes in my pocket. I ignore it, wrapping my jean jacket tighter around myself. It's Lyra. Again. I'm not in the mood to deal with her. I just can't.

I scan the room for available guys, but most of the decent ones are already taken. I catch sight of Felix standing to the side of the keg table, a cup in one hand as he gestures wildly to a few of his buddies. Probably explaining string theory or debating the original origin story of Nightwing or Aquaman or something.

My stomach drops.

"Let's get plastered," I say to Autumn. "Come on."

We down at least three beers each while we dance to the frenetic, pulsing music. Autumn doesn't have any sense of rhythm, but I try to mimic her anyway, and we nearly choke on our laughter.

I catch Simone staring at me from across the room. She still hasn't forgiven me. Screw her. She can pout in her corner until the apocalypse if she wants to. I'm here to have fun.

After a few minutes, the warm buzzing liquid flushes through me. It's thrumming through my blood, humming in my bones. My body untethered, my head light as air, light as a balloon floating up toward the ceiling.

I just want to forget. I need to forget.

Autumn bumps my arm, gesturing with her cup in the general direction of Simone. She's dancing now, her mane of spirals shaking, brown skin gleaming with sweat. A gaggle of guys surround her, all trying to get her to dance with them. But Simone goes into her own world when she dances.

She doesn't see anyone else.

"You know what that reminds me of?" Autumn asks.

"No, but I'm guessing you're about to tell me," I yell over the thumping music.

"When anacondas mate, up to fifty males form a writhing ball around a female. The orgy can last up to a month."

"Geez Skittles, sex is all you think about, isn't it?"

She ducks her head, her hand fluttering to her face. "I'm just saying."

Dominic strides up to us and slips his arm around my shoulder. He smells like Axe spray and cigarette smoke. "Dance with me."

I motion toward Autumn. "I'm already taken. You're welcome to join us."

He raises his eyebrows and grins. "Oh, a threesome. I'm in."

Autumn has to turn away so he doesn't see the mortified look on her face. I grab her arms. "Shake it off. Let's dance."

We dance through a bunch of songs, until my heart is pounding and the warmth of my body heat drowns out the chill. Dominic keeps trying to grind against me, but I swing my hips and whirl away. There's no way I'm gonna mess up like that again.

Dominic refills my cup. But it's not enough. There's something off. The darkness still skims beneath the surface of my skin. Guilty thoughts flutter flap against my skull. Lyra's unread texts burn a hole in my pocket.

I stop dancing and pull Dominic aside. "Do you have anything?"

He digs his hand into the front pocket of his hoodie. "Wanna share a joint?" He lights it and hands it to me.

I grab the joint and take a long drag. But even this isn't enough. I need that spinning underwater nothing. "Molly? Oxy or K? Anything?"

He frowns. "No, sorry. I've only done Molly a few times. It messes with my head. Dance with me. Whatever's on your mind, I can change it."

"Forget it." I stalk off. I need Reese. I despise him, but I need him. I lean against the wall, the cold of the cement seeping through my jacket. My phone buzzes again. Damn it.

I fumble for my phone, about to tell her to leave me the hell alone.

Only I don't. I stare down at the screen, my gaze glued to the last text.

3 3

---

# LYRA

I lie in the chair for what feels like hours, my body bent in on itself, my chest heaving. I grieve for my father, my mother, for all of us—for what we were and what we should have been.

I grieve because I am an orphan, abandoned by my parents. Because they were lost to me even when they were still alive. Because I was just beginning to find my father, and now he's gone.

He lies in the bed. I can barely bring myself to look at him. His flesh looks waxy. His limbs aren't yet stiff with rigor mortis, but he is a corpse. He is no longer my father. I force myself out of the chair and stumble from the room.

The house is silent and dark, the walls closing in on me. I am completely, utterly alone. Without parents, without a sister. Fresh grief washes over me, sucking me under. I sag against the wall, forcing myself to breathe. My whole body's shaking, shuddering. I don't want to be alone. I need to talk to another human being. I need my sister.

I pull my phone out of my pocket and send her a text, another one to join the dozens I've already sent her today. *I wanted to tell you in person. Dad is...* I hesitate. Typing the words seems like some kind of betrayal. But I have to. She has to know. *Dad is dead.*

I have several unread texts from Ethan. He's messaged me off and on for

the last three days, his words like a lifeline connecting me to the outside world.

He answers on the second ring. "Hey, you." I sink down to the cold tile floor.

"Hello? Are you there?"

"My—" My throat clogs. My voice comes out in a rasp. "He's dead."

Ethan blows a mouthful of air into the phone. "I'm so sorry, Lyra."

"He's just lying in his bed. He's dead and he's just lying there like everything's normal, like he's just sleeping."

"I'm coming over."

"No. I mean, you have Hadley."

"She's already sleeping. My mom's home. I'm coming over. I'll be there in ten minutes."

"No, really. Don't worry about it. I just—I needed someone to talk to."

"Just hold on, okay? Hold on." Ethan hangs up. The phone slips from my fingers and clatters to the floor.

Everything inside me is raw and throbbing. I try not to think, not to feel. I focus on the uneven tiles, imagine composing an image through the Nikon's viewfinder. I can almost discern different shapes in the mottled, discolored squares. I've found a top hat, a dragon, and half a face when the doorbell chimes.

Ethan doesn't say anything when I answer the door. He pulls me into his arms.

I stiffen. I haven't been held like this in years. Instinctively, I try to pull away, but Ethan squeezes tighter. He's so strong, his biceps flexing beneath his sweatshirt as he hugs me. Warmth trickles down my spine, like something deep inside beginning to unfreeze.

Ethan pulls back and peers into my face. "You okay?"

"Thanks for coming. I don't—I don't want to be alone. I'm sorry. I know that's stupid."

"It's not. You're not alone. I'm right here."

I take a step back, ducking my head so my hair falls across my face.

"Let's go inside."

He waits with me while I call the hospice nurse and the RoseHill funeral home director. My stomach hardens into an iron brick. I can't imagine the long list of tasks awaiting me: calling the insurance company, the IRS, credit card and mortgage companies, notifying everyone of my father's death, arranging the funeral, picking out the casket.

I slump at the kitchen table, my hands clenched in my lap. Ethan sits next to me, a warm, solid presence. Just the nearness of him is comforting.

"Do you think he found peace, before he died?"

"If your father never found his peace in life, he will now."

I close my eyes, will the tears not to fall. "You believe there's more? After this?"

"I do. I'm not going to tell you it's God's will. Death is never God's will. But I believe in faith. I believe death isn't the end."

He seems so sure. I long for that, for something as simple as faith. Something to hold on to. "How do you have faith, when everything's falling apart around you?"

He touches my shoulder. "I believe faith is seeing light with your heart, when all your eyes see is darkness. We have hope."

Right now, I can't see any light, only darkness. I've been frantically swimming in a black sea of grief, struggling not to go under. And now I'm sinking down, down, down into the depths. I want to have faith that there's more. More than this.

I raise my head, suddenly heavy as a fifty-pound weight.

"You're exhausted."

Things are going blurry, getting fuzzy around the edges. "Lux means light. Did you know that?"

"You need to rest," Ethan says. "Come on, let's get you to bed."

"I don't want to be alone." "I'm right here," Ethan says.

But I am. I'm alone with my grief. My family is dead. Except for Lux. She would understand. She's in this drowning sea with me. At least, she should be. Where is my sister?

Where is she?

$$3\ 4$$

## LUX

I read the words once, twice, three times. I still can't seem to understand them. They blur and zigzag across my vision. *I wanted to tell you in person.*

*But you need to know. Dad died.*

Dad died. Died. Dead. Dad is dead. A great howling grief roars up inside me. I thought I had more time. I thought I could put it off until tomorrow. Then the next tomorrow, and the next. I've lost my chance. I never even said goodbye.

I nearly drop my phone as I shove it back into my pocket. Lyra wants me to come back home. But for what? He's already dead. It's too late. Everything is always too late.

The black hole opens up. Its surging gravity grabs me, and I fall right in. I'm falling so fast there's nothing to grab on my way down.

I shove off the wall and head to the keg table, gulp down another cup full of beer. It burns on the way down. I fill it again. I turn and nearly plow into Felix Avery.

"Oh, hey," he says, looking down at his shoes, his curly brown hair falling into his eyes. He's wearing a faded red T-shirt that reads, "Never Trust an Atom. They Make Up Everything."

"Felix," I breathe. And suddenly I want him. I need him. I need him to want me. *I need. I need. I need.* "I've missed you."

"Yeah? You haven't acted like it."

"I totally have." I lurch toward him. "You wanted to talk, before. I'm ready to talk."

He kicks at a chunk of concrete with his boot. "Seriously?"

"Please, Felix. I messed up, okay. Just—can we talk?"

I think I see him nod. It's hard to tell, with the room shimmering and undulating around me. I put my drink down on the keg table and grab his arm. "You look smashing tonight. Come on. Let's go find a room."

He frowns. "Just to talk?"

"Um, hello? Isn't that what I just said?"

I'm leading him toward the double doors when Raj Patel steps in front of me. Jayda's with him. "Hey, man," Raj says. "Where are you going?"

"She asked me to talk." Felix sounds unsure.

"Is that really a good idea?" Jayda asks.

"After what she did to you?" Raj echoes.

Anger swarms up my throat. "Just who the hell do you think you are?"

Jayda's face is all scrunched in concern. "She's using you, Felix. That's what she does."

"Hello? I'm right here."

Raj shakes his head. "She's just going to break your heart again, dude. Come on, let's go."

"Are you going to let them talk to me like that?"

Felix looks at them, then at me. He sighs heavily. "Just like, five minutes, guys, okay?"

They both hesitate. Felix doesn't move.

"Um, hello? Get out of here," I snap.

They finally shuffle back to their seats. They keep staring at us, scowling and whispering to each other. Screw them.

"You need to pick better friends." I press my hand against his chest. I can feel the heat of him, the pulse of his heart surging against my palm. "Let's go."

"We can talk here."

"Who said anything about talking?"

He looks at me, confused. I see hurt in his gaze but I ignore it. I lean in and focus on his eyes, deep brown and fringed with thick lashes, and his mouth, kind of pouty and turned down a little at the corners like a disobedient puppy.

I'm so close I can count his eyelashes, can read the braille of pimples along his jawline. I stretch on my tiptoes and put my mouth on his. His lips open for me. Whether he wants them to or not, they do.

"What are you doing?" he says in a choked, whispery voice.

I press myself against him. He's thin but strong, all hard, wiry muscle.

"Kiss me," I murmur, my breath fluttering against his cheek, my lips inches from his.

People are watching us, especially his bodyguards in the corner. They're glaring daggers, but I don't care. Why would I care? It doesn't matter what his stupid little friends think. He wants me. Me, not them. Me, not her. That's all that matters.

My pulse beats in my throat and I remember how neatly my shoulder fit beneath his armpit when he put his arm around me. I remember how he always kissed with his eyes closed, but I kept my eyes open so I wouldn't miss anything, not a single effing thing.

What I remember most is how his breath hitched in his throat, how he gave this little gasp the first time we French kissed. I loved the way his eyes went all soft and bright at the same time.

I remember all his kisses, each and every one. How he always pulled me into him and the first thing he did wasn't to grab all over me like the other guys before him. The first thing he did was hold me. He tilted my head back and knotted his fingers in my hair and kissed me until I saw stars and galaxies and universes all exploding behind my eyes.

I remember it all. My heart thrashes against the cage of my ribs like it wants to escape this prison I've made for it.

I miss him. I miss us. I miss the feeling he gave me, like it was just me and him, and everything else faded away. Like we were the only shooting stars in the sky.

He's still not kissing me. He's not moving away either. I breathe in the clean scent of him. He smells like Spearmint gum and laundry detergent. I want his mouth on mine. I want his arms around me.

I kiss him again, harder this time, prodding at his mouth with my tongue, waiting for his lips to give way.

His mouth closes. He steps back. "Lux. I can't."

"What are you talking about?"

"I need you to stop."

"What? Don't you miss me?"

"Look. You really did hurt me. I wasn't even breaking up with you. And then—then you went and—" He shakes his head and turns away.

Tears scald my eyes. "I'm sorry. I'm a terrible, horrible person. I hate myself, okay? Does that make you happy?"

He encircles my wrist and removes my hand from his chest. "No, it doesn't make me happy. It makes me sad."

I flinch. "You aren't going to forgive me?"

His gaze flits over my shoulder, like he's looking for someone to ride in and rescue him. "I care about you, Lux. A lot. But—"

"But what?" I snarl. "You like Jayda's boobs better? Her ass?"

"No! Of course not. I think—" He sucks in his breath. "You made out with another guy, Lux. Right in front of me. I can't deal with that. It hurts too much."

"I'm sorry. I'm totally and completely sorry! What do you want me to do? Tell me and I'll do it!"

"I can't keep up. It's like you switch back and forth between liking me and hating me, sometimes in the same day. I'm sorry. I just can't."

I stare at him, my eyes glittering slits of rage. I have never been treated this badly. "You know what? I don't need you. I don't need you or anybody else. I won't bother you and your precious life anymore. I could have a gun pointed at my own head and I'd still rather shoot myself and splatter my brains all over the floor than be with a self-righteous prick like you! You think I'm a loser, a dependent, needy, psycho freak—is that it? Is that what you really think?"

"No! I—"

"Guess what, asshat? I don't need you!"

"Lux. Listen to me—"

"Kiss my sweet ass!" I whirl away, leaving him staring after me in shock.

I'm done. I'm so done with all of this. I need to crawl out of my own skin. Right this second, I don't care how much I despise Reese.

I need what he has, the white nothingness he can give me. I crave it. I have to have it, or I will tear my own flesh right off my bones.

I pull out my phone and text him to come get me. My car's here but even I know I'm too wasted to drive. A moment later, he tells me he's coming.

I throw back another cup of beer and then another, gulping it down, until it's warm and sloshy in my stomach. My bones are loose inside my skin.

My gaze drifts over the crowd. Felix is across the room, sheltered by none other than Jayda, his self-appointed guardian angel. Pain explodes inside my ribs. My hands ball into fists. I'm going to stomp over there and do something horrifically stupid, and I don't even care.

Before I can move, Simone steps in front of me.

"What do you think you're doing?" Her hands are on her hips, her face twisted in a scowl. Autumn stands a little behind her, shivering and blowing into her cupped hands.

"What do you care?"

"What's your deal, Lux? Why are you acting like this?"

I shrug, but my heart's beating fast. "You don't care about me, Simone. You've barely spoken to me in weeks. Why the hell is everyone always blaming everything on me? What's *your* problem?"

"Um, can we just calm down a little bit?" Autumn asks.

Simone points her finger at me. "Look, Chica. Felix is back there crying. Again. That certainly wasn't my fault. You can't just treat people like crap whenever you feel like it."

"Oh yeah? Watch me. I don't need any of you." I head toward the front doors. They both follow me.

"Where're you going?" Autumn asks.

"To the only person who hasn't betrayed me."

"What? You mean—Reese?"

"Ding, ding, ding. Skittles wins the prize." I bang into the crash bar and shove the metal door open. Outside, the clouds have cleared. The stars are shards of light against the black velvet sky. The cold air pricks my exposed skin.

My head pounds, swirling with angry, hateful thoughts. And beneath it all, the dark whisper: *Dad is dead. And you killed him.*

"You're voluntarily spending time with that scrawny-ass punk?" Simone stomps her feet against the cold. "Please tell me you aren't that stupid."

I whirl on her. "I guess I am that stupid, *Simone.* You've got me all figured out."

"Please, Lux," Autumn whines. "Reese is sketch. Just come home with me instead, okay? We can leave right now."

Two headlights swing up the long dirt road as Reese's Thunderbird pulls up. Something gives inside me. I'm only a few minutes away from burning up every single dark malignant thought. Only a few moments from a relief that will obliterate every craptastic moment of this night— the party, Felix's stricken face, Simone's anger, my own smoldering self-loathing. I need this more than anything I've ever needed before.

"Lux!" Simone yells at my back.

I jerk open the passenger car door and climb inside. I don't look at them. I sense them both staring at me through the window, but I don't care. I don't care.

"Hey Princess," Reese puts the car into gear and we drive away.

His car stinks of weed and cigarette smoke. I thrust out my hand and he gives me what I need, no questions asked.

I listen to the hard, pulsing base of Aerosmith pumping through the car stereo. I wait for it to grip my brain, to thrust me out of this awful tilting world and take me away, far away.

But it doesn't come. "I need more," I say in a voice I barely recognize as my own.

Reese smiles. When we get to his apartment, he gives me more.

He lays out a square mirror, a small glass bowl, a lighter and razor blade, and a couple of small straws on his end table. I watch him empty a few pills into the bowl and smash them up with the blunt end of the lighter. He crushes it into a fine powder, then scrapes it into four match-stick sized lines on the mirror with a razor. He uses the straw to snort two lines.

"You sure you want to ride this wave, Princess?" he asks, tilting his head back.

I should feel afraid. I should hear warning bells clanging in my head. But I don't. Reese shows me what to do. I fall back into the bean bag. Waiting for it to come for me.

It does. My thoughts start to disintegrate. Break apart. Maybe this time my mind won't come back. Maybe it'll just be gone.

Maybe this time the oblivion won't release me. I'll just cease to exist. Vanish. Disappear. Like spontaneous combustion. An exploded star. A supernova.

And then it comes. Like a bomb going off between my eyes. Shock-waves mushroom inside my brain, radiating out, detonating fireworks.

It's like a wild dream unleashed. Riding the rushing, raging current of my blood, pulsing through arteries and capillaries, sweeping me away.

It's liquid fire whooshing between my ears. It burns everything away. Wiping my mind. Incinerating every memory, every voice, every thought. Every dark and dangerous truth—gone.

Everything consumed in the brilliant, fiery white light.

35

LYRA

The funeral is five days after Dad's death.

The funeral director, a small, compact woman with clouds of apricot hair and sympathetic eyes, took care of almost everything. I didn't care what flowers were used, the type of wood or design of the coffin, or the best time to hold the funeral. I asked for a short, outdoor service next to the grave. The funeral director, who Dad spoke with long before his death, planned the rest.

It's 1:30 p.m. on Sunday afternoon, the first week of April already almost gone. The last three days brought warm air and rain. The air is thick and spongy, the fresh green grass and buds on the trees and bushes sparkling with diamond droplets. A slight breeze ruffles my hair.

It's a day much too beautiful for death.

I stand next to Ethan in front of the gaping hole in the earth. It looks like a wound. The strip of turf that'll cover the gash in the ground lays beside the grave.

After the service, a backhoe will fill in the hole, and in a few hours, the gravesite will look no different from any of the others. To anyone passing by, it'll look like my father's been dead for years.

Pastor Torrès, the pastor Dad met with in his last several months of church attendance, presides over the service. He stands opposite the grave, his hands crossed over the Bible he holds in front of him. He's tall and trim, his dark hair and beard almost completely silver. His eyes seem kind, his voice smooth and lilting. He's talking about finding God's comfort in grief, but I'm not really listening.

There are only a few dozen people here: Ethan and his family, a couple of truckers Dad worked with, the postman, and a handful of people I've never seen before. They must be church members.

Off to the side, Isabel Gutierrez stands with her thin arms folded in front of her chest, her face pinched, almost scowling. She's next to her mother, Maria. Maria is dressed all in black with a wide-brimmed hat and a veil shielding her face. She makes a wet hiccupping sound, like she's trying desperately not to sob.

"... for we shall not weep for long," Pastor Torres says. "Because we have the assurance that we will see Jacob McKenna again. For Jacob believed, and we believe, and we know that the reunion in Heaven will come soon, sooner than we ever know ..."

Should I be crying like Isabel's mom? I've lived in varying states of grief for over two months. Every tear has already been wrenched from my body. I have nothing left.

The funeral is simply a finality, an official farewell. I've already said goodbye a hundred times. My limbs are heavy, my head throbs. I'm drained, emptied. I just want to get this over with and go somewhere else.

As Pastor Torrès drones on, I think about Lux. I haven't seen her since she took off again three nights ago. I've texted and called her a dozen times today. No answer. I've barely spoken to her since Dad died. When I tried to talk to her, she fled out the front door or locked herself in her room or screamed at me until I was the one who fled. She's a towering inferno of rage.

My own anger at her burns bright as a flame in the center of my chest. She never even said goodbye to Dad. Now she's missing his funeral. And the most terrible thing? I'm not even surprised.

Pastor Torrès finishes his speech and asks everyone to bow their heads for prayer. The sun beats down on my head as I listen to this stranger bless me and Lux and ask God to be with us.

Do pastors have more clout with God? Has this pastor ever doubted? What does he do with that doubt? Bury it? Test it? Ignore it and chalk it up to faith? Does he struggle with anger, forgiveness?

The prayer ends. Ethan nudges me gently. Above me, the sky is a milky blue ribboned with clouds. The trees rimming the graveyard are furred with buds and leaves like tiny green stars.

I step forward and drop a bouquet of daisies—my mother's favorite—onto the lid of the coffin. Wherever my father is now, he would want a piece of Eve with him.

Several other people toss flowers into the grave. Most people voiced their condolences to me before the service started. Now free of their obligation, they begin to drift back toward their cars.

Ethan turns to me, Hadley hitched on his hip. She's wearing a dark blue dress with her little red purse clutched in her hands. Ethan's dressed in a matching navy blue suit that emphasizes his broad shoulders. "You okay?"

I force a smile I know doesn't reach my eyes. "I will be."

Isabel trudges toward me, her hair piled up in a bun, the dyed blue strand tucked behind her ear. She stops in front of me. "Thanks for coming," I say.

"At least he's not in pain anymore." She looks pale and drawn, her expression strained.

I nod mechanically. "I guess so."

"My mom always says everything happens for a reason."

"Well, that reason sucks."

She snorts, wipes a hand across her forehead. The black dress she's wearing hangs off her, the loose fabric bunching around her too-thin waist. I can see the knobs of her elbows and knees.

"Are you okay?"

"That's just like you, isn't it? Always thinking about someone else," she says, her face blank, expressionless. "I'm fine. And you'll be fine, too. Sooner than you think."

I have no clue how I'm supposed to respond to that. "Thanks, Isabel, for coming."

She blinks, staring off over my shoulder. "I'm sorry for your loss."

She turns and slogs through the dewy grass, her heels sinking into the earth.

Ethan touches my shoulder with his free hand. "You need some time?" Ethan's mom kindly offered to host a dinner at her house after the service. That's where we're headed now. How death and eating go together, I'll never understand.

My gaze slips past Ethan and snags on Maria Gutierrez, still standing on the other side of the grave. A knot forms in my stomach. She's the only person who hasn't said a word to me. "Just a minute. I'll be right there."

I walk toward her. "Maria?"

Her shoulders hunch inward. She turns slowly to face me. "Yes?"

Up close, I can see the woman's features behind the netting of her veil: her small, pinched face incongruous with her wide, generous mouth. Her eyes are black and shiny as olives.

Maria tilts her head, her eyes flicking to the side as if she's searching for an escape route. "I'm sorry. I shouldn't have come."

"Why not? You used to babysit us. You were friends with my mom."

She twists a handkerchief between her fingers. Her hands are the hands of an old woman, thin and veiny. "You don't know who I am?"

I just stare at her. "You're Maria Gutierrez. Isabel's mom." But even as I say the words, I know it's the wrong answer.

She opens her mouth, closes it. "I should go. I'm so sorry."

"Wait." As she turns, I reach out and touch her arm. She actually flinches. My stomach turns over. Whatever this is, it's bad. "Tell me."

Her watery gaze searches mine. Then her shoulders straighten. She lifts her chin. "I'm sorry to tell you this way, here. It was never my intention to hurt you, please know that. But—I loved your father."

It's like skipping a stair, that sudden disorienting rush of vertigo. The solidness you expected and trusted, suddenly, catastrophically gone. "What?"

She opens her mouth as if to say something else, then closes it. She blinks rapidly behind her veil, her eyes gummy and streaked with mascara. "Your father and I had an affair."

"You're lying." But the truth settles over me like a cold, unrelenting fog. The puzzle pieces slowly click into place, one after another. My father's guilt. The way he reacted when Isabel stopped by. The sins for which he so desperately sought forgiveness.

I'm struck with the same gut-punch of betrayal Mom would've felt, if she'd known. It was true after all, the fear she'd gnawed and worried like a rotting tooth all those years.

Something wrenches loose deep inside me. "When?"

Maria clasps her hands, twisting the handkerchief between her fingers. "It started nine years ago. Your father ended the affair, but we never stopped loving each other. I never stopped loving him."

I close my eyes, force myself to open them. The sun is the same. The sky, the trees, the faint scent of manure and the soggy grass sinking beneath my heels.

Everything is fuzzy, disconnected, like I'm actually somewhere else and this is all some horrible dream. But I'm not. It's not.

"When? When did he end it?"

She hesitates for just a moment. "Right after your mother died."

Reality shifts beneath me like water, my memories realigning to fit with this new information, this ugly truth. My mind scrambles to connect the dots, link the timeline. "You were sleeping with my father when my mother killed herself."

"Eve didn't know. Jacob—your father—he was sure of it. Eve couldn't love Jacob, not like he needed. She was sick." "No thanks to you," I spit out.

Her mouth tightens. "I told you. She didn't know."

"How would you know?" My voice is rising, carrying on the wind. Mourners from a nearby gravesite glance our way. For once, I don't care what anyone else thinks.

"We were discreet."

I can't listen to this anymore. "You don't belong here."

"You should know, I've barely spoken to Jacob in eight years. His choice. It was his penance, sacrificing our love. Your father had a real chance at happiness. Instead, he lived and died alone."

I barely resist the urge to slap her across the face.

I can't take in air through the vise constricting my lungs. I thought I wanted answers. I thought I wanted to know every secret of my past. I was wrong. "I need you to leave."

I feel a presence at my side. Ethan, standing next to me. "Everything okay here?"

He's so strong, so warm and safe and steadying. I want to sag against him. I want to throw my arms around him, press my head against his chest and feel the beat of his heart. But I can't. "This woman was just leaving."

Suddenly Isabel is here, too. She takes her mother's arm. "Mamà, we need to go."

Maria dips her head, fresh tears streaking her cheeks. "I'm truly sorry for your loss, Lyra."

Isabel tugs at her mother, and they both turn away. I watch them make their way across the grass toward their car. Isabel glances over her shoulder, throwing me a knowing look. Her expression is a mix of disdain, pity, and resentment.

It hits me, then. This is why she despises me. She knows. She knows her mother ruined my family. She knows my father ruined hers.

My stomach churns. Acid surges up my throat.

"Are you okay?" Ethan asks.

"I'm fine," I say, the words heavy as stones in my mouth.

My bones are brittle, hollowed out, on the verge of cracking wide open.

---

I barely make it through the wake. My face is a mask hiding the fissures opening up deep inside me. Dad cheated on us, on Mom. He betrayed her when she was at her weakest, her most vulnerable.

When she needed him most, he was gone.

And now here I am in my empty house, alone and trembling with fury. There's no one to scream at, nowhere to aim my grief-stricken rage. He's dead. He abandoned me in death just like he did in life.

I need to leave. What's left for me here? I gave up a semester of college to care for the man who betrayed my mother, who betrayed us all. A voice in the back of my head whispers, *What about Lux?*

What about her? I made a promise to my father, but he broke every promise he'd ever made to his wife, his daughters. What binds me to that promise now? Misguided loyalty? The old burden of familial responsibility?

I'm sick and tired of being the only one trying to hold this family together. It's over. We failed.

I failed.

I throw my suitcase on my bed and smash my clothes inside. The gallery is in three days. I can still make it. I can slip right back into the rhythm that is my life, find my way back to the map of my future.

I charted my way here, I can chart my way back. I write my own destiny. Not my mother's or my father's or my sister's. Only mine.

Lux doesn't even want me here. She missed Dad's death, skipped out on the funeral. Maybe she's better off. The house is paid for, she can stay here. Get herself a job, pay her own bills. Live life on her own terms.

It's what she wants, anyway. She cut her ties to this toxic family. Now I'm free to do the same.

I pause in the darkroom to grab my camera. A half dozen prints still hang on the rack. There's one of Lux at four or five, grabbing onto Dad's neck as he gallops around the yard. They're both laughing, eyes bright. She's so small in the picture, so young and vulnerable.

That girl is gone. The girl I used to be is gone, too. Who we were, who we could have been. All those possibilities burned to the ground. There's only our own fractured selves. Only now.

By the time I sink into bed, I've already emailed Dr. Wells and booked a flight to Tampa for two days from now.

Two days until I'm gone for good.

# LUX

Sunlight bleeds through the seams of the blinds over the front windows. I wake up slowly, my mind groggy and thick. The sun hurts my eyes. Everything aches.

The events of the last few days come back jerky, in slivers and chunks, and then faster, like a spray of vomit. Dad died. He died and I wasn't there.

And there's something else, some other fact I can't seem to dredge up from the fuzzy mire of my mind. My head throbs like it's been split open with an axe.

I sit up with a groan.

"Mornin', Princess," Reese drawls.

Things blur and drift into focus. I'm sitting on the floor next to a fancy glass coffee table, my fingers sinking into plush white carpet.

Reese sprawls on the leather couch on the other side of me, one hand stuffed into the pocket of his basketball shorts, the other gripping a remote. He flicks through sports stations on the massive curved-screen TV. This is Floyd's house.

"What happened?" My mouth feels stuffed with wet paper towels.

"We partied," Reese says.

I don't even remember what I took. I'm falling fast and I know it. Liquor isn't enough. Weed isn't enough. The pills and the powder aren't enough. Ever since Dad... I can't go more than a day without the itch beneath my skin, my mouth going dry and metallic.

I'm scared to look at myself in the mirror. The gray shadows beneath my eyes. The sickly pallor of my skin. I put on my make-up in the dark. "I feel like death warmed over."

He just laughs again, the sound sharp and unpleasant.

"What time is it?"

"Almost noon. You got totally blitzed last night."

"I slept here?"

"Yep."

There's a string of drool stuck to the corner of my mouth. I wipe it away with the back of my arm. I can fit the last several days into my memory, but how I got here, what I did—those questions sink into a black void.

The funeral. It's today. It must be. Or was it yesterday? I remember getting ready, pulling on my tights, wrestling into the fitted black velvet dress with the rosettes along the bust line.

But after that? Nothing.

I shift, trying to find a comfortable position. My side aches. I'm sore all over. I glance down. I'm still wearing the black dress. It's bunched up around my thighs, and my tights are ripped above my knee.

I try to remember, my heart plummeting. "Did we—?"

He shakes his head, his eyebrows flatlining. He looks angry. Like I did something wrong. Maybe I did.

My ears are tinny. My mouth is dry. I need something to drink, but I don't move. "What the hell happened?"

His gaze bounces off me. He shifts uncomfortably. "You and Floyd."

"That's impossible." I scramble through my brain, trying to pull out any memory, but there's nothing there. Fear and disgust lodge in my throat like I've swallowed a mouthful of staples. "No. I would never."

"I walked in and he was all over you," he says in a strained voice, like he wants to be anywhere but here, doing anything but this.

My stomach lurches. I scramble to my feet. The world is suddenly brittle, hollow, so easy to shatter. "Was I passed out? Did he—?"

"Did he rape you?" Reese says. Something crosses his face—pain? Regret? Jealousy? "No, Princess. Not that. But I walked in and he—"

I sense movement to my right. Floyd walks through the kitchen archway into the living room, rubbing what remains of his hair with a plush white towel. For a second, he looks like someone's dad.

Then he lifts his head and meets my gaze. His face is expressionless. His eyes are blank.

Instinctively, I take a step back, my legs bumping against the coffee table. For the second time in as many weeks, fear settles in my stomach like a block of ice.

"Did I just hear someone cry rape?"

"Look, I don't know what you think happened, but I would never—"

"No one *raped* you," he says, leaning in close. His breath stirs the hairs on my neck. "I doubt that's even possible."

I try to swallow the fist in my throat. "Shut up."

He just shrugs.

"Then why don't I remember?"

He comes closer, staring at me through half-lowered lids, like he's watching for the pulse in my neck so he can strike. "Nothing happened you didn't want to happen. You were asking for it. Screaming for it."

My brain says shut the hell up but I can't stop myself. "You're lying."

He circles my neck with his thick fingers, his thumb resting in the center of my throat. His fingers are cool and dry.

I try to jerk my head away, but Floyd holds onto my neck, his bland face inches from mine. "I could do anything right now," he says.

I'm splintering, breaking apart, my mind severing itself from my body. This isn't happening. He would never really hurt me. He looks like a stuffy librarian or the uncool high school history teacher. He looks exactly like the kind of person you forget you've met three times already.

But my brain registers how dilated his pupils are, the flush in his cheeks. He likes this. He's getting off on it.

"You're hurting me."

His smile is menacing.

I remember the skulls in his display cases. I struggle to think over the shrieking inside my head. He is a bear, a wolf, a snake, a predator like any other. Maybe if I'm still as a corpse, he'll lose interest and leave. The seconds tick by in my blood.

After a long, agonizing minute, he lets go.

"Frankly," he says, his voice dripping with disgust, "If I knew you were just gonna lay there, I wouldn't have bothered."

It's like a sucker-punch to the gut. Hot sticky humiliation flushes through me. I sag to the floor, sucking in tiny clots of air.

Floyd settles on the couch next to Reese, his legs crossed. Reese's gaze skitters away from me and lands on the television. Both of them act bored, like nothing just happened, like the fabric of my world wasn't just torn to shreds.

I wrap my arms around my legs, tuck my chin into my knees, and rock. I squish my eyes shut and watch the white fuzzies dance across the back of my eyelids.

I want to crawl out of my own skin. Acid stings my throat, my stomach churning. I need to get out of here. I need to be somewhere I can actually think.

I wait until I can hear my own voice over the slamming of my heart. "Take me home, Reese. I want to go home!"

"You sure? You sure as hell didn't want to be home yesterday."

I glare at him. My head pounds so loud I can barely make out his words. "What are you talking about?"

"You were crazy upset. Like, psychotic or something. Don't you remember? You forgot your old man's funeral."

My heart stops beating. "You're lying."

"Check your phone."

My phone is sitting on the glass coffee table. I flick through the texts. And there they are, six or seven messages from Lyra, dated yesterday afternoon.

*Where are you?* 12:55 p.m.

*You're late!* 1:10 p.m.

*The service just started. Hurry up.* 1:17 p.m.

*Get your butt here now.* 1:26 p.m.

*I guess you really don't care about anyone but yourself.* 1:42 pm.

I remember. I was nervous and guilty and ashamed. I got wasted, taking every single thing they handed me. I partied right through my own father's funeral. Darkness swirls inside me.

My thoughts skitter, stampeding across my brain. I scramble to my feet, stumble down the hall, and puke my guts out in the toilet.

"Hey." Reese stands in the bathroom doorway, his fists jammed in his shorts pockets. His face twists in a tangle of competing emotions — revulsion, guilt, regret. "You okay, Princess?"

"What do you care?" I snarl into the toilet.

"I do," he says, his voice catching.

"Go away." I push away from the toilet and fall back against the bathroom wall. No. No, no, no. The self-loathing is like a living thing, black and ugly.

I slam my head against the drywall. Lights streaks across my vision. I do it again and again. I can't get the darkness out of me. I can't get it out.

"Stop! Don't do that!" There's something in his eyes, something I haven't seen before. A flash of pain. He looks younger, sadder. "You were right, okay? You were pretty much passed out. You looked like a rag doll."

"Get the hell out!"

But he doesn't. He comes into the bathroom and squats down next to me. "He didn't do anything, I swear. I was in the kitchen making a seven-layer bean dip. When I walked in, he was sitting next to you, pushing your dress up. He heard me. He stopped what he was doing, pulled your dress back down. He made some lame joke about girls always wanting it, especially when they're unconscious."

I let out a low moan.

"I kept an eye on you the rest of the night. I swear to you, he didn't touch you. He wanted to, but he didn't."

I clamp my mouth shut to keep the scream inside. "I can't remember."

"Look, I know you think I'm a scum-sucking piece of crap. I'm a dealer, not a monster. Whatever you think of me, I'm not that guy. I wouldn't have let him ... He didn't do anything, okay?"

I shake my head back and forth, frantic. The vortex is opening up beneath me, that gaping black hole. I'm free falling.

Here, Princess." He hands me a baggy with three capsules. "This will help you. I promise."

I tear open the bag with trembling fingers. He has everything I want. Everything I need. What's the point? What's the point of any of it?

My skin crawls. I'm filthy. I'm trash. People like Floyd know it. I'm cheap, something to use once and throw out, like garbage. This is who I really am. A nothing, a nobody.

Everyone hates me. They should hate me. I'm a terrible, awful human being. I push away everything I love and wallow in the ugliness.

All I do is hurt and destroy anything good in my life.

I ruin everything I touch.

I don't deserve to live.

# 37

# LYRA

"Is this the spot for all the cool kids now?" I slip into the traffic-cone orange booth of Bill's Bar and Grill. We pretty much ignored this place in high school.

It's not as run-down as I remember. The walls are all red brick and decorated with giant framed pictures of old-Hollywood celebrities: Marilyn Monroe, James Dean, Nat King Cole. "Sorry I'm late."

Ethan's mom is watching Hadley, so we have the booth to ourselves. Ethan grins at me, the corners of his mouth curling like he knows exactly what I'm thinking and feeling. He smells faintly of oil and grease.

"They got the veggie burgers Hadley loves. My mom is turning her into a good little vegetarian." He makes a face. "I guess it's healthier or something."

"Sure. Whatever helps you sleep at night. What are you reading?" I ask, nodding at his phone.

"Don't make fun of me. It's called *What to Do When Your Toddler is an Asshole.*"

"What?"

"Don't knock it. Little kids can be terrors. The book has all these tricks for getting said terrors to sleep through the night. It's all about the schedule. Who knew? Oh, and you can get them to eat broccoli if you blend it up in a smoothie. You can totally hide vegetables in brownies."

"That's horrible. Stop reading that crap, please. Imagine the trust issues she'll have when she figures out you've been deceiving her all this time. 'Brownies do not actually taste like spinach and kale, my darling. They're a delicious gift from the food gods I've been keeping from you your whole life.'"

"Very funny."

I grin at him and pick up a laminated menu.

Darcy Ackelsen walks up to our table, her gold hair tucked into a messy bun on top of her head. Even in her loose overalls and ratty green apron, she looks like she's just been transported here from the runway.

"And of course, Darcy works here, too," Ethan says, a grin in his voice. "That's reason enough to hang here."

"Hey," I mumble. My stomach clenches jealously. Which doesn't even make sense. I'm leaving. Packing it up and hightailing it out of town. I want this. I want to escape. Why should I feel even a speck of jealousy over Darcy? If she and Ethan become a thing, what do I care?

I don't. It's none of my business, none of my concern. And yet, my heart still flutters in my chest when I look at him. What the heck is wrong with me?

"Hey, guys. What's up? What can I get you?" she asks, her pen poised above her notepad. Even in the dim light from the bulb hanging over the table, her skin glows, ivory white and flawless.

Instinctively, my hand flits up to cover my own flawed, freckled skin.

"What's good here?"

"The mushroom burgers are fantastic."

"Great. I'll have that. And coffee. Lots of coffee."

"Make that two."

Darcy collects our menus and leaves us in peace.

"Hey, you okay?" Ethan asks, peering at me beneath his thatch of dark hair.

I clear my throat. "Yeah, fine. Anyway, thanks for coming. I just wanted to say thank you." I push the wrapped present I brought across the table.

Ethan grins. "You got me a gift? I'm touched."

"Chill out. It's for Hadley, too."

Ethan rips off the silver wrapping paper and lifts out the 11 x 14 framed photograph of Hadley cupping the rock in her pudgy fingers, her face bright, her eyes glowing with joy and curiosity.

Ethan just stares at it for a long moment, his mouth working but no sounds coming out. "Oh, wow. This is fantastic." His finger brushes across the glass. "Thank you, Lyra."

Heat flushes my face. "I'm glad you like it."

"Whatever competition you entered, you'll win."

I'm sure my face and neck are a deep scarlet. "I wish I had an ounce of your confidence. The gallery is tomorrow. All the art is displayed and people are coming from all over, important curators and magazine editors. The winner will be announced at the event. I can't win if I'm not there. That's why—" I swallow hard. "That's why this is goodbye. I'm flying out tonight. I need to be there. This is huge for me."

"When are you coming back?"

I look out the window. Dusk drapes everything in purple shadows. "I'm not."

"What?"

"The funeral is over. I've made arrangements for everything else. Lux can keep the house. It's time to return to my life, go back to school."

He's staring at me, I know he is. I keep my gaze averted, barely seeing the cars in the parking lot or the huddled shapes of the trees beyond the road.

I pretend this is what I want. I mean, it is what I want. It's just not *all* I want.

Not anymore.

He doesn't say anything. The silence stretches so long, I think he must be able to hear the thump of my heartbeat. I grab the container of sugars and start organizing the packets: Equal, Splenda, Stevia, then the white real sugar ones.

Darcy brings us our sandwiches, enormous burgers smothered with mushrooms and melted Swiss cheese, the buns glazed with oil. My stomach twists in on itself. Suddenly, I'm not hungry.

"We'll miss you," he says, his voice husky.

I crumple a yellow Splenda packet in my fist. "Me, too."

He takes bite of his mushroom burger, wiping off the bits of lettuce stuck to his chin. "What about your sister?"

"What about her?"

"She seems like she's in trouble."

My phone buzzes on the table next to my plate. I ignore it. I don't want to hear her excuses. I can't deal with her right now. "Lux *is* trouble."

"That's not what I mean. Like, real trouble. Darcy told me she's been getting completely wasted. She missed the funeral."

"That was her decision." I fight down the nausea clawing up my throat. "She made her choice. She wants to live her own life. So fine, I'll let her go."

"You don't think something's wrong?"

"Is anything ever right when it comes to Lux? She does what she wants. She never thinks about anyone else. Besides, she hates me, okay? She doesn't want me around. She's made that crystal clear."

"Still."

"I can't stay here," I choke out. I've got to escape while I still can, while some part of my heart can still be salvaged. "Not a second more."

His forehead furrows. "What's going on?"

How can I explain what it's like? My whole life is a lie. I've been betrayed by every single person in my family: my mother, Lux, even my father.

He cheated on Mom. He left us when we needed him most. Not because he was scared or guilty, but because he was selfish. He was weak. He kept the ring on his finger, he kept the address, but in his head and his heart, he was already gone. He abandoned us.

I clench my jaw. "My dad wasn't who he said he was. He betrayed my family."

I can't let myself think about that. If I do, my bones will crumble, my heart disintegrating into dust. I thought I wanted answers, I thought the truth could set me free. But it can't.

The truth is a raging fire that burns everything to the ground.

I don't want any part of the ashes.

# 38

# LUX

"Tell me what you want," Reese says. "I'll get it for you."

I take the pills. Chew the capsules. Snort the powder. I take whatever he gives me.

Then I ask for more.

"Be careful, Princess," he says.

But I can't hear him.

I leave the bathroom and lurch down the hallway, leaning against the wall for balance. I find the display room and curl up on the floor, surrounded by menacing, ochre-stained skulls. They leer at me with their empty eye sockets.

I stare up at the skulls. What lives did they live, when they wore skin? They look so peaceful. So still, ancient and wise. I can join them. I should join them.

My vision spins. Stars exploding and dying right before my eyes.

The fever fire roars through me. It's jet fuel, propulsion, launching me into a brilliant, blinding stratosphere. It's starfire lit beneath the mantle of my skin.

I've swallowed a star. Not a star, a supernova. Imploding on itself. Bursting open from the inside.

I remember Mom telling me about supernovas on a night when lightning shattered the sky and rain pummeled the roof over our heads. When a star's core collapses, the shockwave from the explosion rushes through every fiery plasma layer. The supernova blasts apart, a hundred million pieces ricocheting through the universe.

My thoughts are shooting stars. Darting, crashing, careening through my skull. Heat pumps through me. Blistering my brain, melting my eye sockets, scalding my pores.

My mind fractures. I'm sinking fast. Into the darkness, the swirling vortex. The star collapsing, caving in on itself. The black hole so gigantic, so powerful, not even light can escape.

I cradle my phone in my hands. Would anyone miss me? Does anyone even care?

Black fire surges through my arteries, veins, capillaries. Smolders through every nerve, every synapse. My sister. My blood. The only thing I have left. Will she even miss me?

Pain slams into me. I carried my secrets all this time. Like Dad, like Mom, I'll carry them into the grave. And then it will end. The splintering shrieking in my brain will stop.

Go quiet.

A silence like drowning.

The black hole sucks me down, down, down.

I curl into a ball, covering my ears with my hands. I won't have to run anymore. Won't have to *be* anymore. Won't have to live inside this hateful, loathsome skin.

My heart explodes.

What they don't tell you: for that brilliant, shattering moment, a supernova shines as brightly as a whole galaxy of stars.

3 9

———

LYRA

E than stares at me for a long moment. The space between us fills with the clink of dishes in the kitchen, the murmur of the couple in the booth next to us. The bell over the door jangles as a new customer comes in.

"I don't think you really feel that way about Lux," Ethan says.

"How do you know? She made her choice."

Ethan doesn't speak for a moment. He stirs a French fry in a puddle of ketchup. "I know you're grieving. And you probably have every right to be angry—"

"I do."

"You have every right to be angry. But I'm sure there's more to the story. Everyone handles things differently. Some people just aren't as strong. I have a feeling very few people are as strong as you."

"It's not about being strong. It's about doing the right thing."

"Exactly what I'm talking about. When your dad had his heart attack, you didn't even think about not quitting school, did you? I bet the thought of hiring a nurse never even entered your mind."

"Yes, it did."

"But it wasn't even a decision you had to make, was it? You knew what you had to do and you did it."

I shrug, staring down at my uneaten food.

"Most people aren't like that. 'Doing the right thing' is a struggle every step of the way. People want to protect themselves from the things they're scared of, like death, and responsibility. And guilt."

"You think I don't feel all those things too?"

"I'm sure you do. I'm speaking from the perspective of someone who's made some huge mistakes myself. It must be hard for Lux. She probably feels like an absolute loser next to you."

I sip my coffee. It's cold and gritty. My throat feels coated in grime. I think of her, purposefully missing Dad's funeral. I think of my promise to Dad. But I don't owe him anything anymore. "She hates me."

"You're her sister, the only family either of you have left. She needs you."

My heart twists. Guilt spears me. "But she's so—she's so—"

"Hard to love?" Ethan says wryly.

"Exactly. She wrote me off a long time ago. Right or wrong. Maybe right, I don't know." I remember Lux at Mom's funeral, her little body hunched in a ball on the hallway floor. Her face looked fake, false somehow, like it was made of plastic, like it wasn't real at all. She was always so emotional. She cried and screamed at everything. But that day, she didn't cry at all.

She was a stone girl, with a stone heart.

No, maybe I'm remembering it wrong. Maybe the stone girl was me.

"My dad made me promise." I rub my eyes with the palms of my hands. "He wanted me to find her, to save her."

"And?"

"And it feels like it's too late."

My phone buzzes on the table. Another text.

"You sure?" Ethan nods at the phone.

I stare at it, everything it represents, everything it might or might not mean. Was I the stone girl? Am I? Is this who I am? Who I want to be?

This time I tap the screen. This time I read it. *Sry I nevr said gdbye.*

"I'm not spying," Ethan says, but he is. He leans over to read the message.

My heart clenches, my pulse pounding in my ears.

Ethan reaches across the table and grabs my hand. A spark of electricity zaps up my arm and jolts my heart. "Look. She's messed up, no doubt. But love is messy. Love scrawls outside the lines. It never fits inside the small little box we plan for our life."

I shake my head, emotions warring inside me, a confusing assault of fear and love and resentment and guilt and obligation. "My suitcase is in the car. My plane leaves in an hour. The gallery is tomorrow …"

"All important facts. But?"

My heart is hemorrhaging pain. My escape hatch is right in front of me. I can taste my future, it's so close, so alive. This is my dream, my big chance. If not now, then when? The rest of my life dissolves before me in a gray, impenetrable fog.

Because there's Lux.

"You think I should stay."

"I'm not telling you what to think. I'm simply offering up some brilliant advice. Normally I'd charge, but you know, Hadley has a soft spot for you."

"You think you're always right, don't you?"

"Glad you're finally seeing the light."

I try to smile at him, but inside me, things are falling apart. I'm breaking into pieces.

I think of Dad, whose memory brings a stab of grief, then bright, white-hot anger. He was weak. He checked out when we needed him most. He didn't protect us from Mom during her bad times. He didn't keep us safe.

And after her death, he was a ghost, consumed by his own guilt, grief, and lost love. A ghost can't comfort you, can't hold you in the middle of the night when your heart is disintegrating.

And Mom. My love for her is tangled with sorrow and resentment and pain, so much pain. No matter what I did, I couldn't keep her here. She left us, too.

Now here I am, facing the same choice. To stay. To go. To go or stay. To escape and save myself. Or stay and step into the muck and mire threatening to drag me under.

I see my mother, leaning close, her hair smelling of jasmine as it falls over my face and shoulder, curtaining us both, the night sky above us a cavern of cascading light.

*Wish I may, wish I might, which star will you wish on tonight?*

And then, another text: *I'm sry for evrythng.*

My heart stops. I reread the text. Read it again. This doesn't sound like her. Not at all. Unless ... I text her back: *Where are you?*

No answer.

*Are you okay?*

No answer.

I call her number. It just rings.

*Just let me know you're okay. Please.*

Nothing.

I clutch my phone. No. *No, no, no.* Not again. Not her.

"I think she—" I can't speak the words aloud. They're nails in my throat.

Ethan doesn't hesitate. "Let's go get her."

I look at him. "I don't know where she is."

"I do." He jumps up from the table and disappears around the corner. A moment later, he returns, dragging Darcy with him. "We need to know where Lux is."

She sticks the end of her pen in her mouth and chews. "There are a few different parties tonight, but ..." her voice trails off. She eyes us warily.

"We're not the cops, Darcy. Come on, you know me. This is important."

"Please," I say, my voice raw.

Darcy rolls her eyes. "Only for you. Lux hasn't been partying at the usual places lately. Rumor has it she's gone straight to the source."

"Meaning?"

"This guy Reese is the dealer for everybody around here, everybody at the high school, anyway. Lux's been slumming it heavy with him for weeks now. But the guy Reese goes to for his stash is like a middle-aged dude named Floyd something. I've never met him, but I've heard a few things. Real sleazy. He's bad news.

"Sometimes some of the real hardcore guys hang out at his place. Like, all night benders. I heard he's having a party tonight. If I was a betting girl, which I definitely am, I'd put my money on his place. She's in crazy deep lately. More than I can handle, for sure."

I'm already up, grabbing my phone and jacket. "Can we get the address?"

"Text it to me," Ethan says, tossing a twenty on the table. "Thanks, Darcy. We owe you."

"You can take my next shift at the shop," she calls after us as we hurry out of Bill's.

I turn to Ethan. "You don't have to do this."

"Just get in the car."

For once, I listen without saying another word.

4 0

———

LYRA

I hunch in my seat and peer at the mailbox numbers slipping by in the light emanating from our headlights. We're about fifteen miles outside of town on a rutted dirt road that makes the car groan and sputter.

The houses are spaced far apart, tucked in between dense trees and scabby cornfields. We pass a house with cars crammed in the driveway and lined along the street. It's a pretty yellow colonial, well taken care of.

"You think that's it?"

"Yeah. That truck's blocking my view of the address, but I'm pretty damn sure." Ethan circles the block and parks on the side of the road just behind the last of the cars.

I take deep breaths, trying to keep myself from trembling. What if we don't even get through the front door? What if she's already ... but I can't let myself think these things.

Only an hour ago, I planned to jump on that plane and jet out of here like a coward, but that was with Lux still here, still doing whatever the heck she does. Still okay, still alive. The thought of my sister dying or dead wraps my heart in iron chains.

I have to do something.

I have to find her.

I unbuckle my seatbelt and glance down at myself. What would Lux do? I pull off my jacket and my long-sleeved top. My last layer is a white tank top edged with lace. I tug it down until I'm showing some cleavage, my chest veiled with freckles.

Ethan clears his throat. "What are you doing?"

"You want to get past the front door, don't you?"

"I'm officially impressed. What about me? Do I pass?"

I take in his worn leather jacket, the tousled black hair falling to his neck. "Barely. It'll have to do."

We walk up the large white porch. A seam of yellow light splits the dark front window where the curtains meet. I ring the bell. A few moments later, the door opens.

"How can I help you?" a man says pleasantly.

Ethan steps forward, puffing out his chest, starting in on his strong, "I've got this" act. Only he doesn't have this. He'll ruin it. Instinctively, I know that's not the right play.

Ethan says, "We're looking—"

I grab his arm, tug him back. "We're here for the party."

The man is dressed in pressed khakis and a white button-down shirt. He leans against the door jamb, his arms folded across his chest. He looks like a high school math teacher: thinning acorn-brown hair ringing his bald head, heavy jowls, a poochy gut. "What party would that be?"

I shrug, trying to look nonchalant. "We're friends of Reese. He invited us."

His lips curl in what looks like a smile, but nothing reaches his eyes. "Reese did, did he? What're your names?"

"I'm Lauren, this is Matt."

The man's gaze falls on me, traveling slowly up and down my body. "Lauren, huh?"

"Yes," I force out, praying my voice sounds natural. He must be Floyd. Beyond him, I can just barely see the living room. A pair of feet stick out from the end of a leather couch, several prone bodies scatter in front of a huge TV.

"Shut the door!" someone yells.

"It's freezing out here," I say, shivering for effect.

The man steps back. "Well, if you're friends of Reese. Take off your shoes please, this is high-grade carpet. The house is yours. But no loud music. We wouldn't want to attract any undue attention, now would we?" He actually winks.

"Nope," I say brightly, leaning down to slip off my boots. I feel him staring. The hairs on the back of my neck stand on end. "Thanks."

"No problem." The man turns away from us and settles into the love seat in front of the TV. A skinny girl wearing a deep scoop neck top and a leather miniskirt scoots into his lap. Even with her clumpy mascara and purple lipstick, she doesn't look older than sixteen.

Ethan takes my arm. "Let's go."

The air is heavy with cigarette smoke, the sickly-sweet stench of weed, and another thicker, burned plastic smell. The music is low and thumping.

No one's dancing, no one's really moving around at all. They sit and slouch and slump on chairs, couches, and beanbags.

We pick our way over several people collapsed in the hallway. I open a door to a bedroom with a bunch of people slouched around a coffee table littered with empty baggies, a couple of joints, and a bong. No Lux.

A trio of stoned faces turns toward us. "What's goin' on?" someone mumbles.

"Where's Lux?"

One of them blinks stupidly at us. "I dunno."

"She's here, isn't she?" I can't bear the thought of having to go through this all over again at some other doper's house.

"Yeah, yeah. She was in the kitchen jus' awhile ago." The guy shrugs, takes a wet swig from a dark glass bottle.

I turn and leave the room.

"Bye, bye now," someone says behind us.

We find the kitchen, all fancy marble and shiny steel. A half-dozen people sit around the table playing strip poker. Two girls lean against the counter by the sink, guzzling beer and giggling uncontrollably.

"Have any of you seen Lux?" I ask.

"Who?" A straggly-haired guy with a joint in one hand and a splay of cards in the other looks up at me.

"Lux McKenna. She's short, with a nose ring and long red hair."

"Reese's girlfriend," Ethan says.

The guy nods. "Reese's girl. I know her."

"Is she here?" I repeat, trying to keep from screaming, from grabbing them all by their throats and shaking them as hard as I can.

"I saw her earlier," one of the girls at the sink says. "She was blitzed out of her mind."

"Great. Thank you so much."

"I think there's a room we missed," Ethan says in a low voice. He's standing so close, I can smell the scent of cinnamon gum on his breath. I fight down the urge to grab his hand, to hold on and not let go.

We walk back through the hallway, checking each door. I reach for the handle of the last door on the right. It catches, like it's locked. I jiggle it hard. It unlatches and swings open.

The room is dim, draped in shadows. I take in four walls covered in display cabinets, with some kind of animal bones or—are those skulls?

My gaze jerks to the form lying prone in the middle of the white expanse of carpet, her ruby red hair spread like a halo around her head.

We found her. My breath catches in my throat. I lean down and pull on her arm. "Lux, get up."

She's lying on her side, her legs curled, one arm tucked beneath her torso, her hair almost completely covering her face. I pull back her hair to reveal a circle of yellow puke. There are chunks of vomit around her mouth. She's not moving.

Adrenaline floods through me. "Help me turn her," I say in a voice I don't recognize as my own. Ethan squats down on the other side of Lux and helps me flip her onto her back.

Lux's eyes are glassy and gaze unseeing at the ceiling. Her pupils are pinpricks. I slap her across the face. "Lux!"

She doesn't respond. Her skin is gray, her lips and fingertips tinged blue. Vomit crusts the corners of her mouth. Her breathing is so shallow, I can barely see the rise and fall of her chest.

Terror grips me. "Lux, wake up!"

My yelling draws a crowd.

"Hold up," one of the poker players says. He's stripped to the waist, his chest so skinny it's almost concave. "She's just sleeping it off."

"What was she on?"

No one answers. I twist around to look up at them. "What did she take!"

They just shrug, stare at us like they're waiting for a show.

"What the hell is wrong with you people?" "Lyra," Ethan says.

"Call 911!" My voice cracks, half shouting, half crying.

Someone says, "I don't know—" "Call!" I scream.

Ethan has his phone out, already dialing the numbers.

The rest of the room scatters. I hear shouting and the jumble of footsteps as the news spreads, not that someone's dying, but the cops are on their way. Car doors slam and engines rumble to life as everyone escapes the house.

I gather Lux into my arms and rock her. Her skin is too damn cold. "What should we do? Do we make her puke it up?"

Ethan presses the phone to his ear. He shakes his head. "No. The operator says to keep her on her side, in case she vomits again. Keep her mouth and airway open. Make sure she's still breathing. The ambulance is coming."

I cradle Lux's head in my arms. Her body is soft, floppy as a doll's. I smooth her bangs back from her face. It's been years since I've been this close to her. Even with her heavy makeup, she looks young, so very young.

I count the faint spray of freckles across her nose, each strand of her glorious red hair. My heart constricts. How could I have been so ready to abandon her? "You'll be okay. Just hold on. Please, please. Don't do this to me. Just hold on."

"What do you think you're doing?" Floyd looms in the doorway.

His arms hang loose at his sides, his face bland and nearly expression-less. Only his eyes seem different. Hooded. Blank.

"What do you think?" I snap. "We called 911. The paramedics are on their way."

"Get out of my house." His voice is low and dangerous.

Ethan pulls himself to his full height, squaring his shoulders. "No."

"Did you not hear me? Get the hell out of my house."

Ethan steps in front of me and Lux, blocking Floyd from entering the room. "We're not leaving her."

Floyd takes a step closer to Ethan, until they're only inches apart. "You're trespassing on my property. I have a gun and I have no qualms about using it."

Fear shoots through me. "Ethan—"

Ethan doesn't flinch. "We aren't leaving."

Floyd seems to notice me kneeling next to Lux for the first time. His expression flattens, his eyes going hard and shiny. "You little bitch."

Ethan puts his hands against Floyd's chest and pushes him back. "*You* need to leave. Now."

We all hear the sirens in the distance. Floyd lets out a string of curses. Without another word, he turns and leaves, probably to dump or bury his stash or whatever it is drug dealers do when they're about to get caught.

Someone brushes past him, a skinny guy with a thin, hawkish face.

"You called the cops."

"We called an ambulance," Ethan says. "You must be Reese."

"What happened to her?" He sways on his feet. His pupils are huge.

"She overdosed," Ethan says, more calmly than I ever could've.

Reese's face tightens. "Will she be okay?"

"No, you idiot!" I yell as the sirens grow louder. "Does she look okay to you?"

Lux groans, her eyelids fluttering. I pinch her cheek. "Lux! Can you hear me?"

The sirens wail louder. I look up at Ethan. "Can you go stand by the street, so they know where to go?"

Ethan takes off. Reese still stands there, staring down at us with a shocked, desperate look on his face. "I didn't think—She was upset. I was trying to help her feel better, that's all. Will she be okay?"

"What do you think?" I stroke Lux's hair. Her eyes roll toward the back of her head as she sinks back into unconsciousness.

After Mom's suicide, I thought I'd prepared myself for anything. For years, I thought Dad's death would be the other most awful thing, the unavoidable tragedy, the inevitable drop of the other shoe. I didn't think it could get worse.

I'm unprepared, totally defenseless. I can barely form thoughts over the terror pulsing through my brain. My chest is going to explode.

The paramedics arrive. They brush me aside in a flurry of activity and noise. Ethan shoves his way back into the room.

He grips my hand and we watch the paramedics bend over Lux's body, checking her airway, her vital signs. They inject her with something in a syringe, then snap an oxygen mask with a bag attached over her mouth and lift her onto a stretcher.

Their movements are efficient, their words clipped. A woman with glasses and brunette hair scraped into a ponytail gives Lux oxygen while the second paramedic wheels the stretcher out of the room.

I follow them on trembling legs. "Please. Can I come, too?"

"What's your relation?" the woman asks as we step outside.

My breath puffs out in foggy jets. Lacy clouds scrim the wide white moon. Above me, the stars are strands of diamonds scattered across the velvet sky. So many stars. Millions and millions of them.

The thoughts skittering around in my head coalesce into a single gleaming realization. It's not that the truth isn't important. It is. But it isn't truth that sets you free.

It's what you do after the truth burns your world to the ground.

What do you do with those smoldering coals in your hands, the ones melting the skin of your palms? Do you hold on? Or do you let go?

I wanted the truth and I got it. My father betrayed us with his affair, with his weakness, even with his death. My mother betrayed us when she refused to get help for her illness, when she chose to abandon us.

These are my truths, my own set of burning coals.

The girl lying unconscious on that stretcher holds her own secrets, maybe ones even worse than I know. But it's not her truth that will set me free.

It's mine.

"Please," I say. "She's my sister."

# 41

# LYRA

We've been waiting for hours. A nurse led us from the ER waiting room to a waiting area on the second floor. There are several couches and two coffee tables stacked with back issues of *Better Homes and Gardens* and *Golf Digest*.

Ethan sits beside me. He's trying to interest me in various dessert and appetizer recipes, since we got bored with our phones an hour ago. The clock on the wall above a fake potted plant reads 1:36 a.m.

"This blueberry crumble cake looks gangbusters," Ethan says, thrusting the magazine at me. "What do you think?"

I barely glance at it. My brain keeps spinning like I'm trapped in a deep-sea whirlpool. "I hate blueberries."

"What? No blueberry muffins? Blueberry pancakes? Who hates blueberries?"

"I do. I can't even eat blueberry Pop Tarts. What's taking them so long?"

"It's a hospital. Slow is what they do. Lux is okay, I know it. They just haven't gotten around to telling us yet."

"I hope so."

"I know so. What about coconut? Here's this three-layer coconut concoction that looks like a frothy wedding dress."

"I hate coconut."

"Do you like anything?"

"Spinach."

"I know that's not true. Come on. Three favorite foods. Go."

"Okay fine. My mom's baked mac and cheese. Strawberry short-cake with fresh strawberries. And my dad's homemade hot chocolate."

"I'm totally sold on that hot chocolate. It was like fuzzy pajamas and a warm fire and Christmas morning all rolled into one."

I manage a half-smile. My gaze strays back to the clock. Only five minutes have passed. My skin feels stretched out. My eyes are gritty. "Is Hadley all right without you at night?"

Ethan waves his hand. "She's fine. When I called my mom around eleven, she was screaming up a storm in the background. She's two. It's what she does."

"You don't have to stay, you know."

"I'm staying."

"You've already done so much."

"No worries. You can buy me brunch. Or make me one of these pie things."

"Deal," I say. "But seriously, you aren't obligated or anything."

Ethan closes the magazine and looks at me. "Come on, college girl. Haven't you figured out by now I want to be here with you?"

My heart sputters in my chest. I look down at my hands, study my cuticles like they're the most fascinating thing in the world. "Well, you know. Thanks."

"Well, you know. You're welcome."

"Lyra McKenna?" The nurse calls from her seat behind the counter of the nurses' station. She hangs up the phone she' s been holding to her ear.

I stand up. "That's me."

"I'll shoot up a prayer to the Guy Upstairs for you," Ethan says.

"I doubt it'll do much good."

"You might be surprised."

"Maybe so. I'll take anything right now." I take a deep breath, steel myself, and make my way to the counter. "I'm Lyra McKenna."

The nurse smiles in my direction but doesn't make eye contact. She has a weary, withered face, like she's lost the will to care anymore. "Please wait in the glassed-in room behind me. The doctor will be in to see you shortly."

"Why do we need to be in a separate room? Is it bad news?"

The nurse shakes her head, still not looking at me. "Not necessarily. It's for privacy purposes."

I walk into the small room and sit down in an upholstered chair. I look out at Ethan through the glass. He raises one hand. I can't bring myself to do the same.

The wait is only ten minutes this time. I stand up as a short Indian woman in a white lab coat enters the room. Her large eyes are a rich, deep brown in her round face. She looks far too young to be a doctor, to be in charge of keeping my sister alive.

She grips my hand in a firm handshake, introducing herself as Dr. Sandeep. "Your sister has stabilized."

I lock my knees to keep from sagging in relief. "Thank God. She'll be all right?"

"She came close to slipping into a coma a few times. Your sister experienced respiratory depression, bradycardia, and hypotension. If you hadn't found her when you did ... But yes, her odds for recovery are excellent. She was administered naxalone at the scene. We pumped her stomach and stabilized her fluids. We'll monitor her for a few days for withdrawal, then she can go home."

"What happened?"

Dr. Sandeep clasps her hands in front of her stomach. "Alcohol is a central nervous system depressant. Mixing it with another depressant such as opioids greatly increases the risk of an overdose. Mixing multiple substances is like playing Russian Roulette. When taken in excessive amounts or in combination, they depress normal function such as breathing and heart rate, sometimes to the point of death."

"Opioids?"

"Why don't we have a seat?" Dr. Sandeep says, gesturing at the seat opposite her. I sit down. "Your sister was at risk for hypoxic brain injury, when the brain is deprived of oxygen for too long. Symptoms include mild to severe impairment of balance and coordination, senses such as hearing and sight, and thinking, concentration, and memory. Liver damage is also a concern.

"However, we are hopeful the long-term effects will be minimal. You reached her in time. She's extremely lucky."

There's not enough oxygen in the room. "She knew it could kill her."

Dr. Sandeep shakes her head. "I don't know her motives, Miss McKenna, if that's what you're asking. Do you think she was trying to end her life?"

I rub my temples with my knuckles. "We've been through some rough stuff. Our dad just died. My mom committed suicide, but that was years ago. Lux is really angry. Her behavior has been—erratic. And tonight—" I swallow. "She was sending me these weird texts, and I just thought—I just knew."

"Child survivors of suicide are five times more likely to commit suicide themselves. You should consider in-patient treatment for your sister, for possible suicidal ideation and addiction. We have a psychiatrist who will see you during rounds tomorrow. He'll give your sister a psych eval, and then he'll have more specific suggestions for you."

I clear my throat, blinking rapidly. "Thank you."

Dr. Sandeep glances at her watch. "Your sister is in room 313 when you're ready to see her. I believe she's sleeping now. We have a chapel on the third floor, in case you'd like to use it."

I stand alone in the glassed-in room for several moments after the doctor leaves. Did Lux really want to die? Did she do this to herself on purpose?

*You already know*, a voice whispers inside my head.

I take a deep, steadying breath and walk out into the waiting area. Ethan is gone. There's a text on my phone. He's grabbing some food in the cafeteria. *Want some blueberry muffins?* I send him a smiley emoji and message that Lux is okay. For now.

I don't want to disturb her if she's sleeping. She needs her rest. She's alive, and safe. For now, that's enough.

I need to get away from the florescent lights, the harsh antiseptic smell of the hospital. I head up to the third floor.

There's only a small sign on the door designating the chapel, and I walk past it twice. I open the door to a room about the size of my bedroom, with two rows of five wooden pews separated by a narrow aisle that leads to a bare table at the front. A cross hangs on the white-washed wall behind the table. Wall sconces give off a soft glow.

I'm alone. I slip into the last pew on the right-hand side. My eyelids are weighted down. I'm drained of emotion, physically exhausted, my body screaming for sleep. It's past two thirty in the morning.

Thoughts and images flit through my mind: my mother's face turned toward the light coming from a window, so beautiful, so tortured, those fathomless eyes I could never read. Dad lying in his bed, his closed eyelids bruised purple, his mouth slightly opened, his thick cheeks sagging against the pillow. And Lux, so small, so vulnerable, crumpled in the hallway after Mom's funeral.

What did Lux think about every time she snorted or sniffed or smoked or whatever she did? Did she think about her family? Did she dwell on all the painful, ugly things and let that drive her toward oblivion?

I understand the lure of forgetting, the appeal of drowning out whatever sorrow or guilt or responsibilities threatened to overwhelm her. I've felt it myself.

Were things that bad for her? Or was it our mother's blood flowing through her veins that drove her to it, a defective gene or faulty chromosome passed to the next generation?

I groan and rest my forehead against the back of the pew in front of me. Only hours earlier, I was ready to leave her behind for good. Lux decided to do the same thing. And she almost succeeded.

Almost, but not quite.

*Thank you.* I'm not even sure whom I'm thanking. God? This is a church of sorts, after all. A chapel for the desperate. How many promises were made in this room, how many deals, pledges, and pacts offered, if only so-and-so would live? *I'll never drink or smoke or steal or cheat on my wife again.*

This is a room for bartering souls and sins.

But it's not only that. There is a quiet, a calm, a serenity here. Dad believed. Did he find peace in the end? Or was he racked with guilt even with his last breath? What about Mom? Love wasn't enough to save her.

I grip the pew and lift my head, gazing at the simple wooden cross hung on the wall. It seems like an easy thing, choosing to believe. I want to believe there's more, that there's somewhere better than this, a place free of grief and pain and endless, aching sorrow. I long to have faith in something more than my own pathetic, broken soul. *Please save her. Save us.*

Our past is a sea of wreckage, a ship smashed on the rocks. We've both lost more than anyone should ever have to lose. We're both orphans, bloodied and bruised. Survivors.

But we are not completely adrift. We have each other. We can find Polaris, the North Star, the only fixed point in the infinite sky.

It can guide us home.

42

LUX

I wake up fast, like someone grabbed me by the hair and yanked me from a dark underwater womb up into harsh, blinding sunlight. I gasp and sit straight up. The IV pulls taut in my arm, the needle stinging as it tugs against my vein.

I'm in a hospital bed, a thin blanket bunched around my waist. The other half of the room is cordoned off by a crinkly curtain hanging from a track in the ceiling.

Lyra sits beside me in a blue plastic chair. "Finally awake?" she asks, closing the pages of a magazine and placing it on her lap.

I lift my IV-free arm and scrub my hair back from my face. My teeth are furry. My greasy tongue sticks to the roof of my mouth. Everything about me is stale and unwashed.

"How do you feel?"

"Awful. Like I've been run over by Dad's eighteen-wheeler."

Lyra smiles grimly. "You look almost that bad."

"Thanks so much."

"You can breathe okay? Everything's working properly?"

"Mmm, yeah. What happened?"

Lyra stares at me without blinking. "You mixed opioids with alcohol.

You overdosed."

When I try to think back, the memories are blurred, disjointed. Acid spikes up the back of my throat. I feel sick. "How long have I been out?"

"Since last night."

"Oh." It seems like it's been days since the party. "What about Phoenix? Does she have food?"

"I've been feeding her and doing the kitty litter. She literally tried to bite my toes off. That thing's not a pet. She's feral."

"Half-feral," I say groggily. "I'm taming her."

Lyra's jaw tightens. "We can talk about that later. What happened?"

I shake my head, waves of dizziness washing over me. I ease back against the bed with a groan, trying to shift into a comfortable position. "I wasn't thinking, obviously."

"You could've died."

"I know."

"Were you trying to?" Lyra asks, her voice trembling.

"No. Of course not." But my head is thick with fuzz and half-formed thoughts. A memory agitates the corners of my mind.

"I found you, Lux. I was there."

"You found me?"

"You sent me some crazy texts. I was worried. You were unconscious, barely breathing."

My throat burns. "Why does it hurt to swallow?"

"They pumped your stomach." Gray smudges rim Lyra's eyes, her unruly waves flattened against her head. She looks like she hasn't slept in days. "Lux. You nearly—" She sucks in a breath. "You almost died. How could you—?"

"Sorry to disrupt your perfect life by, you know, almost dying."

"That's not what I meant."

Every bone in my body aches, my throat burns, and my brain is clogged with cotton balls. It hurts too much to think. I don't want to think. I don't want to know. "I get it, okay? It's my fault. It's always my fault."

Lyra's lips press into a thin line. "You aren't even listening to me."

What else did I expect? She's always letting me know just how much of a screw-up I am. And she's right. I always have been, since I was ten years old. "I get it, Lyra. You don't have to rub it in."

"Why are you doing this?"

"Doing what?"

"You always push me away. Even now, when you nearly—"

"Just stop it, okay? Can you please just stop?" I curl clumps of blanket into my fists. Shame and longing twist inside me like battling snakes. Half of me is desperate for her presence, craving her love and attention. The other, bigger half wants to push her aside and run away as hard and fast as I can.

Except I can't. I'm trapped.

The machine next to me beeps incessantly. The murmur of nurses' voices filter through the opened door. On the other side of the crinkly white curtain, someone snores.

The smell of other people's sickness stings my nostrils. A headache pounds against my skull. I just want to close my eyes and sleep, sleep for days. Maybe forever.

Lyra is silent for a long moment. She tears strips from the magazine in her lap. Little pieces fall to the floor. "You're right."

"I just can't right now."

"No—I've been too hard on you. I was just so ..." Competing emotions flit across her face. She takes a deep, shuddering breath. "You really scared me, Lux. I thought—I thought I'd lost you."

"I'm right here, very much alive."

"I just—I need to know if you're okay." There are tears in her eyes.

My gut clenches. My first instinct is to lie, but for some reason, I don't. I can't. "I don't know."

Lyra hesitates, then nods. She stares down at her hands. "I'm here, Lux. Okay? I'm right here."

A nurse knocks on the open door and bustles into the room. "You're up. Excellent. How are you feeling?"

I rub the heel of my palm against my eyes. I feel like I was buried alive and had to claw my way back to the surface. "I'm still breathing. Score one for small victories."

"I'm Nurse Gibbens. Have you urinated on your own yet?"

Lyra stands up quickly. "And that's my cue to go." The nurse chuckles and checks my IV.

I don't think I'll ever laugh again. Fear and anxiety tighten my throat. I don't want her to leave. I'm terrified of being alone. "Where are you going?"

Lyra looks down at the magazine she's twisting in her hands. "Home.

I'm dead on my feet. I promise I'll come back first thing in the morning. We'll talk more then."

I swallow hard. Something inside me whispers, *Don't leave me!* But all I manage to say is, "Okay."

Lyra touches my hand, then walks out of the room, her thick red hair swinging down her back. I watch her leave.

That empty, hollowed out feeling returns, howling inside me. The memories are there, submerged just beneath the surface.

I don't want to remember.

I don't want to know what I've done.

43

# LYRA

Lake Michigan shimmers in the sunlight like the shards of ten thousand mirrors. The strong breeze nips at my exposed skin and tugs my hair across my face. I tighten my cardigan around myself and dig my bare toes into the cold, wet sand. It's hard to believe it was snowing only a few short weeks ago.

In Michigan, spring sneaks up on you. It's the second week of April and seventy degrees, but the wind is chilly. A few other families are scattered down the beach, everyone playing in the sand, avoiding that gorgeous, freezing water. We have an entire section of the beach to ourselves.

Lux is still in the hospital, but she's stable. She's alive. I feel like I can relax for the first time in weeks. I carry my Nikon, snapping pictures of everything.

I fill the viewfinder with image after image of the glittering water, the orange sun in the blazing white sky, the beach grass clumped on the dunes, the seagulls pecking at the sand along the shoreline. And of course, Hadley and Ethan.

Hadley sits on her plump bottom a few feet back from the waves. She's wearing a knit sweater already caked with sand as she gleefully waves a shovel in each fist, her laugh like a burst of sunlight shattering the sky. My chest nearly cracks open from the haunting beauty of that sound.

"She brings happiness wherever she goes, doesn't she?" I say, walking up to Ethan. He's sprawled on a pink and purple Tinker Bell blanket.

"She really does," he says. "Take a break. You haven't sat down yet."

I sit, my blood buzzing with the awareness of how close my body is to his. I open the picnic basket I brought, the same one Mom used to bring on our midnight picnics. My stomach twinges.

"I brought a few things." I pull out potato salad, PB and honey sandwiches, grapes, and chocolate chip cookies.

Ethan pops an entire cookie in his mouth. "These are gangbusters! Are they homemade?"

"Yeah. And the blueberry crumb cake you liked from that magazine at the hospital. I made you some to take home to your mom."

"Are you serious right now?"

I spent the morning baking. I wanted to say thank you, to show him how I felt. "It's no biggie, really."

He pulls a sand-covered package of Doritos out of a beach bag stuffed with towels, sunblock, and brightly colored sand toys. "This is all I brought. A meal fit for a king."

"Doritos make great dippers for the potato salad."

"Seriously, Lyra. This spread is amazing. You didn't have to do this."

I shrug, my cheeks tingling. "It's my pleasure."

Ethan takes a huge bite of PB and honey sandwich. "No, I assure you. The pleasure is mine."

I grab a handful of grapes. "You're welcome."

Ethan takes a grape out of my hand, his fingers barely brushing mine. Heat creeps up my throat. I'm not used to someone so close to me, especially not someone like Ethan. I have no idea what we are, if we're anything at all. I remember how he stood up to Floyd, so strong, so confident, so protective. My mouth goes dry.

"This Tinker Bell blanket is amazing." I rub the sand-covered fleece. "The pinks and purples really bring out the color of your eyes."

He grins. "I'm partial to Dora the Explorer and Doc McStuffins, too. Very flattering color combinations."

"You have exquisite taste."

"Why thank you. I'm also a fan of country music, the Green Bay Packers, and Bill's infamous mushroom burgers."

"Okay, I take it all back. The Packers? Seriously?"

"Don't knock 'em. I'll be a Brett Favre fan 'til the day I die." Ethan stretches out on the blanket, leaning back on his elbows. The breeze blows strands of black hair across his eyes. We watch Hadley run back and forth on the beach, grabbing clods of wet sand and flinging them at the water.

"Don't throw sand in anybody's eyes!" Ethan calls after her.

"There's like, nobody within one hundred feet of us."

He shrugs. "All the books say I need to instill good habits while she's young."

Hadley dashes up to us. She shoves one hand into the Doritos bag and grabs two cookies with the other.

"Hey!" Ethan says.

Hadley giggles and scampers away, shoving both cookies in her mouth at the same time.

"Good habits, huh?"

"We're starting tomorrow. Obviously."

My phone buzzes in my sweater pocket. I pull it, shielding my eyes to read the number. It's from my advisor. Again. Over the last several days, Dr. Wells has left me several concerned voicemails. I was ineligible for the award and my chance at the internship due to my very noticeable absence at the gallery show. Why did I tell him I'd be there if I was just going to flake on him? He embarrassed himself in front of the board, et cetera, et cetera.

My stomach tightens. I hate that I've disappointed him. He's a good man, a great mentor. Will he even still want to mentor me next semester?

I put my phone away and sigh.

"Are you okay?"

"The gallery. I missed it. I lost the competition, the prize money, the internship." I made my choice. But still, that burning ache beneath my ribs won't dissipate. My dreams are disintegrating beneath my fingers.

My throat thickens. I lift my camera again to hide my face, the scalding heat behind my eyes.

Ethan puts his hand on my arm. "I felt the same way when I dropped out and lost my athletic scholarship. It sucks. But that doesn't mean your life is over. Or even your art."

"I know that. I'm just afraid ..." My voice trails off. I don't know how to explain it. I stare at Hadley through the viewfinder. "I don't want to turn into my father. I can't. He gave up his own dreams when I was born. So did my mom, for that matter. When I was a kid, I always felt like I was the reason for their unhappiness."

Ethan snorts. "Now that's hubris if I ever heard it. And you said I was the one with the enormous ego."

I lower the camera to glare at him. "And that's funny?"

"Okay, not funny. But one act, one choice, doesn't determine a person's entire life. Your father could've gone back to school in the evenings. It wouldn't have been easy, but it could've been done. He could have joined online photography groups, submitted to competitions. Geez, he should've at least taken pictures for himself, for his own joy. He didn't have to quit altogether."

I nod slowly. "I guess you're right."

"Forgive me for speaking ill of the dead. I don't mean to sound harsh. But you can't just hold on to one version of your future, just one thing you think will make you happy. Because if you lose that, then what? If you keep holding on to what's already gone, if you can't let go—you become trapped. Bitter."

I stare at the brown sand beneath my toes. "It's like the monkey and the marble."

"What?"

"I learned about it in Intro to Psych. In the jungle, trappers put out glass jars with a single marble inside. The monkey comes by and wants the marble. He shoves his little hand in the jar and grabs it. But with his fingers clasped around the marble, he can't pull his fist out. That's how he's trapped. He wants that marble so badly, he won't let go. All he has to do is open his hand, leave that shiny round promise behind, and he's free."

"If there's anything I've learned in the last three years, it's this. There's more than one kind of happiness. And more than one way to get there. But you have to let go of that shiny marble of your future you wanted to have. You have to let it go."

"Have you?"

He shields his face with his hand as he watches Hadley frolic by the edge of the water. "It's a long, hard process. But yeah, I'm getting there."

"Neither of my parents could do that."

"A lot of people don't." He touches my arm again, sending an electric shock through my entire body.

I pick up a handful of sand and rub the granules between my fingers. Seagulls wheel overhead, swooping and diving over the water.

I think about my parents, my past, how our world always felt so precarious, like it could so easily slip away or come tumbling down on us. On my own small, brittle shoulders. How it always felt like it was up to me to keep it all up, keep the balls in the air, the plates spinning, the darkness at bay.

"They're both dead, but it still feels like I have these weights on me, dragging me down, anchoring me to all this darkness."

"You think your sister feels the same way?"

I open my mouth, but I don't know what to say. She'll be discharged from the hospital in two days. The doctors recommended in-patient treatment. They spouted all these psychological terms I heard but didn't understand, every word another rock in the pit of my stomach. "I don't know."

"Maybe you should ask her."

"Getting close to her is like trying to hug a porcupine."

"Is it possible she thinks the same about you?"

Anger jolts through me. "Just whose side are you on, anyway?"

"Take it down a notch, would you? I'm simply asking questions."

I take a steadying breath. "She's just so—I can't understand her. She can be so thoughtless, irresponsible, so downright cruel. I don't get it."

"People in pain can be hard to understand."

"She's hurting, I know that. She tried to—" My words catch in my throat. I remember how she looked, her body crumpled in a heap on that pure white carpet.

I thought she was dead. I thought I was too late. "I have another chance now. A chance I lost with my parents. I want to make things right. I have to."

"Good."

"It's just—I don't know how."

Ethan raises his eyebrows and pops another Dorito into his mouth. The rims of his lips are orange. "Can you talk to her?"

"When I try, she screams at me or runs away."

"Don't take this the wrong way, but how do you talk to her? You've got some sharp edges yourself, you know. Not that I don't like that, I do. But if I were her, I'd feel all that anger coming off you in waves. It can't be easy for her."

"There you go, taking sides again."

"I can still be on your side and empathize with her."

A shiver runs through me. "Are you? On my side?"

He shifts his body. "You haven't figured that out yet, college girl?"

The blush travels up from my chest and neck and blooms a hot, furious red across my face. Instinctively, I turn my head away.

His hand touches my chin. Gently, he turns my face toward him. "I'm on your side. Okay? And why do you keep turning away and hiding your face?"

I shrug, blushing even harder. "It's not much to look at. You know, all these freckles. My big nose."

"What are you even talking about? I love every single one of your freckles. You're beautiful. Whoever said you weren't?"

I can barely force the words out. "Oh, I don't know. Every guy in high school."

A slow smile spreads across his face. "Boys don't appreciate the sophisticated or unique. And I know of which I speak, having recently been one." This close, his amber eyes glisten in the sunlight like pools of gold. He smells so very male, like sweat and soap and grease.

I must be one shade of boiled lobster red, from the tips of my hair to the freckles at the base of my throat. My heart jackhammers against my ribcage. My belly explodes in fluttering wings. "Ethan—"

Hadley runs up to us, kicking a spray of sand across the blanket. She's got a round stone clutched in her fist. "Yook, Daddy!"

"Awesome, Chipmunk."

She presses the stone into Ethan's hand. "Urse!"

Hadley watches with a critical gaze as Ethan opens the red polka dot purse and slips it inside. Satisfied, she scampers off to find more treasure. Two wet, sandy circles splotch the bottom of her pink sparkly sweatpants.

"More 'gifts'. My dresser is covered with rocks, pinecones, dried leaves, and sticks," Ethan says ruefully. He turns back to me, that wry grin still on his lips. "Now, where were we?"

Before I can protest or think of all the ways this is a terrible idea, he leans in and kisses me. He tastes like Doritos, but his lips are soft and his fingers graze my cheek and his hands are warm and strong.

I feel like I've been thrust beneath the surf, wave upon dizzy wave unfurling over me. My whole self is melting beneath his touch, beneath his kiss.

The sand is gritty between my toes and the breeze whips my hair and the water is a soothing murmur. Every sense is sparkling and alive.

I don't think I breathe until he pulls away.

"Now do you believe I'm on your side?"

I take a ragged breath. My mouth is unable to formulate words.

"Maybe you need more convincing?" I manage to nod.

"Happy to help." His lips are on mine, his eyes glowing flames. My stomach somersaults. Every nerve in my body sparks. Part of me can't believe this is actually happening. I'm the frizzy-haired dork, the artsy girl no one notices. Now here he is, Ethan Kusuma, noticing *me*. He's kissing *me*.

I don't know what this is or what it means. All I know is my head is swimming, my blood buzzing. I just want to stay here, kissing him, feeling his presence, his fingers on my face sending electric charges through my whole body.

Suddenly I'm hungry for his touch, his kiss, his everything. The numb parts of me are tingling, coming back to life, awakening a desire I didn't even know I had. I scoot closer, tucking myself against him. I kiss him back, hard.

We stay like that for what seems like hours, electricity surging in my blood, my bones singing. I'm warm and safe and happy. For now, at least here in this moment, with him.

"Daddy?" Hadley's voice breaks in. I pull away. Hadley stands inches away from my face, peering at me with confused, curious eyes. She puts her chubby, sandy hand on my mouth, like she's trying to figure out what we're doing.

Laughter bubbles up inside me, and pretty soon we're all giggling. Hadley's face breaks into a radiant grin and she hurls herself into my arms. I hug her back, feeling the solidness of her, the softness.

And the coldness of her skin. "Ethan, she's freezing."

Ethan puts his hand on her cheek. "You're right. I didn't realize how cold it was, seeing how we were sharing body heat. Time to go, Chipmunk."

Hadley's whole body stiffens. "Noooooooo!" she shrieks. She jerks out of my arms and throws herself to the sand, rolling around and flailing her fists in despair.

Ethan and I stand up. "It's time for supper, and bath, and stories. Remember those? You love stories."

But Hadley just screams, her shrieks picked up by the wind. A few couples further down the beach look our way. Ethan's brow furrows. "In the *Everything A to Z Guide to Toddlers*, it says not to take her anger personally. We shouldn't reward her tantrum by holding her. She has to stop crying completely before I pick her up."

"What? I can't hear you over the wailing."

Ethan smiles tightly. "I knew you'd get it."

He collects all the sand toys while I stuff the snacks into the bag, roll up the blanket, and tuck it under my arm. I think about what Ethan said, about not taking it personally. Hadley's little body can't handle her oversized, out-of-control emotions. It's her fear and hurt and sadness coming out as a tantrum, as anger. I understand that.

Most of us grow out of tantrums. But maybe some of us don't. Maybe they just change, become darker, angrier, with steeper consequences. Maybe beneath all of Lux's anger and resentment is fear, and loss. Two things I know plenty about.

Hadley keeps shrieking and screaming. Her face is so red it's almost purple. Tears streak her face. She beats at the air with her fists.

Ethan watches her, pain and indecision on his face.

I touch his arm. "She needs you. Just pick her up. To hell with the experts."

He gives me a sideways glance. "Seriously?"

"For the sake of our eardrums, please. Pick her up."

Ethan scoops Hadley up and wraps her in his strong arms. She flails against his chest, screaming her fury at him. He pats her back and murmurs soothingly. After a minute, her little body collapses. She wraps her arms around his neck and presses herself against him, sniffling and hiccupping.

"You don't need the books, Ethan. At least, you don't need to follow every single thing you read. You're good at this."

"Really? 'Cause it doesn't seem like it," he says grimly. "Most of the time, I feel like a spectacular failure."

"You're not."

He shakes his head. "I'm not used to feeling like this, like I'm out of my element and I have no clue what I'm supposed to do. Anything else, I can study it and figure it out. Like a car's engine or a playbook. I studied the plays, re-watched the game tapes, put in the hours at two-a-days and in the weight room. I knew what to do to improve, get better.

"But here? This? It's like I'm blindfolded, stumbling around in the dark, cracking my shin open on the freakin' coffee table."

"No, you aren't."

His expression is strained. Suddenly I see how tired he is, the creases below his beautiful eyes. "It shouldn't be this hard, this exhausting. I must be doing something wrong."

"You aren't doing anything wrong. Parenting is hard. It just is. Anyone who says it isn't is either lying or they have a live-in nanny."

Ethan snorts. "You think?"

"I do. Seriously, you're amazing. Do you not see the way Hadley looks at you?"

He rubs her back. "I love her more than anything. More than my own life."

"It shows."

Hadley hiccups, burying her snot-covered face in his neck. "That's my girl," he murmurs. The love between them radiates with a light so bright, it almost hurts to look at.

"See? Show me one book that can do that."

He turns to me. "Thank you, Lyra. Truly. How do you know so much?"

"Even when my mother was physically present, she wasn't. I took care of things. I took care of Lux." But even as I say the words, I know they aren't completely true.

I see Lux, her knobby knees squished against me beneath the table, her tiny hands squeezing mine, inventing one of her stories. I remember my heartbeat slowing, the choking fear receding as I focused on her intent little face, her eyes blazing as she spun a fantasy world around us, wrapping us up in visions of fairies and castles and Greek gods and mythological creatures.

It wasn't just me taking care of her. Sometimes, it was the other way around. We took turns, back then.

Maybe we can again.

"Ready to go?" Ethan asks, hefting the bag of sand toys. Behind him, the sun is a yellow ball sinking over the horizon, barely skimming the surface of the water.

"Ready," I say.
And I am.

# 44

## LUX

I feel like a piñata someone's attacked with a baseball bat. I didn't think short-term use would cause such nasty withdrawal, but I was wrong.

I've survived four nights of tremors, insomnia, muscle cramps, and nausea. Lyra is an amazing caretaker, as always. She barely leaves my side. She sits by my bed, bathing my sweating skin with cool washcloths. She brings me copies of *US Weekly* and downloads new games on my phone.

But there's nothing she can do about the fierce need burning through my veins like acid. The symptoms peaked yesterday, but it still feels like I've been dragged through a blender. I'm pale, dizzy, and shaky. My bones ache.

Every day, the tangled memories in my mind clear more and more. I remember way more than I want to.

The doctors poked and prodded and tested me. They gave me a psych eval. I don't know if I passed. *Do you want to hurt yourself? Yes. Do you have feelings of low self-worth? Yes. Do you ever feel like tearing your own skin off? Yes, yes, yes.* Lyra sat beside me when the doctor made her recommendations, throwing around terms like self-harm, addiction, personality disorders.

The words float around in my brain like a toxic soup.

The doctor recommended a three-month in-treatment program at Sunny Meadows Mental Health and Addiction Treatment Center. It sounds like some terrible psych ward horror movie, where the nurses tie patients to the bed and torture them. No one believes them because they're crazy anyway, right? But I'm not crazy. I'm not foaming at the mouth or throwing myself into walls or obeying the voices in my head telling me to saw my arm off.

I just sit and listen to them talk, let the words wash over me. Lyra asks all the questions. She promises to take care of me, to get me treatment. I'll be discharged tomorrow.

"You need help," Lyra says after the doctor leaves.

"I'm fine." But that's such a whopper of a lie even I can't swallow it. "I'm not crazy."

"No one said you were."

I cross my arms over my chest and stare at the TV bolted to the wall, Jeopardy on mute. "I'm not going anywhere with padded rooms and restraints and pills that make you drool."

"You tried to kill yourself—"

"It was an accident."

"We both know it wasn't." There's tension in her voice. And pain. "Please, Lux. Let's not do this. I'm sorry I was so pissy before. But this is important. When I read those texts you sent that night—I knew. We barely made it in time. You nearly died. If nothing changes, it will happen again."

"You don't know that."

"Yes, I do." Lyra smooths her hair behind her ears. Her face is pale beneath the freckles sprinkled across her face like nutmeg. "This twelve-week program sounds good. The hospital is in Tampa, only a few miles from my university. This can seriously work."

"I can't move away. What about school?"

"You dropped out, remember? After the hospital, you can get your GED or take distance classes or even find a school there to finish up your senior year. We'll figure it out after you're better."

"We can't afford it," I say, throwing up every roadblock I can think of.

"Dad had a life insurance policy. We'll use the money to pay for your treatment."

"It's gonna be thousands of dollars. That money should pay for your college or a house or something."

Lyra's face tightens. "You getting better is the priority. That's what matters. Don't you understand?"

"I can't." I don't know how to explain the terror that explodes inside my chest at the thought of signing myself into a mental hospital. I'm not crazy.

I'm not Mom. I'm not her. I'm not.

I'm fine. I'm fine. I'm fine.

The memory of that night seeps into my brain like poison. Taking the pills. Snorting the powder. Learning what Floyd had tried to do. The white-hot flame of shame incinerating my bones, muscles, tendons, skin.

The whole thing is a black blot in my brain I'm desperate to forget. But I can't. I can't forget any of it.

So much of my past is shifting shadows. But these things, the things I despise most about myself—these memories are always clear and sharp as shards of glass.

"What if Mom got help? Real help? Everything could've been different. If she—"

Her words cut off as the door opens. Simone and Autumn clatter in, huge bouquets of orange roses and yellow lilies and bobbing Get Well Soon balloons in their arms.

"We're here!" Autumn calls. I can barely see her head past the balloons as she and Simone drop their gifts at the foot of the bed.

"How you feeling?" Simone asks, adjusting her square-framed glasses. She's wearing green cargo pants with a black tank top, her mane of corkscrew curls as wild as ever. Autumn's got her usual hoodie on, her hair tucked back in a French braid. They look so out of place in this cold, ugly hospital room.

"Look! We brought you a money origami book!" Autumn thrusts a book entitled *Extreme Origami* into my hands. The picture on the cover is of a scorpion formed out of a single dollar bill. "I know you're all advanced and stuff, but using dollars seemed like a fun new thing to try, right? Here's five bucks to get you started."

"Don't spend it all in one place," Simone drops two Twix bars in my lap. "One of those has my name on it."

"I think you're in good hands." Lyra stands up and straightens her clothes. "I'm gonna go home and take a shower. I'll come back tonight."

"Okay," I mumble.

"We've been waiting forever to visit you." Autumn unscrews the lid of the Faygo she brought with her and takes a swig.

Simone plops down in the blue plastic chair next to the bed. "You hungry? We can smuggle in some Taco Bell."

I tear off the Twix wrappers and divvy up the single bars. I take the last bar, break it into thirds, and pass the pieces to my friends. "The hospital food isn't that bad, actually. Except for the mashed potatoes that literally came in a square shape and jiggled like Jell-O. I was afraid to taste it."

"Gross." Autumn makes a face. She pops the Twix piece in her mouth.

"Ahhh. Much better."

"Lots of people are asking about you," Simone says.

"Felix?"

Simone nods. "Yes, Felix, too. But don't get your hopes up." "I'm so not," I say. But I so am.

Autumn chews on the end of her braid, her face scrunched up. "So, are you like, okay?"

"Autumn!" Simone hisses.

Autumn rolls her eyes. "What? It's too important not to ask."

"I'm okay. I'm fine."

"What happened?"

I take a breath. What do I tell them? Will they stick around once they hear the worst of me? "I had too much to drink. I took some stuff I shouldn't have."

"Everybody's talking about it," Autumn says softly. "Reese told people you tried to kill yourself."

I flinch. Autumn stares at me intently. I avert my eyes and open the origami book and look at the dull green and white animal shapes without really seeing them.

"He actually sounded pretty broken up about it," Autumn says.

"Whoop-de-freaking-do," Simone says. "Someone give the drug dealer an empathy award."

I think about the way his eyes got all soft when I gave him the origami bat, how his face looked desperate and angry when he told me what Floyd tried to do to me.

"Is that—is that what happened?" Autumn asks again.

"I'm not crazy."

They both look at me, waiting for whatever it is I need to say.

"A bunch of horrible stuff happened," I say in a rush. I'm not going to lie anymore. I'm not going to wear that mask that's been slowly suffocating me, strangling my breath. I need to tell the truth. I have to. "Everything with my dad and my sister just brought back all these terrible memories, about my mom and stuff. I just—I lost it."

Simone lowers her brows. "It was on purpose?"

How can I explain to them what it's like? How the space inside my own head is a battlefield. What it's like when my mind wants to murder itself.

I can't. I don't know how. I can't speak those things. I can only nod my head.

Autumn grabs my hand. Tears gather in the corners of her eyes. "I'm so

sorry, Lux."

Seeing her tears activates my own. My eyes burn. My throat closes up. "I'm the one that's sorry."

Simone looks furious. "How could you do that? Why didn't you say something? Why didn't you call me?"

"We weren't talking. I didn't even know if we were still friends."

"Lux!" Simone shouts. "It was a fight. You know, that thing normal people do? Then they make up and get over it? You think every fight is the end of the world. I would've been there in a heartbeat. Autumn, too. We're your *friends*."

"I know." Snot bubbles in my nose. I wipe it away with the back of my arm. "I'm sorry."

"You never told me you felt that way," Autumn says.

"I just—I didn't know what to do. I felt like—like everyone would be better off if I was gone."

"Never. We'd be devastated, Lux."

"Swear to us," Simone says, her voice hard. "Freakin' give us a blood oath, right here, right now, that you'll never do that again."

My heart is going to burst. I have the best friends in the whole world. I don't know why either of them want anything to do with me, but they do. They still want me. They still love me. "I swear," I choke out.

Simone glares at me. "I'm not even joking. I'm bringing a knife next time we visit."

"I said I swear! I'll be fine. I—" Suddenly I remember Floyd, his cold, flat eyes taking me in, his breath on my cheek, his thick fingers pressing on my throat. "Something else happened. Before the party ..."

Autumn squeezes my hand. "You can tell us."

"I got trashed. I mean, I don't remember most of the night. When I woke up, I realized my dress was all bunched up."

The room is silent.

My heart beats in my throat. "I thought at first it was Reese."

Autumn shifts on the bed. "But it wasn't."

"No. It was Floyd, the guy who deals to Reese, who owns the house."

I swallow hard. "He's like, forty."

Simone stops fidgeting. Her body goes still. "What did he do?"

Shame and humiliation burn through me. "I don't remember," I whisper. It's the one terrible thing about that night I still can't recall. When I try to search for it in my mind, it's like looking into a bottomless black pit. There's nothing there, only darkness.

"What about Reese?" Simone stalks the room in tight, savage circles.

"He said he walked in. That Floyd was trying to push up my dress —but it didn't happen. He stopped it. If Reese hadn't been there ..."

Autumn grips my hands so tight my fingers go numb.

"It's a damn good thing Reese isn't so worthless after all," Simone says.

The words curdle in my throat. I force them out. "I still feel horrible.

Dirty."

"Oh, no you don't," Simone says.

"I'm just another drunk girl who—"

"Shut up right now," Simone says.

I lower my head. I'm repulsive. Junk. A piece of trash to use and throw out. "I'm damaged. Tainted."

"That's not true!" Autumn says.

"Don't you dare say that," Simone says fiercely. "Do you hear me?"

"I hear you, but—"

"You hear me, but you're not listening. You. Are. Not. Tainted."

I try to nod, but I can't. They don't know what I am. They don't know the half of it.

"I'm going to kill him," Simone snarls, her eyes bulging. "I'm going to bust out his large intestine and wrap it around his slimy neck and choke him with his own—"

"Let's try to avoid murdering people, okay?" Autumn says.

"Why? Do you know the abysmal rates of incarceration for sexual assaults of any kind? Why mess with the broken, archaic judicial system when you can just put a bullet in his brain for free?"

"Simone!" Autumn hisses. "You're not being helpful!"

Simone snaps her fingers. "What's that species of spider, Autumn? You know the one I'm talking about."

"Tarantulas, black widows, wolf spiders. After mating, the female cannibalizes the male. Some female tarantulas just eat the guys without mating at all."

"Yes!" Simone pumps her fist in the air. "We need to do that. Maybe not the cannibal part. But the killing part. So much yes."

"Ignore her." Autumn looks at me, concern darkening her face. "This is not your fault."

I shake my head, about to argue, to spit out more words like barbed wire in my throat.

The nurse sticks her head in. "Visiting hours end in five minutes, ladies."

The silence stretches between us. On the TV, the three contestants write down their final answers on their blue screens. Even without sound, the famous Jeopardy music hums through my brain.

Simone clears her throat. "That disgusting creep? He's responsible for every single thing he did and everything he wanted to do. It doesn't matter what you did or didn't drink. You weren't able to give consent. That's wrong. It's wrong and it always will be. Full stop."

"You didn't do this." Autumn stares at me intently, her gaze not leaving my face. Her dark eyes drill into mine. "Do you understand? This is not your fault. You have to believe that."

I manage a small, trembling smile. "I'll try, Skittles."

Simone says, "At least he's going to prison. He deserves way worse."

"What?"

"Reese rolled on him. That guy Floyd got arrested on major drug trafficking charges. He's in jail."

Relief floods through me, from the top of my scalp all the way down to my toes. "Good."

Autumn gets off the end of the bed, comes over, and grabs me in a tight hug. "We're right here. We're your friends, and we love you."

Simone leans in and squeezes my shoulder. "What she said. You'll get through this. If you need us to, we can always cut off his head with a cleaver. Just say the word."

My heart fills up and overflows. I've treated them horribly, especially Autumn. Yet here they are, still loving me. Lyra's here, still loving me.

I don't deserve it. I don't deserve any of it.

## 45

## LUX

Phoenix stretches on my bed, legs extended, claws out, kneading my pillow. She's seven months old now and full-size. Her sleek coat ripples in the early morning sunlight slanting through my window. She rules the house, going where she pleases, sprawling on the couch or her absolute favorite spot, right in the center of my pillow.

It's been over two weeks since I left the hospital. The day they discharged me, I asked Lyra to bring me clothes from home. I stuffed the black velvet dress and the ripped tights and my underwear into a plastic grocery bag and threw it in the trash on the way out of the hospital.

I took the longest, hottest shower I've ever taken in my life, scrubbing every square inch of skin until it was pink and stinging. I can rub the smell of him off my flesh, but I can't rub that black blight from my memory. Maybe I don't want to.

Reese can be a total asshat, but he did the right thing when it counted. Ordinary acts of courage happen every day. There's no fanfare or celebration. It doesn't make the news. But still, the world—in some small, perceptible way—is brighter.

A week ago, I went to the police station. Lyra, Simone, and Autumn went with me. I don't know what they can do. There's no proof, no evidence. But I told my story. When I was finished, the female cop touched my shoulder. "Even though it's unlikely we can prosecute your case, you can still have justice. We have plenty of evidence related to his drug trafficking charges. He's going away for a long time."

This will have to be enough. It is enough.

What I mostly feel is tired. A tiredness like a deep ache in my bones. And the need. The need is always there. Rustling beneath my skin. But I ignore it. I fight it.

It's grueling, excruciating, like climbing the same damn mountain every single day. My body is exhausted just trying to recover from everything I've done to it.

Everyone else is celebrating the end of senior year, the start of the next big thing. Simone's going to Michigan State, Autumn to U of M. I heard Felix got that scholarship to Notre Dame he wanted so bad. I'm the only one treading water, fighting as hard as I can just to keep my head above the surface.

I reach out and lay my hand gently, carefully on Phoenix's back. She flinches, hesitates, then softly arches against my hand. After a minute, her purring starts, growing until it vibrates her entire body.

Her whiskers brush against my fingers. "That's my girl," I whisper. Phoenix leaps off the bed. She stalks off, tail high in the air. She still won't let me hold her. She goes frantic, writhing, spitting, and swiping at the closest object, usually my bare skin.

I don't need her to be a lap cat. I don't need her to be anything more than she is. She's tough. She's a survivor. She's like me.

I turn back to the pile of clothes strewn across my bedspread. I pick up an old reindeer Christmas sweater I haven't worn in three years and tuck it inside a cardboard box. If it was up to me, I'd grab handfuls of clothes out of my closet and drawers and just stuff them in boxes. Way faster. But no. Lyra wants organization. Lyra wants neatness.

In the two weeks since I've been home, I've helped Lyra pack up dozens of boxes, listed furniture on Craigslist, sold Dad's old Honda Accord on Autotrader, and hauled bags of donated clothes and knickknacks to Goodwill. She's decluttering before we put it on the market.

The house I grew up in seems to shrink, becoming emptier every day. The echoes ring louder and louder as we remove all the things that made it a home—curtains, bedspreads, pots and pans, rugs, candles, lamps, clocks.

There are ghostly squares on the walls where picture frames used to hang, the yellow paint around the frames faded from years of sunlight. The rooms look strange now, so stark, so blank.

I asked Lyra what that meant for me. "I don't know," she said. "I want you to come with me to Florida and go to that treatment center. We can rent an apartment together. But I can't force you to do anything. If you won't come, I hope you'll see a therapist here. I'll give you some of the life insurance money to rent a place and go back to school. The choice is yours."

"I'm not going to any crazy psych ward," I snapped.

She looked hurt. But she didn't yell back or scream at me. "You get to choose, Lux."

My future is wide open. The weight of it is crushing me.

Staying alive takes so much work. Not just staying alive. Not just surviving, but really living.

I grab another shirt off the bed. It's a cute oversized teal shirt with silver sparkles that I always wear with my gray skinny jeans. It's the shirt I wore on my first date with Felix.

He kept touching the sparkles. I slapped him away, playfully, flirting, until I grabbed his hand and kept holding it. He leaned in and kissed me, but our noses bumped and we both started giggling hysterically.

That's when I knew this would be different, that he was different from all the other guys. An ache starts deep in my chest. There's still something I need to do. If I put it off, I'll wuss out and never do it.

I toss on some clothes, tug a brush through my bangs, and line my eyes with kohl. I drive to his house, my knuckles white on the steering wheel. The air is chilly, low-hanging fog drifting above the ground.

My heart stutters in my chest when he opens the door. "Hey."

"Hey yourself," Felix says, standing in the doorway in gray boxers and an oversized vintage Star Wars T-shirt that says, "May the Mass Times Acceleration Be with You."

My heart throbs just looking at him. He's so good, so wholesome, like he belongs in a Norman Rockwell painting or should star in a commercial eating all-American apple pie.

He runs his hands through his tangled mop of curls. "I wasn't expecting visitors."

"I guess it's a bit early in the morning."

"Lux, it's eight a.m. on a Sunday. Most people in their right minds are still sleeping."

"Oh, sorry." I grin sheepishly. "I can come back." "It's all right," he says with a sigh.

A sleepy voice from inside calls, "Who is it?"

He hesitates. "Just a friend, Mom."

I'm hurt and relieved at the same time. At least he said, 'friend.' "I won't take long. But I need—I'd like to talk to you. Please."

He squints at me, examining my face. "Okay. Five minutes." He comes out onto the porch and shuts the door behind him. "We can sit on the swing."

He sits on one end of the porch swing and looks out across the driveway. I put down my messenger bag and sit on the other end. There's a wooden end table with a glass ashtray and a purple lighter next to it. Nervous energy buzzes through me. I grab the lighter and slip it in my pocket.

Felix clears his throat. "So . . . ?"

It's hard to look at him. I imagine us cuddling on this same swing, talking long into the night. I imagine epic make-out sessions, both of us wrapped up in one oversized blanket.

The space between us seems solid as a brick wall.

"I screwed up." Once I start, it all comes bursting out. "You're the best thing that's happened to me in like, forever. I like you so much, Felix. I can't even ..." I take a deep breath. "I have a problem. I know that. I can't seem to keep good things in my life. I do bad things. I mess up. Everything I care about, I end up hurting. But I don't want to. I don't even know how it happens. It's like I lose control or something. I don't know how to explain it."

Felix just stares at me, eyebrows raised.

"It's like, I've been hurt so much, I just assume everyone else is gonna hurt me too." I shove my bangs out of my eyes. "I get so afraid, I just—I hurt them back. Or maybe I do it before they've even done anything to me."

"It felt like you stabbed me and then twisted the knife," he says softly. "Like you were trying to do as much damage as possible. On purpose."

I flinch, but I have to keep going. I have to see this through. "I thought you didn't like me anymore. My Dad was dying of a heart attack. My sister had just come home, and I thought she hated me. My head was like this boiling cauldron of terrible, horrible thoughts."

"I'm sorry for you, I really am. I know you've had a lot going on. I would've been there for you, you know. If you'd just talked to me."

My heart jolts. Maybe there's a chance. Maybe I can win him back. I move a little closer. "I know. I'm so, so sorry."

He looks at me, wetness in his eyelashes. His face looks stretched, pained. "I forgive you."

I want to weep with joy. I scoot closer, ready to fling myself at him, to kiss every inch of his body, to wrap him in my arms and never let go. Hot blood thunders through me and I'm remembering all the times we touched. All the times we hugged and held hands and kissed. All the times I fell asleep to the comforting sound of his heartbeat against my cheek.

"I love you," I say breathlessly. I don't mean to say it. It just slips out. I know immediately it's so right, so true. I do love him. I love him so much my body hums with it.

Felix shakes his head, a curl falling across his eyes. His face contorts. "Lux—"

"I know it's weird for a girl to say it first and everything. I can't help it. It's true. I love you."

"I can't."

I freeze. Go still and cold. "What do you mean?"

"I really, really liked you."

"Liked. As in past tense," I say, my voice flat.

"I still have feelings for you." His face is etched with regret, his eyes filled with sadness. "I probably will for a long time. But, Lux, you hurt me so much. What you did ... I understand you were in pain. I understand you're sorry. But it was too much. I don't think it's healthy for us to be together."

My heart splinters, each shard aching, throbbing, pulsing. I know I hurt him. Seeing it now, written across his face, across his whole body —it tears me apart.

I did this. I caused this pain. This rift, wide as a canyon between us. I can see it in his eyes. There's no way to cross it. It's too late.

I blink, willing away the tears. But they come anyway, hot and burning. "I'm so sorry." He shakes his head, looks away.

The whole world breaks into pieces.

I did this. I ruined us. It's true. That fear always curled like a fat, black slug inside me. It's real. I destroy what I love. I hurt everything good in my life.

I'm broken. I'm broken like my mother. If I don't do something, I'll shatter. And the shards of me will cut and scar every single person within reach.

I take a deep, ragged breath, fighting to stay in control. To keep my splintering heart together for just a few more minutes. "I made something for you," I say before I can change my mind. I wanted to give it to him after we'd made up. But that's not going to happen. I can see that now.

I hurt him. I hurt him so badly that we can't be together. Not now, maybe never.

I pull the piece out of my messenger bag, where I tucked it carefully in its own pocket. I hand it to Felix. It's the final version of the large origami gray squirrel I've been working on for weeks. It took more than a hundred folds to create it, to develop the depth and soft sleekness of his fur. It took me hours and hours. It's one of my best.

Felix whistles. "Wow!"

"It's Squirrel Girl," I force out. "Superhero of the day."

"You remembered," he says softly. "Thank you, Lux. Truly."

I make my face approximate a smile, even though I'm crumbling inside. "I hope it makes you think of me."

"I'll miss you."

"I know." I make myself stand, my legs wobbling. I take the purple lighter out of my pocket and set it gently on the end table. I don't look at him, don't look at anything. I turn and walk carefully down the porch steps.

The sun rising above the treetops burns away the fog. It shines too brightly. It should be raining, pouring, the sky as gray and cold as my grief-stricken heart. But it isn't.

Everywhere around me, the beginning of May signals new life. The jeweled greens of new leaves and lush grass. The hazy blues of a sky quilted with clouds. The yellows of daffodils and dandelions, the purple of violets and the delicate white of Queen Anne's Lace. I should feel brand new, reborn, alive with second chances.

But I don't. I feel like I'm drowning.

I know this is right. I know I can't be with Felix. I'm not ready. I'm not okay. I can't fix us because I'm the one that's broken.

I'm broken and I need to be fixed. No. I need to fix myself.

I climb in the car and drive away. My vision blurs. My heart plunges into an ocean of pain. My lungs are suffocating.

I'm drowning.

And I don't know how to swim.

## 46

## LYRA

I knock on Lux's bedroom door.

"Come in," Lux says.

She's been back from the hospital for almost three weeks. Long enough for the tremors to stop, the sunken gray color of her skin to fade. Long enough for us both to be ready, finally, to talk.

Lux is lying on her bed, earbuds hooked in her ears, working on one of her origami pieces. She's only got a few points completed, but the star is already forming beneath her fingers, the paper a rich, shimmery gold.

Her cat is curled into a furry ball in a nest of her hair.

"How're you feeling?"

Lux lifts her shoulders. "I've been worse."

"Good, I guess." I clear my throat. "I was hoping maybe we could talk."

An expression I can't read passes over her face. Lux yanks her hair out from beneath Phoenix, sits up, and swings her legs over the bed. Phoenix leaps to her feet, hissing and spitting. Her yellow eyes are trained on me, her gray fur standing on end along the ridge of her spine.

"I think she hates me."

Lux hovers her hand over the cat's back. "It's okay," she murmurs.

Slowly, her hackles lower. Her hiss dwindles to a low growl in her throat.

"I do believe you're actually taming that thing."

Lux smiles weakly. She's dressed in the green striped flannel PJs I got her for Christmas the last time I was home. She's not wearing any makeup, and her unwashed red hair hangs lank around her face and shoulders.

She looks unbearably young.

"How about I make Dad's homemade hot chocolate?"

Lux attempts another smile, but it slides right off her face. "Comfort food at its best."

"Yeah."

Lux gets up slowly, as if a great weight is attached to her spine. She cradles the half-finished star in one hand and follows me into the kitchen. She slumps at the table.

I wipe my palms on my jeans and open the cupboard, pulling down two pans. I grab the Ghirardelli dark chocolate bar and the milk from the fridge. "I'm trying not to be judgmental," I say to the counter, suddenly unable to meet my sister's gaze.

I will be understanding. I will not flinch from her spikes. I will take the pain. Because I love her. Because she's all I have left. If we can't save each other, then we're both lost. "I'm going to try my best to just listen."

"That'd be a first."

I add whole milk, cinnamon, sugar, and vanilla into the pan and simmer, stirring the whole time. Stay calm. I must stay calm. Things already seem like they could blow up any second, and we haven't even started yet. "What do you mean?"

"You never listen, Lyra. You always judge. You've decided how things are before I even open my mouth. What's even the point?"

I try to remember Ethan's advice. What would he do? "I may have behaved that way in the past—"

"You always do."

I grit my teeth as I break up the chocolate bar and add it to the double boiler. "That doesn't seem fair."

"No?" Lux's gaze crackles, burning holes in my back. "You think you know everything, up there on your marble pedestal. You're all pompous and justified, judging everyone else for their mistakes."

"Now, wait just a minute. That's unfair—"

"Is it? You stew in your self-righteousness, Lyra. It's what you do. You think you have everybody and everything figured out, but you don't. You never even ask. Not really, not like you actually want to know. You never even tried to talk to me unless you were telling me what to do. You never tried to understand."

The pain radiating off her is palpable. I bite my tongue so hard I taste coppery blood. I will not respond. I will not be defensive. I will listen. "I didn't know you felt that way."

"You won't talk to me," she says again. "You never even tried."

"I'm trying now, Lux," I say, glancing back at her.

She folds the gold paper, twisting it this way and that. Her fingers move deftly, making diamond and triangle folds, shaping a form she already knows in her heart, in her bones.

I whisk the chocolate into the milk. "This isn't easy for me. But I'm trying. I'm here."

She just looks at me.

"We only have each other. If we don't figure this out ..."

She sighs. "I know."

"You talk, and I'll listen. I won't judge you, I promise."

"What do you want me to say?"

"The truth."

"You don't want to know. Trust me."

I hand Lux a mug and move to the kitchen table. I cup my hands around the hot mug and breathe in the steam. I keep my voice even, relaxed. "We've had enough secrets in this family to last a lifetime. Maybe we should try something else this time."

"I screwed up. Is that what you want to hear?"

"Just tell me what happened. Start with Dad's heart attack."

"Fine. Whatever." Lux stares down at her mug, her mouth taut. Half-moons of fatigue darken the skin beneath her eyes. "We fought about everything. What were we fighting about that night? I don't even remember. Something about what I was wearing. He'd gone all religious, quoting the Bible at me. I couldn't stand it. He was the last person in the world to be getting all high and mighty. I said things."

"What did you say?"

Lux shakes her head. Her eyes take on a far-away, glazed look. "I shouted, screamed at him. I said he was a homewrecker and a hypocrite. I said he had no right to say anything about what was right or wrong because I knew what he did, I knew he'd done the worst possible thing. I said he killed Mom."

I suck in my breath. But I don't speak. I listen.

Lux keeps talking. "I didn't even notice for a minute. I just kept screaming at him. He slipped down against the wall. He grabbed his arm and made these hitching sounds in his throat, like he couldn't talk. Then his eyes were still open, but they weren't looking at anything. I freaked. I called 911. I couldn't stand it, waiting there with him like that. I couldn't do it. I was so scared that he was dead, that I'd killed him."

"So you left him."

"I left. I had to. I didn't know what else to do. You never would've left. I know that." Bitterness spikes her voice. "You're the perfect daughter. You would've done everything right, just like you always do."

"I didn't—"

"I know what I did, okay? I'd give anything to take it all back if I could."

"You never talked to Dad."

"I'm sorry. I'm sorry, sorry, sorry. I always meant to go in there, to talk to him, but why would he ever want to see me again? He should've hated me. He didn't though, and that just made it worse. I got scared and I ran away. I got scared and I let Dad die without ever saying I'm sorry."

"He wanted to see you."

She makes a choked, strangled sound in the back of her throat. "I know."

"You acted like you didn't care."

"I couldn't—it's hard to explain. It was too big, like something big and dark about to swallow me whole. I just couldn't ... I did what I always do. I screw up everybody's lives and run away and hide, and then I try to fix things when it's too late. That's my life story."

"You could've talked to me."

Lux's eyes are raw and red-rimmed. Her face is drained of color. "Yeah right. At least I know what I am. I know you hate me. I deserve to be hated. It's not like I could ever say something that would change that."

Tenderness creeps through, first small and light and then stronger, and faster, filling me up. "I've never hated you."

"All I've ever been to you is trouble. I'm a screw-up, always have been. You had to leave your scholarship to take care of Dad, and I couldn't even talk to him."

I left her alone. I got to leave, to escape, to chase my dreams. She was stuck here, alone in this house haunted with memories. She and Dad both trying to flee a past they couldn't acknowledge. "Lux, I—"

"Maybe it was better if Dad could pretend all he had was you," Lux says. "That's what I told myself. Then he died and I missed my chance. And I didn't plan to miss the funeral, but guess what? I managed to eff that up too."

Her words bleed together. She hiccups, struggling to keep the sobs at bay. Her fingers quiver as she twists the paper in her hands, folding and unfolding, creasing and uncreasing. "That night, when I realized I missed the funeral ... It's not like there was any reason to have me around. I ruin everything I touch."

Something shakes loose inside me, rattles around inside my bones. I jump to my feet, grab the hand towel next to the sink, and bring it to her. "You really felt that way?"

Lux buries her face in the towel. Her shoulders jerk and heave. "I still do," she says into the cloth.

My heart bursts open. I crouch down beside her and wrap my arms around my sister. Lux stiffens. "I didn't know. I wish you'd told me."

Lux pulls away. Tears leak down her cheeks, snot bubbling in her nose. "You wouldn't have listened. You wouldn't have heard me."

I want to yell, *That's not true*, but I can't. I know I can't. I feel Lux's absolute loneliness, her isolation, her prison of self-loathing and regret. "I'm listening now."

"When it's too late," Lux says, blowing her nose into the towel. She rubs her eyes and cheeks with her fists.

I shake my head. We've lost so much. But not everything. Not yet.

This is what I know: sometimes you need to let go. Let go of the anger and the bitterness. Let go of the fantasy of a perfect life, a perfect mother. Let go of the idea that people are better than they are.

And sometimes you need to hold on. Hold on to hope in the face of despair. Hold on to love despite the disappointments, the betrayals, the bone-crushing pain. Hold on to family, even when it seems like they're the ones leaving you.

The trick is knowing which is which. The trick is figuring out when to let go, when to hold on, and how to tell the difference. Maybe that's part of growing up. Maybe it's just part of being out in the world, choosing to live with your heart wide open.

"Not for us," I say. "It's not too late for us."

Lux closes her eyes. "You say that because you don't know it all. What happened with Dad—that's not even the worst thing. You might not hate me now, but you will."

I sit back in my chair. I get that feeling, that black prickling energy that comes to me sometimes in the darkroom when I'm near to some-thing, when I know I almost have it right, am so excruciatingly close to discovering something new and brilliant and maybe a little bit treacherous. "What do you mean?"

"I'm talking about Mom," Lux says in a voice aching with misery. "It was me. I'm the reason she killed herself."

# 47

# LUX

This is it. There's no going back now. Only forward, into the savage unknown. This is me, cracked wide open. This is me, raw and skinless.

I'm utterly terrified.

I stare at my sister. She stares back at me. "Tell me," she says.

How can I? How can I share everything I haven't been able to say for years? Haven't said. Have been afraid to. *I want. I need. I'm scared.*

I do this, or the black hole sucks me in. I do this or I explode. Dissolve into dark matter. I'll be gone, only the reflected light of an already dead star.

Like Mom.

The memories are honed steel, sharp as razor-edged claws. They take hold and drag me back.

I was nine years and two months old that day in October, when I found the letter. The wind sheared the red and yellow leaves from the trees, hurling them through the air and slapping them against the windows. The leaves were wet and stuck to the glass like brightly colored stars.

Lyra was gone for the afternoon, on a field trip to a museum in Grand Rapids. Mom was home, sitting at the kitchen table with a cup of coffee and the newspaper opened in front of her. She wasn't reading it. Her eyes were glassy and unfocussed when she looked at me. My stomach knotted uneasily. Still, I asked her to play.

"Not now," she said, even though she wasn't even doing anything. If Lyra had asked her, she would've said yes. She always said yes to Lyra.

I escaped to the closet, where I started rummaging through the pockets of Dad's jackets. He had two: a bright blue windbreaker and an old, greasy green flannel one Mom was always harping on him to throw away.

The flannel jacket was his favorite, but it was the windbreaker he took when he left three days ago on another long haul. I liked the feel of the worn flannel and the faint scent of cologne, sweat, and gasoline.

"You took things out of his pockets," Lyra interrupts. Her brow furrows. "You took things from us. Mom's ceramic box in your closet. It's filled with stuff you stole. My pearl earring from that last Christmas."

Heat creeps up my neck, but I don't look away. "Yes."

I expect her to get all red and furious, but she doesn't. She doesn't ask why. It's like she knows already. Her lips press together, but she nods for me to continue.

I counted the handful of change in the right pocket of Dad's coat: two quarters, thirteen pennies, three nickels. In his left pocket, my hand closed around a neatly folded sheet of paper. I sat cross-legged on the carpet and read the swirly handwriting. I was only ten, but I knew.

"It was a love letter," I say aloud. "A love letter addressed to Dad, to 'Jacob, my love.' Signed 'Forever Yours, M.G.'"

A shadow passes across Lyra's face. She doesn't look surprised. "What did it say?"

I make another petal fold, my fingers shaking so hard I can barely burnish the crease. "It said she loved him. She talked about him leaving Mom, about building a new family. They were making plans. I knew that meant *we* wouldn't be a family anymore. It was Mom's fault."

The letter was worn around the edges, well creased and softened with the oil of many fingerprints. They hadn't used messaging or email, either assuming hard copies were safer or just caught up in the romance of it, who knows. But he'd held that paper a hundred times if not a thousand.

I imagined him on those long, lonely nights on the road. Sitting up so high in his big rig, pausing to pull out the letter, gently cradling it in his hands. Reading and rereading the feminine, loopy script.

The knot in my gut turned into a ball of snarled steel. It was like a giant hand twisting up my insides, turning them inside out. My fury wasn't aimed at Dad.

It was aimed at Mom. She was the one always apologizing, always begging for our forgiveness. She must've done something to make Dad so desperate to leave us. She did this. It was her fault.

I walked down the hallway with the unfolded letter clutched in my fist. I entered the kitchen and went straight to Mom. She was bent over the newspaper, her hair dull and snarled around her bony shoulders.

I thrust the paper in front of her.

Looking back, it doesn't make sense. I hoarded the bent paper clips and used gum wrappers I'd stolen from Dad like precious treasures, hiding them away so no one would find them. The letter, my most dangerous secret—I simply gave it to her.

The 'why' is a black ink spot staining my mind. An oily darkness swirling beneath my consciousness. Did I seriously want to hurt her that badly? Was my heart that bent, that cruel? My greatest sin, and I didn't even think twice about it.

"What did Mom do?" Lyra asks. Her expression is unreadable, hard as stone.

I close my eyes. "It wasn't as bad as you think. Not then."

Mom read the letter several times, her gaze jerking over the words, her fingers white, the blue vein in her forehead pulsing. I stood in front of her, hands limp at my sides. I looked out the kitchen window at the trees losing their leaves, the golden stalks of corn bending in the wind.

Mom asked, "Where did you get this?"

I told her.

"Just now?"

"Yes, Momma."

She smoothed the letter in one hand and tapped the newspaper with her finger. "How apt," she said in a strange voice. "My horoscope for today says, 'You must widen your horizons and change your perspective to see where you need to go. You must open yourself up to do what is needed to move on.' Do you see? The stars always know."

"What's mine say, Momma?"

"Go to your room now." Her smile was too wide and too bright, almost grotesque in its falseness.

I obeyed. I brushed the manes of my Breyer horses, lining them up side by side on my dresser. I folded a crane out of buttery yellow paper and set it on my nightstand. The house descended into an eerie silence.

I don't know what thoughts winged inside my mother's head. Something shifted inside her, a critical tipping point. In its insidious silence, its invisibility, it was the most dangerous thing of all.

When Lyra got home, Mom was already sequestered in her bedroom. Lyra opened two cans of Spaghettios, and we ate it cold, the way we liked it. After supper, we watched TV, the volume turned down low.

I didn't warn my sister. I didn't say anything at all.

The next morning, Lyra packed our lunches and we met the bus like we usually did on days Mom didn't get up. After school, I had flute practice and took the late bus home alone. Lyra was already there.

There was a fire truck and two police cars parked in my driveway. All the kids leaped from their seats and pressed their noses to the bus windows.

I remember the sky was a harsh, cloudless blue. I remember my breath steaming against the glass.

My body went cold, a coldness that penetrated my bones. I stayed in my seat. I wished the bus driver would pull away and keep going down the road. Instead, he put the bus in park and walked with me across the driveway up the steps to my house.

He left me with a police lady in a blue uniform. She squatted in front of me and kept patting my shoulder.

"Where's my mom?" I asked.

"Your mom was hurt. She—"

"Where's my sister?"

"Your sister and your father followed the ambulance to the hospital. I'm going to take you to the hospital to be with them." She looked at me with a bleak pity in her eyes that told me everything.

I knew in that instant exactly what I'd done.

"Honey, are you okay?"

I was drowning in a black, seething sea, my body dragged under and pummeled by the waves. My lungs were exploding, desperate for air.

It was grief, but it was also something worse.

The police lady shook me gently. "Honey, can you hear me?"

The girl who was finally able to nod was not the same girl who'd stepped off the bus three minutes earlier.

That girl was sucked down beneath the black waves.

That girl did not come back.

She was lost. Lost for good. For forever.

4 8

---

## LUX

I blink back the dark swell of memory, keeping my gaze on the table. I'm afraid to look at my sister, afraid of the horror and revulsion I'll see etched across her face.

"Oh, Lux."

I can't speak. I don't know how.

"Why didn't you tell anyone?"

The tears dry on my cheeks in salty streaks, tightening my skin. I work my jaw, running my tongue over my lips. Finally the words come, slow and halting. "What was I supposed to say? 'Oh by the way, I'm the reason Mom offed herself?'"

"You can't seriously think that. You were ten years old."

"Old enough to know what something like that would do to a person like Mom. I knew. I knew it would hurt her. I wanted—I wanted to hurt her."

"You were a kid."

I make the final fold in the eight-pointed star, untuck the edges and fill out the center. I set it on the table, gently, between us. "Still."

"All this time you've believed it was your fault." Lyra talks fast, almost eager. She takes a swallow of her hot chocolate and wipes her mouth. "You hid yourself so deep. I couldn't find you. But now I get it. I see you."

"That's a good thing because . . . ?"

"You were so young when Mom died. No one was there for you. I was caught up in my own grief, Dad in his guilt. There wasn't any air left for you to breathe."

Emotions I can't define plunge over me. My heart tugs loose inside my chest. I expected rage, scorn, rejection. I've been preparing myself for it for years. Now here's Lyra, finally seeing all the dark inside me. And she's not gone. She's still here.

I grip my mug, my fingers shaking. "It was my fault."

"No, Shortcake. It wasn't. I used to believe the same thing. I thought if I was good enough, she'd be happy. But that's impossible. She was sad, and sick. I've learned so much being back here, thinking about everything that happened. Maybe the letter sent her over the edge that day. But, Lux, she was going over anyway. It was only a matter of time."

I shake my head. "No. I don't believe that. If not for that letter—she never would have left us. She had her moments when she was so happy, like she could float right off the ground if she wanted to."

"And when she came back down?"

"You mean her 'vacations,' when she was sad?" I remember her smile, so bright, her eyes like emeralds. The way she'd scoop me up into her arms and whisper a secret fortune in my ear: *You will find your dreams among the stars* and *You will be an explorer and find great fortune in this life and the next.*

Lyra stares at me in silence for a long moment. Then she leans forward and rolls up the right sleeve of my shirt.

"What are you doing?"

She pushes it up past my bicep. "Look."

I glance down, see the same pale skin, the same white, raised half-moon scars I've always had. "What?"

She shoves up the sleeve of her plaid shirt, revealing her own faint scars. "That's how she grabbed us, when she lost it."

I shove back from the table. "No."

"Maybe you were too young, or maybe you just chose to forget," Lyra says softly.

"How can you say that? Mom was a good mother. Yeah, she was depressed, but she never—" I stop. Because she did. A memory pierces me: the sudden, sharp sting of nails digging deep, her beautiful face contorted, mask-like.

Lyra reaches for my hand. "Mom loved us, but there was something wrong with her. She was sad. She was angry. Sometimes so much that she screamed at us, grabbed us. Hurt us."

"No! That can't—"

"It's the truth whether you want to see it or not, whether she's dead or not."

Grief strangles my throat. "You're lying."

Lyra looks at me, sorrow welling in her eyes. She looks so much like our mother, like how I remember her. Her skin is a white sky studded with fiery stars. "You know I'm not."

I fold my arms on the table and drop my head, my shoulders heaving. Lyra scoots her chair closer. She rubs my back, tentatively at first, then harder. "Mom was broken. She had doctors and medication, and she refused both. She had a family. Instead of fighting, she chose to abandon us."

"No," I whisper.

"Yes. She tried to kill herself three times."

"No."

"Her illness had nothing to do with us. It had nothing to do with Dad's affair, or you giving her the letter. Do you understand?"

It all seems too much, too overwhelming to take in. "Maybe," I whisper.

I think of that last time I saw my mother smile, before she sent me off to my room. At the time, it seemed real. I could feel its light, its warmth.

Now I realize the warmth was just the final, fading light of an already dead star.

"It wasn't your fault," Lyra says, that old familiar conviction back in her voice like she believes it enough for the both of us. Like that's enough.

And maybe, for now, it is.

Neither of us speak. The house creaks and pops. The refrigerator hums. Every sound seems amplified in the emptiness. It doesn't seem like our house. I can't shake the feeling that we're strangers wandering the rooms of a place long abandoned. We don't belong here anymore.

Lyra clears her throat. "I'm sorry I've been such a terrible sister."

"Was that an actual apology I just heard?"

A grim smile tugs at the corners of her mouth. "I want to be better. I want to do better."

My heart balloons in my chest, pressing against my rib cage. For the first time in forever, I see a glimmer of hope. Maybe there is a path out of all this darkness. Maybe Lyra can help me find it. "Me too."

"I love you to the moon," she says.

My fingers tighten around my empty mug. I can still smell the rich scent of hot chocolate reminding me so much of Dad. I miss him so much, now that he's gone. It's up to Lyra and me to make sure we don't forget the good things, too. "I love you all the way back."

Something changes in Lyra's face. "When I thought you'd—" She takes a shuddering breath. "You can't do that to me. You have to get better."

I stare at my hands, at the chips in my turquoise nail polish. A dark thread of fear winds through me.

The thing about change is that it's hard as hell. There's no easy out. No escaping. I'll feel it all. There's no relief, no popping a pill to make it all go away. It's always there, a monster chained to my leg.

I don't get to leave. I don't get to run away. It's myself I can't escape from. The fear, the anger, the pain and the guilt, that deep oppressive loneliness like a mountain of bricks on my chest.

I'll feel every single thing.

"I'm scared."

She reaches across the table, grabs my hand. Entwines her fingers with mine. "You're not alone."

# LYRA

"This is it," I say. Dread curdles my stomach.

Lux and I head to Florida in three days. Ethan is leaving tonight for Chicago to be a groomsman for the wedding of one of his former teammates. We have only this afternoon to say goodbye.

Ethan's mom is watching Hadley. All morning, he helped me load the last of the furniture into a rental truck, which we delivered to the Goodwill in Dowagiac.

It's the middle of May. The afternoon warmed up into the 80s, Michigan's humidity sticking my hair to my neck with sweat. My arms burned as we carried our couch down the ramp and set it down in front of the donations drop-off bay.

I stared down at the worn, plaid fibers, remembering my parents shouldering it through the front door and down the hallway, brand new and sheathed in plastic, when I was ten. Ten years ago. A whole decade, a generation, a dozen lifetimes past.

Now, the muscles in my back and arms ache, reminding me afresh of all that is lost.

"Hey, you with me?" Ethan says, squeezing my knee.

We're in line for the automatic carwash at Suds'N'More in Dowagiac.

"Sorry," I say. The Honda clicks onto the motorized track, and I shift into neutral and release the brakes. I cleaned and vacuumed the interior yesterday afternoon, decluttering what felt like years' worth of Lux's junk.

I ordered the Deluxe Gold package, with extras like an undercarriage flush with rust inhibitor and foam polish and sealant wax. I want it pristine for our road trip back to Tampa.

I want a fresh start, for both of us.

The inside of the van darkens as the conveyer belt pulls us into the tunnel. We pass beneath an arch with nozzles spraying liquid chemicals over the hood, the windshield, the roof.

Ethan squeezes my knee again. His hand on my bare skin sends electric sparks sizzling up and down my leg. "I'm going to miss having you around, Freckles."

"Really? You're going to start calling me that again? And I thought we'd made so much progress." I try to be light and funny, but it comes out flat.

"Sorry." He unclicks his seatbelt, turns toward me, and leans over the center console. He buries his hands in my hair on either side of my face. Instinctively, I try to duck my chin, but he gently forces my head up. "Lyra."

My stomach flutters. I'm feeling so much more than I want to be. I feel everything. And it's scary as hell. "You're not under any obligation to text or call or anything. I had a good time. I think you did, too. Let's leave it at that."

"Leave what at what? You think this was just a spring fling?"

Liquid drips down the windshield. High pressure nozzles spray the tires, and a soapy chemical smell fills the car. I nod.

"Sometimes you don't seem that smart, college girl."

"Wasn't it?"

"Not to me."

I feel his fingers in my hair, on my scalp. I swallow hard. "But I'm not—I'm not good enough."

"Good enough for what?"

I don't answer. I can't. Huge brushes descend over the van on all sides. The colorful cloth strips slap against every surface, making soft, wet sucking sounds.

"Good enough to love?" he asks.

I can't answer that either. It hurts too much.

"Love isn't something you have to earn," he says quietly. "Love is something you give away."

"You don't love me."

Ethan's face softens. "Not as much as I'd like to. Not as much as I will."

I want to believe every word he says, butt he doesn't want me, not really. "You don't understand. I'm not—"

"When you love someone, you can't pick and choose what parts of them to love. You can't pick and choose what parts of your life to live. You're either all in, or you're not. And Lyra, I need you to know this before you leave. I'm all in."

I stare at him, stunned.

The van slides beneath another arch of high-pressure nozzles. The sprayers blast against the side windows. It feels like the whole world is crying. "But I'm leaving. Florida is a long way away and—"

"We have this new technology? It's called a smart phone. We can IM, Skype, Facetime, whatever. It doesn't cost that much to hop on a plane.

You only have a year left, Lyra. After that, who knows? Chicago, New York, wherever your art takes you. Hadley and I can follow. Most universities offer engineering degrees."

The entire English language escapes me. "But what—I don't . . . I can't—" I sputter.

Ethan tips my chin up. "All you have to say is yes."

All the hard, brittle things inside me are weakening, breaking apart, shattering into shards of light.

"And Lux?" I whisper.

"We'll figure it out as we go."

"But she comes with us?"

"She comes with us, if that's what she wants." He traces my nose, my chin, my cheeks with his fingers. "I know it's probably not what you planned, a ready-made family with a whiny, stinky-butt toddler in tow. It's totally okay if you don't want—"

I lean against my seatbelt and kiss him. His lips stretch into a grin beneath my own. I breathe in the smell of him, the clean, warm scent of cinnamon and soap, a hint of engine grease.

I don't believe in soulmates. I don't believe in "the one." I'm not even sure how much I believe in love. Love is not infinite. It's not all-powerful or all-consuming. Love is like everything else, like beauty and memory and flowers and even stars—it fades. It dies.

But maybe it doesn't have to. Maybe love can be different. Love can change things. Love can change everything.

After what seems like an eternity, Ethan pulls away. He traces his finger down my neck, across my collarbone, leaving a trail of fire. "I could stare at your face forever. I adore every single one of your freckles."

"My mom used to say they were like tiny red stars. She said I had galaxies etched in my skin."

"Your mom was right."

I face the front, trying to hide the goofy grin spreading across my face. Automatic blowers move over the van on a mechanical arm. Water droplets streak upward across the windshield, then disappear.

I think about my mother, about what she would say if she could meet Ethan. My boyfriend. I think she would like him. She would approve. She would be happy with the choices I've made.

I touch my own cheek, the memory of her so close, the sweet smell of her jasmine shampoo, her river of hair falling around me. *The stars reveal your past and whisper your future,* she told me that chilly night when the moon was so bright everything was bathed in silver.

When we lay on the blanket, the hard, bumpy ground beneath us, the canopy of the heavens unfurled above. *But look at you. You have the stars written on your skin. You have the past, the present, and the future already within you.*

I was wrong about the past. Wrong about everything, really. Memory isn't captured within the four sides of a photograph. It isn't frozen within a one-dimensional space. Memory is shifting. It changes, transforms, takes new shapes, adding layers of rich, deep meaning. Memories merge and condense with time, experience, and the act of retelling.

Two people can experience the exact same events yet have vastly different memories of what happened. I mostly remember the sadness, the anger, the pain. Lux remembers the laughter, the whirling spinning ride in a galaxy of stars.

It can be both. I can have both.

This is what I know: one truth doesn't have to cancel the other out. Eve was both a wonderful and terrible mother. I can remember her both ways. I can love Dad for his homemade hot chocolate and his jokes and his love of photography he shared with me. I can love him and still feel anger at his weakness, how he escaped into work and an affair instead of protecting us.

I can love Lux as my sister, loud and fun and charming and wild. I can love her and still hate her self-destructive choices, her recklessness, her secrets.

I can hold both versions of the people I love in my memory and in my heart.

I reach across the seat and twine my fingers through Ethan's. My hand fits perfectly inside his larger, calloused one.

I blink several times as I shift into drive and pull out of the car wash. The car slips out of the tunnel into bright sunlight.

# LUX

"I don't know about this," Autumn says, staring uneasily at the tattoo needle.

She takes a swig of her diet Faygo and wipes her mouth with her arm. "It's kind of a life goal of mine to avoid as much pain as possible."

"Some pain is good pain," I say.

Autumn, Simone and I arrived at Pierced Hearts Tattoo Parlor twenty minutes ago. We're staring at several papers tacked to the wall with sketches of common tattoos—the usual hearts, Chinese symbols, tramp stamps, and the like.

Adele plays from an iPod dock on a table covered with tattoo portfolios. Artsy black and white close-up photographs of tattooed body parts adorn the pumpkin-orange walls. Simone sits in a wheeled chair, rolling back and forth across the black and white checkered linoleum.

While we wait, we look through the portfolios. Autumn picks out a small jewel-green hummingbird she wants on her ankle. "Hummingbirds are so adorable," she sighs.

"I know, right?" I scan a row of dolphins in various diving and leaping poses.

"Did you know that during mating season, the long-billed hermit male hummingbirds use their needle-sharp beaks to stab their rivals in the throat?"

Simone stares at her. "Seriously? Hummingbirds whack each other to death with their face-knives?"

I punch Autumn's arm. "Thanks a lot. You've pretty much ruined every cute and cuddly creature in the animal kingdom for me."

She grins. "You're welcome."

A pretty Asian lady walks out from the back room. She's wearing a frilly lemon-yellow dress. "I'm Mae."

Another girl walks out, a few years older than me and heavy-set. Thick blue-black hair dusts the tops of her shoulders. Her eyes are a stunning cobalt blue. "Hey," she says, sticking out her hand.

"This is my new assistant, Sidney," Mae says. "She's working here for the summer, and she's very talented."

I squint at her. "You look familiar. Did you go to Brokewater High?"

"I graduated three years ago. You have a sister in my class?"

"Yeah, Lyra. The red hair give it away?"

"Something like that."

"Sidney attends the Art Institute of Chicago. Very prestigious." Mae pulls up the sleeve of Sidney's T-shirt, revealing a silvery blue, jewel-toned butterfly caught in mid-flight on her upper arm. "She came in with this glorious butterfly drawing a few years ago, wanted me to tattoo it on her. I said, 'You this good? You work for me. So, trust me when I say you're in good hands."

"What're you thinking of?" Sidney asks me.

"It's gonna hurt!" Autumn says in a singsong voice.

I hand Sidney the drawing. I need to do this. I need the pain.

I will manufacture my own self. I will take up certain aspects of my past and discard others. I couldn't choose my history, but I can choose my present. I can chart my future. I can map it out on my skin.

"Let's do this."

I sit back on a reclined, padded chair. The white paper crinkles beneath me as I shift my weight. Sidney snaps on her disposable gloves. She gathers the ink, needles, a towel, then pulls up a rolling stool next to the tattoo machine. She slips the headband magnifier over her forehead and adjusts the overhead light.

I listen to the buzz of the tattoo machine, focus on the first pinpricks of pain. The room smells like ink, disinfectant, and incense. Sidney doesn't make inane small talk. She doesn't say anything. After awhile, Simone and Autumn make a run to the café next door for mochas and brownies and more diet Faygo for Autumn.

The tattoo needle jabs into the skin on my forearm. Pain flashes behind my eyes. My whole arm burns as I watch the origami star take shape. The points slowly emerge, flaring out in each direction. The dark blue ink etches the shadows of the folds. Beneath the tattooed image, the words: "It is not in the stars to hold our destiny but in ourselves."

"Shakespeare, right?" Sidney says. I nod. She's quiet for a few minutes. "We all have our hard-won truths. It's good to remember, to have it imprinted on your skin."

Being me is like walking around with no skin. Skin is a boundary, a protection, armor from the toxins and the germs. Without skin, you're raw. Exposed. Flayed. Your organs glisten. Your veins pulse.

I'm tired of being skinless.

Pain sears me. But it doesn't matter. I can endure it. I will create my own skin, a skin within which I can bear to live.

I will build it through hard work and unbearable pain and my own relentless will.

I'll build my skin with images, with words and colors and signs and messages that will remind me.

In the darkest dark, there is light inside me.

# LYRA

I sit on the bare floor in front of the living room window, staring out into the darkness. I can barely make out the shadowed cornfields stretching to the tree line in the distance.

Lux isn't home yet. It's past midnight. Everything is silent and still. It feels like the whole world is sleeping.

On nights like tonight, the sky is a swath of black velvet studded with diamonds close enough to touch, close enough to believe in. The moon is a gleaming disk suspended above the house, moonlight splashing the trees and bushes in shades of pearl.

It's Saturday night, our last day in Brokewater. Tomorrow, Lux and I leave for Tampa. We're driving the bulldog on an eighteen-hour, twelve-hundred-mile road trip to our new life.

The house we grew up in sold the first week it was on the market. It's time to be rid of it, rid of the shadows and ghosts that live in the walls, that sleep beneath the floorboards. We'll never be totally free until we leave.

I glance again at the time on my phone. Lux left at seven, agreeing to be back by eleven. Every minute that passes, my gut winds tighter and tighter. I lean my forehead against the cool glass and sigh, my breath leaving a circle of fog.

She hasn't texted or called. She could be dead by the side of the road somewhere. She's fine. I know that. She always is. She just never *thinks,* just lets herself get caught up in the moment.

It's me who's left to worry, me who stays up late, anxiously waiting for Lux to wander home in her own sweet time.

I make the shape of a star with my finger in the splotch of fog. I wipe it away and breathe on the glass again. My eyes burn, but I won't sleep until I know she's safe. How many more times will I have to do this?

Lux is still hurting. She's wounded, battling a darkness stronger than I know. And when she slips, I'll just have to be there.

It's after one a.m. when Lux's car finally squeals into the driveway. She gets out, stumbles and then steadies herself, and moves a few paces away from the car. She doesn't come inside.

She wraps her arms around herself and begins to dance in the moonlit yard. I remember watching her with my mother all those years ago. They danced in the rain, Lux standing on my mother's toes, water dripping into their upturned faces as they laughed, spinning round and round.

I place my hands on the window, cupping the image of my sister swaying on the grass, her hair dark and glistening in the moonlight, her gaze upturned toward the sky, starlight on her face.

We have both been scarred. We have both been blessed.

We have each other.

And in the end, this is enough.

# AUTHOR'S NOTE

It takes great courage to fight our demons. It takes courage to recognize our triggers and our weaknesses and work toward self-care and mental health. But we can do it, for those we love and for ourselves. I know what it's like to feel like you're locked in a battle with your own mind. For every person struggling, know that you are not alone.

You are not defined by your mental health. You do not have to be trapped by the past. You can chart your own future.

Please consider the following resources if you or a loved one needs help.

**National Suicide Prevention Lifeline**–Please call the toll-free Lifeline at 800-273-TALK (8255) to speak with a trained crisis counselor 24/7.

**Crisis Text Line** – Text NAMI to 741-741 Connect with a trained crisis counselor to receive free, 24/7 crisis support via text message.

**National Domestic Violence Hotline** – Call 800-799-SAFE (7233) Trained expert advocates are available 24/7 to provide confidential support to anyone experiencing domestic violence or seeking resources and information.

**National Sexual Assault Hotline** – Call 800-656-HOPE (4673) Connect with a trained staff member from a sexual assault service provider in your area that offers access to a range of free services.

# ABOUT THE AUTHOR

Kyla Stone is the *USA Today* Bestselling author of over 25 novels. With over two million copies sold worldwide, her books have been translated into several languages, and her *Edge of Collapse* series has been optioned by Sony Studios for television.

She lives in Michigan with her family and spends her days writing apocalyptic, survival, and psychological thrillers. Her favorite treats while writing include dark chocolate and coffee.

When she's not writing, she enjoys reading, hiking, playing board games, and traveling around the world. She loves adventures, including rappelling down waterfalls in Costa Rica, off-roading on the dunes of Lake Michigan in her blue Jeep, skydiving and parasailing in the Dominican Republic, and scuba diving in Roatan and Belize.

She loves to hear from her readers.

Email her at Kyla@KylaStone.com

# ACKNOWLEDGMENTS

Although writing is a solitary pursuit, a book is never written in a complete vacuum. The advice and encouragement of several people helped shape and polish the final drafts of this book.

Deep thanks to my beta readers, who pointed out my authorial blind spots and offered amazing suggestions: Becca Cross, Mallory Burgey, Miranda Navarro, Katrina Carlson, Kay Karolyshyn, Elizabeth Oakes, Jazmin Cybulski, Miranda Russell, Jeremy Steinkraus, Jennifer Murphy, and my first reader, Leslie Spurrier. To Ashley Cotoy Ruiz, who called me out on an error and then graciously read the whole book for authenticity in the characters of Lux and Eve.

To my dear friend, Jim Chambers, who read the first raw version of this novel over a decade ago. Your perceptive feedback and wise and steadfast encouragement made this a stronger story—and warmed my heart.

To my developmental editor, Danita Mayer, for the time and attention you devoted to my characters and their journeys.

Deep gratitude to Dr. Rachel Harris, both a friend and an expert, who took the time to check my manuscript for medical errors. To Dr. Daniel Collins, who also offered his medical expertise and experience. And to Dave Nyce, for lending me his expertise in darkroom techniques and photography. Any mistakes are my own.

To my children, whose unconditional love keeps me going. And to my husband, Jeremy, whose unwavering support sometimes translates into taking over chores and grocery shopping while I write frantically to meet publication deadlines. Thank you from the bottom of my heart.

# ALSO BY KYLA STONE

*Edge of Collapse* Series:

Edge of Collapse

Edge of Madness

Edge of Darkness

Edge of Anarchy

Edge of Defiance

Edge of Survival

Edge of Valor

*Nuclear Dawn* Series:

Point of Impact

From the Ashes

Into the Fire

Darkest Night

*The Last Sanctuary* Series:

No Safe Haven

Rising Storm

Falling Stars

Burning Skies

Breaking World

Raging Light

Queen of Fate and Fury

Beneath the Skin

Before You Break